Cassandra

by

Jann Rowland

One Good Sonnet Publishing

This is a work of fiction based on the works of Jane Austen. All of the characters and events portrayed in this novel are products of Jane Austen's original novel or the authors' imaginations.

CASSANDRA

Cover Design by Marina Willis

Published by One Good Sonnet Publishing

ISBN: 1987929349
ISBN-13: 978-1987929348

To my family who have, as always, shown
their unconditional love and encouragement.

ACKNOWLEDGEMENTS

Creative endeavors are never
A walk in the park.
Slaving away,
Starving for inspiration,
Any encouragement is always appreciated.
Numerous people help every day,
Dispensing support,
Replete with confidence-building words.
Affectionate thanks to all!

Chapter I

To understand Fitzwilliam Darcy, it is necessary to investigate the past events of his life which shaped him, molded him into the man he would become. Born the son of the owner of a large estate in Derbyshire, Darcy was brought up with every physical advantage. The estate produced income exceeding ten thousand pounds per annum, a figure which did not include any of the other satellite estates or the other sundry investments which through shrewd management had greatly increased the family fortune. Though untitled, the Darcys were an old family, well-placed within society and possessing connections to its highest levels. There were few in the kingdom of any consequence who were not familiar with the Darcy name.

As for Fitzwilliam Darcy's family, his father, Mr. Robert Darcy, was a dutiful, sober man who brought up his son to care for the estate by the sweat of his own brow instead of leaving the majority of the work to a steward like so many others of his station. The elder Mr. Darcy's wife, Lady Anne Darcy, was the daughter of an earl, and she was graceful, intelligent, and caring, at ease speaking with anyone of any background. Add to this a much younger sister, born when Darcy was twelve, and one would think his family life idyllic.

Unfortunately, his beloved mother, never of a robust constitution, passed a mere two years after the birth of his sister, her body weakened by the ordeal she had endured to bring new life into the world. His father, having loved his mother with every ounce of his heart, seemed to die at the same time, and though physically he lived on, it was if he walked the path of life without knowing—or caring—where it took him. The elder Darcy finally succumbed to an apoplexy, leaving Fitzwilliam Darcy as the proprietor of one of the largest estates in the kingdom at the tender age of two and twenty.

Darcy, having inherited his father's disposition, took these tragedies hard, and the mourning period for his beloved parents was spent in solitude, with little more than his young sister for company. That, coupled with the betrayal of his childhood companion, served to give him a slightly jaded view of the world. George Wickham had grown up to be a very different sort of man than his father, the elder Darcy's late steward, and it was with relief that Darcy severed all connection with the man after the elder Darcy's death for the modest price of a few thousand pounds in lieu of the living mentioned in Robert Darcy's will. It was fortunate, to Darcy's mind, that he never heard anything again from Wickham.

When Darcy once again reentered society after his period of mourning, he could not find any pleasure therein, for it seemed to Darcy that he was not sought after for who he was, but rather for the advantage that marrying him would bring to some young debutant. The young men were no better, as it was clear that the privilege of claiming a connection to the Darcy name—and by association his Fitzwilliam relations—was a highly sought after prize. Indeed, Darcy might have become even more reclusive and reticent had he not had the good fortune to meet a young woman who would coax him from his shell and breathe life into his austere existence. Perhaps more importantly, she helped him regain his faith in humanity.

She breezed into his life with all the force of a gale, thawing his heart and enlivening his life in a manner no one had ever managed to do before. Their meeting, achieved by chance, was ever after a source of fond remembrance and amusement, a light in his life through the dark times which would come.

Darcy had not intended to do more than stalk about the floor at the annual ball held by his aunt, Lady Susan Fitzwilliam. In fact, dancing was a compliment he never paid to any young woman if he could avoid it, as even a request to stand up for a set was enough to start rumors of attachment and raise the expectations of the lady so favored.

It was thus while he was engaged in such behavior that his cousin approached him to call him out for it.

"I say, Darcy," said Fitzwilliam in his ever-teasing manner, "it seems that you have once again settled for stalking about the floor, even though it is your own aunt's event."

"You neglected to mention my stupid manner," said Darcy.

Fitzwilliam laughed. "I shall endeavor to remember it the next time we have this conversation. Come now, Darcy. Can you not find some enthusiasm for *any* young woman present? My mother would not have invited anyone who was unsuitable."

"No she would not. But suitable does not necessarily equate to a lack of insipidity or an interest in the man rather than the position."

"You are quite determined to be displeased by all, even if you have not been introduced to most of them," said Fitzwilliam with a shake of his head.

"I do not need to be introduced. They are all the same."

"Now that is unfair." Fitzwilliam gestured to a location to the side and continued: "Come, let me introduce you to the young lady sitting along the wall there. She is a new acquaintance, and as *I* could not keep up with her quickness, I do not doubt that she would suit *you* quite well indeed."

Following Fitzwilliam's gesture, Darcy took stock of the young woman. She appeared to be tall and graceful, though as she was seated, it was difficult to tell. Her hair was a fetching shade of chestnut, done up in a typical woman's style, and her face was comely, with a clear complexion and full lips. She watched him through dark eyes which seemed to express intelligence, and Darcy could immediately see from her manner that she had heard every word which had passed between them. There was no choice—to refuse to be introduced now would be rude.

Annoyed with Fitzwilliam for putting him in this position, Darcy indicated his willingness, and the thing was done. What Darcy could not have imagined at the time was how profoundly this introduction would impact his future life.

The young woman was, in a word, a gem of the first order, and one he would never have even thought to secure an introduction to if he had been left to his own devices. Once Fitzwilliam performed his office, he excused himself, citing a previous commitment to dance the next with another young lady, and though Darcy glared at him, Fitzwilliam only chuckled and departed, leaving Darcy with his new acquaintance and an inability to fathom what he should say. Darcy despised small talk.

"I must say, sir," said the young lady, "I rather thought most people attend a ball with the intention of enjoying themselves. To you, it seems to be a punishment."

"I find that I do not, as a rule, find such functions as this to be to my taste," said Darcy. "In fact, I find most of those who attend to be . . . well, let us say that I find their manners trying."

"Please, Mr. Darcy, you do not need to behave with circumspection with me. Please say what you will. I shall not be offended."

In spite of himself, Darcy responded to her smile. "Very well. In truth, I find most people of society to be false. Most pretend to be something other than what they are, either for material gain or to impress those of a higher standing. And as disguise of every sort is my abhorrence, I cannot be happy in such society."

"There is no recourse but for me to agree with you, Mr. Darcy. I could not have said it any better myself."

Their conversation continued from there, and though Darcy initially thought the young woman was agreeing with him to obtain his good opinion as any other young woman would do, he was forced to discard such a notion within the first twenty minutes of speaking with her. Within the half hour, Darcy had actually asked the young woman to dance, and by the end of the evening, he had danced with her twice, something which was so far out of character for him that it was remarked upon with great fervor.

Darcy found himself surprised at his response to his new acquaintance. He found himself drawn to her like he had been drawn to no one else. She was, for lack of a better word, *genuine* in a way that drew his attention like a moth to the flame. She was refreshing in her penchant for honest observations, she was not shy of sharing her opinions, and for all that, she was demure and conducted herself in an impeccable manner. She was also in possession of many of the accomplishments which were often attributed to young ladies of society, as she soon demonstrated in the time which followed. Darcy quickly found himself enamored with her.

Within two days after the ball, Darcy had called on the young lady, and within the month, they were officially courting. A mere three months later, Darcy had proposed, and they were married in a ceremony attended by what seemed to be half of the members of high society. And for once, Darcy did not concern himself for the unwanted attention. The demands of society and the attention of the masses soon faded away in favor of his love. As she gazed at him with such devotion, Darcy found himself unable to look away.

The first year of their marriage was sublime. After their spring wedding, Darcy took his bride to the lake country, where they spent several weeks in the area at a lodge the Darcy family had owned for decades. Their solitude was spent deepening their relationship and coming to know each other ever better, making their marriage of hearts a true union of body, spirit, and soul. When they finally left the lakes, they retired to Pemberley and could not be budged from the great estate. Darcy's sister, Georgiana, joined them from where she had been staying with the Fitzwilliams since Darcy's wedding, and he had all the pleasure of seeing his wife and his sister coming to love one another as true sisters.

If there was any blemish in this perfect world Darcy and his new bride had managed to build for themselves, it was the reaction of one of his family members. It was, of course, his aunt, Lady Catherine de Bourgh, who took it upon herself to journey to Pemberley to express her dissatisfaction for his choice of wife. Of course, the only reason his wife was deemed unsuitable was the fact that she was not Lady Catherine's daughter Anne.

Though Darcy's new wife had the patience of a saint, Darcy could not consider himself to be so blessed, and it took only a moment of Lady Catherine's diatribe before Darcy's temper snapped. His aunt was forcibly removed from the premises and informed that all connection between them was hereby severed, and that she would not be admitted should she try to return. Her screeches attested to Lady's Catherine's fury, but Darcy was implacable. Lady Catherine did not return.

The rest of the year continued and the Darcys' happiness only increased. Darcy was careful to show his new wife his love for the estate, and many hours were spent riding its length and breadth. Darcy attended to the harvest, overseeing it in person, as was his wont, and his wife presided over a grand harvest ball, such as had not been held since before Lady Anne's death. Darcy's family, along with that of his wife, joined them at Pemberley for the Christmas celebration, and to every other happiness was added the society of those dearest to him.

When the calendar turned to the New Year, the Darcys left for London. With laughter and love for her husband, Mrs. Darcy teased him of his aversion to society, and their teasing led to the typical sort of encounter between a man and his young wife who could still claim to be besotted with each other. Regardless of whether Mrs. Darcy's suspicions were correct, she forever after considered that day to be the day on which their child was conceived.

As it was, it would be some time before the couple was aware of the fact that Mrs. Darcy was with child. They stayed in London for several months, enjoying the events of the season—or as Mrs. Darcy put it laughingly, *she* enjoyed them while her husband merely tolerated them. Darcy loved his wife so much that he was willing to do anything to give her pleasure. But when they became aware of the pending new addition to the family, they were both only too happy to leave society behind and return to Pemberley to await the birth of their child.

Those summer months, the second year of their marriage, were perfect, and Darcy would remember them for years after as one of the happiest times of his life. Mrs. Darcy's pregnancy progressed smoothly, and she glowed with health and happiness, vitality and vigor. Ever the dutiful man, Darcy continued to care for his estate, but as the summer progressed, he found much leisure time in the company of his wife. Each new event was experienced and savored: the first movement of his child, the creation of an extensive wardrobe—far more clothes than Darcy thought the child could ever wear—the visitors who came to wish them joy were all savored, stored away as future memories of their little family.

Mrs. Darcy's lying in began one beautiful morning in September. As was the custom, Darcy waited while his wife labored to bring his child into the world. He was joined in his vigil by his uncle, the Earl of Matlock, and the earl's two sons, Major Anthony Fitzwilliam and the Viscount James Fitzwilliam. It was long and difficult for the fretful young Darcy, but he was confident in the ultimate outcome. Word finally arrived of his child's birth, and he was escorted into his wife's bedchamber to meet the new arrival.

The first hint that anything was amiss was the visage of the doctor who had attended the birth at Darcy's insistence. While Darcy did not doubt the midwife's competence, it seemed only prudent to have a doctor present to assist with any unforeseen complications. Darcy's fears were about to be realized.

"Mr. Darcy," said the doctor, calling his attention as he entered the room.

The doctor motioned to the side of the room and indicated by his expression that they needed to speak. Darcy obliged, though a feeling of utter dread was welling up within his gut.

"Your child is well, Mr. Darcy," said the doctor. "The delivery was hard, but she does not appear to be affected by the ordeal."

The man paused, and though Darcy's inclination was to scream at him and demand that he speak rather than hesitate, he could only hold his breath in suspense.

"I am truly sorry, Mr. Darcy, but there is nothing I can do for Mrs.

Darcy."

Eyes wide and horror-filled, Darcy stared at the man with incomprehension.

"The birth was long and difficult, sir," continued the doctor. "Mrs. Darcy is bleeding within her body. It is beyond medicine's ability to repair. I cannot help her."

Voices screamed in Darcy's head, all vying for his attention, but to the outside world, he appeared to be numb with incomprehension. His beloved wife was to be taken from him so soon? How could such a thing be?

Gently, the doctor encouraged him to see his wife, and Darcy turned and woodenly approached the bed on which his beloved lay. Her color was chalk white. Her hair was limp and damp. Her eyes, though alert, spoke of her pain. She was altogether lovely; Darcy could not imagine a more beautiful sight.

"Will," said she as he approached and knelt beside her bed.

Darcy smiled; she was the only one who had ever referred to him in such a manner. "You have done well, my love."

Previously unnoticed, a bundle beside his wife stirred, and the small child within opened her eyes. He found himself staring at a perfect duplicate of his beloved wife. He smiled at the child, which she seemed to consider with a seriousness of someone many times her age, before her eyes once again closed in sleep.

"I require your promise, Will."

His attention brought back to his beloved wife, Darcy gazed at her, drinking in the sight of her. For the first time, he recognized that this would be the last opportunity he would have to gaze into her beloved eyes. Her agony, now evident upon her features and in her eyes, appeared to be increasing. Darcy wondered if she had been given something to dull the pain. But when he tried to turn away, she insisted upon his attention.

"Promise me you will care for our girl. She is precious. She will be the light of your life if you let her. Promise me."

Tears blurred Darcy's vision. Surely this could not be happening. He could only shake his head in denial. This was not possible.

"Promise me!"

The repeat of her plea pulled Darcy from the depths of his despair. Though his wife still pleaded with him urgently, her eyes had become dull, unfocused. Her head rested back on the pillow; she had not the strength to raise it. Her insistence demanded his agreement. He could only give it.

"I promise. She will be a testament to our love."

With a final smile and a sigh, his wife's beautiful eyes closed for the final time, and her breath grew still.

Mrs. Darcy was interred in the Darcy family crypts two days later. It was a blustery day, but Darcy could spare no thought for such mundane matters. The grieving husband and father accepted the condolences of all his acquaintances, but he did not truly see or understand those to whom he was responding. Soon, the mourners left him alone, and in the company of his sister and his cousin, Major Fitzwilliam, he stayed at Pemberley, trapped in a world he could not have imagined entering only a few months previously.

The reality of his wife's death refused to settle in. He awoke in the morning reaching for her, only to find her place empty. He found himself turning to inquire her opinion, only to remember she was not there. He found himself looking for her at the oddest times, only to discover his nightmare was reality. Nothing would ever be right again.

It was well Darcy had a capable and loyal steward, for the harvest that year could not hold Darcy's attention. Though he did not know it at the time, the steward, good man that he was, recognized his master was in no condition to make decisions and approached Darcy's cousin whenever something occurred which was beyond his purview. Between the two men, they determined what was best to be done by discussing the matter, reviewing what Darcy had decided in the past in similar circumstances, and following his example. Darcy, when he later learned of this, was grateful for their diligence.

But in that horrible autumn, he was aware of virtually nothing; little penetrated his consciousness, even though Fitzwilliam sat with him every day and informed him of the doings of the estate. He drifted in the hallways of remembrance, his thoughts filled with his wife and the happiness they had shared. Her laughter, the teasing lilt of her smiling lips, her loving way of speaking with him all ghosted past his eyes, memories of happier times, phantasms sent to torment him with images of what was, what might have been. For a time, Darcy had difficulty distinguishing between reality and fantasy, and he thought he might go mad with grief. But his sadness was never expressed. He shed not a single tear.

At length, when the demands of duty called Major Fitzwilliam away, he came to take his leave, little though Darcy understood it at the time.

"Darcy," said the major, "I have come to take my leave of you."

Darcy did not even raise his head to acknowledge his cousin. Indeed, he had barely heard him.

"I shall leave you and Georgiana, for I must return to my regiment in London. As we are being dispatched to the continent, I doubt we shall meet again for some time."

"You cannot leave," said Darcy, his voice rusty with disuse, though still uncomprehending. "Everyone I love, taken. There is little left. There is nothing. I cannot bear it."

"Our parting shall not be forever. I promise you."

"I promised . . . I promised *her*."

Perhaps it was the brokenness of his tone, perhaps it was the utter devastation of his countenance, but in that moment, his cousin's patience with him snapped, and Darcy felt himself forcibly removed from his own personal hell by the force of Fitzwilliam's strong arms.

"Darcy, you must pull yourself together! You cannot continue to live like this. Your sister needs you. Your daughter needs you. Pemberley needs you. Your wife would not wish you to give up. We all loved her, Darcy! She would not be pleased with what you have become!"

Feeling like a drunkard Darcy stared at his cousin. And all at once, the weight of the last months came crashing down on his shoulders. His knees buckled, and a sob escaped his lips.

Of the rest of that night, Darcy was never able to remember anything more than slivers of memories, impressions of the strength of his cousin's arms supporting him, the cathartic tears which flowed from his eyes, and the ever-approaching darkness which beckoned him into its arms.

When he awoke the next morning, his cousin was gone. But Darcy felt more like himself. He was refreshed in a way that he had not been since before the terrible day of his wife's passing. Perhaps most importantly, he felt like he was able to face the day; he felt able to face his life. The sadness was still there. Darcy knew that he would never be free of it. But it was now the sadness of reminiscence, the ache of longing rather than the crippling sorrow of loss which had held him in its grip. His wife had lived her life well and had not wasted an instant. Neither would he. He would live for her memory. He would live for his daughter.

Though his resolution was made with the best of intentions, Darcy found that following through with it was more difficult than he imagined. His duties as the master of Pemberley were the easiest to resume, and he took them on without hesitation. His relieved steward quickly acquainted him with the events of the past several months, the yields of the harvest and other estate business, and Darcy familiarized himself with the reports from the stewards of the other estates. Before long, he was fully in command of his assets and ready to make the decisions so essential to the continuing prosperity of his family.

Where he struggled, perhaps unsurprisingly, was in his relationships with others. His closeness with his sister was soon restored, and he received visits from his relations with perfect civility and even an eagerness to once again be acquainted with their lives. Lady Catherine he kept at arms' length, not forgetting the woman's behavior to his dear wife. But with respect to society, Darcy had no interest in once again putting himself in the public's sight, knowing the attention he had endured before his marriage would interrupt his tranquility. He lived a reclusive life at Pemberley, eschewing all forms of society, content with his work, his society with his young sister, and the occasional visits of his dearest family.

The worst part of his life was his interactions with his child. Time and again, he berated himself for his inability to involve himself with his daughter's life, but regardless of his frequent resolutions to do better, he could not stand more than a few moments in her company. She was a bright and precocious child, full of life and energy, happy and smart. But her looks were those of his dead wife—her eyes haunted him, her hair as it grew was the exact shade of his lost love, and her face, her laughter, and her very being were all reminders of what he had lost. The mere sight of her caused *her* visage to appear before him, and he was helpless before her. His only recourse was to flee. He never fell to the temptation of drowning his sorrows in the bottle during those years, but those days on which he could force himself to see the girl saw him often drinking more than he should. He hated himself for it, but he was helpless.

When more than two years had passed since Mrs. Darcy's death, Darcy was once again visited by his cousin, newly returned from the continent where he had distinguished himself in the fight against the tyrant. The arrival was greeted with joyous anticipation, and both Darcy siblings welcomed him with pleasure.

Fitzwilliam was, by nature, a garrulous sort of man, and he spent the evening in the company of his cousins regaling them with tales of his adventures. For a man who had experienced the horrors of war, Fitzwilliam seemed, in essence, unchanged from the man he had been before, and if he had acquired a little more of a haunted look about his eyes, he was still happy and eager to acquaint his cousins with all that had happened in his life. His stories were still entertaining, and Darcy suspected their content was edited in order to preserve the sensibilities of his younger cousin. Not having had much about which to smile these previous years, Darcy was quite happy to have him returned to them.

After Georgiana had sought her bed that evening, the cousins retired to Darcy's study for a nightcap, and after they had both settled into two comfortable armchairs with their drinks, they chatted well into the evening. Though Fitzwilliam had not been injured during his time of service, Darcy took care to confirm that his cousin had not been harmed in any other way, and once that matter was resolved to his satisfaction, he allowed Fitzwilliam to direct the course of their conversation. Of course, what Fitzwilliam wished to know about was the state of Darcy's life.

"You need not concern yourself for me," said Darcy in answer to Fitzwilliam's thinly veiled questions. "I am perfectly well, I assure you."

Fitzwilliam regarded him with healthy skepticism. "You are?"

"I have fulfilled all my duties. Pemberley's yield has increased these past few years, which has helped everyone in the area. The higher prices driven by the war have not hurt my revenues either. Georgiana gets on with her new companion and my daughter continues to grow." Darcy paused, thinking of the matter. "I am continuing to live. It is what I must do. It is what *she* would have wanted."

"I can see that everything is well cared for, Darcy. I never doubted that for a moment.

"How are you coping?"

A shrug was Darcy's only response. When pressed, however, he could only say: "Please leave off this inquisition, Fitzwilliam. I am grateful you pulled me from the hell I had inhabited after her death, for I truly believe I was well on my way to madness. Had she discovered the matter, I have no doubt Lady Catherine would have used it for her own advantage."

Fitzwilliam snickered as he sipped his drink. "I understand from father that you still refuse to admit her to your society."

Darcy snorted. "She journeyed here again not long after your departure, but I would not allow her entrance. Her letter denouncing my lack of civility was the last letter from her I opened; every missive since then—and there has been at least one every month—has been consigned to the fire unopened."

"I do not blame you," said Fitzwilliam. "I understand James has attended her every Easter these past years to look over the books of the estate. The old bat had wanted you to take on the task."

"No doubt so she could throw Anne in my way."

"That, dear cousin, is a wager I would not touch even should my life depend on it."

The cousins laughed together, and thoughts of Lady Catherine and her insipid daughter filled Darcy's mind. It was not as if Anne was vicious or unprincipled, but years of existing under her mother's thumb coupled with her general ill health had left her colorless and mousy, a shadow of a girl rather than a real, living person. Darcy felt sorry for her, but as Lady Catherine's late husband, Sir Lewis, had possessed the poor judgment to leave the estate in his wife's hands until her death, there was not a whole lot anyone could do about Anne's situation.

"So when will you reenter society?" asked Fitzwilliam.

"I will not," said Darcy, his resolve putting an end to any suggestion this was a welcome topic. "Subject myself once again to the cloying attentions of every fortune hunter in society? I will not do it. My daughter—" Darcy's voice choked up at the very mention of the girl. "She may inherit the estate when she comes of age. I shall approve her marriage to any young man who agrees to take on the Darcy name. I am through with society."

"It is not sound, Darcy," said Fitzwilliam. "You know this, little though you wish to own it."

When Darcy refused to speak on the matter any further, his cousin sighed and then said: "To say nothing of your daughter, whose time in society is still many years away, Georgiana needs your involvement for her own introduction to be a success."

"Your mother and father may escort her."

Fitzwilliam, however, was not daunted by his unfriendly tone and the flashing of his eyes. "You know it will not be the same. Yes, mother and father have standing and fortune to recommend them, but if there is any oddness perceived on the part of her brother and guardian, it might materially damage Georgiana's chances of making a good marriage."

"Then I shall simply barter a marriage for her with a good man, and save her the trouble of having to deal with society.

"It will also save her from the torture of falling in love," said Darcy in an almost inaudible tone. He stared into his glass, seeing images he had long consigned to the furthest reaches of his memory. He wished he could forever expunge them from his mind.

"Darcy," said Fitzwilliam, and against his will, Darcy's attention was drawn to his cousin and away from his waking nightmare.

The expression of utter compassion with which his cousin regarded him was Darcy's undoing. It spoke of love and friendship, brotherhood, and all those things which bound them together and had done so since they had been small boys. Fitzwilliam was the one person in the world who possibly understood Darcy better than he did himself. He knew he could have no secrets from his cousin.

"Tell me, cousin, can you honestly claim that you would rather not have loved at all? Can you state without a doubt that it would have been better had your mother and father behaved as many in society and withheld their love? What of Mrs. Darcy? Would it have been better to never know love, rather than to have had the time you spent with her, however brief?"

"No," said Darcy after struggling with his emotions for some minutes. "But that does not make the pain any less."

"Nor should it." Fitzwilliam rubbed his chin for a moment, his eyes unfocused, before he seemed to come to a resolution. "You know, I had considered pursuing your wife myself instead of introducing you to her."

"And why did you not?" This was something Darcy had always wondered, and he eyed his cousin with keen interest.

"Because I knew she would be perfect for you. I knew that you would form a connection with her, and light and life would be brought into your world. I would have loved her—I did love her, as the wife of my cousin. But I could not have loved her with the depth you possessed.

"Tell me now—was I wrong to have introduced her to you? Was I wrong to think you would have wished never to meet her, rather than have been blessed with the time you had, no matter how brief?"

"No, you were not," rasped Darcy.

"Then continue to live your life. Let each day be a tribute to her. She would not have wished for you to hide yourself at Pemberley, close yourself off to all people, all forms of love."

Fitzwilliam watched him as he considered the matter. Somehow his cousin knew exactly what to say. He always knew what to say.

"There is no need for you to enter society again as if nothing has changed. You may even make it known that you are not looking for a wife."

"I doubt that will be much of a deterrent."

"Perhaps not. But it may dissuade those with nothing more than casual interest. You have always been able to handle the mercenary before. Georgiana is still only fifteen, so you have time. Go to London this season, and even if you do not partake in social events, connecting with old friends will once again be to your benefit."

For some reason, Darcy felt like he was standing on the edge of some great precipice; the sensation that the whole course of his life would be altered by his decision here today was strong, and though he could not account for it, he did not doubt that something momentous was occurring. Whether this feeling was in any way real did not truly matter. Deep within the recesses of his heart, Darcy knew Fitzwilliam only spoke the truth. It was time to live again, even if only for his dearest sister. If he could help her find her happiness in life, loved in a marriage to a good man, he would be happy indeed.

For the moment his mind shied away from similar thoughts of his daughter; that was a matter which he still had many years to consider. But for Georgiana's sake, he would do as Fitzwilliam asked.

"Very well. We shall go to London early in the New Year."

Chapter II

What remained of that autumn was a time for Darcy to come to terms with his decision to reenter society. He still intended to keep his participation to a minimum—surely his appearance at a few carefully chosen events, coupled with the renewal of his friendships with several old acquaintances, would be enough to ensure Georgiana's acceptance when the time came.

It was an adjustment to his way of thinking. He had not thought he would *ever* return to his life, or once again partake in society in even the smallest way; it was a testament to his relationship with Fitzwilliam that he would even consider such a thing, as all the pleas from his aunt and uncle had been steadfastly refused. But even the thought of once again putting himself in the way of London's fortune hunters filled him with dread, and more than once he considered calling it off altogether.

The one thing that stopped him was not even his cousin, for Fitzwilliam had not been able to stay long before he returned to London and his duties. It was Georgiana.

"I cannot tell you how happy I am we shall return to London, brother," said Georgiana.

In fact, Darcy had been ruminating on the matter, and was actively considering telling his sister that they would not return to London at all when she had spoken.

"You are?" asked he, and he marveled at her excitement, which was such that she had missed the way his voice came out as a croak.

"Of course I am, brother," replied Georgiana happily. "I am sure I am not the most social of creatures, but I do long for the theater, concerts, the museums, and all the other activities which can be found in London. Though I am not out, there will be ample sources of amusement to keep us entertained while we are in residence."

Darcy was surprised. Georgiana had always been a quiet and timid child, ill at ease meeting others and content with her own solitude. In short, she was a little too much like Darcy himself.

And then Darcy was forced to consider what she had said. When Georgiana put it that way, it was not the daunting task he had been dreading. He had always enjoyed music and the theater, and there were many sights to see in London which his sister would enjoy. The thought of stepping into all that without any hesitation did fill him with a bit of dismay, but it was not as debilitating as the thought of the full season and all the social obligations which came with it. A slow build up would be best to become accustomed to being with people again, and he felt certain that regardless of her seemingly newfound interest in such things, Georgiana would agree with him wholeheartedly.

"And how long have you wished for such a change in our routine?" asked Darcy, curious at this sudden change in his sister.

"Mrs. Annesley has told me of her experiences in London during our lessons," said Georgiana, her manner beginning to show an enthusiasm he could rarely remember seeing from her. "I wish to see the menagerie, the Royal Academy, and maybe even the races at Epsom!" Georgiana smiled and ducked her head a little self-consciously. "I would even like to see an opera. I've read much of Herr Mozart's works, and I would love to witness such sublime music mixed with theater."

A gentle smile settled over Darcy's face, and he was overcome with a reminiscence from the past. Mrs. Darcy had loved the opera, and her especial favorite had been Mozart's *The Marriage of Figaro*. They had seen it in London at Covent Garden mere days after their marriage. Even now, Darcy could remember the expression of joy in his wife's eyes as she had watched the story unfold on the stage, could hear the sound of her voice as she sang much of the music quietly along with the actors. She had possessed a beautiful voice. Darcy's tastes in music ran more toward the symphony and the concerto, but he had indulged her for nothing more than his pure love of her. He had to confess he had enjoyed the music as well, though he had always considered the story to be a little frivolous.

For the first time, however, this memory was characterized by fond remembrance of a significant event in his life rather than the crushing sorrow and sense of loss. He indulged in the memory for several moments before he realized he was not searching for a way to keep his composure, and though he was grateful for the sudden strength found within, the realization caused a sort of sad acceptance. His time with his wife was fading into memory, mere wisps of the past. But he would *never* forget her. Of that he was determined.

It was mere days in advance of the Christmas holiday when Darcy received a letter from one of his friends, Charles Bingley. Despite his close friendship with the man, Darcy opened it with a hint of trepidation, knowing Bingley's manner of correspondence was atrocious and his letters nearly always illegible. Bingley was one of the few friends who he had seen these past two years. He was a younger man Darcy had met at Cambridge and his family's fortune had been made in business. He still had many concerns in the York area which required his attention from time to time, but though he was attempting to leave that world behind and purchase an estate, he had been obliged to journey north several times, during which he would stop and meet with Darcy, usually staying only a night. Darcy valued his friend's visits.

For a wonder, Bingley's letter was actually readable. It seemed like he had leased an estate to learn something of its management, and there had met his angel and was engaged to be married. Darcy shook his head; Bingley had always been less than astute when it came to fortune hunters, and his head had often been turned by a pretty face.

Darcy quickly penned him a reply. In it, Darcy congratulated Bingley for his upcoming nuptials, while informing his friend that he would be unable to attend the wedding. Instead, he proposed that they meet in London during the season where they could renew their friendship. He could only pray that Bingley had made a wise choice; Darcy could do nothing further concerning the matter. Surprisingly, for Bingley was not a diligent correspondent, a reply arrived with alacrity, expressing all Bingley's anticipation of meeting again in the New Year.

That Christmas season was characterized by family as the Fitzwilliams—including his aunt, uncle, the viscount, Colonel Fitzwilliam, and the earl's daughters and their husbands—descended upon Pemberley. The season was joyous and the company good, and if Darcy felt the melancholy of remembrance settle over him, such feelings arrived late and did not stay with him as they might have before. The Fitzwilliams were a close-knit family, loving and happy, and

Christmastide had always been a family favorite. Darcy's mother had loved Christmas, and his childhood memories of the season were happy. It seemed that Georgiana had inherited her mother's love, and as he was charmed by her enthusiasm, he allowed her to do as she wished. The results were a testament to her passion, as Pemberley was liberally festooned with all manner of holly, mistletoe, and other greenery.

"So I hear you are returning to London," said James the Viscount Chesterfield that Christmas night. They had remained in the dining room after the ladies had withdrawn as was the traditional practice.

"Your brother left me no choice," replied Darcy. He had always gotten on well with James; they were not close in the manner Darcy was with Colonel Fitzwilliam, partially due to the viscount being five years older, but he had always looked up to the other man. That this might be due to James strong character and upright manner—so unlike so many others of his set—Darcy had never really considered.

"Nor should he," said the earl. "You have mourned your wife long enough, Darcy. She was a beautiful woman. But I believe she would not wish you to forever closet yourself at Pemberley. She was full of life—I believe she would wish the same for you."

"As I have recently been reminded," Darcy murmured as he stared into his glass.

"Come, Darcy, it will not be all bad," said James. "There are many amusements in London. You need not even attend balls and such if you do not wish to."

"I do not," said Darcy firmly, not missing the looks of amusement which passed between his relations. "But I believe I will enjoy escorting Georgiana to wherever she expresses an interest to go. And you are right about the variety of amusements."

"That is the spirit, Darcy!' said Fitzwilliam.

"If you are for London, you and Georgiana should visit Snowlock on your way south," said the earl. "Susan would love to have you stay, even if it was only for a week."

Darcy considered the matter. Georgiana would enjoy the opportunity to stay with her relations for a week, and it would allow Darcy himself to become accustomed to being away from Pemberley, without having to deal with going to town immediately. Furthermore, he had not visited his mother's ancestral home for some time, and unaccountably, he found himself wishing to be there again.

"I believe we might be persuaded to accept such an invitation," said Darcy.

"Excellent. We shall count on having you."

What Darcy had not counted on when he agreed to join the Fitzwilliams at Snowlock, was that his aunt might have ideas related to his future felicity in mind. On a cold and snowy morning in late January, Darcy and his sister entered the carriage for the short journey to the south which would take them to the Fitzwilliam estate. When they arrived, they exited the carriage and entered the house, retiring to their rooms to refresh themselves. It was not until they descended to the sitting-room to attend the family that Darcy realized there was another in residence at his uncle's estate.

"Thank you for coming, Darcy," greeted Lady Susan with pleasure

By her side, a tall, slender woman arose, watching him with interest. She was fair of complexion and her long blonde hair was gathered up into an elegant style that accentuated her comeliness of appearance. Those attributes, along with the seeming advantage of poise and grace, rendered her an appealing young woman indeed.

Knowing this was a test for what was to come, Darcy smiled slightly and bowed. "Thank you for the invitation, aunt. Georgiana and I are happy to be here."

"Oh, do desist with this bowing nonsense, Darcy. Unless you think me to be one of those in society who must be kept at arm's length."

Darcy stepped forward and kissed his aunt's cheek. She was a lovely woman, happy and bright, possessing an impeccable sense of decorum and at ease in any company. And even though she had two sons and two daughters full grown, time had been kind, leaving in her visage a mature loveliness which spoke to the uncommon beauty she had possessed as a young woman.

"Darcy, please allow me to introduce Victoria Patterson. Victoria is a relation through my sister's husband. She is staying with us until we return to town for the season. Victoria, this is my nephew, Fitzwilliam Darcy of Pemberley."

Bowing to her curtsey, Darcy dusted off his long-disused sense of civility and inquired after the lady, receiving a tolerable reply.

It quickly became evident that even if she was not about to actively promote a match, Lady Susan was at least interested to see how he got on with Miss Patterson. When they sat down, they spoke for several moments before Lady Susan was called away by the housekeeper, and Darcy watched her go with more than a hint of suspicion. His aunt was not above a little stratagem in order to push events in the direction she wanted.

"I understand your estate is a little north of here," said Miss

Patterson, drawing his attention back to her.

"It is," confirmed Darcy. "The journey is a little more than four hours on good roads in the summer. With the current weather, it consumed more than an additional hour."

"Oh, please do not discuss the weather, Mr. Darcy. It is positively dull to discuss such a mundane matter, and it cannot but call to mind the insipid commentary of many young men in London who only care for their amusements."

In spite of himself, Darcy smiled. "I must confess I have often thought conversation to be lacking in London's drawing rooms. It is as if people of substance do not exist."

"I cannot agree more, Mr. Darcy. Come, what think you of books?"

And thus began a conversation which was far more satisfying than any he had ever had with a young woman who was not his late wife. They spoke for some time, and then when they went into dinner, they carried on that conversation over the meal. And by the end of it, Darcy was happy to find that Victoria Patterson was a different breed than most young ladies of high society. She was intelligent, well-read, handsome, and in possession of impeccable manners.

But despite her many attractions and Darcy's great enjoyment of their conversation and appreciation for her physical assets, he was completely *disinterested* in a closer connection. It was nothing he could put his finger on, no seeming deficiency in Miss Patterson, and nothing in her person or manners which put her in that category. Furthermore, he sensed that she did not wish for anything but a pleasing discussion from him, and for the rest of his visit he was able to simply enjoy being in the company of his family, and in the society of a young woman who was lovely, clever, and wanted nothing more from him.

Only a day or two before their stay was to end, Darcy found himself in conversation with his aunt. She had not played the matchmaker on this visit and she had not attempted to put him in company with her niece, but he had found her watching him at times, and he wondered exactly what her motive was for bring her niece here at that particular time.

"I am happy you have decided to rejoin society, Darcy," said Lady Susan. "I was beginning to despair of you ever showing any interest again."

"It is a stretch to call it 'interest,' aunt," said Darcy, a definite wry note coloring his words. "Nothing less than Georgiana's future and that of my daughter could have pried me from Pemberley at present."

"Then it is well you possess such a sense of duty. And I must tell you that your daughter is the sweetest little creature I have ever met. You must be proud of her."

To hide the shame he felt at his many failures with respect to his daughter, Darcy changed the subject: "I thank you for inviting us, aunt. Georgiana and I have truly appreciated your hospitality."

"You are welcome at any time, of course." Lady Susan paused and looked at Darcy with an expression that made him feel like she was seeing right through him. "And have you enjoyed the company of us *all*?"

Immediately understanding to whom his aunt was referring, Darcy felt an instant of anger, which changed to curiosity when he recalled his aunt had not, in fact, thrown her niece at him during the course of his stay.

"I must confess your *guest* was a surprise. If not for the fact that she is a lovely young woman, I might almost be upset at such blatant matchmaking."

Lady Susan laughed. "Surely you cannot accuse *me* of matchmaking!"

"No, you have been circumspect this entire visit. But I must wonder at your invitation to a young lady precisely at the time when I have left Pemberley for the first time in years."

"You may rest your suspicions, Darcy. Victoria's visit was decided upon before Hugh issued the invitation to you and Georgiana and her stay here began almost as soon as we returned home from Pemberley. I *was*, however, happy that she was here when you came."

"Oh?" asked Darcy. He was more curious than annoyed.

"Darcy, you are going back to London, and you know what society can be like. I was happy Victoria was here because she gives you an easy initiation back into the ebb and flow of conversation and making new acquaintances in as unthreatening a situation as possible. Furthermore, I wished to show you that not all young ladies are cold and calculating. Not all have capturing a rich husband on their minds."

"I assume Miss Patterson is in the market for a husband?"

"No indeed," replied his aunt with more than a hint of amusement. "In fact, Victoria is visiting us as a respite from suitors who will not leave her alone!"

A smile broke out on Darcy's face. "She has had some trouble, has she?"

Lady Susan shook her head. "Her father is the proprietor of a prosperous estate, though a little smaller than Pemberley, but as she is an only daughter, Victoria's fortune is substantial. That coupled with her connections to Matlock and other connections on her mother's side have caused her to be highly sought after since her debut two years ago.

"Unfortunately, with such virtues to recommend her, the attention she has attracted has at times been overwhelming. Two such suitors attached themselves to her near the end of the little season, and have been most persistent in pursuing her. As she was not inclined to either of them, her mother and I decided it would be best for her to stay with us for some time, in order to cool their ardor. We shall be joining you in London two weeks after you depart, and she will stay with us for a time before returning to her father's home. We have let it be known that she is under the earl's protection, and that we will allow for no untoward behavior."

"Do you suppose it will work?"

"Only time will tell," said Lady Susan with a shrug. "At the very least, I believe my husband and sons will take a dim view of any suitors stepping beyond propriety."

Darcy chuckled and then changed the subject. It was, after all, a very good thing to know that his aunt was not indulging in such behavior. Perhaps even more important to Darcy was the lesson of the variety of people who were found in society was not unwelcome. For the rest of their time at Snowlock, Darcy was able to appreciate the company without fear of any ulterior motives, including that of Victoria Patterson. She *was* a beautiful girl, he decided.

It was on a cool but clear day that Darcy and Georgiana departed for London with his daughter following with the nurse in the second carriage, with all the assorted luggage and accoutrements which would normally follow them on a journey of such magnitude. They made good time to London, and soon were ensconced within the homey confines of Darcy House on Grosvenor Street.

For Darcy, seeing the family home in London was fraught with emotions, for it was here he first met his beloved wife, here where he had paid court to her, and here where he had brought her for the first two weeks of their marriage. A sense of nostalgia enveloped him as he roamed through the familiar rooms; the music room, where she had played and sang for him, the sitting-room, where they spent evenings in company, welcoming guests and reading to one another, to the bedroom, where their nights had been filled with passion and love. But after indulging in his memories for a short time, Darcy put those memories firmly from his mind. That way lay sorrow and madness, and he would not return to that state.

The first few days were spent settling in and accustoming themselves to being in London once again. His in-laws visited as he had given them advance notice of their arrival. Darcy had his daughter brought down from the nursery, and he watched as his wife's parents and their younger daughter were reintroduced to his daughter. The ladies fussed over her and the gentleman exclaimed at how much she had grown and how smart she was. Darcy bore it all with dignity, thanking them when required, and agreeing with them, though he had no personal knowledge of the matter with his inability to stay in the same room of his daughter for more than a few minutes.

Within a few days, they had settled inn, grateful they had been left in peace. The true crush of the season had not yet started and Darcy had not put the door knocker up on his door, signaling to all they were not accepting visitors at that time.

Of course, such strictures did not apply to those who were the closest of his friends. Fitzwilliam visited soon after their arrival, and Darcy became reacquainted with a few gentlemen with whom he had been friendly before his withdrawal from society. But perhaps the most welcome of those who visited was his dear friend, Charles Bingley.

Bingley was a garrulous man, tall in stature—though his height was not so much as the men of Fitzwilliam descent were wont to attain—with a shock of short red hair on his head and a spring in his step. On an afternoon not long after Darcy's arrival, Bingley bounded into Darcy's study and greeted him with pleasure, his handshake vigorous and friendly.

"It is good indeed to see you at last, Darcy," said Bingley in greeting. "I have missed your company and wished for your sound advice on more than one occasion."

Privately Darcy thought Bingley was being a little more enthusiastic than was warranted, given Darcy's distaste for society. But it was ever thus with Bingley, and so Darcy allowed him to exclaim his pleasure, reflecting on his own appreciation of once more being in the presence of his friend.

"So you have recently married," said Darcy when he could insert a word.

"I have!" said Bingley, his enthusiasm rising to greater heights. "My wife is an angel. I am a fortunate man indeed."

"And how did you meet this paragon of virtue?"

Ignoring, or perhaps not even recognizing Darcy's slightly sardonic tone, Bingley was a font of words which could not be stoppered.

"My Jane is the eldest of five daughters of my neighbor, a Mr. Bennet, and she is everything lovely, graceful, demure, and elegant. The family is an interesting one, with quite a disparity of individuals amongst them, though they are closely knit."

Darcy wondered if this was Bingley's way of saying the Bennets were in some way deficient, but his friend had not paused to draw breath. Bingley spoke on for some time, telling Darcy about the woman he had married, and dwelling on the seeming multitude of her fine attributes. One might think the woman was a messenger sent from on high for all the boasting Bingley indulged in. At some point, the man actually began to repeat himself, and Darcy sighed, knowing his friend could go on for some time in that fashion.

"The Bennets actually share a connection with you, though it is not a typical one."

When Darcy raised his eyebrow, Bingley chuckled. "The Bennet estate, Longbourn, is entailed away from their daughters on a cousin who is a newly ordained clergyman. This man happens to hold the living at Hunsford, of which I know you are familiar."

"I am familiar with it indeed," said Darcy. "Newly ordained you say?"

Bingley replied in the affirmative and Darcy could only shake his head. "I can only imagine what sort of man he is. My aunt prefers to surround herself with those who will not dare gainsay her, and if they are also disposed to drown her with compliments and behave as if she inhabits a higher plane than mere mortals, she is well pleased indeed."

A great laugh escaped Bingley's lips. "With such words I might have thought you had already met Mr. Collins."

"No, I merely understand my aunt, Bingley. She prefers to keep the distinction of rank preserved, you understand."

"Yes, well the cousin is estranged from the Bennets at present, though I understand he was not even known to Mr. Bennet before. I shall not bore you with the details, however."

Darcy nodded but his mind was engaged in other matters. He wondered if Bingley had managed to get himself ensnared by a fortune hunter. If these Bennets had five daughters to provide for and an estate which was entailed away from the female line, then he could not imagine the daughters' portions consisted of much. Unless, of course, the estate was large and otherwise produced a goodly income.

Darcy decided against saying anything, as he would not cast aspersions on Mrs. Bingley, especially as he had never even met the woman. Besides, it was not as if the matter was his business.

"In fact, I have come today with an invitation for you to dine with us whenever convenient so that you might meet my wife," said Bingley. "Please say you will come—I would so much like to introduce you."

Though Darcy thought to refuse, he knew he could not. If a dinner with Bingley would not provide an evening of which nothing untoward would be expected of him, then he could not imagine the existence of such a thing.

"Please do not concern yourself," said Bingley. "Caroline is living with the Hursts at present, and I do not intend to inform her that you will be dining with us."

"I thank you Bingley," said Darcy, "but you misconstrue my hesitation. I was not concerned about Miss Bingley's attendance."

In fact, Darcy considered Bingley's sister to be a serious impediment, not only to Bingley rising in society, but also to his very respectability. The woman was not poor in appearance—in fact she was tall and handsome, and if a little too slender for Darcy's taste, at least she was the commonly held epitome of loveliness. Unfortunately, the woman could not be described as "amiable" by any stretch of the imagination. The adjectives "catty," "unpleasant," and "mean" all came to mind. Miss Bingley was a social climber of the first order, and though Darcy had met her only a time or two before he had begun to court his wife, she seemed to instantly latch onto the idea that there was no one more suitable to be Mrs. Darcy than she herself. Darcy had hoped that the woman had found some poor soul to take her on in the interim, but as she was living with the Hursts it appeared he would not be so fortunate. Undoubtedly, she would decide she was still the best woman to become Mrs. Darcy.

"I find that I can bear Caroline's absence cheerfully," said Bingley, interrupting Darcy's reverie.

"Surely you have not banished her to the Hursts," said Darcy with a frown.

Bingley laughed. "Nothing so terrible, I assure you. In fact, my sister-in-law—Elizabeth Bennet, who is Jane's closest sister—is living with us at present, and I am quite happy to have her. She has helped my Jane settle into her role as mistress of my house, and she is a joy to associate with.

"But Caroline and Elizabeth do not get on at all. As long as Elizabeth is in residence, I doubt we will see much of Caroline."

Again Darcy hesitated, though this time it was because of the unknown, single young woman who was likely desperate to find a husband.

"Darcy," said Bingley, "would I knowingly subject you to a woman like my sister? My wife is an angel who will make you feel welcome the instant you enter the house. And Elizabeth is a fine woman, and I assure you I have proof that she is most definitely not a fortune hunter. It would please me if you would consent to join us."

Not being able to refuse—and indeed Darcy was curious to meet these women of whom Bingley spoke—Darcy agreed and they set a date for the dinner. The friends spoke for several more moments before they parted. Darcy was forced to own that he was happy Bingley had called and invited him to dinner. The ladies were unknown to him, and Darcy was rarely comfortable when meeting new acquaintances, he expected it would be the perfect opportunity to attend an intimate event where he could be hopeful of being tolerably pleased with the company.

Chapter III

When Darcy told his sister of the upcoming dinner party, he was surprised to see how enthused she was at the prospect of meeting new ladies. As a consequence of his own self-inflicted exile at Pemberley, Georgiana had often been left alone at his estate with only her governess and later her companion for company, and though he knew she did not blame him for her solitude, she was always eager to expand the circle of her acquaintances. Bingley's descriptions of the ladies in question intrigued her all that much more, and Darcy was forced to agree—his friend had given them flaming characters indeed.

"They sound wonderful. I look forward to making their acquaintance."

"I do not believe they are of our station," cautioned Darcy.

"I have not found many of our station I would wish to befriend," countered Georgiana, and Darcy had to acknowledge she was entirely correct. "Given how amiable Mr. Bingley is, I doubt they can be nothing less."

Darcy again was forced to agree with her. When Darcy told her of the date when they were to attend, Georgiana's countenance fell.

"But on Thursday I am engaged to spend the entire day with Lady Emily."

Lady Emily Carrington was the one girl from school with whom Georgiana had kept up an acquaintance. She was a fine girl of Georgiana's age, with happy manners and a sunny disposition, and she came from an impeccable lineage, as her father was an earl. They had been friends since almost the first moment of their acquaintance, according to Georgiana, and they were now as close as two friends could be.

"Then perhaps I could ask Bingley if we can postpone dinner until another day," said Darcy.

"No, brother. You must go on the date you have been invited. I shall have the opportunity to meet Mrs. Bingley and Miss Bennet some other day."

Darcy demurred, stating that Bingley would not mind, but Georgiana insisted. And so Darcy sent a note around to Bingley, confirming his attendance, but citing a previous engagement as the reason for his sister's inability to attend.

The day of the dinner came and Darcy arrived at Bingley's townhouse and was shown into the sitting-room where his friend was waiting for him with two young ladies. Upon his entrance, Bingley smiled and stood, greeting him with a firm grip and a pump of his hand while saying:

"Welcome, Darcy. I am happy you have joined us tonight."

"Thank you, Bingley." Darcy paused, and keeping to protocol, indicated the two ladies who had risen with Bingley and said, "May I request an introduction to the ladies?"

Bingley beamed and beckoned to the two women who came and stood beside him. "Darcy, may I present my wife, Mrs. Jane Bingley," said he, indicating the taller of the two women, "and her younger sister, Miss Elizabeth Bennet. Jane, Elizabeth, this is my closest friend, Mr. Fitzwilliam Darcy."

The ladies curtseyed and Darcy bowed, and when they rose he was able to study them. Mrs. Bingley was exactly the sort of woman Darcy would have thought Bingley would be attracted to. She was tall, though not so tall as Miss Patterson, blonde, and very beautiful. A few moments in her company told Darcy that she was reticent, offering her opinions in a soft tone which, though not lacking in confidence, still spoke to a willingness to allow others of a more forceful nature to take the lead in any social situation.

By contrast, Miss Bennet was darker in coloring, smaller of stature, and much more outgoing than her sister. She was also mischievous, as several times Darcy thought he caught a glimmer of amusement in her eyes, as if she had professed an opinion which she did not espouse merely to provoke a response. Darcy could easily see that she was not what society would deem to be the epitome of beauty, and on that scale he had no doubt she would pale in comparison to her sister. But Darcy had never cared for being fashionable. Darcy could see a definite resemblance between the ladies, and furthermore, the intelligence in her eyes, so dark brown as to be almost black, her high cheekbones and brilliant complexion, her dark mahogany hair, and her playful yet proper manner rendered her to be uncommonly pretty.

"We understand you have a younger sister, Mr. Darcy," said Miss Bennet.

"Yes. My sister, Georgiana, is not out yet, as she is not yet sixteen."

The two ladies shared an expressive look, which seemed to convey some mutual understanding. When she noticed his scrutiny, Miss Bennet said:

"Our younger sister, Lydia, is out and she is not yet sixteen. Of course, she only attends events of local society and does not come to London, but still Jane and I both believe she requires a little . . . maturity before she should be allowed in society. She is . . ."

"Exuberant?" added Bingley helpfully.

Darcy did not miss the younger sister's roll of her eyes. "As always, Charles, you have a gift for understatement."

They all laughed and Darcy looked on with good humor. Though a sister who was somewhat wild could be a detriment to the family, their humor suggested to him that she was not malicious, regardless of her present high spirits. In time, perhaps, she would gain a little maturity as they hoped. For the present, it was just as well that she was hidden away in Hertfordshire. Society—especially that of Darcy's sphere—was remarkably intolerant of poor behavior. Or at least society was intolerant of poor behavior when it was not accompanied by wealth and connections. Darcy personally knew of several who were worthy of the derision of society but were protected by family names or great wealth

"Does Miss Darcy favor any particular activities?" asked Miss Bennet.

"She is especially fond of music," replied Darcy after a moment. While he might usually be made uncomfortable by such questions, he found in this instance he was completely at ease. Miss Bennet's manner spoke of genuine interest which could not be feigned. It was far from the behavior of the Miss Bingleys of the world, who looked on his younger sister as a path to obtain his favor. "She practices quite diligently, and I find her playing to be enchanting, though I own my bias in the matter."

"Then I would be pleased to make her acquaintance," said Miss Bennet. "I do play the pianoforte, though I do not claim to be a proficient. I would love to make the acquaintance of one who is as skilled as you suggest."

"Do not allow Lizzy to mislead you, Mr. Darcy," said Mrs. Bingley, speaking for the first time since they had entered the sitting-room. "She plays with great feeling and everyone who hears her is quite complimentary, though she usually brushes such praise off."

"I do not require you to inflate my conceit, Jane," said Miss Bennet. "I am quite aware of my own level of skill. Besides, Charlotte performs the task of speaking of my perceived level of skill admirably."

A shadow seemed to pass over Miss Bennet's face, and her countenance took on a bit of a distant look, filled with an understated sense of melancholy. It seemed like something she said had caused a remembrance of some sort which was causing her pain.

"It is no flattery, Elizabeth," said her sister. "You do play well, even if you will not own it."

"My sister has expressed a desire to meet you both," said Darcy, attempting to change the subject from one which seemed to cause Miss Bennet discomfort. "She was not able to attend tonight, but she would be happy to receive you at Darcy house."

"Then my sister and I shall be happy to call on her," said Mrs. Bingley.

They discussed the matter for a few moments, deciding on a time and date for the call, and Darcy promised to consult with a sister to ensure it met with her schedule. They had begun speaking on other subjects when the housekeeper entered announcing dinner, and the party rose to go to the dining room, Bingley escorting his sister-in-law, while Darcy escorted Mrs. Bingley.

As there were only four diners, the large table had been converted to the small size necessary for an intimate dinner among friends, with Bingley and his wife sitting at each end of the table as was proper, and Darcy and Miss Bennet sitting opposite one another along the longer sides of the table. There, conversation flowed freely, and largely through the auspices of Bingley and Miss Bennet, as they were by far the most vocal of the party. And though his usual habit was to allow others to speak while he listened—usually with boredom—Darcy found himself well entertained. It was an amicable group, an interesting discussion, and the excellence of the meal made the time speed past. It was most unlike the majority of other dinner parties he had attended.

When dinner was completed, Bingley was of mind to eschew the normal separation of the sexes, but his wife and Miss Bennet laughed at the suggestion.

When the ladies had left, Bingley looked at Darcy and raised an eyebrow. Darcy shook his head and smiled. "Mrs. Bingley is indeed a lovely woman, Bingley. I congratulate you. She seems to be quite well suited to you."

"A fine admission, man," cried Bingley. "I could not imagine finding a better woman for my wife than my dear Jane. The advantages of having her as a wife render whatever disadvantages attached to her situation quite meaningless."

Darcy peered at his friend sharply. "Disadvantages?"

Bingley grimaced, and so he might, if Darcy's suspicions were in any way grounded in reality. "It is nothing—I should not have mentioned it. In truth, nothing matters when I may have such a wonderful woman for my wife."

"Bingley," growled Darcy in warning.

"She possessed little dowry," said Bingley, finally giving in. "As her father is a country squire, she has not the connections that some possess, save an uncle who is an astute businessman. In fact, I believe you would get along well indeed with Mr. Gardiner. He is a gentlemanly man—more so than many other so-called gentlemen I have met."

"She will not raise your standing in society, Bingley," chided Darcy, ignoring the suggestion that he might be introduced to a tradesman. "In fact, with relations such as you say, she may be a detriment."

"It is not as bad as all that. She *is* the daughter of a gentleman."

"She may be," said Darcy. "But you are well aware of the reception your family has received in town and how difficult it has been for you at times. Hurst's connections do assist, though he is not of the first circles himself, but even though your wife is a gentleman's daughter, she cannot provide you with that extra . . . respectability which would allow you to be accepted by a higher level."

"She provides me with something far more important, Darcy."

"I am being quite serious, Bingley."

"As am I."

Darcy paused and looked at his friend. Bingley seemed to possess far more confidence than Darcy could ever remember in the man, and he was confronted by a firmness which seemed out of place on his affable friend's countenance.

"I love my wife, Darcy, and I am grateful she has come into my life. I have seen what you shared with Mrs. Darcy, and I will assume you cannot fault me for wishing to have the same in my life."

"My wife also possessed fortune and connections, Bingley," said Darcy. "It was an eligible match, not only a love match."

"Can you honestly say you would not have loved her had she been lacking in dowry? Would she have been a jot less agreeable to you had she not had a great uncle who is a marquess? I cannot imagine it of you."

Though Darcy did not have as much confidence in his ability to look beyond these things as his friend attributed to him, he could only cede the point. Knowing what he knew *now,* he would have married his wife if she had not possessed a farthing to her name and no connections higher than a country parson. However, though he would have been enchanted by her just as quickly, Darcy wondered if he would have been able to ignore the lack of those virtues society deemed to be so essential, or if his pride would have stood in his way. While he would like to state with unequivocal conviction that he would have, he could not be certain himself.

"I suppose we cannot know," said Darcy out loud to his friend. Then, realizing he had not been gracious, he smiled a little ruefully at his friend. "My apologies, Bingley. I should never have spoken of your wife in such a fashion."

Bingley only waved him off. "Considering the conversations we have had in the past, I confess I had expected you might say something.

"But I cannot repine my choice of wife despite any of these things. She is a wonderful woman, a check on my exuberance, which, as you recall, is one of my defining characteristics."

Darcy chuckled. His friend *was* very lively. Companionable silence settled over the friends and while Darcy was considering the situation, mixed with memories of his late wife, he thought that Bingley was caught up in thoughts of his own of the young woman in the other room, with whom he appeared to be quite besotted. The sight stirred up a feeling of . . . well, not precisely envy. He missed his wife as much now as he had when she had first been taken from him, and though he was happy for his friend for his circumstances, thoughts of Darcy's own lonely existence brought a sense of melancholy on him.

After a few moments Bingley perked up a little—remembering Darcy was there, unless Darcy missed his guess—and looked on his friend with what Darcy could only call soberness.

"How have you been these past years?"

Hesitating—he did not wish for anyone other than his family to know of his near madness after his wife's death—Darcy decided to tell his friend the truth without any details.

"I am well, Bingley. I do miss her, as you must already know. But I am coping. She would wish me to continue living, and what I do, I do for her memory."

"I cannot imagine what you have been through," replied Bingley. "I cannot fathom the thought of losing my Jane."

"I hope you are never required to experience it."

Bingley only nodded; there was nothing further to be said, after all.

"What of marriage? Have you given any thought to remarrying?"

"I do not expect that I shall ever marry again."

"Far be it for me to suggest you might benefit from having a wife again," said Bingley, "but would it not be best for your daughter to have a mother?"

Darcy sighed—that was the one argument he had never quite been able to dismiss when he promised himself he would never again submit to matrimony. In fact, he thought it might be exactly what she would require, given his own insufficiency in the matter.

"One cannot ever be sure," said Darcy, though slowly and with hesitation. "I cannot imagine ever loving another woman as much, and if I cannot give my whole heart, it would hardly be fair to her."

"Many women in society would not care if you withheld your heart."

Darcy smiled. "And I would not wish for such a woman to be mother to my daughter."

A commiserating nod met his statement.

"I believe you are correct in that it *would* be desirable for my daughter to have a mother. But I do not, in the strictest sense, require a son, so I need not marry in order to sire a male heir. Pemberley is not entailed, and my daughter may inherit as well as a son."

"I wish you well, my friend," said Bingley. "As you are well aware, there is nothing quite like experiencing the love of a good woman, and if could find another gem like your wife, I believe it would make you happier in the end. But if you will excuse me, I believe it is time to return to the ladies."

Readily agreeing, Darcy arose with his host and allowed him to lead the way from the dining room. He *was not* envious of Bingley's good fortune, decided Darcy. In fact, he was pleased that Bingley had found someone to love and who would love him in return. Darcy had always recognized that his friend would not be happy in any situation other than one which there was true regard between him and his wife. And if her situation was not what Darcy would have wished for Bingley's advancement in society, he could not rebuke his friend for acting in a way which would ensure his happiness.

When they entered the sitting-room, the ladies looked up at the gentlemen's entrance. Miss Bennet was laughing at something her sister said, and Darcy was struck by the fact that he had rarely seen two sisters who were as physically attractive as the two before him. Jane Bingley was, of course, very beautiful, and her demure modesty could only render her beauty all that much more alluring. And Miss Bennet, though she was not as traditionally beautiful and could not, by any stretch of the imagination be called reticent, was equally lovely with her dark eyes framed by beautiful lashes, and the flush of pleasure which shone upon her cheeks.

"You are returned earlier than *we* had expected, brother," said Miss Bennet, but her sly glance at her sister belied the term "we." Mrs. Bingley flushed, but Miss Bennet continued her gentle teasing, saying: "Am I to understand that you find certain company in this room to be especially appealing?"

"I confess I do," said Bingley with good humor. "You are well aware that I cannot bear to be separated from my dearest Jane for long ere I grow lonely."

"Oh aye," said Miss Bennet, laughing as her sister swatted at her to protest her teasing. "I cannot but commend you for your good taste, sir."

It was in that moment, as Darcy watched their banter, he was struck by the fact that Miss Elizabeth's delight and the intelligence in her dark eyes, rendered her all the more alluring. This was, perhaps, her true claim to beauty, and as Darcy was one who appreciated a woman who was clever and unafraid to speak with him as an equal, he was more than willing to acknowledge her attractions.

The gentlemen sat with the ladies and tea was served, and for a time they sat, speaking concerning inconsequential topics. But while the subjects were those of a typical sitting room, the time was not spent in boredom; no room containing Charles Bingley could be anything but interesting, and Darcy found that the two ladies were able to contribute with ease, one with spirit, and the other with quiet confidence. It was a scene of domestic contentment which Darcy had not seen for some time.

"Perhaps we should adjourn to the music room, if you will oblige us, Elizabeth," said Bingley after some time had passed.

"Mr. Darcy must be used to much finer performances than I can offer," said Miss Bennet, though Darcy thought her display of hesitance was more teasing than reticent.

"And yet you are the only one among us who can fill the office, Lizzy," said her sister.

"We shall not press you if you do not wish it," said Darcy, feeling like he should say something as well. "But if you are of mind, I believe we would all appreciate a little music."

Miss Bennet laughed. "In that case it would be churlish of me to refuse. I will oblige you all, but I warn you, Mr. Darcy, not to expect a masterful performance. My discretion is not at all the work of false modesty."

"But we shall enjoy it nonetheless," said Bingley, and they rose to go to the music room.

It was quickly evident that Miss Bennet was speaking nothing but the truth when estimating the extent of her own talent. Darcy was not proficient with any musical instrument, but he still possessed a keen ear. While Miss Bennet played competently, still there were times when she hurried over a section, perhaps not playing precisely what was on the sheet due to its difficulty. And yet her playing was pleasing nevertheless, as what she lacked in technical execution she more than made up in feeling. It was clear that she enjoyed playing, and perhaps more than that, she felt the cadence of the music, and the emotion she put into it rendered her performance exceedingly pleasing.

But where she truly shone was in the second piece she played, when she sang along with the music. Her voice was a mezzo soprano, clear and free of embellishment, and when the music soared to the higher notes, her voice climbed the heights along with the piano, sounding like an angel soloist amongst a heavenly choir. Hers was one of the most beautiful voices Darcy had ever heard.

After her second song she quit the pianoforte and refused all further entreaties to play with a smile and a laugh.

"I would much rather participate in conversation than subject you all to my continued poor attempts at music."

"On the contrary, Miss Bennet," said Darcy, though he was surprised to hear himself speak, "I have rarely heard anything so lovely. I thank you for consenting to play for us."

Smiling in a mischievous manner, Elizabeth turned a raised eyebrow on him and said: "I thank you for your words, Mr. Darcy, though I must question your knowledge of music. Besides, I have heard it said you have a sister who is *excessively* talented. There is little doubt that I cannot measure up to her with my own meager abilities."

Darcy looked back at her with a frown. "Where have you heard such an account? I had not thought Bingley had ever paid much attention to music or possessed much of an ear to know when talent was being exhibited."

"Aye, it was not Mr. Bingley," said Miss Bennet, and her eyes flashed with amusement. "It was, in fact, Mr. Bingley's sister, the inestimable

Miss Caroline Bingley who spoke of your sister's abilities. I believe it might have been when she was trying to convince my sister that Georgiana Darcy was the only woman in the world for her brother."

Darcy grimaced. "Miss Bingley has only heard Georgiana play once if my memory serves, and that would have been when Georgiana was still quite young. I will own that I *had* considered the possibility of Bingley and Georgiana eventually forming an attachment, but such a thing could not have happened until after she is out, which will not be for at least two more years."

"A responsible elder brother then," said Miss Bennet, and her approval warmed him. "Do not fear, Mr. Darcy; I never took Miss Bingley at her word, and I convinced Jane of the truth of the matter quickly enough. It seemed to me she was after nothing more than a step up in society."

Miss Bingley undoubtedly wished for much more than that, though Darcy had not actually seen the woman since before he was married. A quick glance at Bingley told Darcy that he was engrossed with his wife and had likely not heard Elizabeth's comments. Still, he felt a change of subject would be desirable so as to avoid offending his host.

"My sister *is* talented, Miss Bennet, though I own to more than a little partiality in the matter. But she ought to be so, as she has had masters aplenty and she practices diligently."

"Ah, then I believe I have determined the disparity in our apparent levels of ability! As I have, unfortunately, many interests and many things that occupy my attention, I have often not taken the trouble to practice as much as I ought."

"And yet you play so very charmingly."

"I assure you, sir, it is in the eye of the beholder. Miss Bingley would doubtlessly proclaim my talents to be *tolerable*, but not fine enough to grace the drawing rooms she is accustomed to visiting."

Laughing, Darcy shook his head; she was not far from the truth, he thought, though perhaps she should not speak of her sister-in-law in so cavalier a fashion.

"With my sister, I believe it is a mix of a true love of music, and a desire to gratify her own amusement which has led her to become so diligent. Of course, the admonitions of my aunt, Lady Catherine de Bourgh, on the subject—a relation Georgiana finds particularly fearsome—might also have been a motivating factor when she was still young."

Darcy smiled, remembering fondly the way his father had warned his aunt against frightening his only daughter, and his aunt's subsequent offense. Lady Catherine had refused to speak with his father for months after the fact, a situation which caused regret to none of them.

Miss Bennet nearly choked on her tea. "You are Lady Catherine's nephew?" exclaimed she.

"My apologies, Miss Bennet—I had thought Bingley had acquainted you with the connection."

"I am sure I have heard nothing of the matter."

"She is indeed my aunt, though we have recently had a . . . falling out. I understand your cousin is the parson at Hunsford, which is under her direct control."

There was no mistaking the rolling of Miss Bennet's eyes. "I assure you, Mr. Darcy, I am well acquainted with my cousin's situation, and I have heard so much of Lady Catherine that I feel as if I already know her. In fact, I believe my cousin takes notes whenever he hears her speak, and commits much of her words to memory. That way he may have some little piece of wisdom given from your aunt that he might adapt to any conversation."

Darcy chuckled at Miss Elizabeth's portrayal of her cousin, but she was not yet finished.

"But I assure you, Mr. Darcy, that he always attributes his little homilies to their source, and that furthermore, when he delivers them, he gives them as unstudied an air as possible!"

By now Darcy was laughing openly, and Miss Bennet joined him in his mirth. From the Bingleys they received only an amused glance before the couple was once again engrossed in each other. Perhaps it might not have been the most proper way for the couple to behave, but Darcy was happy for them, feeling a sort of wistful indulgence. Besides, he was most amply entertained by Miss Bennet's anecdotes and the loss of his friend's cheerfulness did not bother him.

"I can well imagine what kind of man Mr. Collins is," said Darcy when their laughter had run its course. "My aunt has a penchant for surrounding herself with those who will not dare contradict her. She prefers her servants, her parson, *and* her relations to be suitably cowed and to follow whatever advice she deigns to bestow on them, regardless of how nonsensical it might be."

"But Mr. Darcy!" exclaimed Miss Bennet, "Surely your aunt is the preeminent lady in all the land, and as a consequence, her advice must be beneficial for all without fail."

Darcy could only shake his head. "That is what *she* believes, Miss Bennet. My aunt is set in her ways and opinionated, and whatever she says must be right and proper, allowing for no contradiction. In truth she is a meddling and intolerant woman, and I dare say she is quite unhappy in her life."

"It is a sad state of affairs then," said Miss Bennet.

"It would be, had she not chosen it of her own accord. As I have said, she is estranged from the Darcys and my uncle cannot tolerate her company. My cousin, the viscount, visits her estate every year to go over her books and deal with matters of business, but he keeps to himself when in residence and is eager to leave. While I hate to speak of a relation in such a manner, in Lady Catherine's case it is only the truth."

"We all have some family members who embarrass us, I suppose," said Miss Bennet, and from the introspection on her face, she was likely thinking of her own family which, if Bingley's information was correct, contained at least one such member.

"Perhaps we do," replied Darcy. "I suppose there is nothing we can do in such circumstances but bear their ridiculous behavior with fortitude."

"*And* hope that others do not judge us for our relations."

Miss Bennet seemed to catch sight of her sister and brother-in-law, and an indulgent smile came over her face.

"Does something amuse you, Miss Bennet?"

"I am happy for my sister," replied Miss Bennet, still watching Mrs. Bingley. "Jane is the best of us, Mr. Darcy. She and I always determined to marry for love, but considering our situation, I had wondered if such a thing would be possible. Jane deserves to be loved. I could not be happier."

It was at that moment when all Darcy's concerns for his friend evaporated. The ladies were wonderful—he had already acknowledged that fact. To hear Miss Bennet speak of love and regard, and not mention what some would consider Bingley's greatest attraction—his fortune—spoke to their characters. With a woman as good as Mrs. Bingley, Bingley had gained far more in his marriage than he would ever have obtained by marrying someone of greater consequence.

"They seem to be . . . rather engrossed with one another," observed Darcy, feeling that something must be said to break the silence.

Miss Bennet's eyes positively danced at his observation. "I assure you, Mr. Darcy, I am quite used to being positively invisible at times when in company with my sister and my new brother. Their absorption in one another at present is not precisely an isolated incident."

A laugh escaped Darcy's lips. "Now that I consider the matter, I doubt that my friend could have loved with anything other than his whole heart, and I am not surprised he would be so devoted to her. He has always put his entire heart into everything he did."

"I can see that, Mr. Darcy," said Miss Bennet.

"Since we must fend for ourselves, what shall we discuss?"

Miss Bennet looked back at him and she smiled, a sight which filled Darcy with contentment. "Perhaps we may discuss books?" suggested Miss Bennet.

"Very well."

They spoke for some time, and Darcy could not remember the last time he had been so entertained.

Chapter IV

When Darcy brought word of the Bingley ladies back to his sister, Georgiana was enthusiastic about the possibility of meeting them.

"Mrs. Bingley is much like you are, my dear," said Darcy as he buttered his toast. "She is reticent and content to allow others to be the focus of attention, though with her beauty, I imagine the notice of others is difficult to avoid. I believe you will like her very well indeed."

"And her sister," pressed Georgiana.

"Miss Bennet is an estimable lady too, but in essentials, she is not at all like her sister." Georgiana gave him a perplexed look. "She is lively and intelligent, and she is not averse to sharing her opinions. I believe you will like Miss Bennet as well as her sister. They are different it is true, but they are both excellent ladies."

"Then I cannot wait until I meet them. You say they are to call the day after tomorrow?"

"If that fits in with your schedule."

"Of course it does!" exclaimed Georgiana. "I would be happy to meet these ladies of whom you speak so highly. Perhaps we might invite them for dinner as well?"

Darcy laughed at his sister's exuberance. "I dare say we might. But first, shall we allow them to visit so that you might become acquainted?"

"Oh, of course, brother. I cannot wait!"

When he left the breakfast room that morning, Darcy could not help the bemusement he felt at his sister's enthusiasm. It was true Georgiana did not have many ladies in her life—she had Lady Susan and her two daughters, of course, but the two ladies had married, and were therefore focused on their own families; Georgiana did not see them often. Other than Lady Emily, Darcy did not know of any of his sister's other friends. Miss Bennet and Mrs. Bingley would undoubtedly be good for her. They would be genuine friends, not like to those who praised her to get close to her brother, much as Bingley's sisters behaved.

Business occupied much of Darcy's time for the next few days, and though he did take the opportunity to walk in nearby Hyde Park with Georgiana, they did not go out much those days. As Darcy had eschewed conducting any kind of business while at the Fitzwilliam estate, there were a few letters from his steward at Pemberley and the other estates waiting for him when he arrived in London. Those required his attention.

But though he completed his tasks with the same diligence for which he had always striven, he found it difficult to keep his attention on his work. For his mind was far more agreeably engaged, and he often found himself meditating on a pair of fine eyes and the light and pleasing figure of a pretty woman.

Darcy was confused. He had only met the woman once, and yet Miss Elizabeth Bennet already seemed to hold his thoughts, and despite all his efforts to the contrary, he simply could not remove her from his mind. It was as if she had with stealth and secrecy slipped her way in, bewitching him into thinking of nothing but her. What was more disturbing was how not even Victoria Patterson had captured his attentions like Miss Bennet had. In fact, he could not remember a woman who had caught his attention since . . .

No, that will not do, said Darcy to himself.

Feeling a restless energy, Darcy rose from his chair in his study and approached the fireplace. Soon his gaze was caught by the flickering and the popping of the fire, and he allowed his mind to wander.

Knowing that way was unfair to both ladies and potentially led to madness, Darcy shied away from comparing Elizabeth Bennet to his deceased wife. Putting the thoughts of his wife away, Darcy considered the woman who had entered his life. And though he might once have been contemptuous of her lack of fortune and connections, age and experienced had changed him, and he was now not so willing to dismiss her due to these deficiencies.

Was Miss Bennet a fortune hunter? No, the suggestion beggared belief. Bingley was not the most astute of men, but he had testified of her integrity with a force which suggested actual knowledge, and though he might be considered to be blinded by love, still his opinion was not to be discounted. Besides, Darcy considered himself to be a good judge of character. Mrs. Bingley was far too self-effacing to possess the cold calculating ruthlessness which being a fortune hunter required. And as for her sister, she appeared to be all that was genuine. In fact, though talk during the dinner at Bingley's house had turned to his estate on occasion, Miss Bennet had deftly turned it away to other matters of more interest to her. Furthermore, Darcy had become adept at recognizing those little veiled questions designed to ferret out information concerning his fortune, marital status, and prospects, and Miss Bennet had not once made any such comments.

Miss Bennet had seemed to be genuinely interested in him, and if her playful banter with Bingley and her genuine happiness for her sister was not enough of a recommendation, then the way they had discussed books, the opinions they had shared, and the fact that she had dared to hold an opinion contrary to his, all spoke to her honest character.

She was not a fortune hunter. The thought was absurd. But what Darcy could not decide was exactly what she was.

Regardless, it was a moot point, Darcy decided. There was no future with her—he had determined to remain single in memory of his late wife. Surely he could not be considering Miss Bennet in such a manner after only one meeting. It was in every way unfathomable.

When the day arrived for Bingley to bring his wife and sister-in-law to meet Georgiana, his sister was a bundle of nerves. As he watched her twist her handkerchief this way and that, Darcy noted the similarities between her character and his own. They were both reticent and uncomfortable in unfamiliar company, and though he liked to consider himself to be a good, upright sort of man, and knew that Georgiana had been raised in the right way, those were not traits which would help them in society. Unfortunately, those similarities between them would not serve Georgiana well, considering how they had prevented him from ever feeling at ease in a social situation.

"Perhaps you should calm yourself, Georgiana," said Darcy.

His sister jumped in response, and she directed a severe scowl at him. "Perhaps you should refrain from startling me out of my wits!"

Darcy only directed a complaisant smile at his sister. "If you were not so intent upon tearing your handkerchief in two, my words would not have startled you."

A flush spread over his sister's cheeks, and she looked down at the fabric which was tightly clasped in her hands. Taking great care, Georgiana loosened the handkerchief from the ball in which she had forced it, and smoothed it out on her lap. But it was useless—the fabric was horribly creased from the mistreatment it had received.

"They are amiable ladies?" asked Georgiana, as she studied her handkerchief.

"Of course they are," replied Darcy, looking on his shy sister with affection. "You do not think a man as amiable as Bingley would marry a woman who was not agreeable, do you?"

"I suppose you must be correct," said Georgiana. Her countenance became a little less fretful and a little more at ease as she pondered his words.

At that moment the door chime rang announcing the visitors, and once again the anxiety rushed over her countenance. It was all Darcy could do not to chuckle at her behavior, but he did not say a word; the visiting ladies would no doubt calm her within moments of stepping into the room.

Soon the housekeeper appeared with Bingley and his family and announced them. Darcy rose to his feet and greeted his guests, and Bingley, with his usual effervescence, took on the task of introducing the ladies to one another.

Curtseys were exchanged and Georgiana mustered some nearly audible attempt at welcoming her guests when Miss Bennet spoke.

"Now this will not do," said she, prompting Georgiana to look up in surprise. "Society is insistent upon imposing their stodgy rules upon us all, but I believe we have dispensed with the pleasantries. Thus, you may call me 'Elizabeth' or 'Lizzy,' as my sisters do. 'Miss Bennet' has always been *my* sister, and though she is now married, it is difficult not to think of her in such terms."

Though clearly shocked at the lady's familiar manner and high spirits, Georgiana allowed a tentative smile and nodded her head.

"As for Jane," continued Miss Bennet, "I shall allow her to choose her own moniker. Since she is an old married woman now, I believe she may prefer stodginess to familiarity."

"Lizzy!" admonished Mrs. Bingley. "Perhaps *you* do not wish to follow the rules of society, but others take them much more seriously."

"Oh, Jane, you forget that I know you too well. You are not one of *them*."

Darcy could not believe his ears as his sister actually giggled and invited the ladies to sit with her. Within a few moments the three ladies were sitting close together on a sofa, chatting as if they were longstanding acquaintances instead of having been introduced only that morning. And it seemed as if formality had indeed been dispensed between them, as he distinctly heard Georgiana call them both by name on several occasions.

"Her ability to put others at ease is so effortless, is it not?"

Starting in surprise at Bingley's voice, Darcy turned to look at his friend, noting that Bingley's attention was focused on the three ladies. Darcy raised an eyebrow in question.

"I love my wife dearly, Darcy, and I am well aware of my own character. I declare I have been fortunate to find the one woman in the world who is most suited to be my wife.

"But though I love Jane with my whole heart, I must own that Elizabeth, though a very different person, is her equal in every way. She brightens a room with nothing more than the force of her smile, and she makes everyone around her feel at home. And she does it without seeming effort, and without any motive other than to make others happy. She is as dear to me as my wife, and I would be happy to see her protected in marriage, if there was only someone to whom I could entrust her."

"She is a wonderful girl," said Darcy, more due to feeling a need to respond than from any particular desire to do so. Not that he disagreed with Bingley, he surprised himself by thinking. "But does she always behave in such a manner to a new acquaintance?"

"This is the first time I have ever witnessed it. Elizabeth seems to possess an uncanny knack for seeing what will make another comfortable. I do not doubt she would refrain in behaving so should she be introduced to your aunt, the countess, but she obviously saw how uncomfortable your sister was, and she acted accordingly to put Georgiana at ease."

Bingley was silent for a few moments, until he once again spoke in a low tone, saying: "She is also her father's favorite. I was given a most solemn charge when she left his house for mine that she would be protected and cherished. It has been no hardship to shoulder those burdens."

Darcy considered the woman before him. Something in what Bingley said told Darcy that he was not aware of the entire story behind Miss Bennet residing with Bingley and his wife in London. But as the matter had not been discussed openly in Darcy's hearing, it would not be polite to ask.

"It is not . . . awkward to have a sister live with you so soon after your marriage?" asked Darcy. It was the only thing he could think of to say.

"Would I not have had my sister with us if Elizabeth's presence did not keep her away?" said Bingley.

"Your sister would not prefer to live with the Hursts anyway?"

This time Bingley actually snorted at the suggestion. "You know how well she gets on with Hurst. Though she and Louisa are thick as thieves, she has difficulty tolerating him for more than a few days at a time, and his tolerance for her is even less. It is a testament to how much she despises Elizabeth that she is willing to live with Hurst as long as Elizabeth lives at my house. I find I am quite happy with matters as they are now. Not only do I have difficulty enduring my sister's airs myself, but I am much too lenient with her. Hurst handles her much better than I do; even though she considers him to be a drunk and a buffoon, when he speaks to her the authority in his voice is unmistakable, and she actually listens and obeys."

Darcy frowned. "That is a rather singular way of speaking of your sister, Bingley."

"And your opinion is any different?"

"She is not *my* sister."

"And you should be happy with the sweet creature who *is* your sister, Darcy." Bingley sighed and gestured in surrender. "I *am* circumspect about such things, Darcy, but though I love my sister—both of them, in fact—I am not blind to their character flaws, especially that of the younger. I do love her; unfortunately, I do not always *like* her.

"I should also warn you that Caroline is aware of your presence in London. Now that you are . . . well, what she would consider to be *available*, she is convinced yet again that she would be the best possible wife and mother to your daughter."

A grimace he could not quite suppress came over Darcy's countenance, and Bingley looked upon him with laughter in his eyes. Luckily Darcy had started courting his wife not long after his introduction to Miss Bingley, so he had been spared the worst of her cloying attentions. But even so, she had tried a few times to impress upon him how she was a better match for him than the woman he had ultimately married. The sheer gall of her assertions never failed to astonish him—she imagined that she was a better match than a woman possessing a greater dowry and connections to a marquess, and moreover a woman he had loved to distraction! If her behavior now was in any way comparable to what he had seen before, it would be difficult to avoid offending Bingley, which was the only reason he would tolerate her at all.

"Do not worry about offending me, Darcy," said Bingley. "I completely understand."

Smiling—Bingley had always seemed to be able to read him—Darcy nodded his acknowledgement. "Unfortunately, though I can keep her at arms' length, I cannot truly cut her from my society as she is your sister. I would ask you, however, to keep her in check as much as you are able."

"For what it is worth, I shall attempt to do so, though you know she listens to me but little. I will speak with Hurst when I have the chance. I do not know how much weight even his word will carry where it concerns her ambitions, but I will make the attempt."

"Brother," said Georgiana at that moment, "I would like to invite our friends for dinner one evening, and thought to decide on a date today. Would Tuesday next fit into our schedule?"

Darcy smiled at his sister, noting her ease with the ladies. "Dearest, you may make the invitation. I shall ensure that date is open for us to receive guests."

Beaming, Georgiana turned back to Mrs. Bingley and issued the invitation which was accepted with pleasure.

"We would be quite happy to attend, Georgiana," said Mrs. Bingley. "We do not have any engagements fixed for that evening."

"I will be so happy to have you come," said Georgiana. "And Elizabeth, you must promise to play for us that evening."

"Only if you promise to return the favor," said Miss Bennet with good humor.

Georgiana agreed, though a little hesitantly, but her manner became excited again. "Perhaps we should practice a duet that we may play in the future."

Laughing, Miss Bennet replied: "You would shame me even further, by displaying my mediocre playing next to your superior skill?"

"Oh Lizzy," said Mrs. Bingley. "Why must you always disparage your talents?"

"Because it is only the truth."

"Do not allow Miss Bennet to mislead you, Georgiana," said Darcy, interjecting himself into the conversation. "I have had the pleasure of hearing her play, and despite what she says, her playing is quite fine."

"I thank you for that bit of flattery, Mr. Darcy."

"Oh no!" cried Georgiana. "I am convinced that there is no other in all the world who is as honest as my brother. If he says your playing is fine, then it must be."

Miss Bennet laughed again. "Then I must live up to your expectations, or I shall prove your brother to be false."

"I am certain you cannot fail, Miss Bennet," said Darcy.

The ladies once again resumed their conversation, and Darcy watched how well they got on with one another. He was content; surely Georgiana was in good hands with these ladies. They were friendly and obliging to a young girl who was young and shy and still required confidence before she could make her debut in society. When he considered the matter, Darcy thought Georgiana would benefit from someone closer to her own age when she came out; Lady Susan was in no way lacking, but her perspective was that of a matron, with many years of experience, and not that of a young girl.

"In answer to your previous question, Darcy," said Bingley, when the ladies were once again engrossed in their conversation, "it is not awkward to have Elizabeth live with us as she is obliging and discreet. She is well able to amuse herself playing the pianoforte, reading, or walking in the park close to my home. She allows us to have our time together when we require it. Again, I refer you back to my sister; do you think Caroline would be content to allow us time to ourselves?"

Again Darcy was forced to acknowledge that Bingley was entirely correct in the matter, though he did not wish to speak severely about the man's sister. Darcy had seen Bingley and his sister interact, and the one word which he thought he could use to describe the woman was "needy." She required Bingley to escort her to this place or to that function and required his attention at all times. Darcy could not imagine Caroline Bingley amusing herself.

"I must confess, Bingley, with your sister in residence at the estate you leased . . ."

"Netherfield," said Bingley.

"Yes, Netherfield. I was only trying to say that I am surprised she was not more vocal in protesting against your attachment to Mrs. Bingley."

"I did not say she was not," replied Bingley, his lips curved with a certain dark amusement. "In fact, after I hosted a ball at the estate in late November, I was required to return to town a day or two later on a matter of business. I will own that part of that business was to begin work on Jane's settlement and to retrieve my mother's ring from my safe. I left Netherfield on my own, but it was not above a day later when Caroline and the Hursts joined me in town."

"Oh?" asked Darcy, entirely able to imagine what had ensued.

Bingley, of course, obliged him. "I have never been witness to such behavior in my life, Darcy." He paused, darting a look at his wife, who was engaged in conversation with the other two ladies, and then turned back to Darcy, speaking quietly. "I have never told my wife of this, you understand, but my sisters spent three days trying to persuade me against her. They used every stratagem they could devise, from denouncing her family, to denouncing her connections, to claiming that she did not love me."

The snort which Bingley released told Darcy what his friend thought of that. "Their histrionics were quite the sight to see, I assure you."

"How did you persuade them to desist?"

"I returned to Hertfordshire. I reminded them of their own ties to trade and informed them I had proof—in Jane's own words—of how mistaken they were about her affections. Then I arose early in the morning of the day I had always intended to return, and left for Netherfield, telling them they could join me when they were ready to welcome my future wife with open arms. But that was only before I left London."

His tone told Darcy that there was something else at work here, and his friend's grim countenance suggested it was not a happy memory.

"Is there something amiss?"

Bingley sighed. "When I returned to Hertfordshire and visited the Bennets, I discovered that Caroline had sent Jane a letter before she departed for London, and in it she told Jane that we were all removing to London for the winter, with no intention of returning."

Turning to look at his friend with awe, Darcy noted the barely suppressed anger, even months after the events he was recounting. It was so far from the Bingley he had always known, that for a moment he was shocked. It appeared that his friend had still not completely forgiven his sister of her interference.

"That was poorly done, Bingley," was the only thing Darcy could say. "Even if she did not agree with your choice, she had no authority to attempt to cut the acquaintance."

"Apparently she felt like her ambitions for high society gave her that authority," replied Bingley. "I was so incensed when I discovered what she had done that I was forced to hold my tongue for several moments in order to avoid saying something not suitable for a sitting-room. Though I attempted to smooth matters over and tell them Caroline was mistaken, Jane was not fooled. Neither Elizabeth nor her father were taken in either.

"It is an uncomfortable experience to be hauled over the carpet by a man whose daughter you hope to marry. Though Mr. Bennet appears to be indolent and indifferent, he is protective of his girls—especially the eldest two—and I was required to give him my solemn assurance that my sister would not be allowed to run roughshod over his daughter *if* I was allowed to pay my addresses to her."

In some small way Darcy was relieved at that intelligence. The image he had received of the Bennets the night of the dinner at Bingley's townhouse was not exactly positive. That a man would act in such a way to protect his daughters was admirable, even if the man had not done the duty to provide for them as he ought.

"I wrote to Caroline that evening, and you would be proud of my work, Darcy." Bingley paused and grinned. "Not only did I take great care to make it completely legible, but I also informed Caroline, in no uncertain terms, that she was not welcome in my home again until she apologized to my future wife. Furthermore, I told her if she could not accept Jane as her sister, then I would have her dowry released to her so she could set up her own household."

Darcy laughed. "I cannot imagine she took that well."

A grin came over his friend's countenance. "No, she did not. She assumed I would capitulate. She was wrong."

"Then she has issued the apology?"

"With her own brand of insincerity, yes. I decided it was too much to attempt to force genuine contrition. Of course she was not happy when it was decided that Elizabeth would reside with us, but by then she understood she was on thin ice with me, and her protests were much more muted in nature. I find that I cannot repine the matter in the slightest."

"Well done, Bingley," said Darcy quietly. "Well done."

The conversation turned to more benign topics and the gentlemen were soon engaged in speaking with the ladies. Darcy was heartened by the sight before him—Georgiana was speaking with her new friends with as much animation as he had ever seen from his sister. They had drawn her out effortlessly, and in far less time than he had expected. Perhaps they were all that Bingley had suggested, though Darcy could not help but wonder about the rest of the family.

Still, it did not signify, he supposed. It was not as if he would ever be making their acquaintance, though if Bingley did purchase the estate he was currently leasing, it might be a possibility.

When the time of the visit had expired, the visitors rose, stating their intention to depart. The Darcys arose with them to see them to the door. The Bingleys walked from the room in Georgiana's company, who was speaking with Mrs. Bingley with some animation, leaving Darcy to follow along behind with Miss Bennet.

As they exited the room, Darcy thought to say something to his companion, feeling it would be rude to remain quiet, but he might not have bothered, for Miss Bennet soon spoke to him.

"Your sister is delightful, Mr. Darcy. I commend you for raising her to be such a wonderful girl."

No words could possibly have pleased Darcy more, offered as they were by a young woman he was quickly coming to esteem, and who spoke from nothing more than a sincere affection for his sister.

"I cannot take the credit," replied Darcy. "She has the most even temperament, and has never caused an instant of trouble."

"Not even an instant?" asked Miss Bennet with a laugh. "That is remarkable, Mr. Darcy. Though I cannot claim sisters who do not cause trouble, I have observed that all young ladies like to have their own way on occasion."

"And in that you would be correct," replied Darcy. He turned and smiled at her. "Georgiana is as much of a young woman as your younger sisters, I would wager. But she is also self-effacing and eager to please. I try to explain why I require certain behavior from her, and she has always accepted what I tell her with grace and dignity."

"Then you are well-matched, sir. You have done an admirable job with her, and I am happy that you have allowed us to be introduced."

Darcy thought that it was *his sister* who truly benefited from the acquaintance, but at that moment a small form hurtled around the corner and nearly collided with Miss Bennet.

"Hold!" exclaimed Darcy, realizing it was his daughter who had suddenly appeared. "What is the meaning of this?"

The girl's nurse rounded the corner in a great hurry, and noting his presence blanched. "I apologize, Mr. Darcy. She escaped the nursery when my back was turned."

"You know you are not to run away from nurse, do you not?"

The little girl nodded, but she looked up at him with big, luminous eyes, and she said: "Want to see Georgie."

"That is no excuse, young lady. You almost ran into Miss Bennet with your ill-advised running."

Miss Bennet, however, surprised Darcy by crouched down so that her gaze was level with that of his daughter.

"I am pleased to meet you, young lady. May I assume that I am in the presence of Miss Darcy?"

The girl nodded and attempted what was, at best, a rather wobbly curtsey.

"My name is Miss Elizabeth Bennet. I am a friend of your aunt

Georgiana and your father."

"I want friend too."

"In that case, I would be happy to be your friend. Now, can you tell me why you have been instructed not to run in the house?"

His daughter's eyes darted up to him, but she soon focused on Miss Bennet and said: "Because I run into papa's friends."

Miss Bennet laughed. "That is a part of it. But it is also to ensure you do not hurt yourself, and so that you might learn to be a lady."

The girl seemed to consider this. "A lady?"

A genuine smile settled over Miss Bennet's face. "Perhaps if you follow all your lessons, listen to your nurse, and grow up a little. If you do all these things, you will become a lady."

"I shall," said Miss Darcy.

Then with another curtsey, no steadier than the first, the girl allowed herself to be led away by the nurse. Miss Bennet turned to him, and Darcy gestured toward where his sister and the Bingleys were waiting for them and watching them, curiosity evident in their gazes.

Darcy did not know what to say. Being in his daughter's company had never been easy, and he found that he was not aware if this was truly how she usually behaved, or if something was affecting her spirits that day. Moreover, Miss Bennet had taken the encounter in stride and had not taken offense, though most of those young ladies of Darcy's acquaintance would have been unhappy to be thus accosted by a young girl. Or perhaps they might have feigned enchantment and praised him in order to secure his good opinion. Miss Bennet did none of these things.

"I apologize for my daughter, Miss Bennet," said Darcy, thinking he should say something, even though he felt certain she had not taken offense. "She is usually not quite so rambunctious."

"Do not make yourself uneasy, sir. My aunt and uncle have young children, so I am quite accustomed to their ways. She seems like a charming young girl."

There was nothing he could say to that, so Darcy merely bowed in thanks. They continued the rest of the way to door, and as the Bingley carriage was already called for, it was only a few moments before the visitors departed.

As she was turning to leave, Miss Bennet hesitated and turned back to him, her head tilted slightly to the side, regarding him with thoughtful curiosity. "If it is not an impertinence, Mr. Darcy, might I inquire to know your daughter's name."

Darcy faltered for a moment, and then for the first time since that fateful day when he was given his daughter and lost his wife, Darcy found the courage to say the beloved name.

"Her name is Cassandra."

Chapter V

Actually saying his beloved wife's name out loud had several unexpected effects on Darcy. The foremost affect was a cathartic one—it seemed like he was now able to speak of his wife without any crippling pain, as had not been the case in the time since she had died. The sadness due to her passing was still there—Darcy did not think he would ever truly be rid of it—but it was now duller, muted, and he was able to think on her with fond remembrance rather than pain.

Unfortunately, it did not help his relationship with his daughter. Regardless of being able to *think* of her without grief, the constant reminder of his loss in the face of his daughter was still painful. Though he had not the courage to spend much time in her company, when he did, those eyes would stare back at him, and it was like his wife was watching him from beyond the grave. He could not bear it, so he continued to keep his distance, much though he was disgusted at himself for his weakness.

The Darcys did not see any more of the Bingley party in the next few days after their visit, and for that Darcy was grateful. He was feeling the power of Miss Bennet's magnetic pull, and her siren call was far too seductive for him with his feelings in such a raw state. A few days away from her would allow him to fortify his defenses and build up an immunity to her.

There were, in fact, no visitors those days. The knocker had not yet been placed on the door, and though the wealthy families in the area might be curious about the Darcys who had suddenly returned to London after several years of absence, they respected his privacy and stayed away. Darcy had no doubt they would be inundated with calls once the knocker was replaced. That was something to worry about in the future, however—for now he was content to continue in his solitude.

There was one visitor who made herself known, however, and the small matter of a missing door knocker was not enough to persuade her to leave without bothering him. In fact, Darcy suspected the woman had never restrained herself in her life. Needless to say, he was not happy to be accosted by someone who was among those he least wished to see.

It started on a typical afternoon. The sun was brightly shining, and though it was still cold as befitted a February day, there was more than enough light in Darcy's study for him to work by without the benefit of candles. He had finished reading a letter from his banker when a sudden commotion in the hallway caught his attention, and a voice—long unheard but never forgotten—invaded the quiet of his sanctuary.

"Where is he? Where is my nephew? I must see him at once!"

Shaking his head, Darcy rose from his desk. Though the standing orders that his aunt should not be admitted had never been lifted from his staff at Pemberley, he had never given those orders to the staff in London, largely because he had not been here in several years. Johnson, his London butler, knowing his master's mind, knew that Darcy would not wish to see his aunt, but he was under no illusions as to the man's ability to bar her with anything less than half a dozen footmen at his back. Lady Catherine was a force of nature akin to a hurricane—the only recourse one possessed was to take cover until she blew over and it was safe to once again emerge.

He opened the door quickly, thinking to save his harried butler, and he noted the man following in Lady Catherine's footsteps as she stalked the length of the hall toward his study, and though Johnson did not attempt to impede her, he followed behind, a grimness to his countenance which was not usually present.

"Thank you, Johnson, I will take my aunt from here."

The man hesitated, but he looked at Darcy and nodded his head before turning and walking away. Darcy knew Johnson had understood his look precisely and would be waiting to evict Lady Catherine when it was time for her to leave.

"Lady Catherine," said Darcy with a short bow.

He waited until she had entered the room, and in order to ensure she did not attempt to take the position of authority behind his desk, Darcy gestured to one of the chairs in front, and sat in his own chair. The narrowing of his aunt's eyes told him all he needed to know of her intentions, and of her opinion of his maneuver.

"I am surprised to see you as I have had no word of your coming. To what do I owe this pleasure?"

The woman, more than usually insolent, turned and sat on the chair he had motioned her to, but one would have thought it a throne the way she perched on it, tall, erect, and proud. Her eyes roved about the room, taking in his study with a single glance, before she turned her attention back to him.

"You will remove your butler from his position and replace him. The man was not of mind to allow me entrance. I will provide you with a suitable candidate to replace him."

"On the contrary, Lady Catherine, Johnson is an excellent butler who has been with the family for many years. You might not have noticed, but the knocker is not up on our door. Johnson was merely protecting the family's privacy and turning away visitors as he ought."

"I am not a visitor!" snapped Lady Catherine. "I am almost the nearest family you have, and I will not be denied entrance to your home—to the home my sister presided over!"

"Given the manner in which we last parted, you *are* a visitor, Lady Catherine," said Darcy, keeping his tone mild but firm. "Your behavior while you are here today will determine your future status in this home."

Eyes wide and nostrils flaring, Lady Catherine appeared to pass from insolence to fury from one heartbeat to the next. "I will not be spoken to in such a manner!"

"Then I suggest you behave with circumspection."

Lady Catherine glared at him with every ounce of displeasure she could muster, but Darcy merely regarded her passively.

"I can see *her* influence still persists," said the woman with a disdainful sniff.

"If you have come here to insult my wife then you can leave," said Darcy, his anger building with every word the woman spoke. "If this was your intent, I wonder why you bothered to come in the first place. She is beyond your contempt now."

"I have no intention of leaving. Not until you hear what I have to say."

"Then you had best say it, for I am quickly tiring of this

conversation."

For a change, though Lady Catherine appeared angry at his words and his less than conciliatory manner, she appeared to restrain herself from a caustic remark. It was evident the woman wanted something from him, and though she was normally confrontational, in this instance she desisted. It did not take much insight to determine what the woman wanted. There was only one thing she *ever* wanted from him. Darcy was not about to oblige her any more now than he had four years earlier.

Instead, she turned away and let her eyes wander about his study in a much lazier manner than she had when she had first entered. Darcy kept his attention on her, aware that her behavior was nothing more than a show.

"How is Georgiana getting on?"

"Georgiana is well," replied Darcy.

"She has returned from school? And does she take her continued studies seriously?"

"She is, as is to be expected, more interested in some subjects than others. I have nothing of which to censure her. Her companion is a lovely woman who attends to Georgiana's lessons faithfully."

"And her musical skills? Does she practice diligently?"

"Most diligently. In fact, it is sometimes a trial to get her to focus on other subjects, so happy is she to sit at the pianoforte as long as she can."

"She should by no means neglect the rest of her education."

"I have already stated she does not. She is more naturally inclined to music. That is all."

"She shall come and visit me for a six-month. She does not have enough female influence in her life."

It was all Darcy could do not to sigh. "I prefer to keep Georgiana here with me."

"You had best think of her needs. Anne and I can provide her with the education she requires. You may as well dismiss this companion. I will assume responsibility for her education."

"I *am* thinking of her needs," replied Darcy with more force. "Georgiana has her companion, she has her friends, and her aunt Fitzwilliam will be here in a matter of days. She has all the female companionship she requires."

Lady Catherine's eyes narrowed, and though Darcy could not account for it, she seemed to be inching toward the understanding that matters would not proceed in the manner she wished. It was rather shortsighted in Darcy's opinion—the woman had never been able to prevail upon him for anything. Why she should believe she would get her own way now was quite beyond Darcy's comprehension.

Lady Catherine would doubtlessly be infuriated if she knew how little Georgiana cared for her. Georgiana had once referred to Lady Catherine as a great whirlwind of spite, and though she should not speak of an elder relation in such a manner, Darcy privately found it to be a rather apt description, and his cousin Fitzwilliam had laughed for hours when she had said it. As shy as she was, Lady Catherine would turn Georgiana into a docile mouse—or another version of Anne—within a week. Darcy would not allow such a fate to befall on his beloved sister.

"I am quite determined on this matter, I assure you," stated Lady Catherine. "I shall not leave until Georgiana's trunks are packed and she is seated in my carriage."

"And I shall not allow her to depart. I am her guardian, and I will decide where she spends her time."

"I can see your guardianship set aside."

Darcy laughed, a harsh, derisive sound, which instantly affronted his aunt. "I would like to see you try," said Darcy, his tone scornful. "As you are well aware, my cousin, Colonel Fitzwilliam, joins me in the care of my sister. You would have to have both of us shunted to the side before you could step in. Furthermore, as my uncle, the earl, supports me, you would have to work against *him* too. And this does not even mention the fact that Lord Matlock himself would precede you if a guardian for my sister was required. I cannot see how you could prevail, but I wish you luck, though I believe you will need something more substantial than mere luck."

"I will not be gainsaid!"

"Lady Catherine, I tire of this," said Darcy. He leaned forward and put his arms on the desk, peering at her, knowing as he did this that he appeared to be looming. "I shall not release Georgiana to your care and I will not allow you to dictate your will upon us. If you have come with no more design than to attempt to enforce your will on my sister and myself, then I will ask you to leave."

"I will leave when I have had my say."

"Then you had best come to the point."

Though the woman looked upon him with considerable displeasure, she apparently decided there was no reason for her to continue on this subject.

"Very well. I have come today because it is clear you have mourned your *wife* long enough. It is time for you to remarry so you may beget the heir that . . . *woman* failed to provide you."

Now we come to it, thought Darcy, a dark amusement coloring his thoughts.

"It is primarily for this reason I shall take Georgiana with me back to Rosings, though I suppose it can wait until after the wedding. It is only proper that a man and his wife have time to themselves after they have married."

"Then there is no reason to entertain the notion of Georgiana going to Rosings at all," said Darcy, and his tone stated that there was to be no further discussion on the subject. "I do not mean to offer for Anne. I shall not marry her, so you had best let the idea rest once and for all."

"Of course you will!" exclaimed Lady Catherine. By her tone she appeared to be trying for a jovial tone, but it only came across as more imperious than was her normal wont. "It was the favorite wish of your mother as you well know."

"I know nothing of the sort," replied Darcy evenly. "My mother never spoke a word of it, and my father expressly told me the choice of wife was mine alone."

"I care not what your father told you. Your mother and I decided on this matter while you were young. You *will* marry Anne. If I am required to drag you both to the altar myself, then that is exactly what I shall do."

"That is an amusing image, Lady Catherine," said Darcy with a snort. "Considering my height is much greater than yours and I weigh several stone more, I think it rather unlikely you could manhandle me to enforce your will."

For the briefest of moments Darcy thought his aunt would lose her carefully controlled composure which she had mostly managed to maintain throughout their entire discussion. But instead of the outburst he had expected, she instead closed her eyes and made a visible attempt to calm herself. When she again looked at him, it was clear she had changed her tactics.

"Anne has much to offer. Her dowry is Rosings itself, of course, and with such an estate added to the Darcy holdings, you would be in a position to be envied. Perhaps you might even be able to qualify for a title, which would further empower your line. These are not benefits to be set aside in a fit of obstinacy."

Darcy sighed. "Aunt, you would be correct, should I care for such things. But I do not. I have plenty to occupy my time with the holdings I currently possess, and I doubt I would have the time or inclination to pay Rosings even half the attention it would require."

"Nonsense!" cried Lady Catherine in another attempt at joviality. "Rosings' steward is capable and independent. And I would be there to continue to watch over it, much as I have these many years."

"If you are so engaged at present, I see no reason to make changes."

"Exactly! You and Anne may do as you will. I will stay at Rosings."

"Aunt, you misunderstand me," said Darcy. He rubbed his forehead, feeling a headache beginning to form behind his eyes. "I do not wish to marry Anne. I do not believe she wishes to marry me. In the end it matters little as I shall not offer for her. Please cease to importune me and put this matter to rest once and for all."

All at once his aunt's attempt at civility fell away from her face like ashes dispersed in a stiff breeze, and an expression of ugliness manifest itself. Had Darcy been in any way in awe of his aunt, he might have found himself quite intimidated. As it was, he merely braced himself for her displeasure, which would no doubt display itself in the worst of her manners.

"You have stated your desires, now you shall hear me dictate what shall happen," said she. "You will marry Anne, and you will marry her as soon as may be. This will not be negotiated upon and there is nothing else for you to say. I have put up with this recalcitrance of yours for long enough. Your wild oats have been sown; it is now time to do your duty."

A rush of anger swept over Darcy like a wave over a dry beach, and he rose from his chair and put his hands on his desk, glaring over it at the meddling old woman. "One more word of disrespect for *my wife* and you will be evicted from this house, never to return. I was duly married to a woman of my own choice who I loved and respected. I was not 'sowing wild oats' as you have the temerity to suggest, nor was I engaged in any behavior other than that which would constitute my own happiness, without reference to you or anyone else."

An ugly sneer came over his aunt's face, and she said in a tone laced with contempt: "*Your wife!* Are you insensible of the fact that the woman perished because she was not meant to be your wife? You were always meant to be Anne's. There can be no other!"

For a moment Darcy could not move. He could not be certain that he had actually heard the woman correctly, that she could be so lost to decency that she would speak of his beloved in such a manner. This paralyzation only lasted for a moment, however, before the red haze of true rage settled upon him.

In a rush of movement Darcy stood and crossed the room in a few long strides. He yanked open the door and bellowed for the butler. The man responded with alacrity, accompanied by two footmen. Then Darcy whirled back on Lady Catherine who had risen in response to his movement, and was regarding him as if he were a madman. At present, Darcy almost felt like one.

"Lady Catherine, you are a stupid, meddling virago, and I shall have nothing more to do with you. Get out of this house, and do not return!"

"How dare you speak to me in such a manner!" cried Lady Catherine. "Do you not know who I am?"

"On the contrary," said Darcy, as he stalked to her as a lion stalks its prey, "I know *exactly* who you are. You are a grasping old harpy who cares for nothing but your own selfish concerns."

"You insolent whelp!"

"Be silent, Lady Catherine!"

It was the shock of Darcy's raised voice which silenced the woman more than his command.

"You have insulted me and mine for the last time, Lady Catherine. You will now leave and you will not be allowed back. If you should dare to return, my staff will have orders to bar you from the premises, and if you should somehow manage to force your way inside, I shall throw you from the house into the street. I am severing all connection between the houses of Darcy and de Bourgh."

"Do you know what this means? Will you ruin us all?"

"I am well aware of the implications, but I care not. I will not publish this separation, but I will not allow you to dictate your will upon either me or my sister. Return to Rosings, Lady Catherine. There is nothing for you here."

"I shall return!" screeched the woman as she turned and stomped from the room, the butler closely following her. "My brother shall hear about this!"

As she marched down the hall, the sound of her footsteps and the slap of her cane echoed behind her, accompanied by the continuous epithets which spewed from her mouth.

Darcy sank into his chair in the wake of her departure. He had not intended to separate all congress between them, but he had thought it a distinct possibility. She was correct in one sense—the matter would become fuel for the gossips should it become known to society, and it would reflect well on none of them.

But Darcy could not repine his decision. The woman was beyond all tolerance, and he would not endure her stupidity for even an instant longer. Lady Catherine rarely left Rosings, so the break should not become common knowledge. At least it would not if she had the sense to keep her opinions to herself, which was anything but a surety.

A sound at the door caught his attention, and Darcy looked up to see his sister peering into the room, a look of apprehension stark upon her pale countenance.

Darcy beckoned to her and she came and sat in the chair next to him. "What did Aunt Catherine want?"

A mirthless chuckle escaped Darcy's lips. "What does she ever want?"

"She frightens me, brother."

"You shall not be required to endure her any longer. I have cut all connection between us."

Georgiana looked up at him with wonder. "You cut the connection?"

"I did. She insulted my wife and her demands have simply become insufferable."

"What will uncle say?"

"I imagine he will wish he had severed his own connection to her before long."

Georgiana could only laugh and shake her head. They sat in this attitude for several moments, Darcy calming from his fury, while Georgiana received comfort. Darcy did not tell her of Lady Catherine's insistence on her going to Rosings, as it would do no good to further alarm her. But Darcy determined one thing—should the woman actually be so audacious as to return, he would follow through with his threat and throw her out. He would not suffer her company again.

The next day, visitors of a more welcome nature came to visit, when Mrs. Bingley and Miss Bennet arrived at the house. Darcy was once again in his study attending to business, when he was brought word that the ladies had come.

Appreciative of the civility though he was, Darcy decided to stay in his study for some time completing the work he did not wish to set aside. He contented himself with asking the housekeeper to inform his sister that he would make an appearance in the sitting-room to greet the ladies, but that he was busy at present. After the woman left, Darcy turned back to his work.

Unfortunately, and as he might have predicted based on previous experience, he was unable to focus on his work. Though Darcy attempted not to think on the matter, he was well aware of the dark eyes framed by beautiful long lashes which were the cause of his distraction. He attempted to put this aside and concentrate, but it was not much longer before he gave up entirely on the notion of completing his work. Sighing, he rose and, making certain he was presentable, left the room.

His sister was entertaining her visitors in the main sitting-room, and though the two ladies had only been there for a few moments, they all appeared to be quite cozy in one another's company.

Georgiana brightened at his entrance. "Brother, Miss Bennet and Mrs. Bingley have come to call."

"Your brother can already see me, I am sure," said Miss Bennet with a laugh.

Georgiana appeared a little silly at the observation, but she laughed along with the ladies.

"Good day, Mrs. Bingley. Good day Miss Bennet. My sister and I are happy you have called."

"Come, Mr. Darcy, do you not think calling again so soon is an impertinence?"

Darcy smiled at Miss Bennet. "I assure you that is not the case. We are always delighted to welcome you at any time you should wish to call."

"You should take care, Mr. Darcy," said Miss Bennet, the light of mischief shining in her eyes, "you may never be rid of us if you continue in such a manner."

Completely disarmed by her humor, Darcy could only laugh, in which he was joined by the rest of the company.

"Oh, I would not wish to be rid of you!" cried Georgiana. "In fact, I would welcome you whenever convenient. I am so happy we have made your acquaintance! I cannot help but laugh at your witticisms."

"And I am happy with your acquaintance too," said Miss Bennet. "But I would hope that my coming here is more than simply humorous in nature."

"No indeed," said Darcy. "You have already shown yourself to be a lady of substance, and we are very pleased to have you as a friend."

"Thank you, Mr. Darcy. I am pleased to have met you and your charming sister as well."

"Is your husband busy this morning, Mrs. Bingley?" said Darcy, turning his attention to his friend's wife.

"Charles had business with his attorney," said Mrs. Bingley. "Lizzy and I decided to visit as we were at leisure."

The discussion then turned to other matters and soon tea was delivered and they were engaged in the business of their tea and refreshments. The conversation consisted of only those matters which were typically discussed in a sitting-room, but somehow Darcy felt that the subject matter was rendered that much more interesting by the company. He could never remember being half so entertained by such things in the past.

When the visit had proceeded on for some minutes, Miss Bennet took the opportunity to turn to him with a smile, as his sister and hers were immersed in a discussion.

"I was happy to meet your daughter when we were here last, Mr. Darcy," said Miss Bennet. "She seems like a dear, sweet girl."

If there was a list of all the subjects Darcy felt he might have liked to discuss with Miss Bennet, his daughter was—to his shame—near the bottom. But knowing it was expected of him, Darcy exerted himself to respond.

"She is . . . quite energetic."

Inside, Darcy could only wince; what he had said sounded so . . . facile.

"She appears to be about three years of age?" asked Miss Bennet. If she had noticed his inability to speak, she had the good manners to conceal it.

"She will be three years in September," said Darcy.

Miss Bennet smiled. "The time passes by swiftly, does it not?"

"It does indeed," said Darcy, and though he did not realize it, he had spoken softly, in a whisper. Of course, he was thinking of something completely different from what she had meant in her reply. He could not help but think of the woman who gave birth to his daughter rather than the girl herself.

"My Aunt Gardiner often tells me that childhood is over in a moment," said Miss Bennet, pulling his attention back to her. "Her eldest is now eleven, and she laments the approaching time when he will be sent to school. She makes it the business of her life to cherish the moments she has with her children before they leave her to make their own way in the world."

"Your aunt is a wise woman," said Darcy.

The visit soon ended after his brief moment with Miss Bennet, and the ladies went away. Darcy returned to his study to attend to his work, while his sister went to practice the pianoforte in the music room. The sounds of her playing wafted through the halls and helped bring him a measure of peace as he worked in his room. But though he was able to concentrate on his tasks, Darcy could not help but realize, deep down under the hustle and bustle of everyday thoughts, that something had changed.

That night, a ghostly figure walked the halls of Darcy house, pacing the hallways, restless and conflicted. It stopped at length in the shadows of the halls, never revealing itself, peering down the dim corridors and into empty rooms.

Darcy was unable to sleep, which had resulted in his stalking the halls of his own home like he was an unwelcome specter rather than its master. Though he had suppressed all thought of his daughter, of Miss Bennet, and of the situation he seemed powerless to ameliorate during the day, his mind, open for sleep, had returned to the subject with a vengeance.

Her words haunted him, mocked him, and called him a coward, a liar, a base, empty caricature of a man, one who had not the strength of character to overcome his personal demons. Darcy could not say that these mocking voices were not speaking the absolute truth. But even so, he might not be so affected by them if he could not hear, on the edge of consciousness, *her* voice, joining in the tumult. It was senseless and ridiculous and so very real.

Once again, the thought of his wife brought back to memory the happy times spent in her company. Darcy had loved her with a strength and ferocity he had not known he possessed. As a child, he had been witness to an excellent marriage, a true meeting of minds and hearts, and one which had brought satisfaction, love, and harmony into his life. No boy could be more blessed than he had been.

On some level, however, as he had lost his mother, matured into a man, lost his father, and then become hunted by every fortune hunter in London, Darcy had wondered if he was capable of such a depth of emotion. He had often times felt that he was not, especially when he considered the simpering debutantes or the cloying attentions of those seeking a comfortable situation. It had often seemed like life was mocking him, teasing him with a glimpse of what could be, only to deny it, to jeer and crow about how little he was worthy of such happiness.

And then *she* had come into his life. His beautiful Cassandra, with her sunny disposition, her ability to induce him to leave his dour persona behind, and most importantly, with the love she had so frequently bestowed upon him. She had saved him from himself. Life had been so wonderful with her at his side.

And yet it had all been snatched away. He had proven that he *was* capable of such great love and devotion. But he would only experience it for a brief season before it was taken from him, leaving him bereft, a shell of a man, and one who had known the heights of sublimity, only to know the depths of despair, the bleakness which would remain with him for the rest of his days.

The one thing which remained of his wife was the little child sleeping in the nursery, and so perverse were the fates, that she resembled his late wife so strongly that he could not even look into her eyes without feeling an intense desire to flee. How cruel life could be!

But his eyes had now been opened—how foolish he had been not to consider it before!—to the fact that his daughter would only be with him for a short season before she too would leave. He had often thought of his daughter's future, or spoken of it in a glib manner with Bingley or his cousin. But he had never truly considered what it would actually entail. The daughter he could not bear to be in company with for more than a few minutes would grow and mature, and would leave him for her own husband, her own children. Her own home.

Darcy knew the thought of her leaving was nothing more than selfishness on his part. When she left him, he would once more be alone, little though her companionship meant to him at present. Georgiana would already be gone to her own life. He would be left to his own devices.

The sad truth was that Darcy wished to know his daughter. He wished to learn her ways and understand her. He wished to know whether she would favor her mother in more than just those traits which continued to haunt him. He wished to know if her smile would be the same, if her laughter would contain the same timbre as his wife's. He did not wish to go through life without knowing the precious gift given to him by the woman who had been her namesake.

The course of Darcy's wanderings brought him, at length, to the nursery door, and he paused for several moments in indecision, his instincts and his desire to know his daughter warring with his fear of causing himself even further pain. The door seemed to be an impossible obstacle to overcome, the handle daunting in the way it separated him from her. Could it truly be this difficult to take this step? Could even watching the girl in her sleep be so intimidating that he would shrink before it like a coward? What had become of the man he used to be?

Shaking his head, Darcy forced his fears away and reached forward, grasping the doorknob, turning it, and passing through, a silent wraith in the stillness of the sleeping house.

The room beyond the door which met his gaze was spacious as befitted the daughter of a wealthy man, and though he had not entered since their arrival in town, he was intimately familiar with it as he had spent many happy hours here himself as a child. The décor was a little different, of course—before coming to town, he had sent instructions to his housekeeper to see the room updated in a manner which would be pleasing to a young girl. Thus, the drapery, the bed pane, and the other assorted decorations were all that which would appeal to his daughter. Her dolls and other playthings were neatly arranged about the play area, and there was a small table and chairs situated to one side of the room.

Beyond that was the door to the other rooms of the nursery—her nurse had her sleeping quarters somewhere beyond that door, and Darcy resolved to take care to remain quiet, as he did not wish to wake the woman in the middle of the night.

All of this passed through Darcy's consciousness in what seemed to be an instant, and he turned to look at the bed and its occupant. By some quirk of fate, the light from the brightly shining moon flowed through the window, alighting on his daughter's sleeping countenance and illuminating her face so that he could see it clearly. She was angelic in repose, her chest rising and falling evenly, her eyelashes fluttering ever so slightly against the downy softness of her cheeks. Her mouth was slightly open as she breathed, but other than her breathing, she moved not an inch. And perhaps most importantly for Darcy's sanity, Cassandra's eyes, the one feature which was so like her mother's, were hidden behind closed eyelids.

Freed of the visible reminder of his wife, Darcy studied his daughter from across the room. It was evident, even in her childish countenance, that Cassandra would be an uncommon beauty when she attained maturity, much like her mother before her. The face of a child cannot be accurately projected onto that of the adult they would eventually be, but Darcy thought that his daughter might be a little longer of face than her mother, whose features had been round, though slightly heart-shaped. Her hair, which was beginning to grow down her back, was a little lighter shade, and though Darcy expected their complexions to be quite similar, their features would be slightly different, though the similarity would be striking.

A slow understanding came over Darcy in that moment, which told him that he was able to bear his daughter's company best now while she was sleeping. It was ironic in a way, and would not help him to know her better. But it would at least allow him the illusion of closeness to his daughter. And perhaps it might even lead to something more in the future.

At that moment the side door to the room opened and the nurse stepped into the room, coming to check on her young charge. Holding his breath against the fear of discovery and knowing that he would frighten the woman half to death and wake the whole house if she noticed him, Darcy shrank back into the shadows of the corner in which he was standing. He watched in fascination as the nurse moved to the bed, fussed a little with the blankets, and then after assuring herself of Cassandra's wellbeing, moved once more toward the door. In her fatigue, she did not once look in his direction, and she exited the room, closing the door as quietly as she had entered.

The weakness of relief fell over Darcy, and he sagged a little. But the thumping of his heart did not slow, and after counting one hundred beats, he made his way to the hall door and let himself out, ensuring his daughter would not be woken by the sound of the door closing.

Once outside, he allowed his breathing to relax, leaning his head against the cool wood through which he had just passed, grateful he had not been detected.

When he felt himself sufficiently capable, he straightened and walked away from the nursery and back to his own chambers. After the excitement of the night and the rush of emotion at nearly having been discovered, he felt that he could sleep now. And though his progress was as yet nebulous, he felt as if he had taken the first steps toward actually knowing his daughter. There was still much to overcome. But for the first time he thought it might be within his grasp.

Chapter VI

Much though Darcy had thought he had achieved a breakthrough of sorts, a reprieve from his sometimes tortured thoughts did not materialize. For that night after he went to bed, he was plagued by dreams of his dead wife, images of what had gone before, and imaginations of what might have been had she lived. The last category was especially trying for Darcy, as he had imagined for years what might have been had she only been able to deliver their daughter safely.

Needless to say, while the images of his wife haunted him by night, he was inundated with thoughts of his daughter by day, and more particularly by how his failure to move beyond his wife's death would affect her for the rest of her life.

In those days he hardly saw anyone. Georgiana, happy as she was with her new acquaintances, her studies, and her music, did not notice much of a difference, he thought, as she accepted his explanation that he was busy and would not be much in evidence. Fitzwilliam would likely have seen his struggles, but as he was busy with his duties, he was not available to comfort Darcy. And as the rest of the Fitzwilliams were not expected yet, he had no one to whom he could turn.

They were long days, filled alternately with longing and loathing, pensive remembrances, and painful recollections. It was as if he could not live the life of a normal human being. He drank more than he ought, sat up late into the night, arose far too early in the morning, and wished for some sort of reprieve to make his living hell bearable.

The one thing he *did* do was to continue to visit his daughter on a nightly basis. Somehow, in the midst of all this turmoil, he found that the fact of going to her room and being in her presence for however brief a moment, was the only time during the day in which he could feel at peace. He timed his visits to avoid the nurse, who he suspected checked on his daughter at set times during the night. He did not know if that was actually the case, but as he did not see her again, he did not think on it any further.

Incongruously, he still could not bear to be in his daughter's company during the day. It was quite obviously silly, but every time he caught sight of his daughter's luminous eyes, his fanciful imaginings told him it was the gaze of his dead wife looking back at him, accusing him for his failures. The promise he had made as she lay dying returned to his mind, and he thought of the way in which he had failed to provide his daughter with the love she required—the love he knew his wife would have unstintingly given. And though the love he knew she needed seemed beyond his ability to provide, Darcy swore many times in those days that she would be protected regardless, and that she would have every advantage he could gift her with.

By the third day after he had first watched his daughter sleep, Darcy was desperate for a change in his spiraling emotions, and he decided to visit his club. The familiar scents, the smell of port and brandy, the slightly acrid scent of cigar smoke, the sight of those of his station, including a few friends he had not seen in many years, were like a balm to his soul, and for a few short moments he was able to forget his troubles and immerse himself once again in the banalities of gentlemanly amusements.

It was when Darcy had sat down to a late dinner that he was joined by Bingley, who he had not seen since the day his wife and sister had been introduced to Georgiana. The man sat down at Darcy's table, greeting him jovially and asking a nearby waiter for the same dinner of which Darcy was partaking. Bingley's food arrived quickly, and the two men ate in silence for some time.

"How have you been, Darcy?" asked Bingley when they sat back with their glasses of port.

"Well enough," said Darcy. "We have not been in town for some time, as you well know, so it is an adjustment."

Bingley peered at him for a moment before he shook his head and speared Darcy with a pointed glare. "Your words might have deceived your other acquaintances, but I fancy I know you better than they."

"I am well enough, Bingley," said Darcy, irritated his friend would not leave well enough alone.

"And the circles under your eyes, the slight waver in your hand, the fatigue I can see written all over your face—none of these things are to be concerned about?"

Darcy was not certain he liked this new and observant Bingley. In the past he had always been able to induce his friend to desist with a word or two, a pointed comment to desist if necessary, if Bingley had even had any reason to disbelieve what he was being told anyway.

"If you prefer not to speak of it, then so be it," said Bingley. "But I would urge you, as a friend, to speak to me of your troubles, for there are few things which are more cathartic than to unburden yourself on a sympathetic friend who will not judge or condemn. You have often provided such a service for me; I urge you to allow me to return the favor."

For a long moment Darcy thought to refuse. He had been taught all his life to resolve his problems by means of his own abilities. But the thought of sharing his troubles with Bingley broke a long-constructed dam within him, and he began to speak without any conscious intention of doing so.

The act of confessing his problems was, as Bingley had suggested, purifying, and it was not long before Darcy felt a burden he had not known existed begin to lift itself from his shoulders. It was, to an extent, embarrassing to acknowledge his weakness to one who had always admired him as a tower of strength, but he knew Bingley was as good as his word. Bingley would not judge. And while he also might not have any answers to Darcy's dilemma, Bingley would at least provide a new perspective.

When he finished speaking, Bingley sat in introspection for some time, and Darcy, drained from his confession, could not muster the energy to speak himself. They sat this way for some moments, but though Bingley was slow in speaking, Darcy knew his friend had something to say—something he might not have said early in their acquaintance.

"I shall not attempt to coddle you or state that everything will work out," said Bingley at last. "You are far too intelligent to be taken in by such prosaicisms. Obviously I cannot offer advice based on equal experience in those trials which have beset you."

A flicker of a smile passed over Bingley's face. "In truth, I cannot imagine what I would do if I lost my dear Jane, and though I am aware it is possible, I also understand that it is no solution to attempt to keep her in a glass house for the rest of her life, even if she would allow me to.

"The fact of the matter is that you have suffered grievously due to the loss of your wife and I can empathize with the feelings which beset you.

"Though I know you are already aware of it, I *will* state that it is patently absurd to imagine that your wife's eyes are looking back at you, despite the similarity. In actuality, if the dead were able to do such a thing, I rather think she would be watching you through her daughter's eyes, beseeching you to love the girl as she deserves."

"It *is* absurd," replied Darcy, though Bingley had given him something to think on. He had not truly considered it in such a manner before. What Bingley said made sense.

"But that does not change what I feel. I wish to move past these senseless feelings, but at the present I know not how to go about it."

"I wish I could advise you, my friend. I would say that with practice you should obtain the necessary fortitude to withstand your daughter's obvious censure. Does not your aunt constantly preach of the benefits of constant practice?"

Darcy could only smile at his friend's jest. "Mentioning *that woman* is hardly conducive to cheering me up."

A curious expression came over Bingley's face. "The scorn in your voice suggests a more than usual level of annoyance. Have you heard from her recently?"

"Even worse," said Darcy. "The woman actually dared to journey to London, insist that I marry her daughter yet again, and insult my deceased wife thrice in the process. One of those insults was to suggest Cassandra died *because* I married her instead of Anne."

Bingley whistled. "No wonder you are affronted. I am glad I missed it; no doubt her diatribe would have been that much worse had I been visiting your house when she arrived. You know she has always detested me for my lowly connections."

A snort escaped Darcy's lips. "You shall not be required to endure her airs again, my friend. In light of her insults, I severed the connection between us and removed her from my home. If she dares show her face there again, I will have no compunction about throwing her into the gutter where she belongs."

"Understandable, but you might wish to take care lest the gossips learn of a family breach."

Darcy only grunted. In fact, there were few subjects he wished to discuss less than Lady Catherine.

"I wish you well, my friend, but I should return home soon," said Bingley.

Thankful for his friend's company, Darcy wished Bingley well and thanked him for listening. But it appeared Bingley was not finished dispensing his advice.

"One thing, Darcy. Though it is a custom of many in fashionable society to leave the rearing of their children to nurses and governesses—and fathers often do not have much congress with their daughters—I would advise you to continue your attempts to come to know Cassandra. I feel you will regret it until the end of your days if you do not make the effort."

And with that, Bingley rose and, after shaking Darcy's hand and slapping him on the back, he donned his hat and departed, whistling a jaunty tune as he went.

For his part, Darcy had been rendered speechless by his friend's words. When had Bingley become so confident, so forceful? Perhaps his marriage to a quiet and unassuming woman was the making of him. It seemed to have done him no harm.

Whatever the reason, a new and erudite Bingley had appeared, and his words only made sense. They spoke to all Darcy had suffered, illuminating his thoughts, even those which he did not wish to acknowledge, bringing them into the open from the darkest corners of Darcy's mind. Though he could not completely define the reason for his ongoing conundrum, Darcy thought he could now place a name to at least one facet of what he was feeling; that facet's name was fear. He feared his daughter's rejection. He feared his wife's disapproval of how he had conducted himself since her death. Most of all, he feared to fail.

But now he knew failure was not an option. He would continue to press forward in his attempts to better himself. If only he could have some hope that success would follow his endeavors.

The next day saw a new visitor to Darcy house, and it was one he had been expecting ever since his aunt's visit. Though Darcy knew his uncle found his sister as trying as Darcy did himself, he also knew the earl would not appreciate a rift in the family. And in this he was right, though the earl would prove himself to be sympathetic to Darcy's plight.

"Darcy," greeted the earl as he was led into the study. "I understand you have been busy since your arrival in town."

Darcy sat back and regarded his uncle. Hugh Fitzwilliam was a great bear of a man, taller even than Darcy, and heavyset, though not excessively so. He was also known to be a kind man, though jealous of his position in society and intolerant of those who believed themselves . . . "superior," in his own words. By that he meant people who sought to climb the social ladder, and those included tradesmen, fortune hunters, and anyone who thought to increase their standing. In this, he was very much a man of his time, though he was not an especially arrogant man.

"I would appreciate it if you would explain to me why you felt the need to sever all contact with your aunt, though I suppose I can guess the reason, at least in part."

"Hello, uncle," said Darcy, deliberately ignoring the question. "I trust your journey to town was tolerable at least?"

"Barely," grunted the earl. "The roads were fair, though it was rough in patches as is common at this time of year."

"And my aunt and cousin? And Miss Patterson?"

"All well, Darcy. My wife has already begun planning for our yearly ball, and James is already looking to escape her matchmaking attempts."

Darcy laughed. "If he would simply get down to the business of choosing a wife he would be spared such machinations."

Earl Fitzwilliam snorted. "That is a conversation I have had with him many times. But though he is as dutiful a son as I could wish for, he insists he will not marry until he finds a woman worthy of marrying. I have some hope to see him attached to the Duke of Westfield's daughter this season, but I suppose we shall see."

"Alice Sutton?" asked Darcy.

"The very same."

As he was familiar with the family, Darcy was also familiar with the Duke's youngest daughter. At the age of seventeen when he had last seen her, Lady Alice had been a pretty girl of many accomplishments, and only a year away from her introduction to society. Though Darcy had not seen her since that time and had no new intelligence of her, he could only imagine that she was a beautiful young woman now, and eminently suitable for one of James's rank. Furthermore, Darcy remembered her as a young woman of good character and impeccable manners, one who actually spoke with confidence about interesting subjects.

"Then I wish James well. As I recall, Alice was a lovely girl the last time I saw her."

"She has only improved as she has matured, I assure you," said the earl.

Darcy only nodded.

"Now that we have dealt with the pleasantries, perhaps you would consent to explain what the deuce your aunt said to set you off. Can you imagine what was waiting for me when we arrived in town yesterday?"

A feeling of dark amusement settled over Darcy. "So she stayed the entire time in town waiting for your return, did she?"

"She did," said Lord Matlock, and though he did not say as much, Darcy thought he was annoyed at Darcy's lack of concern. "It was fortunate the house was closed up, otherwise my staff might not have been able to refuse her stated desire to stay at Matlock house while she waited for our arrival."

"Then she stayed at de Bourgh house?"

"Indeed."

Darcy chortled at the thought. "That cannot have been comfortable. Has the house been used since Sir Lewis passed?"

"It has not, since she refuses to let it out, and there are only a few staff members on hand, and not enough to see to your aunt's comfort in a manner which she deems required. Thus, you can imagine the state she was in when we arrived. My butler tells me she descended upon Matlock house at daybreak and refused to leave until we arrived. As it was nearly four in the afternoon before we arrived, she had worked herself up into a fine state."

"Though I sympathize with your plight, I cannot feel the same for my aunt."

"Come, Darcy, I need you to explain the matter to me."

"Then prepared to be annoyed by your sister, uncle."

"Catherine always annoys me. You may speak without fear I will hear anything but her poor behavior."

And speak Darcy did. He recounted the confrontation in all its detail, and the sighs and exclamations of disgust from his uncle told him adequately what Lord Matlock thought of his sister's behavior. Darcy left nothing out of the discussion, ensuring the earl understood exactly what his reasons were for his decision, and when he had concluded his recital, he finished it off with one final statement.

"I understand your opinion concerning a break in the family, uncle. But Lady Catherine has passed so far beyond the boundaries of acceptable behavior, not only in her dictates, but also in her slurs against my wife, that I will no longer allow her to continue to importune me on that, or any other matter. I will not restore our connection to her regardless of whatever efforts toward conciliation she deigns to initiate, for I have no doubt that whatever she says will be insincere, only designed to appease me so that she might once again attempt to work on me to accept Anne. That will never happen, so she may as well save her breath."

The earl frowned. "That is a rather disrespectful thing to say, is it not, Darcy?"

"Can you dispute it?"

Raising a hand in surrender, Lord Matlock conceded it was true. "But regardless of the state of its veracity, it is not a polite thing to say."

Darcy laughed. "Perhaps not, but I find that I am less willing than ever to give any consequence to the niceties of society, especially when it concerns my aunt."

"I do not blame you, son." The earl paused for a moment, considering the matter—and perhaps more likely considering whether Darcy could be persuaded to recant his decision, but Darcy's countenance must have told him such an effort was less than futile. And thus he conceded the point.

"I trust you will refrain from publishing this abroad?"

"I will say nothing. But I also have no qualms about ejecting her from the premises should she have the audacity to darken my door again."

"For the nonce, at least, I believe you will be spared that. I instructed her to return to Rosings and gave her to understand I would be very *displeased* should she attempt to ignore my directive."

"As long as she does not disturb our solitude, I will allow the matter to rest."

A devilish grin came over his uncle's face. "The best part of this is that I shall direct James to bring your answer to her when he visits at Easter."

Darcy laughed. "I should like to be a fly on the wall for that conversation."

"Exactly, my boy! When you are in my position, you learn the power of delegation, especially when you are forced to deal with demanding harpies such as my sister."

Such a statement could only cause Darcy to laugh again. "I would never disagree with such an assessment, my lord. As long as Lady Catherine does not plague me, I will be content."

The earl nodded. "I will make certain it is so. Catherine is not inclined to listen to many, but inasmuch as I have any influence over her, I will ensure she understands exactly what awaits her should she break your strictures."

Darcy nodded and the subject was dropped. The visit proceeded in a smooth manner from that point on, as the two men settled into a brief conversation of men who were familiar and truly respectful of each other. In actuality they did not converse long before the earl was required to leave in order to go to another appointment. Before he left, however, he fixed a stern expression on Darcy.

"I know that you will not wish to hear this from me, but I shall say it anyway. While your aunt's reprehensible manner of expressing herself is unconscionable, I believe that the gist of her statements are correct. You would benefit from having a wife again."

Darcy frowned, not wishing to discuss this matter with *anyone*, but the earl merely waved him off. "I understand this is not a comfortable subject, and I will not press you. However, you must own the idea has some merit. Not only does your daughter require a mother, but with only one child to inherit, and a girl at that, it would behoove you to attempt to sire a son who can carry on the Darcy name."

"I have thought of these things, uncle," said Darcy. "The thought of paying attention to some insipid debutante makes me want to grind my teeth in frustration. I *will not* marry a woman who is typical of today's society."

"Then marry one who *is not* typical! You found such a woman once—surely you can find another."

Unbidden, the image of Miss Elizabeth Bennet came to Darcy's mind, a laugh issuing forth from her mouth at something he said. Perhaps it *was* possible to meet a woman who would suit him again, though the thought of actually marrying another woman seemed like a betrayal of his wife.

"I shall consider the matter."

"Good. And if I might offer one more piece of advice?"

At Darcy's gesture, the earl continued: "Though you will obviously need to pay some attention to status, do not allow yourself to be led by frivolous things. If you find a woman to whom you wish to pay your addresses, as long as she is a gentleman's daughter, I believe your family—for the most part, anyway—will be supportive. You married a woman of fortune and connections last time and satisfied the need for such things. Follow your own example and look based on the contents of your heart, and do not be put off if she is not a woman of high society."

With that, the earl bid his nephew farewell and departed, leaving a stunned Darcy seated in his study wondering what had happened. Had the earl actually encouraged him to marry a woman, even if she was a fortune hunter?

After Darcy thought on the matter for a moment, he decided his uncle had said no such thing. In fact, all he had said was that Darcy should not worry about status, as he was no doubt confident that Darcy would not be taken in by a woman seeking to marry for nothing more than material advantage. In actuality, what the earl had suggested was nothing more than to allow his heart to rule his choice of a wife, if he should be inclined to marry again.

The earl's regard made Darcy feel warm all over—he had essentially agreed to accept any woman Darcy chose, as long as she was gently born. And for that, Darcy was grateful, much though he still thought it unlikely he would ever marry again.

"Mrs. Bingley and Miss Bennet are to visit again this morning."

Lowering his paper, Darcy looked at his sister with some surprise. "They are to visit again without you returning their previous visit?"

"But I *have* visited them, brother," said his sister. She was buttering her toast as they sat at the breakfast table, and to Darcy's eyes she appeared to be happier and more awake than she normally was in the morning. "Mrs. Annesley and I had a lovely visit with them, and I invited them to take tea with me this morning."

"You know our aunt and uncle have returned to town. I would expect they would visit sometime today."

"Then I shall introduce them to our family!" said Georgiana with enthusiasm. "I am sure aunt would be quite pleased with them, as they are such dear ladies."

Prior to his conversation with his uncle, Darcy might have disagreed with her assessment, but given his uncle's words, he could not dispute it. His uncle and aunt had never been precisely snobbish, but they had always held those of a lesser sphere at arm's length. This promise to accept whomever he chose changed that, Darcy was certain.

In fact, it was his aunt who arrived first, and with her she brought Charity—her youngest daughter who was lately married, as well as Victoria Patterson. The ladies were welcomed with much joy, and soon they were ensconced in the sitting-room.

"Oh, aunt, I have friends I would like to introduce you to this morning. Mrs. Bingley and Miss Bennet will be coming for tea, and as they are becoming very good friends of mine, I am excited for you to meet them."

"Mrs. Bingley?" inquired his aunt. She turned to look at Darcy. "Is Bingley not the name of that friend of yours from Cambridge?"

"It is indeed, aunt. Bingley is one of my greatest friends."

"And he has recently married?"

"Yes, to a young lady from Hertfordshire." Darcy looked at his aunt, wondering if the earl's words would be born out in his wife; the

Fitzwilliams had never precisely disdained Bingley as had Lady Catherine, but it had been clear they did not wish to know him better. "Mrs. Bingley is the eldest daughter of a gentleman from Hertfordshire, and Miss Bennet is her younger sister. She has been staying with them for some months now."

"A gentleman's daughter, you say," said Lady Susan. "Then it is a good match for your friend. I understand he intends to purchase an estate?"

"He is currently leasing an estate near his wife's childhood home, but I believe he will eventually settle on an estate of his own."

"That is well, then. His marriage to the daughter of a gentleman will bring him some legitimacy." Lady Susan turned to Georgiana, who was watching with barely concealed excitement. "These ladies—what sort of women are they?"

"Mrs. Bingley is everything demure and proper, and she is very beautiful. Her sister is lively and fun. I enjoy their company so very much."

Seeming to consider the matter for a few moments, Lady Susan turned her attention to Darcy, a sort of questioning look directed at him. Darcy knew immediately what she was thinking; having met Miss Bingley and Mrs. Hurst a time or two in the past—and having no great opinion of either—Lady Susan was concerned that Georgiana was once again keeping company with ladies who would not provide an adequate example of proper behavior.

Darcy smiled and nodded to allay her concerns. "They are very proper ladies, aunt. I believe you will enjoy their company."

Nodding, Lady Susan smiled. "Then I shall be happy to make their acquaintance."

The visitors arrived soon after, and they entered, clearly surprised to see others in attendance in the Darcy sitting-room. Their surprise was all that much greater when it became clear they were to be introduced to the wife and daughter of an earl, but both ladies handled themselves with aplomb, and were able to accept the introductions with perfect civility. If they were in any way nervous, it was to be expected, though they did not betray it in either their countenances or manners.

Soon after their arrival, the tea service was sent for and they all settled down to their visit. Darcy watched the proceedings, noting the various demeanors of those present. While Lady Charity was enthusiastic, eager to meet and converse with the new acquaintances, Miss Patterson was more curious, and if her eyes travelled from the ladies to Darcy an excessive number of times, he ignored it. As for Lady Susan, she appeared to be determined herself, likely feeling a protective instinct toward Georgiana. Darcy was grateful, however, because she appeared willing to allow the ladies to prove themselves.

"Mrs. Bingley," said Lady Susan at one point after the tea had arrived, "I understand you are from Hertfordshire. Is your home far from town?"

"It is about four hours distant," said Mrs. Bingley.

"And your father is a gentleman? It is my understanding you met Mr. Bingley when he leased a nearby estate."

"That is correct, your ladyship."

"It is curious that I have never seen you before," said Charity. "I believe we are of similar ages—I should have thought we would have met ere now."

"My father is not fond of town," said Miss Bennet. "We are rarely in residence here, and when we are, we usually stay with my uncle."

"Then that would explain it," said Charity. "Will you be staying for long?"

The sisters exchanged a glance, and it was Mrs. Bingley who responded. "My husband wishes to return to Netherfield for the spring planting. It will be the first time he has supervised such an endeavor." Mrs. Bingley turned to Darcy and said: "I do not know if he has spoken with you, Mr. Darcy, but he has expressed a hope you would consent to stay with us and assist. He values your input."

"I would be happy to do so, Mrs. Bingley," said Darcy. "The planting season in Hertfordshire is much earlier than that of Derbyshire, so there should be no conflict."

Mrs. Bingley nodded and thanked him. "We shall be here at least until that time then. After, I would imagine we would be in Hertfordshire for the rest of the spring and summer."

"And you, Miss Bennet?" asked Lady Susan, turning her attention to the younger sister.

"Oh, I am very much at Jane's disposal," said Miss Bennet with her typical good humor. "As long as she can stand to have me with her, I doubt I shall leave."

"Lizzy," said Mrs. Bingley, her tone slightly admonishing. "You well know it is no hardship to have you with me."

"It seems you are very close," observed Lady Susan.

"We are indeed, your ladyship," said Mrs. Bingley. "We have been so since we were girls."

"And what of the rest of your family? Do you have any other siblings?"

"We have three younger sisters," said Miss Bennet.

That fact clearly took Lady Susan by surprise. "Five sisters? Then your father's estate—will it be passed on to you, Mrs. Bingley?"

"There is an entail on the estate, your ladyship. It will devolve to a cousin when our father passes on."

What was not said was that there could not be much fortune to be passed down between five daughters; Lady Susan must have instinctively understood this. Given the fact that the Bennets were not at all known in town, the father must be a country squire of relatively little consequence, which would not bode well for the state of his daughters' fortunes.

As the conversation progressed, Darcy thought he saw a change in Lady Susan's attitude toward the visitors. Whereas she had been wary of them upon their entrance, and her initial questions had been of a probing nature, she gradually relaxed until she was speaking with the ladies with friendliness and ease. Charity had formed an instant connection with Miss Bennet particularly, and they were soon chatting as if they were old friends. And as for Miss Patterson, while she was more reserved in nature, she was also friendly and spoke with animation when she did speak. In all, Darcy was happy with how the visit was proceeding.

When the time was approaching for the visitors to depart, another entered the room to enliven the group.

"Fitzwilliam," said Darcy as his cousin entered.

He rose and shook his cousin's hand, slapping him on the back with true pleasure. He had not seen his cousin since Christmas.

"It is so good of you to finally deign to grace us with your presence. I had thought you might be avoiding me."

"Why would I avoid you, Darcy?" teased the colonel. "You keep the best brandy at hand, so I cannot think of why I might wish to stay away. My general is not nearly as amusing company, but he pays my wages, so I must defer to his judgment, and he has kept me busy with a group of new recruits of late."

Darcy shook his head at Fitzwilliam's irreverence; he had always been thus.

"I see you have visitors, Darcy, beyond that of my dear mother and sister." The colonel greeted his relations and then turned his attention to the two ladies with whom he was not yet acquainted. "Might I beg an introduction to these lovely ladies?"

Miss Elizabeth giggled at such exaggerated gallantry and said *sotto voce*: "It seems like someone considers himself to be a charmer."

The entire company laughed at the observation, Fitzwilliam the loudest.

"Such effrontery, such rudeness! And all from a young lady to whom I have not yet even been introduced."

"I should rather call it 'keenness of perception,' Fitzwilliam," said Darcy, enjoying *someone else* teasing his cousin for a change. "It appears Miss Bennet has already taken your measure."

"Now you must introduce us, Darcy," replied Fitzwilliam. "For how else am I to prove myself if I have not the benefit of acquaintance?"

Darcy shook his head, but readily complied.

"Mrs. Bingley, Miss Bennet, may I introduce my rather flippant cousin? This is Colonel Anthony Fitzwilliam, my uncle's second son, and relation to most in this room, though at times we are a little unwilling to acknowledge the connection."

"Come now, Darcy," said the colonel, "You know you would be bereft without me."

"Fitzwilliam," said Darcy, ignoring his cousin's words, "this is Mrs. Jane Bingley and Miss Elizabeth Bennet. Mrs. Bingley is wife to my friend, Charles Bingley, and Miss Bennet is her sister."

The typical words between the newly acquainted were exchanged, and within moments Fitzwilliam had sat down to join the party. As was his wont, Fitzwilliam dominated the conversation, expressing his pleasure at making new friends, and regaling them with tales of his doings the past few days. If Darcy did not know his cousin well, he might have thought that some of his stories might actually contain a modicum of truth.

The ladies stayed a little longer than was normal for a morning visit due to Fitzwilliam's late arrival, but soon Mrs. Bingley rose, pulling her sister along with her, stating they had some other calls to make that day and that they must depart.

"But we thank you for introducing us to your relations, Miss Darcy," said Miss Bennet with a smile for Georgiana. "We have been happy to make your acquaintance."

"And we have been happy to make yours," said Lady Susan, rising to farewell the visitors. "In fact, I believe we should like to have you to dinner one night soon, if you have a free evening."

Mrs. Bingley flushed at the attention, but she said, in a voice infused with understated pleasure, "I believe we would appreciate that very much, your ladyship. Please inform us of the evening and we will be happy to attend."

"Excellent!" said Lady Susan. "As I believe Georgiana has your direction, I will consult with my schedule and send my card around in the next few days."

The ladies curtseyed and Georgiana left to see them to the door while the rest of the company resumed their seats. For his part Darcy was astonished at his aunt's civility. Lady Susan, much like her husband, had never been overly superior in her behavior, but she *was* conscious of her rank and she acted accordingly. For her to suddenly invite a party which was so far below the Fitzwilliam's normal sphere to dinner, was an unlooked for indication of her approval of the ladies, and likely of Darcy's friendship with Bingley, though he did not think she had ever met his friend.

"The ladies were quite charming company, were they not?" said Fitzwilliam, pulling Darcy from his thoughts. "I should like to know where you have been hiding them, Darcy. I rather wonder that you have not introduced me to them before."

"I have only known them since our arrival in London," Darcy replied. "Bingley leased an estate in Hertfordshire where he met Mrs. Bingley. They have been in London since late January. As you know, Georgiana and I have only been in town ourselves since late February."

"They are sweet girls," said Lady Susan. "Especially Mrs. Bingley. I do not know that I have ever met a lady who possessed a sweeter disposition."

"I hardly think Miss Bennet could be termed 'sweet,'" said Charity, though her grin belied any censure her words might have suggested. "She is rather forward with her opinions, is she not?"

"I think it is a rather refreshing change," said Georgiana from where she had once again entered the room. "I have seen too many women who speak to me as if I am a child with an eye on impressing me so that they may gain access to my brother."

Fitzwilliam laughed. "And I do not doubt that Mr. Bingley's sister is among the worst."

Georgiana grimaced and Darcy looked on her with sympathy. Miss Bingley had met Georgiana only a time or two before his marriage, and she had been all praise for his sister which, while Darcy thought it was entirely warranted, was quite obviously nothing more than her attempt to work her way into his good graces. Since their return to London the butler had informed him that Miss Bingley had been turned away from the house no less than thrice. No doubt she was eager to once again reinstate her campaign to ensnare him.

"My point is," said Georgiana, "that Miss Bennet is always genuine. I have never felt that she had an ulterior motive at any time I have conversed with her. Furthermore, I cannot imagine that she visits with anything other than friendship for me in her mind. They are estimable ladies indeed."

The rest of the company murmured their consent and talk turned to other matters. Within a half hour, Lady Susan had convinced Georgiana to join them on a shopping outing, and soon the four ladies rose to depart. Several times before their departure, Darcy had caught Lady Susan looking at him, and he thought she was of mind to say something—about the Bingley ladies, though he could not fathom what specifically she wished to say—but in the end she left her thoughts unspoken.

A moment before they were about to depart, Georgiana approached Darcy and said in a low tone: "I extended the invitation to dinner as I was walking Mrs. Bingley and Miss Bennet to the door. They were reluctant to accept, given my aunt's promised invitation."

"But they did accept?"

Georgiana smiled. "After much persuasion on my part. It only further proves what I said about the ladies earlier. Can you imagine Miss Bingley doing anything other than accept both invitations with alacrity?"

Forced to confess Georgiana's portrayal of the situation was accurate, Darcy praised her for her initiative. Within a few moments, the ladies departed.

When it was only himself and Fitzwilliam left, the gentlemen adjourned to Darcy's study and his bottle of port, and once Darcy had served them both, Fitzwilliam sat back on his chair, with one of his legs propped up on the edge of Darcy's desk.

"I believe I shall need to visit more often," said he after he had taken his first sip from his glass. "I would have come before now, had I known such lovely ladies were to be found here."

Darcy said nothing in response. In fact, he was himself rather occupied considering once again the rather fine eyes and long, thick lashes in the face of a pretty woman. He had no intentions toward the woman, but that did not mean he was unable to appreciate her fine qualities.

"What more can you tell me of her, Darcy?" asked Fitzwilliam, pulling Darcy's thoughts from the lady.

A bland look was his response, and Fitzwilliam merely chuckled.

"Come, Darcy, I am not searching for a wife at present, as you well know. I am merely interested in those I have met today."

"Then why do you not ask concerning Miss Patterson?"

"Because I have already met the lady. As you are aware, my mother is quite close to her sister, so while you might not have met her previously, I have been acquainted with her for some time. Now, Miss Bennet, if you please?"

"She is the second of five daughters," said Darcy shortly, not quite understanding why he was feeling so particularly reticent on the subject. "Mrs. Bingley is, of course, the eldest."

"And? What are her connections, her fortune? What else can you tell me of her?"

"I know little of her connections," replied Darcy, forcing his momentary irritation away. "I have heard of an uncle here in town, but I know nothing of him. As for fortune, while I do not know the details, I suspect there is little to be had."

Then thinking of the other connection they had, Darcy chuckled drawing his cousin's attention, his questioning glance demanding an explanation.

"The other connection I know of is a cousin—distant, I believe—who is the heir to her father's estate through entailment. He is also the parson at Hunsford."

Fitzwilliam choked on his drink. "She has a cousin who is Aunt Catherine's parson?" demanded he, an incredulous note coloring his voice.

"So Bingley has told me."

"Well, well," said Fitzwilliam as he wiped a trace of port from his mouth and snickered to himself. "If Lady Catherine has installed him, then I cannot have much hope that he is sensible. And that does not speak well to the state of her connections, if that is the best she can boast."

"Are we any better, with Lady Catherine as a much *closer* connection?"

"Touché," said Fitzwilliam. "Be he ever so foolish, a little foolishness is preferable to Lady Catherine's brand of . . ."

"I know," said Darcy in commiseration, when Fitzwilliam trailed off. "I cannot accurately describe Lady Catherine myself. Have you heard from your father about what occurred between us?"

"You have seen Aunt Catherine?"

Darcy grimaced but he readily told his cousin the tale. At alternating times during his narration, Fitzwilliam exclaimed his disbelief and shook his head with exasperation, but at the end of Darcy's telling he was as angry with his aunt as Darcy was himself.

"We always knew Aunt Catherine was selfish and bitter," said Fitzwilliam with a shaken head, "but I never would have suspected her of such . . . unfeeling arrogance. If you had not severed your connection to the woman I would have been required to question your sanity."

Nodding in agreement, Darcy said: "The one benefit to her stupidity is that I shall never be forced to endure her again."

Fitzwilliam laughed. "Now that is something to drink to!"

The cousins raised their glasses in toast and Darcy sipped his, while Fitzwilliam shot his back. When their glasses had been lowered again, Fitzwilliam looked at Darcy with keen interest.

"Now, shall we turn the discussion back to the lovely Miss Bennet?"

"What of her?" asked Darcy, showing his cousin carefully studied indifference.

"Simply that she *seems*, on a very short acquaintance I will own, to be nothing like the simpering debutantes you typically disdain. Add to that she is a comely lass and she is sister to your dear friend's wife, she would appear to be worth your notice."

"Miss Bennet is nothing like Cassandra, Fitzwilliam," said Darcy in a frosty tone.

"I did not say she was. But though I cannot afford to woo her, given her supposed lack of fortune, the same cannot be said of you. And given your requirements in a wife which led you to Mrs. Darcy, I would say that lightning rarely strikes twice. When it does, it would behoove you to make sure you capture it in a bottle."

Darcy could not help but to roll his eyes. "First your father and now you. And this does not even mention your mother's suspicious activities when I lately stayed at Snowlock."

"Oh?" was Fitzwilliam's lazy reply.

With nothing more than a wave of annoyance, Darcy continued: "With everything that has been said, it appears as if you all wish to marry me off again. I fulfilled society's expectations once. I cannot hope to find the perfect woman twice."

"I am not trying to marry you off, Darcy," said Fitzwilliam.

He rose to his feet and indicated his need to depart. But as he was leaving the room, he paused at the open door and turned back.

"All I ask is that you do not close yourself off to the idea of finding happiness again. It may not be with Miss Bennet—this I understand. But there are pleasant ladies out there. You only need to keep your eyes open and recognize them when they present themselves."

And with that, Fitzwilliam left, closing the door behind him, leaving Darcy alone with his thoughts.

Chapter VII

In the days leading up to the dinner with Bingley and his family, Darcy went about his business as he normally did. He attended to his correspondence in the morning, along with the business of his estates and his investments in town, and in the afternoons his time was his own. He would normally spend that time reading or in some other solitary pursuit, though one afternoon he escorted Georgiana to a museum, the first of the cultural activities they had promised to attend. It was engaging and interesting, and he was pleased with his sister's insights, guiding her toward a better understanding in those instances where her knowledge was lacking or her opinion was as yet unformed.

Every night he went to visit his daughter, and though he never stayed more than a few minutes, he began to feel a little better about what he was doing. He told himself it would only be a matter of time before he began to feel comfortable enough to be with her during her waking moments, while he fought off the internal voices which told him that his justifications were mere sophistry, brought on by his need to excuse his cowardice.

It was the night before the party when it became clear to Darcy that he was not as effective in fooling himself as he had previously thought. Darcy had retired to the sitting-room with his sister after she had played for him, and though they were both reading, some small conversation passed between them during the course of the evening. Mrs. Annesley was sitting quietly with her needlework a little apart from her charge, and though she was discreet when in the company of her employer, she was always alert.

"Oh, brother!" exclaimed Georgiana when they had been sitting in this attitude for some time. "I had forgotten to tell you. I began to teach Cassandra simple numbers when I visited this morning."

Shocked, Darcy found it difficult to keep his countenance. "You visited Cassandra?" asked he, though even to his own ears his query sounded more than a little dense.

"Yes, brother. I visit her every morning. Of course she is still too young to count without aid, but as I sat with her we counted her blocks, and she counted along with me when I said the numbers. She is very clever, though I suppose it is not a surprise that your daughter would be so. Still, she is a dear girl, and I do so enjoy having her here with us."

As Georgiana prattled on about Cassandra, Darcy could only listen in dumbfounded stupefaction, while Mrs. Annesley looked on in the background. Unless Darcy was mistaken, he thought that Mrs. Annesley regarded him with sympathy, though it might be nothing more than a trick of the light. It was clear that Georgiana had no notion of Darcy's problems with his daughter, and Darcy was grateful he would not have to explain what was bothering him. Fortunately, Mrs. Annesley was his employee and he could ignore the matter with her, though he knew she was most likely aware of the problem. That Georgiana was interacting with his daughter on a personal basis was a relief. Though Darcy knew he would need to eventually make overtures himself, at least Cassandra was receiving *some* attention from the family.

However, the incident also highlighted the need for Darcy to overcome his inability to see his daughter and quickly. The fact that Georgiana was seeing to her wellbeing and he was not, did not sit well with Darcy.

The next evening arrived and Darcy found himself amused by his sister's excitement, and even more so by her nervousness.

"I do hope Mrs. Bingley and Miss Bennet enjoy dinner," said Georgiana as they waited for their guests' arrival. "I should have asked for their favorites the last time I visited."

"Georgiana," said Darcy in an admonishing tone, "these *are* your friends, are they not? I dare say they will be happy with anything you have arranged."

"And your arrangements have been completed beautifully," added

Mrs. Annesley. "You have nothing to worry about, as I have told you. These are not judgmental ladies."

Darcy could see Georgiana relax and he could not help but snicker to himself. She was maturing beautifully and she would undoubtedly make him proud when she came out into society. For the present, hosting Mrs. Bingley and her sister was a good way for her to receive her first experience in acting as a hostess.

At that moment they heard the door chime, announcing the arrival of their guests, and all at once Georgiana tensed into a ball of nerves. Darcy smiled at her, encouraging her to leave her worries behind, and then rose with her to greet their guests. But those who entered were not who he was expecting.

"Mr. Darcy! It has been such an age since we last met. And dear Georgiana too! I cannot tell you how I have longed to see you both."

By his side Georgiana gaped to see Miss Bingley, followed by her sister and Mr. Hurst enter the room, but Darcy, who was well aware of what the woman was about, was instantly beset by annoyance at the woman's presumption.

"Miss Bingley. How . . . surprising it is to see you here this evening. How do you do?"

"Oh, very ill indeed, Mr. Darcy. It has been far too long and many things have changed, and not all for the better. But now that we are once again in company, I must confess that I can once again wish for the best. I am so happy we have been reunited!"

As Miss Bingley moved on to greet Georgiana, her manners and words as cloying and falsely praising as was her wont, Darcy looked to the other members of the party. Mrs. Hurst was attending her sister and Georgiana and betrayed no sign of understanding—or concern!—that she had inserted herself into a dinner party to which she had not been invited.

Hurst was another matter. Darcy had no great opinion of the man—he was far too indolent for a man of Darcy's active nature, and he had little to say whenever they were in company. He lived for his food and his guns and his port, and little else could rouse him from his customary stupor. At present, however, it appeared the man had come to an understanding of what had happened, as he appeared to be rather embarrassed.

Knowing that as a gentleman there was nothing Darcy could do about the interlopers, he welcomed them into his home and made a note to speak to Bingley concerning his sister's behavior at the first opportunity.

Then the door chime rang again and Bingley, his wife, and his wife's sister entered the room, and it was evident that he was surprised to see his sisters there. And then the mask of annoyance fell over his countenance at the sight.

"Bingley," said Darcy, moving forward to ease the situation before it became a problem. "Thank you for coming tonight. And Mrs. Bingley and Miss Bennet. Georgiana and I are so happy that you have joined us."

"Darcy," replied Bingley, still looking at his sister with considerable displeasure.

The ladies stepped forward to greet Georgiana and the Bingley sisters, and as Darcy was watching the events unfold, he was witness to Miss Bingley and Miss Bennet when the former first became aware of the latter's presence.

Georgiana, having caught sight of the two ladies she had actually invited, turned to them and greeted them with pleasure. "Mrs. Bingley, Miss Bennet! We are so happy you were able to attend tonight!"

Even someone as apt to see what she wished as Caroline Bingley could not have missed the difference in Georgiana's greeting to Miss Bennet and Mrs. Bingley, as opposed to how she herself was greeted. Miss Bingley turned, however, at Georgiana's words, and when she caught sight of the two ladies, an expression akin to a sneer fell over her face.

"Dear Jane!" cried she in a voice falsely infused with enthusiasm. "How fortunate we are to meet you here! I was telling Louisa that it has been some time since we have been much in each other's company!"

Then, in a tightly controlled voice which fairly oozed with contempt, she said: "And Miss Eliza. I thought you might actually be visiting with your relations this evening. How . . . fortunate you are that the Darcys saw fit to include you in their invitation to their superior home and exalted company. I am sure you feel favored indeed."

"Actually, Georgiana, Jane, and I have become great friends these past days," said Miss Bennet in a cheerful tone. "But you are correct that they have a lovely home and are excellent company. I am grateful to your brother for introducing us."

Miss Bingley grimaced and she appeared to be attempting to swallow stinkweed, but she plastered a smile which was even more insincere than her previous attempt, and said: "Yes, Charles is to be commended indeed. But as a friend, I suggest you do try to rein in your impertinence. The circles in which our friends move have little tolerance for such a character trait."

"There is nothing wrong with Elizabeth's behavior," said Bingley, and he gazed at his sister in a pointed fashion. "Her manners are as fine and proper as I have ever witnessed, and the fact that she has become intimate with Miss Darcy in so short a time speaks well to her character. Darcy *is* particular about with whom he allows his sister to associate. Perhaps we should all sit down and enjoy the company, rather than casting aspersions on those who by no means warrant such censure."

The tightening around Miss Bingley's mouth spoke to her understanding of her brother's reprimand, but she merely sniffed and turned her attention back to Georgiana. What followed was a conversation which was one-sided, and if Georgiana's understated glances in Miss Bennet's direction were not an indication of his sister's feelings, her polite but bored countenance in the face of Miss Bingley's prattling were.

The one thing which *did* surprise Darcy was how Bingley had spoken to his sister. In the past he might have been more likely to allow her behavior in the hope of avoiding any unpleasantness; and Miss Bingley was nothing if not unpleasant. It seemed his marriage and the experience he had gained being his own man had benefitted him.

"I apologize, Darcy," said Bingley quietly from where he stood at Darcy's side. "I had not expected to see Caroline and the Hursts here tonight."

Darcy turned a raised eyebrow on his friend. "You did not tell her of the invitation?"

"Of course not," said Bingley, a huff escaping his lips. "I am well aware that to do so will only induce Caroline to assume the invitation includes her as well, which is undoubtedly what happened here tonight. My Jane did not say anything concerning the matter, and Elizabeth and Caroline can hardly exchange a few words without Caroline saying something nasty. I doubt you will be surprised when I tell you that rarely does my *sister* get the advantage of my *sister-in-law*."

Darcy stifled a laugh and Bingley turned his attention back to his sister, rubbing his jaw in thought. "My only explanation is that she somehow managed to gain access to my study and found the invitation there. Jane did mention that she visited a few days ago, but she only stayed for a short time." Bingley turned to Darcy with a grin. "She must have become desperate when she has gone so long since your return without being admitted to your company."

"Perhaps I should not have written that invitation," mused Darcy. "Georgiana's invitation when your wife and sister visited would have been sufficient, after all."

A sigh escaped his friend's lips. "We should not be required to hide our activities from my sister. I suppose I shall be required to begin locking the door to my study again. I love my wife dearly, but she has not a suspicious bone in her body. Her sister makes up for it, but as she and Caroline barely tolerate each other, Elizabeth is not in a position to curtail Caroline's less than proper activities."

"Bingley, I do not hold *you* accountable for your sister's activities." When Bingley would have protested, Darcy waved him off. "She is of age, Bingley, and as you correctly pointed out, she listens to no one but herself. You could not have known she would use some clandestine means to discover your intention to be here tonight. I wonder why Hurst did not take action; his demeanor seems to suggest that he is aware of Miss Bingley's subterfuge."

This time Bingley actually snorted. "No doubt the invitation was presented to him as an extension of our invitation. You know Hurst; the thought of good food and good wine—both of which you can amply supply—would have overruled whatever suspicion he possessed and left him less than inclined to question her concerning the matter.

"But I shall speak to him on the morrow and make him aware that no further invitations which come to *my* house are intended to include *his*, unless I specifically extend it to him."

Darcy nodded in thanks, but their attention was taken by the ongoing conversation and Darcy decided to table the matter until another time. When he once again attended the conversation, it was unsurprising that Miss Bingley was dominating the discussion.

"It has simply been an age since we were last in company, dear Georgiana. How have you been amusing yourself in my absence?"

"I have been quite content, Miss Bingley," replied Georgiana.

For his own part, Darcy could hardly avoid looking skyward at Miss Bingley's pronouncement, and though his sister acquitted herself well, Darcy could see her barely concealed annoyance. And then that annoyance was gone, replaced by . . . well, it seemed to be mischief, though attributing such a trait to his sister was outside the realm of his experience.

"In fact, along with my studies with my companion and my activities with my brother, I have been quite busy in my association with dear Jane and Elizabeth. We have become fast friends these past days."

Darcy was only able to suppress a laugh by the barest of margins. Somehow his sister *had* acquired a bit of mischief in her manners, and it did not take much thought to determine from whom. He was delighted!

Miss Bingley was less so, and she appeared even more displeased when Elizabeth said: "Oh yes, Georgiana has visited frequently and we have returned the favor. We cannot be happier with our new friendship."

"*I* am *so happy* to have made their acquaintance that I *could not wait* to introduce them to *my aunt,* the *countess,*" continued Georgiana. "Lady Susan was *so* impressed with my *new friends,* that she was *eager* to invite them for dinner. Have you received your invitation yet, Jane?"

"This morning, Georgiana," said Mrs. Bingley, and though she presented her usual calm front, Darcy could sense an understated measure of amusement in the lady's manner.

"Then we shall all meet at my aunt's house again!" exclaimed Georgiana with enthusiasm. We shall all be great friends!"

Darcy's feelings at seeing his sister—his *shy* sister!—toying with Miss Bingley could not be interpreted, but at this point he was forced to actually cough into his hand to hide the laughter which was threatening to bubble up from his chest. By his side, Bingley was in a similar state; he was looking away, though his shoulders were shaking. It was, perhaps, not especially kind to enjoy the set down of another in such a fashion, but Darcy could not repine it. The lady was, after all, *most* deserving.

A glance at Miss Bingley showed her incredulous disbelief, which soon transformed to annoyance, but finally settled at cunning.

"An introduction to the earl's wife!" cried she. "Dear Jane you are very fortunate indeed. I cannot wait until my own introduction to her, as I am certain your aunt is nothing but lovely and amiable. I can hardly wait to attend."

"And attend we shall," said Hurst. Though the man had been sitting in his typical indolent manner and seemingly paying no attention to the conversation, it was now clear he had been following quite closely in fact. "We shall be very happy to attend and will indicate our acceptance as soon as we receive an invitation addressed to *my wife* at *my townhouse.*"

"But surely Lady Matlock means—"

"*If* she specifically invites us, she means for us to attend," said Hurst. No one could mistake the pointed fashion in which he spoke, and no one missed the inference, least of all Miss Bingley.

Then Hurst turned to Darcy and said: "If you will inform your aunt that we should be happy to confirm our attendance once our invitation is dispatched?"

"Of course, Hurst," said Darcy with an entirely straight face. "I shall be happy to convey your message."

A sour grimace came over Miss Bingley's face, and she glared at her brother-in-law with anger. Darcy nearly lost his countenance; for her to breach propriety and arrive at *his* house without an invitation was bad enough, but if she attempted to do the same at his *aunt's house,* he did not doubt her blunder would have lasting consequences. Lady Susan *might* maintain enough tolerance to refrain from having Miss Bingley escorted from the premises—though that was in no way certain!—but he did not doubt that word of Miss Bingley's indiscretion would be all over London's sitting-rooms within days of the event. While Darcy looked on the possibility of Miss Bingley's humiliation with a savage sort of pleasure, he would not have his friend damaged by association.

"Then we shall await the invitation with breathless anticipation," said Miss Bingley, but by her tone, not even *she* believed one would be forthcoming.

It was then that Miss Bingley's claws were extended, as she turned to Miss Bennet, and in a voice which suggested advice but was laced with contempt, said: "How fortunate that you have made Lady Matlock's acquaintance so soon after making the acquaintance of the Darcys. Even *your* impertinence must be suppressed when in the company of such illustrious personages."

Far from being offended, Miss Bennet's laughter was indicative of her amusement at the woman's paltry attack. But once again Georgiana surprised Darcy by claiming the first right of response.

"On the contrary, Miss Bingley, Aunt Susan praised Miss Bennet for her liveliness, and my cousin, Lady Charity, was very taken with her indeed. My cousin wishes to further the acquaintance."

"I was very taken with all your relations, Georgiana," said Miss Bennet. "And you have no need to concern yourself for me, Miss Bingley. Lady Matlock is quite obliging and friendly. Such unpretentiousness in a woman who can rightly lay claim to being among the foremost lights of society is refreshing to say the least."

Miss Bingley's answering smile became positively patronizing and when she spoke, her voice fairly oozed with false concern and arrogance. "Of course she is, dear Eliza. But as you have not been brought up amongst superior society, I am concerned for you. Only the best manners are acceptable to those inhabiting the highest levels of society."

"Everyone to whom Elizabeth has been introduced is quite charmed by her, Caroline," said Bingley, and his testy tone suggested that he had repeated himself frequently on this subject. "You may cease to concern yourself for her."

Miss Bingley receded, but it was with little evident grace. The discussion soon turned to other matters and if Miss Bingley was quieter than was her wont, Darcy could not repine the loss of her opinions.

The exchange quickly proved Bingley's assertions concerning Miss Bingley and Miss Bennet's mutual antagonism. Or perhaps it was more correct to state that Miss Bingley detested Miss Bennet, but Miss Bennet firmly kept her reaction to the other woman in check; other than a general sense of annoyance at Miss Bingley's ill-bred attacks, Darcy could make out little of Miss Bennet's opinion of the woman.

Several times during those minutes, Miss Bingley would make some cutting remark—thinly veiled, of course—at Miss Bennet's expense. But Miss Bennet, though she clearly understood the other woman's references, calmly deflected her words, and on several occasions, made Miss Bingley appear to be quite ridiculous. This, Darcy thought, was the genesis of Miss Bingley's dislike—the fact that here was a young woman, apparently without fortune or connections, bereft of a fine education at an exclusive seminary, who did not bow to Miss Bingley's supposed "superior breeding," and seemed impervious to whatever attacks she could devise. It was not long before Miss Bingley fell into a frustrated silence, her eyes often darting toward Miss Bennet in exasperation and barely concealed hatred.

The other interesting item was that though Mrs. Hurst had always in the past been a firm supporter of whatever her sister said, on this evening she was largely silent, and though Miss Bingley seemed to implore her sister for support on several occasions, Mrs. Hurst could not be moved on to make any more than the most banal of comments. Perhaps Hurst had spoken to his wife while Darcy had been preoccupied—he did not know, but it was something of a blessing to be forced to endure only *one* grating voice instead of *two*.

When the evening had almost progressed to the time when the company would be called into dinner, the door to the sitting room opened and the nurse escorted Cassandra into the room.

Darcy could scarcely conceal his surprise, but Georgiana only smiled and beckoned his daughter. The girl came willingly, running into Georgiana's arms.

"I hope you do not mind, brother, but I thought to introduce Cassandra to our guests tonight."

Darcy could only nod in dumb agreement.

"Oh, what an adorable child!" screeched Miss Bingley. "I simply love children, and I believe that your daughter is the most handsome child I have ever beheld! You must be proud, Mr. Darcy!"

"I am," replied Darcy, though he still felt as if his head was encased in a bale of cotton.

"How fortunate it is that she resembles your family so strongly, Mr. Darcy!" continued Miss Bingley. "Her resemblance to your dear sister is immediately evident."

The woman's words were like a dash of cold water on Darcy's face, and it was all Darcy could do not to scowl.

"Actually, Miss Bingley," said he in a tone so frosty even Hurst looked up, "Cassandra is the mirror image of my dearly departed wife."

An awkward silence settled over the company and Miss Bingley blanched as white as chalk. Even she must have realized that she had made a major misstep with her ill-advised fawning.

"Hello, Miss Darcy," said Miss Bennet at that moment, breaking the silence and causing the tension to deflate immediately. "I see you are not running today."

Released from her aunt's embrace, Cassandra approached Miss Bennet and favored the lady with another clumsy curtsey. "Miss Bennet," said she. "Lady?"

"My, my, I do declare you have made much progress in becoming a lady," said Miss Bennet with a gentle smile at the girl. "Have you been listening to your father and your aunt?"

Cassandra glanced up at Darcy and he felt like he was being pierced by the force of her gaze. But though it might have caused pain in the past, this time Darcy felt comforted by the force of those eyes. In that moment, he wondered if he might actually be successful in his quest to know his daughter. It felt more attainable now than ever.

"I listen," said the girl. Her manner was a combination of happy childishness and eagerness to please. "Be lady."

"That is very well indeed. I have no doubt if you act like your aunt Georgiana, you cannot help but follow in her footsteps."

"Of course she will," added Miss Bingley in that syrupy voice of hers. "With an example such as dearest Georgiana coupled with her excellent breeding, she cannot fail to become everything a young lady of society ought to be."

It was fortunate the housekeeper entered at that instant to announce dinner, for Darcy did not know what he might have said in response to Miss Bingley's cloying words. In reality, though he had never had any high opinion of Miss Bingley, Darcy found himself disliking her far more than ever before, and he wished he could order her from his house in shame.

As the company stood, Miss Bennet stayed at Cassandra's level, and speaking with the girl gently, she said: "It is now time for you to return to your room, and unless I miss my guess, you shall soon go to bed. I shall anticipate the time when we might again meet, Miss Darcy."

"Bed," replied the girl. Then she gazed up at Miss Bennet and in a beseeching voice, said: "Friends?"

Darcy could see the emotions—tenderness, joy, affection—in Miss Bennet's countenance when she replied: "Indeed we are friends, Miss Darcy. I shall be very happy to continue our acquaintance."

After another curtsey and a kiss to Miss Bennet's face, Cassandra said her good nights and was escorted from the room by the nurse.

"Now that little . . . display is over, perhaps we should proceed to the dining room," said Miss Bingley with a sneer for Miss Bennet.

"You must simply act naturally with children, Miss Bingley," said Miss Bennet. "My aunt has four children, and they are all well-mannered and intelligent, and aware of their parents' great love for them. They respond well if they know they are being spoken to in a manner which displays true interest and affection."

Miss Bingley only sniffed and turned to Darcy. It was clear she expected him to escort her to dinner, but even if she was not the lowest ranking woman in the room, Darcy would not have shown her such attention. Her behavior since arriving, her attempts to insult an invited guest in his home, and her uninvited presence were all worthier of scorn than consideration. Instead, Darcy turned to Mrs. Bingley and Miss Bennet and offered them his arms as if Mrs. Hurst and Miss Bingley were not even present.

"Ladies? Shall we enter the dining room?"

The ladies took his arms—he did not miss the grin on Miss Bennet's face—and they adjourned from the room. Behind him, Bingley took it upon himself to escort Georgiana, leaving Hurst to escort his wife and his sister by marriage. Darcy did not miss the short words Hurst had for Miss Bingley, though it was clear that she did not listen to what he was saying.

During the walk to the dining room, Darcy attended the fair ladies on his arms, but in fact he was much more focused on what he had seen in the sitting-room. Miss Bennet truly appeared to be at ease with children—though given her ease with virtually anyone of her acquaintance, it could hardly be surprising. The contrast between her behavior and that of Miss Bingley was striking. There was no question of who would be the better mother.

The atmosphere settled after they went into the dining room. Though Darcy had expected a return to the hostilities between the two young, unmarried ladies, it seemed like whatever Hurst had said to Miss Bingley had indeed made an impression, as she was sullen and said little the entire time they were in the dining room. The fact that she was situated in the middle of the dining table while Darcy sat with Miss Bennet and Mrs. Bingley on either side, while Georgiana was flanked by Hurst and Bingley, might have had something to do with her silence, as she had no opportunity for private discourse with either Darcy, which was obviously what she most wanted.

Even Mrs. Hurst, Miss Bingley's usual confederate in such situations, was on the opposite side of the table, and therefore was not in a position to sit with her sister, whisper and spin the webs of their plots as they normally would. Not that Mrs. Hurst appeared inclined to any such conduct; whether the woman had known of Miss Bingley's maneuver or had simply trusted her sister Darcy could not say, but she now appeared to understand the gravity of Miss Bingley's error. While others conversed, Mrs. Hurst largely mirrored her sister's silence, contenting herself to watch and listen. Though Darcy had not attended many such dinners with the two women, he had to own this was by far the most pleasant hour he had spent in either woman's company.

When dinner had been consumed, Darcy decided it would not do to leave Miss Bingley and Miss Bennet alone without the inhibiting presence of Hurst or Bingley, so they all left the dining room together and were soon ensconced in the sitting-room. There, of course, there was no such restriction on private conversations, but after Darcy witnessed Mrs. Hurst snapping back at her sister when Miss Bingley said something, he was satisfied that no plotting would occur under his roof that night.

As the conversation was fluid, in both partners and subjects that evening, it was not long before Miss Bingley managed to single Darcy out. That she eyed him with a sort of determined possessiveness he did not miss, nor did he anticipate her discourse would bring him any sort of pleasure.

"We *are* happy indeed that you have finally returned to town, Mr. Darcy. It has been positively dull here without your presence, and that of dear Georgiana too."

"I thank you, Miss Bingley." said Darcy. "I cannot claim to have missed society and all it entails. I am sure you will agree that I cannot be said to be the most social of men."

"That only increases the appeal of your society, sir," said Miss Bingley. "You are calm and deliberate and you take great care in your acquaintances. In fact, I was surprised . . . Well, I suppose in this instance, since Charles is your closest friend, you could hardly escape the acquaintance."

"I have no notion of what you refer to, Miss Bingley. I am as careful as I ever was concerning those with whom I associate. I have not changed in that regard."

"And your sister?" said Miss Bingley, and unusual note of challenge in her tone. "As she is yet a young girl, impressionable and inexperienced, I would have thought you would wish to curtail any possibility of her making acquaintances with those who are less suitable."

"Again, I cannot make out your meaning, Miss Bingley," said Darcy, this time with a pointed glare. "Georgiana only associates with those of the best character. I trust her judgement implicitly; she would not befriend those who are unworthy."

If Darcy thought the matter would end there, he was to be sorely disappointed, as Miss Bingley only seemed more determined to make her point. Her slight change in tack, however, was not expected.

"We are truly glad you have decided to rejoin society, Mr. Darcy. In fact, Charles had hoped that you would join us in Hertfordshire when he leased his estate. I believe he was anticipating your keen knowledge and advice since he is as yet, inexperienced."

"I believe that Bingley must have acquitted himself well," said Darcy dryly. "He has told me much of the estate and it sounds like it provides an ample challenge. I have nothing but praise for what I have heard of his actions when he was in residence."

Darcy made no mention of Bingley's request for him to go to Netherfield to assist with the spring planting. Should she come to know of the matter, Miss Bingley would surely insist on going to Netherfield herself, and Darcy did not fancy fending the woman off while being a resident of the same house.

A hard look met Darcy's statement; it appeared that the woman was truly upset about something, for she had never regarded him with anything other than a smile and an affectedly deferential manner.

"I understand you wintered at Pemberley."

"Yes, that is correct. It was only before Christmas when I decided it was time to once again re-enter society. Sincere concern for my sister and my daughter guides my actions; if nothing but my own comfort was at stake, I would gladly stay there and never leave."

A look of horror came over Miss Bingley's face, but she immediately shook it off. "I cannot imagine what you can mean, sir. The delights of the season are many and varied. Surely you would wish to partake in society."

"*Some* of the events of the season are a delight, but most I would gladly eschew. Still, Georgiana will come out in a year or two, and I must be ready for her. Other than that, I do not believe I will be very active this season, or for many to come."

It was a measure of the woman's determination to have her say that she did not take the opening which presented itself to flatter his sister. Other than a slightly perplexed look at him, she left the subject altogether and turned to the crux of the point she wished to make.

"Again, sir, your presence at Netherfield was *highly* missed. Charles in particular was desperate for your advice, and I cannot help but conjecture that had you been there, he would not find himself in his present predicament."

"Predicament?" asked Darcy, feigning ignorance, though he was certain he understood exactly what the woman meant. "I can assure you that your brother appears to be as happy and contented as I have ever seen him. Everything appears to be well."

Miss Bingley actually snorted. "And I can assure you that not all is well. This brief period of . . . *honeymoon*, shall be over, and when it is, Charles will realize what a mistake he has made."

"Mistake?" was Darcy's bland reply.

"Yes!" cried Miss Bingley.

Then, seeming to sense that she had spoken too loudly and with too much vehemence—at least she still seemed to possess some sense of propriety—she lowered her voice.

"I am well aware of your unerring sense of proper behavior, sir. I cannot help but think that had you been present, we could have successfully deflected Charles enough that he would not have offered for his unsuitable wife."

Darcy regarded her without expression. "Mrs. Bingley is unsuitable?"

A frustrated growl issued from the woman's throat. "Of course she is!"

"How so?"

"She has not fortune nor connections to recommend her! She came with essentially nothing, her family is ill-mannered and improper, her uncle in town is in *trade* and another is a *country attorney*, her second sister is one of the most impertinent women I have ever had the misfortune to meet, and her younger sisters are quite wild. She is in no ways *suitable*, Mr. Darcy. Surely you can see this."

Peering at her with more dislike now than he had ever felt for her before, Darcy said: "She is the daughter of a gentleman, is she not?"

Miss Bingley actually rolled her eyes at him. "In the loosest definition of the word, yes."

"Is her father a gentleman or is he not? There is no middle ground in this matter."

"Yes, he is," said Miss Bingley, a sullen peevish note coloring her voice. "But—"

"Then I do not know what more to say to you, Miss Bingley," said Darcy. "*If* Mrs. Bingley's father is a gentleman, then by the definition of the word, Mrs. Bingley is the daughter of a gentleman. Thus, you can in no way call her unsuitable.

"Furthermore, though I esteem your brother as much as anyone I have ever met, Bingley *is* connected to trade—the family fortune was obtained through your father's business acumen. Therefore, the daughter of a gentleman, no matter what her fortune or connections, must be a step up for him."

Miss Bingley gasped with horror. "Surely you cannot mean that, sir."

"I am sorry to put it in such a way, Miss Bingley, but society will surely see it that way."

"But he now has his own estate!" cried Miss Bingley desperately. "Surely that counts for something. Jane is below us in every way that counts."

"If what you say of her fortune is factual, then she is below you in fortune. But I must say, Miss Bingley, that the consideration of fortune is by and large the least important factor. There are many impoverished peers, but they are still accepted because *they are* peers!

"I would also warn you, madam," said Darcy, as he turned to leave, "I would cultivate Mrs. Bingley's good opinion, if I was in your position. As your brother's wife, she has an enormous amount of influence in your life. It would not do to make an enemy of her."

"I cannot understand why I would fear to make an enemy of such a mousey creature as Mrs. Bingley."

Darcy turned back to her. "Yes, I would agree that she is not wont to push herself forward, and would be too good to act with malice. But should you disparage his wife, I think your brother would defend her. You may have your own fortune, but if you do not wish to be forced to live off the interest, discretion is your best ally."

And with that final warning, Darcy turned away and joined the rest of the company. If he was never in Miss Bingley's company again it would be far too soon. At least for tonight, he would avoid her, and as she sat by her sister until the evening came to an end, whispering her displeasure, Darcy was content. Mrs. Hurst did not appear inclined to respond. In the future, he would make certain to specify that it was only

Bingley, his wife, and his enchanting sister-in-law who were invited.

Chapter VIII

The very next morning after breaking his fast, Darcy received a pair of visitors who were not unexpected, though he appreciated their effort in the matter regardless.

The previous night had been a success as a dinner, though it had been a complete failure in the company, entirely due to the machinations of a social-climbing woman. The more Darcy had thought of the matter last night, the more annoyed he had become by Miss Bingley's presumption, and he was determined to warn his friend of the possibly calamitous effects his undisciplined sister might have on him in society.

When the two men were announced and had entered his study, Darcy invited them to sit, and then poured them each a brandy, sensing they might need a bit of fortification for the upcoming discussion. As the two men took their seats, the elder spoke:

"Darcy." The man's greeting was more of a grunt, but Darcy, by now used to Hurst's ways, only replied with a nod. Hurst had been an acquaintance before he had ever met Bingley and his sister, though their connection had been a slight one. He had also known Hurst at Cambridge, though their time there had only intersected by one year—Darcy's first, which had been Hurst's last.

"We have come to apologize this morning, Darcy," said Bingley. He appeared to be a little jittery, no doubt fearing their acquaintance might be in jeopardy over his sister's indiscretion.

"While I thank you for the civility, you need fear nothing from me. As I mentioned last night, I do not hold your sister's actions against you."

"That is good of you," said Bingley, his shoulders slumping in relief. "But the fact remains that I am highly ashamed by my sister's actions."

"*I* am highly incensed," said Hurst, though to Darcy's eyes the man did not appear angry. Reginald Hurst was, in Darcy's opinion, a bit of a bore. The man was not a bad sort, simply dull, unimaginative, and with a tightly defined group of interests outside which he would not stray. He really had nothing in common with Darcy, nor with Bingley, for that matter.

"Do you know how she managed to discover that Bingley was to dine here yesterday?" asked Darcy.

"She would not confess to any misbehavior," said Hurst, with a sound at the back of his throat which sounded like a growl. "I interrogated her quite forcefully during our journey home. No doubt she was prying into Bingley's affairs. I have informed her that from this time forward we will only attend dinners when *I* am shown the invitation, and it specifically mentions our names."

"And how did she manage to convince you last night?"

"She presented it as a fait accompli," said Hurst, and this time the disgust in his voice was unmistakable. "She had gone to visit Bingley and when she returned she told us that we had all been invited to a celebration dinner with *your closest friends*, commemorating your return to society."

Darcy nodded. "She gave you no reason to suppose her information was false."

This time Hurst looked positively apologetic. "You set a very good table, Darcy. The thought of dining here pushed all other thoughts out of my head, and it never occurred to me to question her. Of course, I knew as soon as we arrived what she had done, but by then it was too late."

"In Hurst's defense, Caroline has never done this before," said Bingley.

"She is desperate," grunted Hurst. "She has not been able to attract a man to marry her and she is rapidly approaching the age at which she might be considered to be on the shelf. She considers your return at this time to be providential. She believes that your close friendship with Bingley is enough to turn your head in her direction."

"Then she is delusional," said Darcy, with an uncharacteristic bluntness. "I will take this opportunity to reaffirm to you both here and now: I will not offer for Miss Bingley, regardless of the circumstances. I do not esteem her, and to be honest, I do not consider her to be a good influence on either my sister or my daughter. If you prefer, I will speak to her myself to make my sentiments known."

"That will not be necessary," said Bingley quickly. "Hurst and I will speak to her and ensure she understands the situation."

Darcy nodded in thanks, and then turned the conversation to another matter. "Let me also be clear that no invitation shall be forthcoming from my aunt. If Caroline should arrange to somehow gain admittance, the social consequences could be vast. I suggest you rein her in before she does irreparable harm to her own social standing, as well as *yours*."

The two men looked at one another, but it was Hurst who responded.

"I had assumed as much, but I thank you for clarifying the matter. Should Caroline become unruly, I will make the matter clear to her."

The two men spoke of their plans for speaking with their sister, but Darcy did not attend to that conversation, as he was disinterested in the subject. Hurst soon took his leave, though Bingley stayed for some time longer. When his brother-in-law had departed, Bingley sat back in his chair and sighed.

"Do you think your efforts will bear fruit?" asked Darcy of the younger man.

"Not if I know Caroline," said Bingley with a dissatisfied grimace. "As I said, she listens to Hurst when to ignore him would obviously be to her detriment. As for me, it seems she still believes I will allow her to have her own way, though I have proven time and again in the past months that I will not be swayed. I cannot tell you how frustrating it is."

"You may need to take her in hand," said Darcy. "The threat to your standing in society is real."

Frustrated, Bingley ran a hand through his hair. "If you have some occult manner I might use to gain Caroline's capitulation, I would very much appreciate it if you would consent to share it with me. I find myself at a loss."

"You have an aunt with whom she might stay, do you not? Better for her to be banished than for her to make a spectacle of herself."

At that suggestion, Bingley grew contemplative. "You speak of my father's sister," said he. "She is a lovely woman, though Caroline detests her for being so provincial, so dull, and such a spinster. I suppose, if required, Aunt Juliet might be agreeable to having Caroline stay with her for a time, though I doubt she will have little pleasure in Caroline's company."

"You need not even send her," said Darcy. "The mere threat of banishing her to a location which is so unpalatable to her might be enough to ensure her good behavior."

Bingley snorted. "Surely you have far more faith in my sister than is warranted."

"I am merely considering her desire for advancement. There will be no advancement for her in . . . ?"

"Aunt Juliet lives in Scarborough," said Bingley. "But your plan has merit. When Hurst and I speak with Caroline, I will mention the possibility."

The two friends spoke for some time longer, though the subjects were generally more pleasant once that of Bingley's sister had been left behind, and when Bingley departed, Darcy was left to reflect how much he had missed his friend.

Before long, however, his musings turned to his friend's wife and her pretty sister, though a little unwillingly. Mrs. Bingley was a lovely woman, and her sister was her equal in every way. But Miss Bingley's words from the previous evening left Darcy wondering. Had he actually been in Hertfordshire, what would his reaction to his friend's attentions to Mrs. Bingley have been? Darcy could not state for certain, much though the thought caused him no small measure of chagrin. Bingley was his own man and was capable of directing his own life—surely Darcy would have been able to resist meddling in his friend's life.

But little though he wished to acknowledge it, deep down he wondered if he might have warned Bingley away from the woman for the reasons Miss Bingley had espoused the previous evening. Darcy knew he was no snob, but he *was* a member of the highest of society, and those in society valued the same qualities upon which Miss Bingley had based her objections. Perhaps he might have done the same. He had hope, however, that he would have seen Bingley's regard—which his wife quite obviously returned—and would have been able to restrain himself from interfering.

Shaking his head, Darcy pushed such meditations away, knowing the question was of little matter at this late date. Instead, he fixed his concentration on his work and left thoughts of friends, wives, and dark-haired beauties for a more appropriate time.

It was therefore a surprise when his solitude was disturbed once more mere minutes after his friend departed. Darcy had been so intent upon his work that he did not notice the sound of the door chime, and it was only when the door to his study was opened that he turned his attention away from his work.

"I apologize, sir," said Johnson, "but a Miss Bingley is here to see you."

Darcy frowned. For the woman to have arrived so soon after Bingley's departure, she had to have been waiting outside.

"I tried to tell her that you were not home to visitors, but she insisted she had business with you which could not wait."

"That is fine," said Darcy. "You may send her in. And Johnson . . ."

The butler turned back to Darcy in the act of leaving, and waited expectantly.

"Please leave the door open—wide, if you please—and ask the housekeeper to wait outside while I speak with Miss Bingley. It would not do for her to have any . . . notions while she is here."

The butler's exasperated scowl spoke of his opinion of Miss Bingley, but he bowed and retreated from the room. Darcy sat back in his chair and clasped his hands to his chin; though he would prefer to allow Miss Bingley to be reprimanded by her brothers who were tasked with her care, perhaps it was time to disabuse her notions once and for all. He was not at all certain she would give any more credence to his declared lack of interest than she would if her brothers spoke to her, but if nothing else, he could make it clear to her that she was not welcome to visit his house again.

When Johnson returned with Miss Bingley in tow, it was difficult to determine who was following whom, for Miss Bingley breezed into the room before the butler could announce her, in the same fashion as his Aunt Catherine had a few days before. Not a word escaped the butler's lips, but the way he pursed them and glared at Miss Bingley amply showed his feelings.

"Thank you, Johnson, that will be all. If you would remind the housekeeper of my instructions, please?"

A bow and Johnson departed. Miss Bingley was oblivious to all this, though she did look at the open door with impatient annoyance.

"It appears your butler is lacking, Mr. Darcy. He did not even close the door as he left."

"On the contrary, Miss Bingley, I am sure he was taking care for our reputations. You would not wish to appear compromised."

The twisted smile she mustered told Darcy all he needed to know of her opinion on the subject. Mercifully, however, she said nothing more on the matter. However, for the moment she said nothing at all, seeming content to peer around his study with unconcealed interest. Darcy was in no humor to allow her to linger.

"You indicated a desire to speak with me, Miss Bingley?"

The woman's eyes made a lazy circuit of the room until they alighted upon him, and in her gaze Darcy saw much which disquieted him. She was covetous, but of this he was already aware. She seemed to be attempting to read his mood and his thoughts, and she appeared displeased with what she had already seen. And well she might be; Darcy had no doubt Miss Bingley would be horrified to learn of his true opinion of her.

"Miss Bingley?" prompted Darcy, promising himself he would have her removed if she still refused to answer.

"I am here on a matter of utmost importance, Mr. Darcy," said Miss Bingley finally, when Darcy was about to determine to remove her. "After last night, I could not rest without warning you of a matter which might be injurious to you if I did not rouse myself to intervene."

"And what might that matter be?"

"Why that of Miss Elizabeth Bennet," said Miss Bingley.

Darcy was surprised that Miss Bingley would be so direct. Apparently with no one else present she felt that she was not required to adhere to social niceties.

"Though I would not injure you by supposing you are not aware of the situation, as I have more direct knowledge of the woman, it behooves me to make this warning without delay so that you might protect your reputation, and that of your sister."

"Miss Bingley—"

"Surely you must see she is not a suitable friend for your sister!" cried Miss Bingley, her manner proceeding from false concern to desperation in the blink of an eye. "She is impertinent and improper, and I cannot tell you what I suffer with her as a sister. She is known for her flirtatious manners in Hertfordshire, and I can tell you of my certain knowledge of several young men there she drew in, much to their detriment. Is this the kind of woman you wish your dear sister to be emulating?"

"That is quite enough, Miss Bingley," said Darcy.

"But Mr. Darcy—"

"I said that is enough!"

Her mouth snapped shut, but though Miss Bingley was silent, her eyes were alight with seething hatred. Darcy could only shake his head. What could she be thinking?

"I have seen nothing to indicate a lack of proper manners on Miss Bennet's part," said Darcy after mastering his own anger. "Her manners are lively, not flirtatious. She has never attempted to flatter me in any way. Rather, she is friendly to all with whom she comes into contact."

A rolling of Miss Bingley's eyes met his statement. "A man tends to dismiss those flaws of character when confronted by a pair of fluttering eyelashes."

"Indeed?" asked Darcy. "I am thankful for your faith in my powers of discernment. However, I would point out that I have never lost my wits when I have been confronted by *your* fluttering eyelashes."

Miss Bingley gasped, and well she might—Darcy's irritation with the woman was prompting him to reply to her insults with more directness than circumspection. But though it was not precisely proper to speak in such a manner, Darcy could not repine it. Anything less would undoubtedly be ignored at this juncture.

"Miss Bingley," said Darcy as he leaned forward in his chair, and looked her directly in the eye, "shall we be frank?"

Though fear bloomed in her eyes, Miss Bingley favored him with a single imperious nod.

"I understand what you wish for, Miss Bingley, but I will tell you here and now that what you want shall never be."

"Why—?"

"Please do not interrupt me, madam."

Though clearly wishing to speak again, Miss Bingley subsided.

"As I was saying, the friendship your brother enjoys with the Darcy family should be all you ever expect from us, as more shall not be extended. I am not of mind to ever marry again. You should cease to think of me as a potential marriage partner."

Even as he stated his opinion, Darcy was aware of the lie which issued forth from his mouth. The rosy countenance of a pretty young woman, the sparkling ring of her laughter, the intelligence shining from her dark eyes challenged the truth of his words. But though he knew the young woman intrigued him more than any woman other than his dear wife, Darcy was not yet ready to face the reality of his interest. And Miss Bingley did not need to know of it regardless.

"Moreover, you should remember that as the sister of your brother's wife, any statements you make concerning the respectability of Miss Bennet threaten to damage not only her, but you by association."

"I did not choose to be associated with her," muttered Miss Bingley.

"Perhaps not. But you are now connected, regardless. I suggest, if you do not wish to damage your own prospects, that you refrain from making such statements again. And I will charge you now to never repeat them in this house. Miss Bennet is my sister's friend, in addition to being the sister of my dear friend's wife, and I do not take kindly to baseless charges against friends of my family."

"Surely you do not misinterpret her behavior," cried Miss Bingley, her tone all affront. "She does not possess fashionable manners. In fact, she owns it herself."

"If you wish to speak of improper behavior, Miss Bingley," said Darcy, "perhaps it is wise to look no further than what happened last night. For is it not the worst of manners and the highest of presumption to arrive at a dinner to which you have not been invited?"

Caroline Bingley's countenance took on that of a ripe tomato and she stammered, trying to find an answer to such a charge.

"But it is my understanding that you invited Charles, his wife, and his sister."

"Sister-in-law," corrected Darcy. "And you could not have known how the invitation was worded unless you had managed to obtain a glimpse of it."

The woman's sputtered denials told Darcy all he needed to know of how she had obtained her intelligence. He did not wonder at Bingley's sure knowledge of the matter; undoubtedly, this was not the first time it had happened.

"It does not signify," said Darcy over the woman's protestations. "Regardless, the fact remains that you inserted yourself into a dinner at my home last night when you had not been invited. If my sister had meant to invite you and the Hursts, she would have dispatched an invitation to Hurst's townhouse as is proper. Even if there was any ambiguity and you were not certain if you should attend, you should have confirmed it with your brother before presuming to inflict your presence upon us.

"And I must tell you, Miss Bingley, that I do not believe for an instant you truly thought you had been invited. I apologize if I am speaking too directly, but I believe it is required in this instance."

"Mr. Darcy," said Miss Bingley, her tone all injured affront, "I assure you that whatever you think, I have never had any motive in mind other than the sincere desire for friendship, and I wish to keep you from harm. I cannot state emphatically enough that continued association with that . . . that . . . *woman* will only be a detriment to your family. Charles is stuck with her, but you are not."

"On the contrary, Miss Bingley," said Darcy, as he rose to his feet, "I can find no fault with Miss Bennet. Indeed, I have the highest opinion of her.

"Now, this discussion is at an end, and I would ask you not to bring it up again."

Turning, Darcy pulled on the cord to summon the housekeeper, and he smiled to note that she, along with the butler, appeared instantly. Darcy did not miss the look of disaffection and hatred from Miss Bingley, though it did not concern him for an instant.

"Miss Bingley is about to depart," said Darcy to his employees. "Please see her to her carriage."

The butler bowed and departed from the room, while the housekeeper waited for further instructions. For her part, it seemed Miss Bingley was not able to recede without one further attempt at swaying him.

"Please, Mr. Darcy—"

"I said this discussion is at an end," interrupted Darcy, and he glared at her, allowing her to see all the dislike he held for her.

Miss Bingley blanched, but she finally gave up, though with an ill-disguised huff. Then the housekeeper escorted her from the room and Darcy was once again left in peace.

Sighing, Darcy sat down at his desk. He would not wish his friendship with Bingley to be broken, but it was true the man's sister was an impediment. Bingley would need to know of this matter as soon as possible, as it would affect his conversation with is sister. With such a thought in mind, Darcy quickly penned two letters and arranged to have them delivered. Then he returned to his work, which had been interrupted already several times that morning.

Darcy did not expect a reply from Hurst and he was not disappointed in this—the man, on the few occasions Darcy had corresponded with him, was an even more dilatory correspondent than Bingley. His friend, however, sent a response soon after Darcy had informed him of his sister's visit, and through the blots Darcy was able to determine that Bingley and his brother had indeed taken up the matter with his sister. What their success was Darcy could not tell, and as he did not see his friend for the next few days, he was left to speculate.

A few days later, Darcy determined to visit his friend to hear Bingley's accounting of the matter. Though the thought of his friend's sister-in-law had never truly left him during those days, any desire to once again see the delectable Miss Bennet was firmly pushed to the back of Darcy's mind.

Georgiana had seen the sisters at least once in the intervening days and Darcy had heard of their deepening intimacy from his sister in exquisite detail. In short, Georgiana was as enamored with Miss Bennet and Mrs. Bingley as she had been previously, and she was ecstatic that they wished to continue their acquaintance with her. Furthermore, she also carried the intelligence that Charity had met with them on a number of occasions, and she was already cultivating a steady friendship with the ladies. Darcy was content—his own views of the women being reinforced by others of his family was a welcome development.

The Bingley townhouse was not at all distant from Darcy's house, though in an area which was not quite as fine, and Darcy, deciding he would benefit from the exercise, walked the distance rather than calling for his carriage. February had turned to March, and while the weather was still a fickle entity, the day was fine, if a little chilly, and Darcy enjoyed his walk a great deal. The crispness of the air, coupled with the calls of hardy birds and the clean air refreshed him, and he arrived at Bingley's house in good humor.

After ringing the bell, Darcy was greeted by the housekeeper, and when he presented his card, he was conducted into the house and led in the direction of the sitting-room. There, he found Miss Bennet, sitting with some needlework, though of the master and mistress of the house there was no sign.

"Mr. Darcy," said Miss Bennet as she rose to greet him.

"I apologize, Miss Bennet," said Darcy with a bow. "I am afraid the housekeeper did not inform me that you were alone this morning. I actually came to speak with Bingley."

Miss Bennet smiled and indicated for him to sit. "Mr. Bingley is not here today, Mr. Darcy. He left, I believe to see his solicitor. And my sister is not feeling well this morning, and is above stairs. I believe you are stuck with me for company."

In that moment, Darcy was struck by several things at once. The first was that he was happy to see Miss Bennet alone; he had come to see his friend, but the sight of her deep brown eyes drove all thought of his friend from his mind. The second thought was that he could have walked for miles and miles and never seen such a beautiful sight as he was confronted by at that exact moment. The final item which passed through his mind was that Miss Bennet, given the brilliant smile with which she was regarding him, was as pleased to see him here as he was to see her. A warmth filled his being and he bowed low.

"I cannot repine such company, Miss Bennet," said Darcy. "If you are not otherwise engaged, would you like to walk to the park?"

A smile lit up Miss Bennet's face and she agreed with alacrity, asking only for a short time to prepare for their outing. Sooner than Darcy might have imagined, she was ready and they departed.

They set out for the park, the sun shining on their faces as they walked. Little was spoken between them in those initial few moments, but it was comfortable merely to walk in her company, and little conversation was required. Darcy did, however, take the opportunity to ask after Miss Bennet's comfort once they had entered the park.

"You are not cold, are you Miss Bennet?"

Her brilliant smile turned on him and Miss Bennet said: "Oh, no indeed, Mr. Darcy. For you see, I am quite accustomed to walking about my father's estate at all times of the year, though I will confess that the winter weather does curtail the extent of my range. I find today to be pleasantly brisk, though I do not doubt some would say it is too cold."

"So you prefer the country to town?"

"I do indeed, sir." Miss Bennet paused for a moment and then she turned her head, her eyes surveying the stark nature of the trees, bare of the summer verdure. "I have enjoyed living with my sister and Mr. Bingley. My sister is the best of us all, in my estimation, and Mr. Bingley is everything that is amiable, gentlemanly, and good. But I will own that I miss my home too. There are benefits to living in London. But those benefits will never outweigh the feeling of freedom and serenity one gains by being in the country."

"I find I can only agree with you," replied Darcy. "There are some who prefer London and its balls, parties, dinners, and all the other trappings of society. I cannot feel truly at home unless I am in residence at my estate in Derbyshire."

Miss Bennet turned a quizzical look on him. "Mr. Bingley has told us something of your estate. I understand it is very beautiful."

"I am perhaps not qualified to speak concerning the beauty of Pemberley and the peaks."

"If you are not, then I cannot imagine who is."

Darcy was caught up in the infectious nature of her smile, and he returned it with his own. "I misspoke. In fact, I can tell you everything about my home, as I am intimately familiar with it. What I am not, however, is unbiased. I am of the opinion that there is no estate in the kingdom which can compare with the beauty of Pemberley. Though I have often heard others speak of their homes, the reality of what they boast of never matches the fantasy they have created, and something is always wanting."

"Then perhaps you would do me the favor of speaking of it? I would be willing to listen if you will paint the pictures with your words."

Darcy willingly obliged, for there were few subjects on which he could speak with as much animation as he could of his beloved estate. The fairness of his companion did not hurt either, as the sight of her rapt attention could only serve to spur him on to further praise of his beloved home.

The talk of his beloved estate brought to mind remembrances of those of his past, all who had loved it and spoke of it in the most glowing terms. His mother, what he could remember of her, had always loved the estate, as had his father, and even his uncle, while rightly proud of his own lands, would readily confess to Pemberley being the superior in sheer beauty. Cassandra had loved Pemberley from the first time she had laid eyes upon it. And Darcy suspected that Miss Bennet, should she ever be privileged to see it, would love it as much as his late wife had.

"Lambton?" asked Miss Bennet at one point in his narration. "Your estate is near the town of Lambton?"

"It is," confirmed Darcy. "Have you heard of it?"

A wry smile lit up Miss Bennet's face. "My aunt, Mrs. Gardiner, who lives here in London, cannot speak enough of the time she spent in Lambton. She is often wont to describe it as the dearest place in all the world, and as a town of little consequence, except to those who have been fortunate enough to have lived there."

"It is indeed a beautiful little town," said Darcy. "How long did your aunt live there?"

"A decade or so, I believe," said Miss Bennet. "Her father was the curate of the church in Lambton for some time."

"Ah, then I likely do not know of her. My family has always attended church in Kympton, the living my family oversees. While I am familiar with Lambton, I am not at all acquainted with the parson."

"My aunt has not lived there for many years. It is unlikely you would have met her anyway."

"Have you ever visited the north country?" asked Darcy.

"I have not, Mr. Darcy. I do hope to do so in the future. My aunt and uncle have spoken of travelling to the lakes this summer, and they have stated their intention to invite me to accompany them. I hope my uncle's business does not interfere; he is a busy man with many concerns to occupy his time."

"In that case, I hope you are able to go, Miss Bennet. The lakes are particularly spectacular. I believe you would enjoy the experience very much."

The conversation continued on for some time, Darcy sharing his impression of the lake country, while Miss Bennet appeared to be enthralled with what he was telling her. As he spoke, Darcy watched the woman, noting with wonder how different she was from Miss Bingley. *That* lady would have listened with outwardly rapt attention, while not being interested at all in the substance of what he was telling her. She undoubtedly would have found some way to praise him, be it the exactness of his memory, or the manner in which he described those things he had seen. Miss Bennet did none of this; instead, she asked him questions, clarifying that which he told her, or requesting he elaborate on some matter or another. Seldom had Darcy been so well entertained in the company of a lady.

When they turned back to make for the house again, Darcy changed the topic of conversation to Miss Bennet's home. With a skill he had never thought he possessed, he drew from her some recollections of her own, remembrances of the past, and the locale in which her father's estate was situated.

It was, he thought, a rather small estate, providing a comfortable life for its family, but not so much as to make them wealthy. Miss Bennet spoke of the estate with pride, and though he doubted it could equal his beloved Pemberley for sheer beauty, Darcy's admiration was stirred by her love of her home, as he was well aware what familiarity and attachment to one's home could do to inspire feelings of loyalty. Her picture of the estate was charming and, he thought, little colored by bias.

Then her words turned to her family, and though she was reticent on some subjects, she clearly doted on her elder sister and her father.

"You are close to your father?" asked Darcy, when she had made mention of some small anecdote concerning the man.

"Very much so, Mr. Darcy," said Miss Bennet. "My father, you see, taught me much of what I know of literature, debating techniques, current affairs and politics, and other unfashionably male subjects. Since I have little use for painting screens or netting purses, I am indebted to him."

"And your sisters? Have they taken interest in similar subjects?"

Miss Bennet laughed. "My four sisters and I are about as different as five siblings can be. I am the only one who takes interest in such subjects, I assure you."

"That is not to your detriment, I am sure. We are all different, with different interests. It would be a boring world indeed if all those living on it were identical to one another."

"I cannot disagree, sir," said Miss Bennet.

A discussion of literature ensued, and Darcy could not help but be impressed with the young lady by his side. Their tastes in literature were by no means the same, as Miss Bennet owned—with a grin—to enjoying the occasional novel, and as a gentleman farmer, Darcy was interested in books on farming techniques. But they both loved the classics, poetry, and had similar tastes in several areas. Furthermore, Darcy was impressed with Miss Bennet's knowledge and opinions; while they did not always agree Darcy could at least respect her views.

Though unwillingly, Darcy was forced to consider his relationship with his wife and her literary tastes. While Cassandra had not agreed with Darcy at all times by any means, her opinions had aligned with his more often than not. Furthermore, while Cassandra had been intelligent and well-read, Darcy had to concede that it was Miss Bennet who possessed a greater knowledge and more developed opinions. She also had a bit of a devil in her, at times proclaiming opinions which were designed to provoke a response. Cassandra had never done that to his knowledge.

During the course of their discussion, they arrived back at the Bingley townhouse. Elizabeth quickly queried the housekeeper, and was informed that Bingley was still away from home, and that Mrs. Bingley was still resting in her room.

A wry smile met this intelligence and Miss Bennet turned to him. "Shall you wait for Mr. Bingley? I do not believe he will be much longer."

"If you can tolerate my company, I believe I would like that very much."

Miss Bennet laughed. "Tolerate your company sir? I can assure you that you are very welcome indeed."

In fact, Darcy did not see Bingley at all that day. But he was more than content in the time he had spent with Miss Bennet. The woman was a gem, he decided; honest, true, intelligent, and possessed of every desirable virtue. In fact, Darcy was so impressed by Miss Bennet that he thought he might actually be in some danger. The question he could not answer for himself was whether being in her power was what he wished for. Regardless, it was undeniably pleasant.

Chapter IX

The days passed and Darcy was not in Miss Bennet's company at all, and though it allowed him an opportunity to think on his relationship with her further, he found himself missing her presence, her fine eyes, and her intelligent opinions. It was still too early for him to tell, but Darcy thought the woman was becoming essential to his happiness, and while he was not ready yet to think of the consequences of that thought, he could easily spend days considering her fine qualities.

Later that same day, Bingley stopped by, mentioning that he had heard of Darcy's visit from his sister. The first words out of the man's mouth reminded Darcy of his cousin Fitzwilliam, rather than his friend who, in the past, had been more inclined to be in awe of him, and had rarely—if ever—teased him.

"It seems you find my home quite delightful, Darcy. I understand from my housekeeper you spent more than an hour in the company of my wife's sister."

"It was only polite," said Darcy with a bland smile.

"Your politeness is quite extraordinary," replied Bingley, a grin of true amusement suffusing his face. "I will own myself that there are beauties aplenty to be found at my townhouse at present, but I did not know *you* would appreciate them."

"I believe you are overstating the matter, Bingley," said Darcy.

The note of warning in his voice only caused Bingley to grin that much wider, though he held his hand out in submission and changed the subject.

"I assume you came to my house to hear of what happened with Caroline?"

When Darcy indicated his agreement, Bingley sighed. "About as well as you might expect. Though she would not give credence to anything *I* said to her, at least she agreed to abide by the strictures Hurst imposed. And while I will not scruple to suggest that she has given up on her designs, at least she should act in a more appropriate manner."

"And did you tell her of the option to send her to your aunt?"

Bingley sighed and shook his head. "She swore that she would never go live with Aunt Juliet willingly, and when I insisted that is what would happen to her if she persisted, she became indignant."

"It is a difficult situation," said Darcy with a nod. "But you must be firm with her, Bingley. What I said of the threat to your standing in society was not idle speculation. She must be induced to behave appropriately."

"I understand. Now I must simply convince her of that fact."

As they were to dine at the Fitzwilliams' home late that week, Darcy found himself looking toward the dinner with keen anticipation. Darcy had not seen Miss Bennet since the day of their outing to the park, and while he could not have imagined feeling this way only a few short weeks ago, he now found himself impatient to see her again. The woman had wormed her way into his affections in a remarkably short period of time.

During those days, Darcy went about his regular routine. He completed his business efficiently, he spent time with Georgiana, engaged in several more outings with her, which they both enjoyed immensely, and he even visited his club on occasion. It seemed to Darcy that he was once again joining the human race, as if he had left it behind for a time.

At night, he still visited his daughter on occasion, though he did not go to her rooms every night by any means. It became a ritual of peace for Darcy; he was still finding it difficult to be in the girl's presence during the day, but the sight of her sleeping, her hair fanned out and her face angelic in repose, filled him with a sort of tranquility and happiness. And in the dark of those occasions, he truly began to think of what his life had become in the years since Cassandra's death.

The thought of his wife in those times was enough to cause a hint of anxiety. Cassandra had been a woman who loved life, living every minute to the fullest, and in that she had pulled him along, though at times unwittingly. Moreover, if his wife could see what had become of him, he knew she would have been disappointed. She would have had no desire for him to waste away in sorrow; she would have wanted him to live a full, happy, rewarding life. It was no less than Darcy would have wished for her.

Because of his acknowledged fascination with Miss Bennet, his thoughts at these times often turned to what his wife would have thought of the prospect of him feeling an attraction to another woman. In the worst of his musings he worried that she would have felt betrayed by his lack of constancy.

But then common sense prevailed. Cassandra, though he knew she would have wished to live a long and happy life with him, would never have begrudged him happiness after she was gone. Her charge to him at her death—to see to it that his daughter was loved and happy—was a testament to her desire for him to look to the rest of his life rather than wallow in the past. And though Darcy had no way of proving his supposition, he thought Cassandra would have wished for her daughter to experience the love of a mother, even if she was not there herself to provide it.

In the face of all these facts, there was one thing which Darcy came to know as incontrovertible—whatever it took, whatever he was forced to do, he needed to overcome his inability to know his daughter. Cassandra would not have wanted him to behave thus. The only choice was for him to do everything he could to be reconciled to the only thing he had left of her.

In the back of his mind, for all he was still not quite able to acknowledge it, thoughts of a young woman, smiling and joyful, persisted. He knew her presence would assist in bringing him back from the brink. And alongside this knowledge was the yearning building within his soul that told him he would enjoy discovering what a life with the woman would be.

The night of the dinner at Fitzwilliam house finally arrived and Darcy prepared for it. He could not remember ever being so concerned with the state of his attire, but that evening he chose to wear a deep blue suit and white shirt which he felt would look quite well on him. The notion that he took such care with his attire for Miss Bennet's benefit crossed his mind, and rather than chastising himself, he instead indulged in thoughts of how *she* would look. This, of course, heightened Darcy's anticipation at the prospect of seeing her again.

Shaking off his thoughts of Miss Bennet, Darcy left his room and descended the stairs to find Georgiana already waiting for him. The sight of her brought tears to his eyes, and as she had not yet espied him, Darcy was able to take in her appearance. She was dressed in a pale rose gown, befitting her status as a maturing young woman who was not yet out in society. But whereas she had always been beautiful in his eyes, tonight Georgiana positively glowed. How had she grown so quickly, from a babe he had held in his arms to the girl on the cusp of being a woman? Darcy knew not. He also did not know how he was ever to let her go.

And thoughts of letting her go were also a reminder of the fact that he would eventually be required to let his daughter go when she attained a similar age. Darcy was surprised by the fact that the thoughts of his daughter leaving him were far more painful than the reminder of her mother. Perhaps he was finally turning the corner.

Darcy descended the stairs and the sound of his shoes tapping on the marble staircase brought Georgiana's eyes to him, and she approached him, beaming with pleasure.

"William!" cried she. "You are looking very handsome tonight!"

"And you, my dear, are particularly lovely."

Georgiana blushed and ducked her head, but Darcy would not allow her reticence.

"You are becoming a beautiful young woman, Georgiana, and when you come out into society, you will be subject to the attentions of those who *will* speak such words to you. You will become more susceptible to the machinations of those not worthy of your notice if you cannot accept a compliment with composure."

Shyly, she looked up at him and nodded. "Thank you, William. With your help, and that of Aunt Susan, I know I will be able to withstand others' flattery."

"I know you will, my dear. I simply wish for you to remember that if *I* compliment you, my words are heartfelt. Please accept them in the manner in which they were intended."

"I shall. I think my acquaintance with Miss Bennet and Mrs. Bingley will also be to my advantage. They are both such confident ladies."

Surprised, Darcy looked at his sister askance. "You are aware that Bingley does not inhabit the same sphere of society as we do, even though he attends many events due to his friendship with me. And Miss Bennet, though she is everything lovely, will return to her father's house ere long."

Georgiana's responding smile was positively mischievous. "Oh? Actually, I had the sense that she will be a resident of London for quite some time."

"Did she give you reason to suppose that?" asked Darcy, his old defensive reflex with respect to young ladies once again rising in response to a perceived threat.

"Not in so many words," said Georgiana, her amusement growing apace. "But I had thought there was some . . . interest in her from certain quarters. Was I mistaken?"

The studied innocence in her manners was such that Darcy had no choice but to laugh. But though he chuckled for a moment, he then turned a sterner look on his sister.

"I would appreciate it if you would refrain from playing matchmaker, Georgiana."

The hand placed on his arm was so much more confident than Georgiana had ever been before, even with her beloved brother. "I have no intention of being a matchmaker, William. I shall leave you to it. But let me tell you now that should you be interested in a closer connection with Miss Bennet, I, for one, would have no objections."

Then with a smile, Georgiana turned away, and taking her spenser from a nearby footman, she gestured with her head, and led him from the hall toward the carriage which waited in front of the house. Darcy could only stare after her for several moments in bemusement before he followed her. It appeared as if Miss Bennet was gaining much support within the family. It was now up to Darcy to determine if he wished for that closer connection his sister had suggested.

Darcy and Georgiana were the first to arrive at the Fitzwilliam townhouse, and they were ushered in to the earl's welcome, and happy greetings from all their relations. It appeared that all the family were gathered together on this occasion: Colonel Fitzwilliam was present along with his brother, the viscount, and the earl's daughters, Rachel and Charity, were also in attendance with their husbands, not to mention Victoria Patterson. It was something of a surprise to Darcy—Bingley and his relations were truly not of a high enough sphere to warrant such attention.

When Darcy made this observation to his aunt, she only laughed at him. "This dinner is not only an invitation to your friends. With my children now married and in their own homes, it is not often that we are all able to gather together for dinner."

"Not all of your children, mother," said Fitzwilliam.

Lady Susan turned and took in Fitzwilliam's insouciant grin with a shake of her head. "You are a completely different breed all unto yourself as you well know, Anthony, and I am beginning to think that James is beyond amendment."

"So you have finally given him up as a hopeless case?" asked Darcy in a teasing tone.

"She has known *I* am a hopeless case for many years, cousin. I have made my position known too many times for my meaning to be mistaken. Unfortunately, I fear that you are in danger of joining this select group in my mother's estimation."

"Do not be silly, Anthony," said Lady Susan. "Darcy has been married and has a daughter to prove it. What have you to show for your life?"

Fitzwilliam grinned. "A whole host of battle scars."

"Anthony!" cried Lady Susan. "I will not have you talk of such subjects in this house! Save them for your club or your barracks."

"Is he speaking of his scars again?" asked James.

Fitzwilliam only waggled his eyebrows to the amusement of the men and the disgust of the ladies. Darcy laughed at his cousin's antics. He could not count how many times his cousin had lightened a depressing atmosphere with his effervescent ways.

"What can you tell me of these guests of your aunt's, Darcy?" asked the earl, in part to change the subject.

"Bingley has been my friend since Cambridge," said Darcy. "He is a jovial fellow, at ease in any company. His wife is quiet, but obliging, and his sister-in-law is intelligent and vivacious. I believe you will like them."

"Oh yes, father!" said Charity enthusiastically. "They are genteel ladies. I believe you will like them very well indeed."

The earl grunted. "I expected as much, as I know your mother would not invite them otherwise. But I am interested in hearing more of their characters."

Charity was only too happy to oblige, and she regaled her family with tales of her interactions with Mrs. Bingley and Miss Bennet, while Darcy added to the discussion with observations of his friend. When he was not required to speak, Darcy largely ignored the conversation around him in favor of his own recollections of the two ladies, Miss Bennet in particular.

It was not long after the Darcys' arrival that the Bingley party entered, and the introductions were performed by those who were already acquainted with the newcomers. Soon the conversation began, even if it was a little slow to develop.

"I understand you have leased your own estate, Mr. Bingley," said the earl.

Bingley, though unusually reticent that evening, was quick to answer in the affirmative. "It is called Netherfield, Your Grace."

"And do you mean to settle there?"

"I am as of yet uncertain," said Bingley. "Though it is a good size and the owner wishes to sell, I believe we might be more . . . comfortable in another county."

"Comfortable?" queried the earl, a frown coming over his face. "It is close to town, you say it is a good size, good terms. I cannot imagine what might not be comfortable about it."

Miss Bennet laughed and spoke up. "I believe what my brother is attempting to say without much success, is that my mother has a tendency to believe that no one can run my brother's house better than she, and it would be beneficial for their happiness if there were several counties between their home and my father's estate."

For the briefest of moments, it seemed that everyone was startled that Miss Bennet would speak in such a manner, and then the laughter erupted. The earl laughed louder than anyone else.

"You speak your opinions decidedly for one so young!" exclaimed he. "Others might obtain the wrong impression of your family, if you speak in so forthright a manner."

Miss Bennet only grinned. "Mine is not the only family which has a less than desirable member. In fact, I have heard my cousin speak of a woman who sounds positively meddling, overbearing, and possessing of a rather overblown opinion of herself. I believe her estate is in Kent. Perhaps you have heard of her?"

This time the earl positively roared with laughter. "Touché, Miss Bennet. Touché! And can I assume that you have also met this . . . paragon of good manners."

"Oh no, Your Grace. However, given what my cousin has said about her, I almost felt that I have. His was a faithful portrayal, I am sure."

"I can well imagine," said the earl. "I am well aware of what my sister is like, Miss Bennet, and I am also aware of what she looks for in her underlings. I have never met . . . your cousin was it?"

Miss Elizabeth agreed and the earl continued: "As I said, I have never met him, but I have met many of her other servants, so I can well imagine how he presents himself.

"And I fully understand the desire to put a distance between one and one's family," said the earl, turning his attention to Bingley. "Perhaps I can be of assistance, or maybe Darcy here can help. I believe there are many estates in the Derbyshire area which can be purchased."

"I would appreciate that indeed, Your Grace," said Bingley. He was speaking with the earl, a large grin etched on his face, and Darcy was heartened to see Bingley with a more typical demeanor. In essentials, Bingley's character was similar to the earl's, and Darcy thought they would get on famously should they become better acquainted.

It seemed that Miss Bennet's humor served to relax the company, as the conversation flowed more smoothly after her exchange with the earl. Though Darcy was not in a position to speak with her directly, he kept track of her the whole time they were in the sitting-room, and she did not disappoint. It seemed that she had quickly become a favorite of Rachel—she had already been friendly with Charity and Lady Susan—and she was quickly accepted by the rest of the family who had not yet met her.

She truly was a bright light wherever she went, Darcy mused to himself. Bingley would undoubtedly think differently—and Darcy had to own Mrs. Bingley was a lovely woman—but to Darcy, Miss Bennet was the true beauty between the two women. Miss Bennet simply shone.

Dinner passed in an amicable fashion. The earl had escorted both Mrs. Bingley and Miss Bennet into the dining room, and if the laughter which emanated from that end of the table was any indication, he found the company diverting.

"It seems like your Miss Bennet is making quite the impression on father, Darcy," said Fitzwilliam by his side.

Darcy frowned. "By what estimation do you call her 'my Miss Bennet'?"

"I imagine that she would be *your* Miss Bennet should you give yourself the trouble to make her so."

"Perhaps I do not wish it," said Darcy. He was quickly becoming irritated with Fitzwilliam's continued assertions.

"I dare say you are a fool if you do not," replied his cousin. "'Lightning rarely strikes twice.'"

Darcy grunted and refused to answer, and Anthony turned his attention to his sister, who was seated on his other side. The rest of the company was apparently engrossed in their own conversations; he did not think they had been overheard. The tinkling laughter which was issuing from Miss Bennet's mouth appeared to have enthralled those near her, and at the other end of the table Lady Susan was holding court with the diners who were sitting near to her.

All at once Darcy felt a wave of annoyance pass through him. His family had taken up Miss Bennet's standard, and they were not shy about promoting her interests. He wished they would desist. Miss Bennet was indeed a wonderful girl, but Darcy had known the bliss of living with a wonderful girl and she had been taken from him far too early. Why should he consider doing the same thing again? Why open himself up to the heartache?

His eyes drawn to where she sat, Darcy examined her with a critical eye, unconsciously seeking to find some fault with her. She was not precisely beautiful, and her form was not the perfection of his late wife's. Furthermore, her manners, while similar to Cassandra's on some level, were far bolder and even brazen, with a dash of impertinence, and not of the fashionable set.

If she was ever introduced to society at large, Darcy wondered how she would be received. No doubt with derision from the other debutantes, who would hate her for being a rival, while being dismissive of her ability to steal the attentions of any eligible gentleman. No doubt her playful manners would also bring the attentions of the worst rakes of society, those who would see only a mark to be conquered. In those instances, her intelligence would not be of assistance to her. In fact, it might actually be a hindrance.

In short, Miss Bennet, though she was a good woman with much in her favor, was not the kind of woman he should be considering for a wife, nor was she the sort with whom he wished Georgiana to associate. She was in no way suitable, and Darcy would be best if he made that fact very clear to his family at the earliest opportunity.

With these gloomy thoughts Darcy passed the rest of the meal, and with his continuing pique at what he saw as his relations' blatant attempts to promote Miss Bennet, he found his mood worsening. Every peal of laughter, every witty rejoinder, which he could only just make out over the buzz of conversation, made him unhappier. It was a relief when the ladies withdrew from the dining room at the conclusion of the meal, leaving him alone in the company of his dark thoughts. He was determined to ignore any attempts at further conversation from the other men in the room.

Unfortunately, his reprieve did not last long, as the earl soon brought his after dinner brandy and sat at Darcy's side. Their initial conversation was for the most part benign, but it was not very many minutes before his uncle raised his ire yet again.

"Have you thought any more on our conversation, Darcy?"

The red haze of anger descended over Darcy and he snapped: "Will everyone in the family continue to promote the girl to me until I capitulate? I would not have imagined you all would champion her availability as a bride to me; I might have thought it was a conspiracy, if you were not all members of my family."

The earl looked at him, and Darcy could see the confusion in his gaze, which quickly turned to speculation and finally amusement.

"I will thank you not to take that tone with me, Darcy," said he at last. "I must own, however, that I never expected it to affect you to such an extent, even if we *were* all conspiring to match you up with the girl."

"I apologize for my tone, uncle," said Darcy feeling a little repentant that he had lost control of his temper. "But I do not apologize for the substance of my words."

"Darcy, I was not attempting to promote—Miss Bennet, I assume?" At Darcy's curt nod, the earl chuckled. "She *does* seem to have made quite an impression on the family, I will grant you that."

Darcy could only grunt with sour exasperation.

"Still, what if the family takes a liking to the girl? What is it to you?"

"That is what I have been trying to figure out myself," said Fitzwilliam as he sat close to them. "I would have thought Darcy was inured to anything *I* might say to him. Yet something seems to have touched a nerve."

Gazing flatly at his cousin, Darcy said: "If Fitzwilliam's comments, calling her 'my Miss Bennet,' are not enough, Charity cannot say enough about the girl, Georgiana is less than circumspect about how she might make a good sister, and your wife, sir, seems intent upon making Miss Bennet the belle of the upcoming season. I have already fulfilled my duty once. Can you not all leave me in peace?"

The earl's speculative stare unnerved Darcy, but he only scowled and feigned nonchalance, taking a swig of his drink.

"Anthony, away with you," said the earl at length. "I wish to speak with your cousin alone."

"What? And miss the fun?"

A glare was the earl's response, and Fitzwilliam snickered before heaving himself to his feet. "Oh very well. Besides, since you will be speaking of the man's sister by marriage, I suppose someone should occupy Bingley."

Then with an exaggerated bow, Fitzwilliam walked away and, good as his word, approached Bingley and struck up a conversation. Darcy was left at the dubious mercy of his uncle.

"Now, Darcy, shall we discuss this further?"

"I have no wish to, uncle."

"And yet I think we shall. I understand how overt matchmaking would irritate one as independent as you, but there seems to be something else at work here. For I cannot imagine such a reaction from you if you did not possess some attraction for the woman."

Darcy flushed and looked down, but he did not miss the knowing look with which his uncle favored him. Nor did he miss the chuckle which this confirmation produced.

"Do not be angry, Darcy. Given the way you reacted when the lady arrived, I had already noticed how much you esteem Miss Bennet, and unless I am very much mistaken, I believe there is some attraction on the lady's side as well."

"What?" demanded Darcy.

"I do not know Miss Bennet well, so I shall venture nothing further. That was only how it seemed to me. What I would like to know, is why this resistance when I believe she would bring you much happiness?"

"She is unsuitable," said Darcy. "She has no standing in society, she possesses no dowry, and she has an uncle in trade. What more is there to discuss?"

"Those are considerations indeed," agreed the earl. "But I cannot account for how you would balk at the thought of having an uncle as a tradesman when your avowed closest friend is only one generation removed from that profession, and in fact still receives much of his wealth from trade."

"Having a marriage relation actively in trade is quite different from a *friend* whose *father* was a tradesman."

Lord Matlock shrugged. "So if the uncle turns out to be a detriment in society, you hold him at arm's length. But since Miss Bennet is sensible and I have heard her speaking of her uncle in glowing terms, I cannot imagine he is anything but acceptable, other than the unfortunate fact of his profession.

"And perhaps most importantly, such things have never meant anything to you. Why should they rule you now?"

Darcy really had no way to answer such a question, so he said nothing. The earl nodded once as if to confirm to himself what he had been thinking.

"In truth, there is nothing unsuitable about the girl. She is pleasant and happy, intelligent, spirited, and would be good for you, I suspect."

When Darcy started to protest, the earl raised his hand for silence. "Do not assume I am promoting Miss Bennet. I can see the kind of girl she is, and it is for that reason I suggest she would be a good match for you. But you must make your own decision, and I have no doubt you will do so, regardless of what I say.

"But remember our conversation. Whether you consider Miss Bennet as a prospective bride is your own business and I will not attempt to tell you otherwise. If you do decide to take another wife, do not allow fortune and connections to dictate who is suitable and who is not. You have already married a woman who possessed those attributes. I would much prefer to see you happy again than seeing you married for the more practical reasons."

The earl rose to depart and slapped Darcy on the shoulder when he did. But before leaving he once again looked Darcy in the eye and said:

"For what it's worth, I believe Miss Bennet *would* make you happy. She is exactly the sort of unpretentious girl your late wife was. But though they are quite different in essentials, there is something about her . . . a *joie de vivre,* if you will, that your wife did not possess. I believe she would make you very happy indeed.

"But you must do as you will."

And with that, the earl turned away and approached his sons-in-law who were nearby, and within moments they were speaking animatedly between them. Darcy looked about the room and noted that Bingley was being amply entertained by Fitzwilliam and the viscount, and more importantly, that no one was looking to him to join their conversation.

In truth, Darcy wished to be away from his uncle's house so that he could think on his own. His uncle had made many valid points and Darcy would prefer to have the time to think about them in solitude. But such was not to be, for soon the men rose and it was back to the sitting-room where the ladies were waiting for them.

Chapter X

As Darcy considered the matter over the next few days, he quickly came to the realization that he had behaved badly at his uncle's house. It truly did not matter if his family was promoting Miss Bennet to him as a prospective bride. If he was not interested, then it was a simple matter to deflect them. He had been deflecting people who wanted something from him for years. Why should this be any different?

The fact of the matter was that he was attracted to Miss Bennet like bees to nectar, and if others could see it, then that was his own fault. Miss Bennet herself had been nothing but circumspect in his presence, and he had never had the impression, even for an instant, that she was the type of fortune hunting woman who was so prevalent in London society. The mere thought beggared belief.

The question was, what was he to do about it? Had he met Miss Bennet and remained unmarried, other than the fact of her situation, he thought he might have been more willing and ready to take the step without all this hesitance. But the fact remained that Darcy still loved and missed Cassandra, and the thought of replacing her with Miss Bennet—or any other woman—was not something he wished to consider.

But then there were those other points in her favor. Her magnetic, sunny personality. Her lustrous dark hair and beautiful eyes. Her intelligence and propensity to speak to him as if he were simply a man, rather than the holder of a large estate, who she felt she needed to impress. The fact that she spoke with his daughter as an equal and appeared to love children. How could he resist her pull? Unless he was content to be alone for the rest of his life, he would need to marry again, and the idea that he would ever find another woman as perfect for him as Miss Bennet, positively beggared belief.

Though Darcy could find no answers for his dilemma, he decided that it was not imperative that he come up with a solution at present. Miss Bennet was ensconced with the Bingleys for at least the next two months, and Darcy could continue to come to know her at his leisure. Surely in that time the matter would clarify itself in his mind.

Within a few days of his aunt's dinner party, the day of their attendance at the opera arrived, and Darcy considered its coming with equal parts exasperation, anticipation, and trepidation. Though he was fond of the theater, the opera, and other cultural delights which could be found in London, the thought of once again being the focus of attention for every gawker in society caused no little annoyance. But then again, he would be able to once again be in the presence of Miss Bennet, which was cause for anticipation.

On the evening in question, Fitzwilliam arrived at Darcy's townhouse to accompany Darcy and Georgiana to the opera; the earl and countess and the viscount would also be attending, though they would watch the play from their own box. Of course, as was usual for Fitzwilliam, he arrived in a teasing mood, no doubt seeking a response.

"Ah, Darcy," said he as he sauntered into the room. He dropped heavily into a chair and raised his booted feet up to rest on the edge of Darcy's desk. "I see you are prepared for tonight's festivities. And it is not only the delight of the opera, eh?"

"I am sure there are many reasons to anticipate an evening at the theater, Fitzwilliam," said Darcy, keeping his tone bland and his expression even.

Fitzwilliam only laughed. "Now there is the inscrutable Darcy mask I am accustomed to. Well done, old man!"

Darcy only leaned back in his chair and regarded his cousin. Perhaps it was time for Fitzwilliam to receive a taste of his own medicine.

"And are you perhaps anticipating the theater yourself?" asked Darcy in an offhand tone. "Or perhaps the beauties of your father's home are superior at present?"

All Darcy received in response was a flat stare and a terse, "You should confine your fishing to the streams of Pemberley, cousin. You are more apt to catch something there."

"That strikes me as a rather defensive answer."

"Take it how you will," said Fitzwilliam with an airy wave of his hand.

Standing, Fitzwilliam approached a side table and helped himself to a glass of port from the decanter which sat on it. With the glass raised to his lips, Fitzwilliam turned and regarded Darcy, a half frown playing about his features. When he sat on his chair again, the indolence of posture was gone in favor of a straight back and a keen look in his eyes. He regarded Darcy for several moments before he again opened his mouth.

"I have been commanded by my father to refrain from sporting with you, and since I am dependent upon the man, I will restrain myself. I will make one observation and then I will never return to the subject."

"Oh?"

"Yes, Darcy. I know you are struggling over the matter, but let me simply say that if you allowed yourself to feel again, I believe Miss Bennet would make you happy."

With that said, Fitzwilliam's previous ease reasserted itself and he leaned back in his chair and once again put a foot on Darcy's desk. "There, now you are safe from me."

Darcy decided that there was nothing to be done but to ignore Fitzwilliam's words. Instead, he said: "The earl has leveled no injunction against *me* teasing *you*."

A chuckle met Darcy's statement. "Compared to me, dear cousin, you are a mere babe in arms when it comes to the fine art of making sport with another. I suggest you quit while you are ahead."

"So you have no admiration for the delightful and lovely Miss Patterson?"

Fitzwilliam glared at him. "I have no intention of refraining from retaliating if you persist, cousin."

"Very well, then," said Darcy, privately certain that he had stumbled onto something. He would store the information away for the future, in case it was ever needed.

"Besides," said Fitzwilliam after taking another sip of his drink, "I was quite serious when I said I am quite happy to remain a bachelor. I have no desire to subject a wife to my life at present. In the future we shall see."

Darcy nodded sagely and allowed the subject to drop. In truth, he had had only the barest of suspicions when he had canvassed the subject, and that was only from observing his cousin at the dinner at his uncle's house. It had seemed to Darcy that Fitzwilliam had been more than usually chatty that evening, and most of his attention had been reserved for his mother's blonde niece. It might mean nothing, considering Fitzwilliam's own previous acquaintance with her, but Darcy, who knew his cousin better than anyone, fancied there was something more to it.

Soon the time to depart arrived and together with Georgiana, Darcy and Fitzwilliam left the house to go to the theater. Covent Garden was not a great distance from Darcy house, but during the short ride, Darcy was able to think on the situation further. Though he was not able to determine any better now what he should do, at least Darcy felt like he would be able to keep himself under good regulation. The incontrovertible fact was that Miss Bennet was a newcomer to London society, and as such would be unused to dealing with the sharks that swam in those waters. London society could be vicious to the uninitiated, and Darcy would not hurt Miss Bennet for the world.

They arrived at the theater in good time, and when the carriage stopped in front of the building, Darcy allowed Fitzwilliam to alight from the carriage first, before stepping down himself and turning to assist his sister. A glance at the crowd in attendance told Darcy what he had been dreading all along—the theater was particularly well attended that evening, and he did not doubt that he would be an object of interest given his long absence from society.

As if girding himself for battle, Darcy took a deep breath and, taking his sister's arm, he led her through the bustling crowd and into the building. It might have been nothing more than fantasy on Darcy's part, but he thought the throng quieted for an instant when they made their appearance. It seemed like word of his return had spread through the city.

Though annoyed at the scrutiny, Darcy attempted to ignore it; along with his cousin Fitzwilliam he led Georgiana into the foyer where they took up a position in a relatively empty section of the room—or at least as empty as they could find in such a crush. Darcy held his position there with Georgiana, and Fitzwilliam excused himself to secure them some refreshments while they waited for Bingley and his party to arrive. It was while Fitzwilliam was absent that his friend entered the theatre, escorting his wife and sister.

"Darcy, my friend," said Bingley, as he approached wearing a beaming smile, "it is wonderful to see you."

"And you, Bingley," said Darcy.

But Darcy's attention was only nominally on his friend, for the moment she had approached, Miss Bennet had capture Darcy's notice. She was wearing a deep forest green dress fashioned from shimmering velvet, which hugged her curves and accentuated the brightness of her eyes, and the slippers on her feet gleamed when they peaked out from underneath her dress as she walked. Her cheeks held just a hint of rosy vitality, and her hair was upswept in an elegant chignon, her eyes watching him as she came close. And though many other women would have simpered from behind fluttering eyelashes had he given them even half so much attention, Miss Bennet watched him, challenged him, as if daring him to approach and be burned by the fiercely raging brilliance of her being. She was in every way breathtaking.

Darcy knew in that moment he was lost. Whether he ever had the courage to actually act on his feelings was a matter for further contemplation at another time. What he knew now was that he was in Miss Bennet's power, and he imagined that he would never be free. His only saving grace was that he knew the woman would be gentle with him and would not abuse the power she held.

"Mrs. Bingley, Miss Bennet," greeted Darcy in an attempt to wrest his attention back from the beauty before him. "My sister and I are honored you were able to join us this evening."

"*We* are indeed," said Fitzwilliam as he strode up to the party. He handed a glass of punch to Georgiana and a glass of wine to Darcy before he turned and bowed low. "Miss Bennet, I am quite speechless when confronted with your loveliness this evening. If I did not know better, I might think you were a goddess descended from her realm on high to grace us with your presence."

Miss Bennet only laughed. "For one bereft of words, I must say that they come rather easily to your lips, Colonel Fitzwilliam."

A laugh met her statement. "There, you have caught me out!" exclaimed Fitzwilliam. "You seem to have a rare talent for deflating the ego of a gentleman, madam. I am crushed at your rebuke."

"You appear to be rather hearty and hale, for one so defeated, colonel," jibed Miss Bennet.

"And still she continues to toy with me when she has broken my heart!"

A hand over his heart and an affectedly downcast expression were belied by the wink he directed at her. Then he turned to Mrs. Bingley and Miss Bennet was left with Darcy.

"Despite my cousin's overly flippant manner, Miss Bennet, you do look remarkably well tonight."

"Thank you, Mr. Darcy," said Miss Bennet. "You are looking rather dapper yourself, sir."

There, in her eyes, Darcy saw the evidence of her regard he had wondered if she possessed. For the first time he could see it plainly. Whatever else was to happen between them, Darcy knew that he would not be required to suffer the pangs of unrequited love.

But this knowledge also brought caution. For if her affections were engaged, how could Darcy hurt such a woman and cause *her* to suffer by not pursuing their acquaintance to its natural conclusion?

No, it was in every way inconceivable that this wondrous creature should be hurt by his actions. Thus, if she *was* already disposed to think of him in such a manner, he would have no choice but to submit and offer for her. He only needed to confirm what he was seeing to know how he should proceed.

As his focus once more settled on Miss Bennet's face, he saw her slightly questioning gaze, and Darcy realized that he must have stood silent for several moments. Feeling rather slow of thought and not a little apprehensive, Darcy smiled back at her and said: "Do you care for some refreshments, Miss Bennet?"

It was all Darcy could do not to wince at his seemingly disinterested and stupid question. Miss Bennet, however, only smiled.

"I believe I am quite content for the present, Mr. Darcy."

Darcy nodded, still feeling as if he was encased in molasses. He floundered for a moment, searching for something to say. It was a mark of Miss Bennet's own adeptness in society that she saved him from further embarrassment.

"What do you think of the opera we are about to witness, sir? Have you ever seen it performed before?"

"No, I have not, though I am familiar with it, and with most of the music," said Darcy, grateful for her innate sense of the social graces. "And have you seen Herr Mozart's *Die Zauberflöte*, Miss Bennet?"

"I have not," said Miss Bennet. "My father has a copy of the libretto in his library, and I have occasioned to read it. It is a marvelous story, Mr. Darcy, and I am eagerly anticipating the music."

"So you possess an appreciation for the arts?"

"Sometimes I wonder if that is the only reason to come to London."

Darcy lifted an eyebrow, surprised at such a declaration. "I would have thought you at home in any situation in society."

"I do enjoy society, Mr. Darcy. But I prefer to be among those I know well; at least with close acquaintances I can be assured they have no expectations of me other than friendship. I have often observed that there is an artificiality in many which I cannot but detest. It is like society is a game whose object is nothing more than to climb to the highest rung of the ladder, so that one might look down upon all and sundry."

"Mr. Darcy!"

Darcy started, noting in the back of his mind that Miss Bennet did the same, and turned to witness a lime green streak flying toward him. It was, of course, Miss Caroline Bingley, and she approached with a determined gait, the feathers of her headdress towering over those around her, swaying while she hurried.

"How fortunate we are to see you here, sir!" said she. Miss Bingley hurried up and inserted herself between Darcy and Miss Bennet, smiling in what she believed to be a winsome fashion. "I had no notion of your attending tonight."

Darcy was about to rebuke her for cutting between himself and Miss Bennet, when he caught sight of the woman in question. She was looking expressively at Miss Bingley, and when her eyes turned back to Darcy, he could see a mischievous sort of amusement alive in them. Recalling the substance of their conversation only moments before, and knowing *exactly* what Miss Bennet found so humorous, Darcy could only smile into his hand and hold back his laughter.

Miss Bingley, unfortunately, took this as his pleasure in seeing her. "I am so happy we have all met here, sir. We shall be a merry party indeed."

"What say you, Miss Bennet?" asked Darcy. Miss Bennet moved around Miss Bingley to once again stand close to him where she belonged, he noted. "Shall we be a merry party tonight?"

"I believe we shall all be too engrossed in the wonders of Herr Mozart's music to make merry."

A sneer fell over Miss Bingley's face and she turned her head slightly to look at Miss Bennet. "Miss Eliza. I did not notice you here. I assume my brother and his *wife* are here as well?"

The tone in which she spoke of Mrs. Bingley left no doubt in Darcy's mind of her opinion of her brother's wife but though Miss Bennet had all the provocation in the world, she held her temper, other than a slight tightening around her mouth.

"They have come indeed, Miss Bingley. Perhaps you should greet them."

Miss Bingley only waved her hand, her expression suggesting boredom. "Oh, I shall see them at some time or another. I am content where I am."

It was all Darcy could do not to shake his head at the woman's audacity. It appeared his discussion with her had been forgotten the instant she had left his house. He was, therefore, determined not to give into her ill breeding.

"I believe we were speaking of the performance tonight, Miss Bennet?"

Miss Bennet clearly caught his meaning, for she smiled and said: "I believe we were, Mr. Darcy. Now, have you ever heard any of the music performed?"

Thus began a conversation which was as amusing as it was, at times, frustrating. Darcy and Miss Bennet spoke primarily to one another, and though she obviously had little knowledge of the subject matter, Miss Bingley interjected as often as she was able, clearly attempting to disrupt the harmony between them. And those observations which she did at times make were so ill thought out, that often the two principles could not help but share a commiserating glance, even as they attempted to ignore her.

Had the woman learned nothing, or was she so conceited that she felt she had the power to persuade him? Darcy was preparing to take her to the side and demand she desist when he happened to catch sight of Hurst standing behind her in a group which included Bingley and his wife. When Hurst saw Darcy looking at him, he rolled his eyes and looked expressively at Miss Bingley, shaking his head.

Turning to the side to avoid laughing in Miss Bingley's face, Darcy decided that the woman's behavior truly did not signify.

As the time for them to be retiring to their box drew near, Darcy noted the approach of his uncle, aunt, cousin, and Miss Patterson. He turned away from Miss Bingley and greeted them with aplomb, noting Miss Bennet's pleasure in her returned acknowledgement.

"This is your first foray into society since your return to London, is it not, Darcy?" asked the earl.

"Into society of this nature," replied Darcy in a clipped tone.

The earl only laughed. "You appear to be holding up well, despite your distaste."

"Do you not enjoy the opera, Mr. Darcy?" asked Miss Patterson, her head tilted to the side.

"It is more the crush of the attendees I do not like," said Darcy. "I believe we canvassed the subject of my dislike for society previously, Miss Patterson. I enjoy the opera very much, once we are able to retire to our boxes."

"But you are one of the leading lights of society, Mr. Darcy!" cried Miss Bingley. "Surely you must revel in the influence you possess, and long to dispense of your great judgement and wisdom to all who ask it of you!"

If Miss Bingley thought she would be asked for an introduction from the earl or Lady Susan, she was destined to disappointment, as other than a brief look of displeasure for intruding on their conversation, they ignored her. If her rising color was any indication, she felt the lack of their notice severely.

"Your words are positively lacking in any sociability, sir," said Miss Patterson.

"From what I have observed of Mr. Darcy, they are nothing more than the truth," said Miss Bennet.

"And I own it without disguise," said Darcy.

The entire company—with the exception of an aggrieved Miss Bingley—laughed at his statement.

"Then we shall simply have to inject some tolerance for society at the very least into your manners," said Miss Bennet. Her playful tone brought on another laugh from those nearby.

"I believe it would be best if you did not insult Mr. Darcy, Miss Eliza," said Miss Bingley, favoring Miss Bennet with a superior sniff. "His standing in society is such that it would be unwise for someone of your . . . social background."

It was perhaps fortunate that someone else approached the party at that moment, as Darcy was preparing to give Miss Bingley a stinging set down. Unless he missed his guess, several others appeared to be of like mind.

"Miss Patterson!" a voice hissed from the side.

Turning, Darcy noticed that a diminutive man, approximately Darcy's age but already balding and with a noticeable paunch, had approached Miss Patterson and was beseeching her with wild eyes and a possessive stare.

"I simply must speak with you! Shall we not stand to the side for a few moments so that I might address you?"

The countenances of his uncle and the viscount darkened in response to the man's appearance, but it was Fitzwilliam who responded. As soon as the man made his appearance, Fitzwilliam moved to intercept him, and he strode up, his face alight with a thunderous scowl.

"What do you do here, sir?" demanded he.

The man's responding cringe was understandable; he was quite short of stature whereas Anthony was a big man, intimidating when he chose to be so.

"I merely wish to speak with Miss Patterson."

A hint of belligerence had crept into the man's manner, and he drew himself up to his insignificant height, attempting to return Anthony's implacable glare with one of his own. Unfortunately, his rotund form ruined the image he was attempting to present, not to mention the picture of a man, more than a hand shorter than Anthony stood himself, attempting to intimidate him, was more than a little amusing.

"Mr. Rogers, as I told you, I have nothing to say to you," said Miss Patterson. "I believe you already know my sentiments."

"But Miss Patterson!" cried the man in a high, wheedling tone. "Surely—"

"That is enough, sir!" said Anthony. He stood up to his full height and glared down at the little man in front of him, who possessed the sense to cower. "By my count, Miss Patterson has told you several times already that she does not wish to have your attention. Do I need to remind you that she is under my *father*, the *earl's* protection?"

The man licked his lips and his gaze darted toward Uncle Hugh. For his part, the earl performed perfectly, scowling at the man, while the viscount actually stepped forward. The last proved too much, as Mr. Rogers turned and scurried away.

"Come, dear," said Lady Susan to Miss Patterson. "Let us retire to the balcony so that you might recover."

To Darcy it did not appear that Miss Patterson needed to recover in any way, but she readily allowed herself to be led away. James also left to escort the two ladies, and if his posture was any indication, he was alert for any further attempts by the recently departed man to once again approach Miss Patterson.

"One of the infamous suitors?" asked Darcy.

The earl gave him a sour look. "The persistent one. The other appears to have given up, but Rogers does not seem to understand rejection."

"I dare say we shall be required to make him understand," said Fitzwilliam. "The word around town is that Rogers has accumulated such gaming debt as to threaten his solvency and his continued ownership of his estate."

Darcy wrinkled his nose; given his experiences with George Wickham, there was little he hated worse than a wastrel.

"Darcy, I believe I shall sit in my father's box tonight, if you will excuse me."

"Of course, Fitzwilliam," said Darcy.

As Fitzwilliam turned away, Darcy exchanged an amused glance with his uncle. It was clear the earl had also detected his son's interest in the lovely Miss Patterson. Darcy felt a measure of vindication.

"We shall meet you at your house after the opera," said the earl.

Darcy agreed and the earl left in the company of his younger son.

"Oh, Mr. Darcy!" cried Miss Bingley. "A gathering at your house. How fun!"

"I am certain it shall be, my dear Caroline," interjected Mr. Hurst. He strode up to them and greeted Darcy, all while directing a severe glare at his sister-in-law. "However, as you are well aware, we shall attend a gathering hosted by my friend Crawford after the opera. There will be ample forms of amusement for you there."

Miss Bingley glared at him, which he returned with ease and unconcern.

"Quite," said she, before she turned away from him with a superior sniff.

"I do so love the opera," said Miss Bingley to no one in particular. "The sights and sounds of the actors and the orchestra, the voices of the actors, the colors of the costumes; it is all simply exquisite."

She turned a sneering sort of smile on Miss Bennet and said, "You should savor these delights, Miss Eliza. When you are returned to your father's estate, no doubt your ability to partake in such amusements will become nonexistent."

Darcy frowned at the woman, but Miss Bennet only smiled with true amusement. "In that you would be incorrect, Miss Bingley. In fact, I have attended the opera on several occasions with my uncle, as he and my aunt are both great lovers of the theater in all its forms."

"Then you should savor this occasion, as the ability to listen from a box is much superior to that of sitting in the gallery."

The affected air of superiority made Darcy's teeth clench, but once again, Miss Bennet merely deflected the woman with unconcealed humor.

"Again, I must beg leave to disagree. Though we have sat in the gallery before, I have seen both opera and play from a box. My uncle has many contacts among the higher echelons of society and it has given him access to many of the finer aspects of society."

"How fortunate for you," said Miss Bingley.

"Your uncle does business with many gentlemen?" asked Darcy, his curiosity aroused. There were few men of business who were even tolerated by men of society.

"Yes," said Miss Bennet. "He is an importer, and he has many contacts in various locations around the world from whence he obtains his goods. He apparently possesses a knack for obtaining difficult items. I understand that is much to be desired in an importer."

Darcy grinned. "It is indeed, Miss Bennet. I believe I should like to be introduced to your uncle when the opportunity presents itself."

Miss Bennet inclined her head an indicated she would be happy to introduce them, while Miss Bingley simply appeared scandalized that he would deign to request an invitation with a man from the detested vocation.

The bell rang at that moment, calling the attendees to their seats. Darcy smiled at Miss Bennet and extending his arm, said, "Shall we?"

"Of course, sir," said she, laying her hand on his arm."

"Oh, there is nothing better than viewing an opera from your box, Mr. Darcy," said Miss Bingley. "It is at such an exquisite location and the acoustics are so fine. Perhaps we might all view the opera together."

As she spoke, she strode up to Darcy, simultaneously directing a venomous glare at Miss Bennet, while appearing to smile at Darcy himself. It was a curious combination to be sure.

"Indeed it is a fine box, Caroline," said Hurst. The man was smiling at her, but it was not in pleasure—he was no doubt feeling dark amusement at her blatant machinations. "Shall we retire to our box as well? We will wish to be seated before the curtain rises."

"But Mr. Hurst, there is plenty of room in Mr. Darcy's box, and—"

"And I have rented a box for our own use tonight, Caroline," interjected Hurst.

Turning, he extended his arm to his wife who took it with her typical disinterest, and then he led the two women away, saying: "Let us go, my dears. We do not wish to be late."

Though Miss Bingley cast a longing look or two back at Darcy, she seemed resigned to her fate and allowed herself to be led away. That did not stop her from glaring again at Miss Bennet, but for her part, Miss Bennet merely watched them depart, an amused smile playing around her mouth.

"Shall we, Miss Bennet?" asked Darcy.

At her assent they turned toward the upper levels, following Bingley and his wife up the stairs. "I fear you becoming arrogant and conceited, sir," said she as they walked.

Seeing the curve of her lips, Darcy was enchanted all over, and he inquired as to her meaning, which she did not at all scruple to withhold.

"Why, with such blatant attentions from such a lady as Miss Bingley, I rather wonder that you do not attain a superior air yourself, sir. Given Miss Bingley's anecdotes which she did not scruple to relate to us so kindly when we were all in residence in Hertfordshire, I understand she inhabits the very pinnacle of society."

Though her speech was delivered with great gravity and seriousness, the twinkle in her eye was unmistakable, and Darcy could not keep himself from chuckling at her sortie.

"I am sure she must have proclaimed her superiority for all to hear," said he. "But I claim more of an acquaintance with Bingley. His sisters claimed the acquaintance through him, but in truth I do not know them very well."

"Miss Bingley would be very sorry to hear that, sir."

For most of the rest of the evening, Darcy could hardly focus on what was happening on the stage. He was familiar with *The Magic Flute*, but though he tried to concentrate on the music and the story, he found it impossible to do so. The reason, of course, was the beauty seated by his side.

It was a revelation to witness Miss Bennet's true joy in the opera. She laughed and clapped, watched the performers through eyes shining with mirth and interest, and for much of the performance, she appeared to sing along with the performers, as if she was intimately familiar with the music. It appeared to Darcy that she had been more than a little reticent when she had spoken of her knowledge of the opera. In fact, Darcy thought she knew it very well indeed.

But though she had been enchanting before, she was nothing less than intoxicating now, and as he sat in the theater, the lights dimmed to allow for the stage to be seen with clarity, he felt the tingle of her presence by his side. He thought that had it not been highly improper and had he not known in advance that she would slap him for his temerity, he might have crushed her form to his side, reveling in the close contact between their bodies. He felt afire with desire, drunk on the sweet nectar that was her presence, and desperately wishing for more, like a man trapped in a parched desert with nothing more than a single swallow of water. He thought he might go mad.

When at last the interminable night came to an end, Darcy escorted Miss Bennet from the box to the exit. He said nothing, and Miss Bennet appeared to be content with the silence between them. Not even the saccharine presence of Miss Bingley at the exit before Hurst essentially forced her into his carriage was able to pull Darcy from the spell of her presence.

At Darcy's townhouse the company enjoyed a late dinner, and conversation flowed freely. Though Darcy watched it all and especially attended to Miss Bennet's words, he said not much himself. He felt particularly slow of wit, and wondered at the affect this diminutive woman seemed to have on him. He was in her power. But it was not an unpleasant experience. Far from it, in fact.

Throughout the entirety of the evening, Darcy's thoughts kept returning to his time with his wife, and he wondered at the feelings which coursed through his veins. He could not ever remember being *this* affected by Cassandra, even though he had loved his wife with a passionate fervor. It was all so confusing. He did not know if he would ever be able to make sense of it.

Later in the evening when they had retired to the sitting-room, Darcy found himself to be in close proximity with Miss Bennet. Though he was still feeling an inability to make any sort of intelligent conversation, Miss Bennet's patient attempts to induce him to speak finally bore fruit. She questioned him on his childhood and his travels, all while avoiding mention of his marriage or his wife—for this he was grateful, as he was as yet unequal to speaking of such subjects. Through it, Darcy felt himself able to open up, and he spoke of many things, including anecdotes of his cousins, his recollections of his childhood, and some of the travels he had undertaken as an adult. But it was when the talk turned to Miss Bennet and her family that it truly became interesting to Darcy.

"And what of you, Miss Bennet. Have you travelled?"

Miss Bennet smiled. "Oh no, Mr. Darcy. My father detests travel intensely. The only times I have gone anywhere was in the company of my aunt and uncle, who have invited me to accompany them on occasion. The only other opportunity I have had—"

Miss Bennet's voice ceased abruptly and she fell silent. Darcy watched her, but as she seemed more hesitant than embarrassed, he prompted her to continue.

Taking a deep breath, Miss Bennet regarded him with a hint of a rueful smile. "My dearest friend, Charlotte Lucas, is lately married, Mr. Darcy. She wished for me to visit her, and had issued an invitation for me to come to her. Had I gone, I would be there now."

"And why did you not go?" asked Darcy, intrigued.

"It seemed that her husband was not exactly happy with her invitation to me, so I felt obliged to decline it."

"Does the man possess something of a grudge against you, Miss Bennet?"

For a moment, Darcy wondered if she would answer. She looked away from him for a moment, and he thought he detected a hint of higher color about her cheeks and neck. Her courage, however, won out, and soon she turned back to him with a rueful smile.

"You might say that, Mr. Darcy. For you see, my friend married my cousin, William Collins, who is the pastor to your aunt lady Catherine de Bourgh."

Darcy frowned. "I do not follow why he should wish to avoid you, Miss Bennet."

"That is because you do not possess the entire story, Mr. Darcy. In fact, a mere three days before proposing to my dear friend Charlotte, Mr. Collins proposed to me."

His jaw dropping, Darcy regarded Miss Bennet with disbelief. "Three days?"

"Yes, Mr. Darcy. And he had only been in residence for a week before he made his proposals to me. Furthermore, he could not understand that I was in earnest when I rejected him, and he importuned me on the subject several times even after I refused. There were many advantages inherent in his position in life, you see, not limited to his current good fortune as the recipient of your aunt's condescension, and his status as future owner of my father's estate. It appeared that he believed me to be waiting with grateful anticipation for the offer of his hand."

For a moment Darcy could not speak. Had he really come that close to losing her before he ever had a chance to secure her?

Then he realized as the thought entered his mind that not only was she not yet *his*, but the woman he knew could never have married such a man as he expected Mr. Collins to be.

"So he objected to your visiting your friend?"

"Not in so many words, sir, but his inference was clear."

Nodding, Darcy said: "I can see how the situation might be uncomfortable. Though I have not much hope for the man's sensibility, given what I have heard of him, I must acknowledge that I would have to agree with him in this matter; it would be awkward indeed for him to accept you into his home in such circumstances. But still—to propose with such haste. What could he have been thinking?"

"I believe he was following your aunt's instructions to the letter, sir," said Miss Bennet.

"My aunt's instructions?"

"It seems he visited us based on your aunt's advice. You see, my father had never even met him before his visit, due to a longstanding dispute with Mr. Collins's late father. Your aunt recommended he approach us to 'heal the breach,' as he put it."

"That would seem to be a worthy goal."

"Yes, I dare say it is. However, that was not the only instructions she imparted. She charged him to marry, as it is incumbent upon him, as the pastor in her parish, to set the example of matrimony. And she specifically suggested that he look to his cousin's daughters as a way of making amends, though I rather think that the 'making amends' part was his own addition to the scheme."

"Make amends?" exclaimed Darcy.

"For inheriting the estate and leaving his cousins homeless."

Darcy watched Miss Bennet with wonder. "While the offer to marry a daughter and take care of any remaining daughters is commendable, he can hardly be held accountable for being designated as your father's heir."

"Exactly, Mr. Darcy. But it was clear that he thought it required to make the matter right."

"But how did he settle upon you?" asked Darcy, still a little confused.

"Ah, I believe that was my mother's work. For, you see, Jane was already being all but courted by Mr. Bingley, and as I am next in line, she must have thought that it was my duty to submit to her will. In fact, she likely would have had much more success with my younger sister, Mary, who is moralistic and pious. Mary might even have done well with him, as there is something pompous in her manner which I believe would have matched Mr. Collins quite well indeed."

A laugh escaped Darcy's lips at Miss Bennet's portrayal of her sister. "I must trust your judgment on the matter, though I cannot imagine any woman would be comfortable under the direction of my aunt."

"I know I could not, though my mother expected me to do my duty."

Darcy's attention was caught and he gazed at her, a question in his eyes. She seemed to understand it, as she said:

"The reason I am in London, Mr. Darcy, is because my mother is still vexed with me for not following her directive and marrying Mr. Collins. Had Mr. Bingley not already been courting my sister my answer might have been different, though I cannot imagine a life with Mr. Collins for a husband. As they were well on their way to an understanding, I felt equal to refusing his entreaties. My mother resents me to this day."

Miss Bennet fell silent for a moment, but Darcy, sensing she had something else to say, did not interrupt. After a moment, she looked up at him, her eyes shining with suppressed pain.

"After my refusal, Mr. Collins made certain to inform me that it was not likely I would ever receive another proposal, and my mother was quick to agree with his sentiments. It was her constant diatribes insisting that I will never marry which drove me from my home."

"But that is patently absurd!" cried Darcy, though he had the sense to moderate his tone so as to avoid drawing attention to their conversation.

"Is it?" asked Miss Bennet. "I am well aware of my position in life, Mr. Darcy. I have little in the way of dowry, and naught but connections to trade to tempt a potential suitor. My mother's opinions may be ineloquently stated, but in essence, she has the right of it."

A frown settled over Darcy's face. Though Bingley had made comments about his wife's family, and Darcy had made inferences from Miss Bennet's words, there was clearly much he had not yet been told. The man of duty in him could not but wonder at the difficulty which had been forced on this woman when the responsibility for the family's future security should rightly have belonged to her parents.

Seeing her a little discomposed over his silence, Darcy hastened to assure her of his continuing regard.

"You have not yet told me the whole story of your family, but I must own that I am a little disappointed. It seems like your mother wished for you to sacrifice your happiness to assure her own security."

"And you would not be incorrect, sir. That is why I refused Mr. Collins's proposal and would not recant, though my mother was strident in voicing her opinion."

"That could not have been comfortable," murmured Darcy.

"No, but I am blessed with plenty of fortitude. And you must not blame my mother, sir. She has lived with the threat of the entail for many years without an heir, and she fears for her future. Furthermore, my mother is not precisely . . ."

Miss Bennet paused for a moment, clearly searching for words. When she finally spoke again it was with a regretful smile. "What I am trying to say, Mr. Darcy, is that my mother is of limited understanding. All she sees is the presence of a suitor which might save the family, and she gives no thought to compatibility, happiness, or anything else. I suppose I must attribute it to the fact that her marriage with my father has not been a happy one. This leads her to suppose that it is security which is important, rather than any other consideration."

"And you disagree."

An even look met his statement. "I would much rather be forced into genteel poverty than to be demeaned for the rest of my life by a sycophantic fool with whom I had not the hope of finding happiness."

"What of your father? Should he not have provided for his family in the event that he did not produce a son?"

Miss Bennet sighed. "I love my father very much, Mr. Darcy, but I am not blind to his faults. He brought me up as his companion, teaching me, debating with me, sharing with me his love of the written word. He loves nothing better than his books and his library, and both provide a barrier from my mother's nerves. To hear him speak of it, he always intended to father a son, but as the number of girl children mounted and my mother's nerves became ever more frayed, he retreated more and more into his library. He is a good man, but life's circumstances have worn him down. Yes, he should have provided for us. But he has not."

"He obviously did not force you to marry your cousin," observed Darcy.

"No, and I knew he would not. My father is an intelligent man and I knew he would not wish me—his favorite daughter—to be caught in such a disagreeable marriage. When my mother attempted to persuade him to insist upon my marrying Mr. Collins, my father told me, 'From this day forward you must be a stranger to one of your parents. Mrs. Bennet says she will never see you again if you do not marry Mr. Collins, and I will never see you again if you do.'"

In spite of himself, Darcy could only laugh at such a portrayal. It appeared that Mr. Bennet possessed a droll sense of humor, even if it was directed at his wife. The dutiful man in Darcy wondered at the man's oversight. In the back of his mind, however, a little niggling voice told him that he had been on the same road when Cassandra died. Had he not been a prisoner in his own mind for months after her death, only to be redeemed by the love and determination of his cousin? He could well imagine how a man might be pushed to such an end.

"It seems then, Miss Bennet, that you have weathered some storms in your journey through life."

Miss Bennet laughed. "You make it sound as if I have had a difficult life. I assure you that it is not so. No one's life is perfect, and I cannot count my own to have been so. I have been born part of a privileged class and I have been loved by my parents, despite their different personalities and ways of showing their love. I cannot but think that I have been anything other than blessed."

"And so you have, Miss Bennet," said Darcy. "But let me assure you that your mother and your cousin are wrong. You have much to recommend yourself—not all virtues are those which society deems to important."

Miss Bennet flushed and thanked him, and though she would not hold his eyes, they did dart up to his. Darcy fancied he could see more of the depth of her regard for him swimming there amongst the tears prompted by her story.

This was perhaps what fanned the flames of his love for her more than anything else—her indomitable will and her ability to see the good in every situation. Many women would have given into a mother's demands and many would have railed against fate or cried long hours when confronted by situations which she had conquered.

It might be said that she had acted foolishly to have rejected a man who could have ensured her future security, but Darcy could only admire her for persevering and holding up her principles.

"Then I am happy you were able to escape such a fate," said Darcy, warmly watching her. "If you had not, I would not have the pleasure of your company in London."

"I am happy too, Mr. Darcy."

More and more Darcy was becoming convinced of her burgeoning feelings for him. And if Darcy was not certain it was love yet, he knew that at the very least she welcomed his presence. It could lead to much more.

Chapter XI

It is strange the way the mind plays tricks upon one. Darcy was very much a man who relied upon what he could see and what he could hear, and he considered himself to be a rational man, normally not overly affected by the emotion of the moment. And perhaps most importantly, he was not affected by flights of fancy.

That was why the situation in which he found himself was so confusing and so beyond his experience that he found himself paralyzed, unable to act.

His attraction for Miss Bennet was real and so very powerful, that Darcy was becoming convinced that to not offer for her would be foolish. But even though his heart screamed at him to make her his wife, Cassandra still loomed in the back of his mind, and he could not quite determine what he should think about espousing feelings for another woman. Perhaps it was his fancy speaking, but he would have thought that looking upon another woman would feel like a betrayal of Cassandra. The reality, however, was the distinct impression that had Cassandra been able to express her feelings to him, that she would have told him that she was happy for him.

Whether this was all just his fanciful imaginings Darcy could not say. But one thing was clear to Darcy, which perhaps he had not seen before.

Cassandra was gone, and though he would have happily spent the rest of his life with her, it had not been fated to be. He was still alive, and he was deserving of happiness in his life. Miss Elizabeth Bennet could provide him with that happiness.

For the next several days, Darcy saw much of Miss Bennet, and of Bingley and his wife. They exchanged visits on several occasions and they also shared several outings. That Georgiana was enamored of Miss Bennet was not in question—his sister took every opportunity she could to speak of her new friend's virtues. Darcy might have been annoyed at his sister's presumption—for though she had not spoken of the matter, Darcy knew that she wanted Miss Bennet as a sister—he found himself charmed by how well she and Miss Bennet had come to know one another.

One day, a week after they had attended the opera together, Darcy was tied up with business concerns, forcing him to reluctantly forego greeting his guests, though he knew that Miss Bennet was to visit his sister that morning. Thus, he ensconced himself in his study with his letters of business and concentrated on completing his duties as soon as may be.

By the time he finished, it was late in the morning, and as he had not heard the bell ring for some time, Darcy thought perhaps there were no visitors in the house. A quick visit to the music room did not reveal any evidence of his sister, which he found strange, as Georgiana could usually be found there after her friends had departed.

Thinking she had retired to her suite, Darcy ascended the stairs to the family apartments, intent upon finding her and hearing about her morning. He had entered the hall near the family quarters when he heard the sound of laughter accompanied by girlish giggling.

Startled, Darcy stopped and peered down the hall, noting the open door further down the hall where the nursery was. The laughter sounded again.

Darcy strode forward, assuming Georgiana was visiting with Cassandra, when his momentum was again arrested by the sound of laughter. This time he could clearly hear the timbre of the woman's voice, and he knew it was not his sister. And given the rich sound caressing his ears, he felt sure he knew exactly who it was.

Feeling like he was sleepwalking, Darcy pressed forward, drawn by the sound of the voices. He paused at the edge of the door, strangely hesitant to step forward and look inside. But to leave without seeing for his own eyes what was taking place in his house was unthinkable. Darcy gathered himself and looked around the corner.

What he saw melted his heart. There, on the floor of his nursery, sat Miss Bennet, her legs tucked demurely by her side. There were books at her side which indicated that his daughter had already experienced Miss Bennet's ability to entertain through stories. At present, they were engaged in playing with several of Cassandra's dolls, which were arranged around a low table. The table was topped by a delicate little tea set, one which Darcy thought he remembered from when Georgiana had been a girl.

"Be careful, Cassandra," said Miss Bennet as his daughter reached for one of the tiny cups. "If you knock the saucers off the table, they'll break."

"Break?" asked the girl.

"Yes, my dear," said Miss Bennet. "This set is beautiful, but it will break easily. You must be gentle with it."

"Gentle," said Cassandra, and she put the cup she had been holding down on the table very carefully.

"Is this the first tea party you have ever hosted?"

The girl nodded her head vigorously. "No play alone."

"That is wise."

Under Miss Bennet's patient tutelage, Cassandra learned the proper way to pour the tea and she learned to serve all of her guests. The assorted dolls watching the procedure seemed to be impressed with how quickly she understood her duties. And Miss Bennet, though allowing Cassandra to play and serve the dolls herself, corrected where necessary, guided when Cassandra seemed uncertain what to do, and assisted when Cassandra's attention seemed to wander.

A powerful feeling welled up within Darcy's breast. His daughter, he could see, was not only a mirror image of his departed wife, but her mannerisms charmed him with their similarity to her mother's, and her enthusiasm was catching. She also appeared to be intelligent, as when she spoke her words were clearly spoken and easy to understand, though she still could not put many words together in a sentence. Seeing her like this, Darcy knew he could not go through life without knowing this beautiful child.

And Miss Bennet . . .

The sight of her actually playing on the floor with his young daughter was one Darcy knew would stay with him for the rest of his life. He did not know another gentlewoman who would do anything more than coo at his daughter, pronounce her to be a lovely child, and then expect her nurse to convey her back to the nursery with alacrity. Not Miss Bennet. Instead she could be found on the floor of the nursery, playing with her, teaching her, showing her love and affection, and being with her when Darcy had found himself unable to do likewise.

Though he had known of her worth prior to this incident, it was forced upon his consciousness once again. This was a woman who was unlike any other of his acquaintance, and he could not imagine how he could have resisted her allure. Though Darcy had determined that he would not compare Miss Bennet to his wife, he could not help but acknowledge that even though Cassandra had been a lovely woman and would have been a wonderful mother, Darcy did not think she would have been found playing with her daughter on the floor.

"Elizabeth!"

At the sound of Georgiana's voice calling for her, Miss Bennet looked up and spotted Darcy by the door. She froze for a moment in astonishment, but it soon gave way to embarrassment.

"Mr. Darcy," cried she as she scrambled to her feet. "Georgiana had business with your housekeeper, and I told her I would visit your daughter. I was charmed by her manners and thought . . ."

Miss Bennet trailed off, and seeing she was rambling, Darcy moved to reassure her.

"It is quite all right, Miss Bennet," said he as he stepped into the room. "You presented a pretty picture sitting here with Cassandra."

He grinned at her, prompting a tentative smile in response. "In fact, I would hazard a guess that you have done this before."

All trepidation seemed to leave Miss Bennet's manner. "Indeed I have, Mr. Darcy. My aunt has two young daughters and as I visit with my aunt and uncle often, I have had many occasions to have tea parties with them."

"Elizabeth?" asked Georgiana as she stepped into the room.

"It appears you have arrived at a fortuitous time, Georgiana," said Darcy, smiling at his sister. "Cassandra and Miss Bennet were about to have a tea party. Shall we join them?"

Georgiana looked at him as if he had grown another head, but the silence was broken by his daughter as she reached up and tugged on Miss Bennet's dress.

"Lizzy, tea cold!"

"Cassandra," said Darcy in a warning tone.

But Miss Bennet only smiled and crouched down to look the young girl in the eye. "Miss Darcy, I shall return to our tea, but you must remember that you must be silent and respectful when the adults are speaking."

"Yes, Lizzy. Tea?"

Smiling, Miss Bennet agreed and she sat down with Cassandra, and Darcy soon joined them, sitting on the other side of the table. Georgiana appeared confused, but when Darcy beckoned to her, she sat down with a smile.

"Shall I order some cakes too?" asked Georgiana.

The other two adults laughed when Cassandra bounced up and down in excitement. "Cakes!"

And a wonderful time was had by all. Perhaps the most important, from Darcy's perspective, was that he was able to sit and laugh with his sister, his daughter, and their guest, and not once did he experience an unwelcome memory of his wife. Truly, it seemed like Darcy was finally able to put the past behind him. And he could not but own that it was largely due to Miss Bennet, her endless optimism, and her excellent example.

The incident in the nursery only firmed Darcy's resolve. There was not another woman in the land who could compare with Miss Elizabeth Bennet, and the powerful feelings which had been growing within his breast were threatening to burst forth. Pemberley would once again become a happy place with her installed as its mistress, and Darcy could not help but think that his days would be filled with bliss.

If a cautionary note entered his mind during that time, it was that he had already seen one wife succumb to childbirth—could he really risk losing another in such a way? Furthermore, his dearest mother had never been the same after Georgiana's birth. It seemed like he was fated to lose those he loved best when they brought new life into the world.

But as soon as these thoughts entered his mind, he pushed them away with anger and determination. Childbirth was a risk which all women accepted to experience the joy of their own children and the perpetuation of the human race, and not all women were so frail as to perish in the process. His aunt, Lady Susan, for example, had brought four healthy children into the world and she had always recovered from childbirth quickly. And what was more, Miss Bennet came from hardy stock—her own mother had birthed five children successfully. Surely that had to count for something.

Those fears would perhaps always live with him and for a short time he wondered if it was not worth it to risk losing a loved one again. But then reason overcame his hesitation. If what he had experienced with Miss Bennet in the nursery was any indication, he thought that she would willingly face it for the chance to have children. And now that Darcy was beginning to experience what life could be like with his own daughter, he now knew that he would welcome more children. He especially longed for a son, who he could raise and train to become the next generation of Darcy masters of Pemberley.

Only a few days after the impromptu tea party, Darcy embarked upon the next step in what was to become his quest to secure Miss Bennet as his bride. Until that time, he had only met one member of Miss Bennet's family. Nothing he had heard of the rest of the family gave him any indication that they were people he would wish to know, other than perhaps Mr. Bennet. But apparently Miss Bennet had other relations for whom she was not required to blush.

"It is only Mr. and Mrs. Gardiner," said Bingley. The man had shown up at Darcy's house that day to extend an invitation to dinner, at which the sisters' aunt and uncle were also to be present.

"I believe you will like them exceedingly," continued Bingley. "Mrs. Gardiner is a sensible and friendly woman, and Mr. Gardiner is a man of keen intelligence and shrewd judgment. I dare say if you met them without knowing who they were, you would take them for people of fashion."

Darcy hesitated, not knowing if he should accept. Bingley was one thing—though his background and fortune was steeped in trade, he at least was not actively engaged in that profession. Mr. Gardiner, on the other hand, was an unabashed tradesman.

But it seemed Bingley had left him little choice, so he agreed and promised that he would attend.

"Excellent!" said Bingley. So to dinner with the Gardiners the Darcys would go.

When the evening arrived, Darcy and Georgiana stepped into Bingley's townhouse and were met with true pleasure, and there the introductions were accomplished. Mrs. Gardiner was handsome, with not a hint of grey appearing in her dark hair, while her husband was clearly genial and friendly, his countenance bluff and open. Though it was difficult to determine, Darcy thought that Mrs. Gardiner was perhaps only five years his elder, while her husband was no more than five years older than she.

"I am happy to make your acquaintance, Mr. Darcy," said Mr. Gardiner. "Charles has had nothing but good things to say of you, and our Lizzy and Jane have echoed his sentiments quite fervently."

"The pleasure is mine," said Darcy, surprised even then that his words were nothing but the truth. "Your nieces have spoken of you in glowing terms."

The company was invited to sit, and Darcy could see that Georgiana was immediately made comfortable by the combined efforts of the sisters and Mrs. Gardiner. He was quick to realize that Mr. Gardiner was indeed and intelligent man. He had come half fearing that the image he had in his mind of Mrs. Bennet—vapid, mean of understanding, loud, and uncouth—would be mirrored in her brother, no matter how much Bingley had told him otherwise. But here was a good and intelligent man, who obviously doted on his wife and nieces.

"I must say, Miss Darcy," said Mrs. Gardiner, after they had been sitting for some time, "that you resemble your lady mother quite closely."

"You knew my mother?" asked Georgiana, eyes wide in surprise.

"I could not claim an acquaintance with her. But I spent much of my girlhood in the village of Lambton, with which I believe you must be familiar."

"Indeed, we are! It is not more than five miles from Pemberley!"

"And the dearest place in the world, in my opinion." Mrs. Gardiner smiled. "Though I did not know your mother as a friend, she often came to the village, and I spoke with her on more than one occasion. She was always very kind, happy to speak with a lowly preacher's daughter."

"You were the daughter of Lambton's parson?" asked Darcy.

"Yes, Mr. Darcy. I understand you were not as familiar with my family as you attended church in Kympton, but the Darcys are well known in Lambton."

"That is true. But I remember when I was young my mother was often involved in charitable endeavors in Lambton."

"That is where I was fortunate enough to speak with her, Mr. Darcy."

Darcy digested this little tidbit of information with interest. "Have you ever seen Pemberley then, Mrs. Gardiner?"

"Only the grounds, Mr. Darcy."

Mrs. Gardiner turned and smiled at her husband who took up the conversation.

"Assuming my business allows me enough time away, we had thought to travel north this summer, perhaps as far as the lakes. And as my wife cannot fathom passing through Derbyshire and so near to Lambton without stopping there, we had thought to visit the area and tour the great houses along the way."

"You would be very welcome to visit Pemberley, Mr. Gardiner."

And Darcy meant it. He had accepted Bingley without any real thought, because he was a good man, and also because he was a gregarious man, something Darcy had never been himself. But in meeting Mr. and Mrs. Gardiner he was reminded that there were good people at all levels of society.

"Thank you, sir," said Mrs. Gardiner. "I would love to see the house, if it is no inconvenience."

"Not at all. The house is often open to visitors in the summer. If I am in residence, I would be happy to greet you."

Of course, Darcy did not say that he hoped their niece would be installed as Pemberley's mistress by that time, but he thought it. Everything in its proper order.

"Are you perhaps fond of fishing, Mr. Gardiner?"

The light which appeared in Mr. Gardiner's eyes told Darcy all he needed to know, if the man's words did not.

"Indeed, I am. I do not get much of a chance to indulge in it now that I live in London, but when I was a youth I was accounted an accomplished angler."

"In that case, I hope you will set aside some time to fish on Pemberley's grounds. The fishing there is excellent."

"Of that I can attest!" said Bingley with a laugh. "Darcy invited me to Pemberley soon after we met, and I dare say we terrorized the fish nearly every day I stayed there."

The company laughed at Bingley's words, and Darcy could only laugh along with them. Bingley *had* been rather eager when he had visited that first time. It brought to mind better and happier days, before life, death, and sorrow had caught him in their grip, seemingly never to let him go.

Soon after, they were called in to dinner, and the conversation continued to flow. Even Darcy and Georgiana, who, along with Mrs. Bingley, were the most reticent, were induced to participate along with the rest. Darcy could not remember a better time in the company of happier people.

When the ladies separated from the men at the end of dinner, the three who remained behind sat back in their chairs in the dining room and sipped from their glasses. The conversation was fluid, moving from one subject to the next without guidance or forethought, and Darcy was surprised by how comfortable he was in the company of a man who was essentially a stranger. Mr. Gardiner was indeed an intelligent and astute man. His opinions were thoughtful and expressed with a sober intelligence, and he was an open-minded and tolerant man. His business acumen was unquestioned, and when he and Bingley spoke of some common interests in the business world, Darcy found that he agreed with them concerning many things.

Thus, when Mr. Gardiner turned and eyed Darcy, his words were so sudden that Darcy was momentarily caught by surprise.

"Mr. Darcy," said he, "I had not thought to be having this conversation for some years yet, but I believe that I must, though Elizabeth is under the protection of our Bingley here." He indicated Bingley with a gesture of his hand in which he held his glass, before he raised it to his lips for another sip. "What are your intentions toward my niece?"

Shocked, Darcy gazed at him in wonderment, at the same time Bingley snickered into his glass.

"Intentions?" gasped Darcy.

"You *have* been rather blatant about it, Darcy," said Bingley. "I saw your interest in her from the first. But though I have been able to witness it growing over time, I am not surprised that my uncle was able to detect it after one meeting."

"It was not difficult," said Mr. Gardiner. "I suspected it before I ever came here tonight based on some of the things I had heard. Besides, I am accustomed to reading people to discern their intentions. It is a tool of the trade, I suppose."

The first thought which passed through Darcy's mind was that he did not care to be questioned by a tradesman. The man was beneath him socially by a very great margin; for him to call someone of Darcy's heritage out was no less than preposterous!

But then his reaction was tempered by the reality of the situation. Social standing did not guarantee depth of character, and though they had spent enough time in one another's company this evening to take the measure of one another, Elizabeth—Miss Bennet—was a beloved niece. Of course he would wish to protect her and her interests. It also spoke to a firmness of character and determination to do right by her. And for that Darcy could only respect the man.

"I can assure you," said Darcy, "that I have nothing but honorable intentions. She is . . ."

Darcy paused, thinking of the woman who had invaded his thoughts these past weeks. The last thing he had expected when coming to London for the first time in three years was that he would fall in love again. But it had happened, and the words did not exist which could adequately express his deepest feelings for Miss Bennet.

"She is a wonderful woman, Mr. Gardiner," continued Darcy at last, "and I have nothing but respect for her. Georgiana is enamored of her, and my family thinks highly of her indeed."

Mr. Gardiner watched him, apparently waiting to see if he would say anything further. When Darcy was silent, Mr. Gardiner let out a hint of a sigh, and he focused on Darcy again.

"Mr. Darcy, might I speak frankly?"

Curious, Darcy nodded for him to continue.

"It is obvious you are an honorable man, sir, and it would be ludicrous for me to oppose you, even if I was inclined to do so. There is no question you can provide our Lizzy with the best things in life and that she would never want for anything as your wife.

"However, I believe that in Lizzy's case—and I have no doubt my brother Bennet would echo my sentiments—she requires something more substantial than physical comforts. You speak of your family's regard for her and your sister being smitten with her, but for yourself you only spoke of respect. Respect is an important aspect of a relationship indeed, but what I wish to know is whether you love her."

"I—I believe I do, Mr. Gardiner."

"You *believe*, sir?"

Darcy paused, trying to put his feelings into words. Mr. Gardiner waited patiently for him to speak, but as he was struggling, Darcy chanced to look up at Bingley, and the man nodded to him, his countenance a study of complacency. Bingley, great friend that he was, apparently had no doubt in Darcy, and the feeling washed over him and calmed him.

"This has been difficult for me, Mr. Gardiner," said Darcy in a quiet tone. "I was not expecting to discover a woman who interested me in London. In fact, I had determined to never marry again. I loved my wife very much, and her loss was hard."

"I understand that, Mr. Darcy," said Mr. Gardiner. "Your feelings are natural, and it is to your credit that you espoused such feelings for your wife."

"That is why I have struggled with the feelings which have suddenly come over me," continued Darcy as he nodded at Mr. Gardiner with gratitude. "Miss Bennet is . . . She is the brightest star I have ever seen. I have tried not to compare her with my late wife, but sometimes such comparisons are inevitable, and I can only say that though they are different, I believe that she can assume the role as my wife and mother to my daughter admirably.

"I am not expressing myself well—this I know. What I am trying to say is that I believe I love your niece. I would very much like to discover what we can be to each other together.

"I have no doubt in *her*. It is *myself* I have always doubted."

"It is a difficult thing to doubt oneself," said Mr. Gardiner, at the same time Bingley said: "I never thought I would see the day when you would own to a lack of confidence."

Darcy could only laugh. "It is not so much a lack of confidence, my friend. I . . ."

Pausing, Darcy tried to search for the words, but for some moments they would not come. Mr. Gardiner and Bingley waited patiently while he tried to find the words he wished to say, and on each he could see an expression of compassion, as if they knew what he wished to speak of. And they likely did.

"I cannot explain it, my friends," said Darcy finally. "I lack neither confidence nor suffer from an overabundance of indecision." Darcy then smiled. "I suppose that last is not completely correct. You must understand that I had never intended to marry again. Furthermore, I had no notion of meeting any woman in London who would interest me so quickly or completely as Miss Bennet. I hardly knew how to react.

"And the thought of another woman taking my late wife's place has caused me to hesitate when I have rarely hesitated in my life. I cannot explain it, other than to say it is something one must experience to understand. And I heartily hope that neither of you are ever in the position in which I found myself three years ago. It is not pleasant."

Mr. Gardiner looked on him with sympathy. "My wife has given me four beautiful children over the years of our marriage, and though she has always recovered quickly, I will confess that I have worried for her excessively. I cannot imagine living my life without my dearest companion by my side."

"Nor can I," said Bingley in a quiet voice.

The three men sat in silence for some time, Darcy thinking of his wonderful wife who had left him far too soon, while Mr. Gardiner and Bingley were quite obviously thinking of the women who filled large roles in their lives. But underscoring all Darcy's ruminations were thoughts of the vibrant lady who had appeared, unlooked for, and who might perhaps fill the role his dearest wife had once filled.

"In that case, young man," said Mr. Gardiner, "I see no need to interfere. I trust Lizzy to act in a manner which will ensure her happiness, and I have every indication that you are an honorable man."

"Thank you, Mr. Gardiner. I simply need to divine the state of her feelings."

Mr. Gardiner only smiled. "If what I have witnessed tonight is any indication, I have no doubt of the state of her feelings, Mr. Darcy."

At this declaration Darcy felt warm all over. He had thought he had earned her regard, but the confirmation was welcome indeed.

Chapter XII

With a resolution borne of unshakable determination, Fitzwilliam Darcy rose the next morning and made his way to the breakfast room. There he met his sister, and after sharing a greeting with her, he proceeded to eat his usual breakfast before he retired to his study to complete the work of the day. It was a light day with respect to matters which required his attention, and he was soon finished and free to amuse himself in whatever manner he saw fit. And he had a specific activity in mind.

After querying the butler about the whereabouts of his sister—and learning that she was engaged with her companion in some lessons—Darcy made his way down the hall from his room toward the nursery in which his daughter resided. There, he opened the door and allowed himself in.

When Darcy had previously been in the nursery for his daughter's tea party, he had been quite focused on his daughter, and even more so on the person of Miss Bennet, and the only other times he had been in the room recently, it had been too dark to truly see what the room contained. It was large and open, like a sitting room in one of the suites of the house, with tables and shelves filled with all manner of implements of play, including several childish pictures, obviously drawn using charcoals by his daughter. Her dolls and other toys were stored in a neat manner over on the right side of the room, and the tea set which had served such a prominent role the last time he had visited had been placed in a location of honor in one of the cabinets.

When he entered, the nurse arose, and though she hid her reaction admirably, Darcy could see the surprise evident in her manner as she curtseyed and greeted him. For her part, Cassandra took no notice of him; instead she was concentrating on playing with a small doll clutched tightly in her hands.

"I do not wish to disrupt your routine," said Darcy, smiling at the nurse to put her at ease. "Perhaps you could indulge in a short respite while I visit my daughter."

The nurse was clearly surprised, but she was not about to gainsay her employer. Darcy quickly arranged for her to return within half an hour and dismissed her.

Turning to his daughter, Darcy approached carefully and sat in a nearby chair, watching Cassandra as she put her doll through some paces which looked designed to mimic walking. He watched her for a few short moments before deciding to address her, knowing that his time was precious.

"Cassandra?"

The child looked up at him for a moment, considering him, before she went back to her play. Darcy watched her for a moment, wondering how he should proceed. This child, though precious and obviously receiving much love from Georgiana and the nurse—not to mention Miss Bennet—had never truly known her father. He was not certain she knew precisely who he was.

Deciding the direct approach would be best, Darcy fixed his eyes upon the doll, and taking it as inspiration, said: "Is that your favorite doll?"

"Yes," said Cassandra.

"Does she have a name?"

"Yes."

Darcy suppressed a chuckle. It seemed his daughter had inherited a brevity of speech from him. Or perhaps she was not comfortable with him. If the latter, it was incumbent upon him to resolve; after all, it was his fault she did not know him.

"What is her name, Cassandra?"

The child stopped her play for a moment and regarded him. Her steady, searching gaze with which she regarded him seemed to Darcy like he was being measured.

She must have found something acceptable in him, as she soon turned back to her doll and said: "Lilly."

Darcy smiled. "Can you show me?"

Once again Cassandra turned her eyes upon him and seemed to study him for several moments. Then, reluctantly it seemed, Cassandra rose to her feet and she approached him, holding her doll out for his inspection.

"See?"

Making a great show of studying her toy, Darcy reached out and accepted the doll from her, turning it this way and that, noting the fineness of the porcelain features, the painted black hair, and the lovely floral dress in which it was dressed.

"She is lovely, Cassandra. I can see why she is your favorite doll."

The child actually beamed at his statement, and Darcy felt the warmth of having said the proper thing. Beckoning to her, Darcy indicated his lap, saying: "Will you not sit with me?"

Once again the child seemed to pause and consider the matter, and Darcy held his breath; this was a greater test of her trust, he knew, and he wondered if he was not pushing the matter too quickly.

His concern was quickly put to rest, however, when she stepped forward and climbed up into his lap, nestling herself in his arms. She showed a small measure of her great aunt Lady Catherine when she imperiously held out her hands for the return of her doll, accepting it into her hands gratefully when he chuckled and allowed her to take it.

"What is Lilly doing now?" asked Darcy as the child resumed her play.

"Walking," said the girl, once again putting the doll through her paces.

"Does she walk a lot?"

"Yes."

With great patience, Darcy continued to speak with his daughter, carefully listening to her responses, attempting to come to know her. As he had noted before, she spoke quite well for a girl who was not yet three years of age, and though her words were childish and she spoke with a slight lisp at times, they were clear and easy to understand.

Within a few moments of Darcy's arrival, Cassandra started to become more animated and shortly she was showing him her domain. He discovered that she loved to play with her blocks, and they were soon on the floor building towers and castles, laughing when the blocks fell over due to being too tall. It was the happiest time Darcy had spent in this room for many years—since Georgiana had been a child.

As he observed his daughter, Darcy was once again struck with how closely she resembled her mother. Her eyes were an exact likeness of his wife, and her high cheekbones and the color of her hair were identical. But there were also parts of her features she had inherited through her Darcy heritage, most notably her strong jaw and prominent nose. The combination would render her to be uncommonly pretty when she attained a greater age. At present, it resulted in a beautiful child.

When they had been playing together for some time—a greater length of time than Darcy had arranged for the nurse to be away from her duties, he thought—a sound alerted him to someone entering the room and he looked up to see Georgiana smiling in the doorway.

"Hello, brother. I can see you and Cassandra are quite busy."

"Indeed we are. We have been attempting to design the perfect edifice to withstand attack."

Georgiana quirked an eyebrow at his words. "That is not precisely a ladylike activity."

Darcy only grinned at her. "Perhaps not, but Cassandra seems to enjoy it. I had thought to send to Pemberley for my set of tin soldiers to complete our fortress."

Laughing, Georgiana hiked her skirts and sat down close to them. As she did, Darcy noted the nurse watching through the open door to Cassandra's room where she was tidying what looked to be an already immaculate space. Darcy could only nod to the woman gratefully—she had obviously seen his interaction with his daughter and tended to other duties to allow him more time with her.

"Papa!" cried Cassandra.

A section of the castle had fallen over, and his daughter's little hands were clutching the blocks, looking at him beseechingly. His focus was not on the blocks in her hands, it was the deep, clear eyes which looked up at him from behind her cherubic face, and the fact that she had addressed him as her father. She had obviously known of his role in her life, but she had never called him by name. Perhaps she had never had the opportunity. Perhaps she had not had the courage to do so in the rare times he had allowed himself to see her.

Out of the corner of his eye, Darcy caught a glimpse of his sister watching them, happiness shining in her countenance, and one single tear rolling down from the corner of her eye. Darcy felt misty-eyed himself as his emotions welled up from within. Foremost was his feeling of gratitude that he had—with the help of certain others—managed to push his way past his fears and come to know this precious child. And a love, long buried though never forgotten, welled up within him for this tiny slip of a girl. He would know his child. He would never shy away from her again.

"All is well, dear girl," said Darcy in a voice choked with emotion. "We shall rebuild it stronger and more secure. Then I shall send for the soldiers to defend it. No one shall ever break it down again."

Beaming at him, Cassandra offered up the blocks which he took with great reverence. And together, with Georgiana's assistance, they began building their edifice, block by block. Each piece was placed with care, anchored in solidly on the blocks below, a structure built to weather the storms of life and the attacks of those who meant them harm. In time, Darcy knew they would share the love only a family could share. In time, he thought they would heal.

The following days were the most blissful Darcy had spent in many years. Darcy visited and played with his daughter every day. He read books to her, he helped her with her dolls and attended tea parties, they played at the blocks and even with the soldiers, when they arrived, and in time she even grew comfortable enough with him that she would climb all over him, whooping and laughing when he would pull her off and tickle her. And the times when she would throw her arms around him and kiss him on the cheek made it all perfect. They were finally becoming a family.

But this was not all. He saw his friends and family many times in those days, and was even able to reconnect with some old friends from Cambridge, some of whom he had not seen in many years. All in his life seemed to be turning aright, and when he felt the presence of his wife and basked in her approval of his attempt to live again, he could not think the matter was nothing more than a feeling. He was certain his wife was looking down on him, perhaps exasperated that it had taken him so long to understand, but happy that he finally had. His life was growing full again, and many times he felt it necessary to say a prayer of thanks for his deliverance.

Of more immediate import to Darcy's future happiness was the ever growing presence of Miss Elizabeth Bennet in his life. He was able to see her every day, as visits between his house and the Bingleys' house were nearly a daily occurrence, and they took much joy in one another's company.

If only the presence of Miss Bingley was not so . . . ubiquitous was the only word Darcy could think of when confronted with the ever-present woman. It seemed that Miss Bingley was seeing all her hopes and dreams slip away, for a second time, no less, and she had determined to do everything she could to be spared the ignominious fate of being passed up by him a second time.

That Darcy looked upon her with exasperation was evident to everyone but the woman in question. Hurst made the offer to take her into the country to spare Darcy her attentions once and for all, but as she was behaving in a more or less proper manner, Darcy informed the man that he could handle her. More than once he was tempted to take Hurst up on the offer, but he decided to exercise patience and refrain from being the one who caused her banishment from society.

His tolerance was sorely tested, however, when she attempted to make Miss Bennet appear to less advantage with cutting remarks and mean-spirited innuendo. That Miss Bennet fended her off with good cheer and humor was the only thing that stayed Darcy's hand. She kept to the stricture he enforced about not calling on Georgiana—though not without hinting at the restoration of her visiting rights—which meant that the only place they were free of her presence was when the Bingleys visited Darcy house. But she had a knack for imposing upon them whenever they were anywhere else, particularly when Darcy and his sister visited Bingley's townhouse.

On a particular morning, Darcy arrived with Georgiana to visit the Bingleys, and they were welcomed with great enthusiasm into the sitting-room, where the residents of the house were waiting for them. Darcy had a particular errand that morning which he needed to complete, but the sight of Miss Bennet's smiling countenance and bright eyes sent all such thoughts flying from his head. It was not long before he was sitting by her side, entranced by her witty conversation and the way her fine eyes flashed when she laughed.

It was not long before an innocuous comment by his sister alerted Miss Bennet to the fact that Darcy had been spending time in his daughter's company recently. When she heard this, Miss Bennet turned to Darcy, and arching an eyebrow, said:

"You find it diverting to play dolls with your daughter, sir?"

Darcy laughed, unable to take offense at her words, even if they had not been said in a disarming, amused fashion.

"Dolls and tea parties are not the only facets of Cassandra's playing," replied Darcy. "In fact, I have discovered that she is not only an expert block builder, but that she is also an intrepid defender of castles once they are finished.

A delighted laugh escaped Miss Bennet's lips. "Mr. Darcy! Are you suggesting that your daughter has been playing with toy soldiers?"

"The very ones I played with as a child myself."

"And would you not call such behavior more than a little unladylike?"

"Some might, but I cannot find it within myself to believe that she is being done any harm by playing with toy soldiers. She still loves her dolls and her tea set, and we engage many other activities one would attribute to the play of a little girl, but she is also happy to play with her father."

"I am happy to hear it, sir," said Miss Bennet. She hesitated for a moment, as if debating with herself as to whether she should speak, and then she squared her shoulders and she said in a soft voice, leaning forward so he could hear: "I am happy to hear it, sir. I had the sense . . . That is, I thought there was some difficulty in that area when I first arrived in London."

Though he debated whether he should speak so openly of such a subject, especially when it would reveal a great weakness, deep down Darcy knew he could keep nothing from this woman. And thus, he found the words spilling from his mouth before he was aware he had begun to speak.

"It *was* difficult, Miss Bennet. You see, Cassandra . . . she is the very image of my late wife. Every time I looked upon her, it was as if I was looking at my wife."

"Surely you did not blame your wife's demise on your child."

Darcy shook his head. "I did not blame her. It is merely that she was an ever-present reminder of what I had lost."

"And now you have overcome those feelings?"

"I have," said Darcy. "With the help of others—my sister and my relations, and in no small amount due to your wonderful example too, Miss Bennet."

A fetching blush spread over her face and down her shoulders, intriguing Darcy, making him wonder how far down it spread. Such pleasurable contemplations nearly caused him to miss her next words.

"I have not done anything, Mr. Darcy."

"On the contrary, Miss Bennet," said Darcy, looking at her, fancying his eyes revealed the contents of his heart, "I believe you have had much to do with it. Your tales of playing with your nephews and nieces, your example of playing with a young girl who you had only met a few times, your wonderful manner with my daughter—all these things helped to inspire me.

"And once I was able to see that the eyes looking on me were filled with trust and a desire to be loved, how could I resist? I believe my wife would wish me to be happy with my daughter, and I cannot but imagine that she is looking down from on high with a smile on her face."

"I believe you are correct, Mr. Darcy," said Miss Bennet, though he had the distinct impression that she was agreeing with his last statements rather than taking any credit for his transformation.

Then, she changed the subject. "I am happy your daughter is so comfortable with blocks and castles and toy soldiers. Perhaps she would consent to have me join her play some time in the near future."

Darcy laughed. "Am I to assume you are familiar with these things?"

A grin spread over Miss Bennet's face. "I did say I have four younger cousins, did I not? And two of them are boys, not that the girls will not join with their brothers at times.

"Besides, though it may come as a shock to you, when I was a girl, I much preferred to play with the boys than the other girls of my age."

"Miss Bennet!" cried Darcy. "That is a shocking thing to confess. I must say that I will be required to reconsider your suitability to be an influence on my young daughter."

Darcy paused, watching as she gazed at him with amusement, before he said: "Unless, that is, you can add the climbing of trees to the list of your accomplishments."

"I can, Mr. Darcy," said Miss Bennet, her grin growing ever wider. "In fact, I was widely considered to be the champion tree climber when I was a girl, though it was much to my mother's chagrin."

"I can attest to that," said Mrs. Bingley.

Darcy looked over, and saw that the other three were watching them with something akin to indulgence evident in their countenances. Miss Bennet seemed to see the same thing, as her glare at her sister promised retribution.

"In fact, I remember one specific instance where our neighbor, Sammy Lucas, challenged Lizzy to a race up to the top of a great tree along the borders of our fathers' estates, and was quite put out when Lizzy beat him to the top by a full minute!"

Miss Bennet laughed. "And subsequently became so frightened at the thought of being so high in the air that he could not come down by himself. As I recall, father had to climb the tree himself and coax Sammy down, as Sir William would never be one to climb up a tree. His civility would never allow it!"

By this time both sisters were in stitches, and Darcy grinned at them, assuming there was something about this Sir William which caused them to laugh.

"Mama was chagrinned that she had birthed a daughter who was so wild as to climb trees. She was inconsolable for some time after."

The two ladies shared a commiserating glance and the subject was dropped between them. Darcy thought it likely that Mrs. Bennet's inability to forgive Miss Bennet for refusing her cousin was still a sore subject for her, so he turned their conversation back to what they had been discussing previously.

"In that case, Miss Bennet, I must conclude that you are indeed a fitting companion for my daughter. I assure you that we would be happy to have you join our play at any time convenient."

A smile crossed Miss Bennet's face again. "I would be happy to, Mr. Darcy. But I must warn you that when I play with toy soldiers, I take no prisoners. You have been warned, sir."

"In that case, we shall see who the better soldier is, Miss Bennet."

"Thank you, Mr. Darcy. It warms my heart to see you giving your daughter the love she deserves. She is such a sweet, happy child."

This was the moment Darcy had been waiting for. He held her gaze with his own, and in a slow and deliberate voice, he said: "I thank you for your compliment, Miss Bennet. She is quite a dear child indeed. But she is not the only sweetness in my life."

Such a blatant statement of regard might have sent some women into paroxysms of delight. Others might have responded with a coquettish batting of the eyes, or a flirtatious touch on the hand. Miss Bennet did none of those. Instead, she regarded him—a hint of color appearing on her cheeks, it was true—steadily and honestly, and as Darcy looked into her shining eyes, he knew that she returned his feelings in every respect. But she was not about to allow such a statement to go unanswered.

"I think there are some who would wonder if you have been overset by madness, Mr. Darcy," said she in that irresistibly arch manner of hers. "I have been called many things in my life. But I believe this is the first time anyone has referred to me as being 'sweet.'"

"Then they were not paying attention, Miss Bennet. There is a playfulness to your manners, it is true. You are not the typical shy and bashful female, and for that I am profoundly grateful, I assure you. But your attentions to my daughter, your easy friendship with Georgiana, your ready acceptance of and eager interaction with *me*, all indicate your sweetness in my opinion."

Miss Bennet cocked her head slightly to the left. "Sweetness mixed with a hint of starch?"

Darcy could only grin. "I would not have it any other way. Both are essential facets of your character, and part of what intrigues me so much about you is how honest and forthright you are. I would not change you at all."

"Then I thank you, Mr. Darcy," said Miss Bennet quietly.

And all at once Darcy saw what he had not seen before. Miss Bennet generally presented to the world such a picture of stubborn courage and self-sufficiency that it was easy to think she did not possess any worries or fears, and suffered from no lack of self-confidence. While that might be true in a general sense, Darcy now knew this episode with her mother *had* affected her, to the point where she was forced to question her own worth. She had said her mother told her she would never marry and that she had refused the only proposal she was to receive. Underneath her tenacious confidence, she must have wondered if they were not correct.

Well, they would *not* be correct, Darcy decided. He would offer for this exceptional young woman and show her what she was worth. He would show all who lacked the ability to see what she truly was.

"You are very welcome, Miss Bennet," said Darcy, "though your thanks are hardly necessary. It is nothing more than the truth. In fact . . ."

Suddenly Darcy was tongue-tied. He had determined that he would offer for her and he was more than sure of his own feelings in the matter, but though he had already gone through this once, it appeared the second time was no easier than the first.

Taking a deep breath, Darcy focused on the woman before him, noting her slight smile, the dazzling brightness in her eyes, and the beauty which shone forth from her very character. It was not a difficulty to speak words of love to this woman.

Thus Darcy took a deep breath and cast a glance at the other three occupants of the room, noting that they were not paying any attention to Miss Bennet and himself, as they appeared engrossed in whatever they were discussing. He turned his attention back to Miss Bennet and said:

"Miss Bennet, I have not spoken ere now for various reasons, most of which I believe you must already understand. It is not because I was uncertain about you. It is because I was not sure of myself. Now I am sure.

"I find you to be the most intriguing and beguiling woman of my acquaintance, and should I be given my heart's desire of a lifetime to study you, I know it shall prove insufficient. But I would like to obtain that opportunity. Thus, do I ask too much in requesting a courtship from you?"

"There is nothing I wish for more, Mr. Darcy," said Miss Bennet. "I accept your offer and anticipate this season and the opportunity to know you better. But I have one condition."

"Oh?" said Darcy, not concerned in the slightest.

"I would wish to keep this between us for the moment, to allow us to savor our new understanding."

"You would have me keep it from Georgiana?" asked Darcy.

Miss Bennet colored. "If you wish to tell Georgiana, I am in agreement, for I shall be unable to refrain from telling Jane. What I wish is to avoid my mother's notice for the time being."

Darcy nodded—he had expected her to wish to avoid telling her mother for the nonce. It was a stipulation he could agree to with very little consideration, as he was no more eager to have her called back to her father's estate than she apparently was to return.

Before he could say another word, however, the distinct timbre of a detested voice rang out through the room, ending their intimate tête-à-tête.

"Mr. Darcy! And dear Georgiana! How lovely it is to see you here."

Into the room waltzed Miss Caroline Bingley, followed closely by her sister and Mr. Hurst. On Hurst's face was an expression of resigned apology. This had happened often in recent days; the Darcys would arrive for a visit, and soon after the Hursts and Miss Bingley would enter seemingly by chance. Darcy wondered if Miss Bingley had an informant in the house or if she sat in some out of the way corner of the street, waiting for their appearance, and then returning to the Hurst townhouse and dragging her brother and sister out to meet with the Darcys yet again. It did not seem the woman would ever abandon her quest.

Miss Bingley strode forward and sat down on a nearby chair—the fact that Miss Bennet was sitting with Darcy on a rather small sofa precluded her sitting next to Darcy himself, though Darcy had almost expected her to attempt to push Miss Bennet aside. She leaned forward and batted her eyelashes at Darcy, shamelessly showing off her décolletage to his gaze.

"It is fortunate that we have met you here, sir. There is no one other than you and your sister that I would wish to visit. I cannot imagine she has seen much beauty or breeding here, of all places, and I am happy to meet with your dear sister at any time convenient and assist her in her growth in the social graces."

"On the contrary, Miss Bingley," said Darcy, not possessing the humor to deal with Miss Bingley today of all days, "everything at your brother's house has been agreeable. In fact, I had come here today . . ."

Darcy stopped what he was saying abruptly, wishing he had thought before he had spoken. But now all eyes were upon him and he could hardly refuse to continue what he had been about to say.

"My apologies, Mrs. Bingley," said Darcy, "but the matter completely vanished from my mind when I arrived here."

A soft snort from Bingley drew Darcy's attention, and he looked at his friend, noting Bingley was shaking with mirth. Bingley obviously understood why Darcy's attention had wavered in that critical moment, and he found the whole thing amusing. Privately, Darcy agreed with him, though he was annoyed with himself for not taking care of it the moment he had arrived. It might have saved an awkward scene.

"That is quite all right, Mr. Darcy," said Mrs. Bingley, her angelic smile never wavering.

"I have brought with me an invitation," said Darcy, reaching into his jacket pocket and producing a small stiff sheet of paper which he handed to her. "Bingley, you are invited to the annual ball at my uncle's house to be held Thursday next."

"Oh Mr. Darcy!" cried Miss Bingley before anyone else could say a word. "How delightful and how thoughtful for your aunt to have included us in her soiree!"

The clearing of Hurst's throat brought Miss Bingley up short and she glared at him. Hurst only returned it with a bland look of his own.

Apparently seeing that she was not about to be able to influence her brother-in-law, Miss Bingley turned back to Darcy and plastered a saccharine smile on her face. "May I ask if Mr. and Mrs. Hurst and I have been included in your aunt's generous invitation?"

"I believe the common practice is to send an invitation to those invited to their residence, Caroline," interjected Hurst. "I do not believe Louisa has received such an invitation."

Miss Bingley turned and pierced Hurst with a baleful glare, but she might have been staring at a stone wall for all the effect it had on her brother-in-law.

Feeling he had no other choice but to respond as it was his slip which had caused the issue, Darcy said: "I will ask my aunt if you have been invited, of course."

"Thank you, Darcy, but please do not put your aunt to any trouble on our account. I believe we have been invited to the Stanbridge ball the same evening. We may amuse ourselves there with tolerable ease."

Darcy coughed into his hand to avoid a laugh. Stanbridge, though Darcy was acquainted with him, was *not* a member of the first circles, and his ball, though likely well attended, would not attract the cream of London society. Aunt Fitzwilliam, by virtue of her status as wife to an earl, would throw a ball which was attended by only those of the highest standing—Bingley and his family was invited *only* because he was a close friend of Darcy's, and because the Fitzwilliams had detected Darcy's partiality for Miss Bennet. Though there may be others in attendance of their general sphere, the Bingleys would be among the lowest rank.

But Miss Bingley would not see that, could not see that as the daughter of a tradesman, many would look down on her and consider her unworthy to attend; all she saw was the bright lights of society and the chance to climb the ladder ever higher. Well, that and the opportunity—in her own mind, of course—to further make her claim on Darcy himself. Darcy shuddered at the mere thought of being *captured* by Miss Caroline Bingley.

"It is no trouble, Hurst," said Darcy. "I will let you know if she confirms your attendance."

For once Hurst did not seem to be inclined to provoke his sister-in-law, as he did nothing more than incline his head in thanks.

Whatever intimacy Darcy and Miss Bennet had managed between them was now lost with the inclusion of Miss Bingley. Darcy could hardly whisper sweet nothings in Miss Bennet's ear while Miss Bingley watched them like a hawk, and interjected her own comments in whenever she could. And though Darcy was content with what had passed between them earlier, there was one more matter which he had wished to canvass with Miss Bennet. He now needed to wait until he had the appropriate chance to do so.

A few moments of speaking once more in their odd three-way sort of conversation was apparently all Miss Bennet could stand, as she soon excused herself to speak with her sister. Miss Bingley directed a smug smile at her retreating back, which quickly turned to chagrin when Darcy stood and bowed, citing a desire to speak with Bingley.

The new conversation groups were thus formed, and other than Hurst's apology for once again arriving when the Darcy party was here, the gentlemen's discussion was largely banal in nature. It was not much later that Darcy began to think of returning to his own townhouse when his attention was arrested by a sight which caused him to scowl. Miss Bingley had managed to separate Miss Bennet from Georgiana and Mrs. Bingley, and she was speaking to her, a hard, unpleasant sneer directed at the other woman.

Noting that Hurst and Bingley were in the midst of a discussion of a new hound Hurst had acquired, Darcy edged away from them and closer to the two ladies in an attempt to hear their conversation. What he heard did not please him.

". . . you are doing, Miss Eliza. But I warn you that it shall not work.

Mr. Darcy is much too intelligent to be taken in by the likes of you."

"If he is too intelligent to be taken in by me, then I can only suppose he possesses the same ability to avoid *your* web, Miss Bingley."

"*I* have been intimate with Mr. Darcy for many years now, Miss Eliza. I am certain you cannot understand the depth of connection which exists between our two families."

"The depth of connection between Mr. Darcy and *your brother*, perhaps. I have seen no particular fondness in Mr. Darcy's manner for you, Miss Bingley."

"You could not possibly understand."

"I understand that the connection you attempt to portray exists only in your imagination. I have no right to comment on the state of Mr. Darcy's feelings for you, nor would I attempt to do so. But I suggest you do not attempt to dictate to the man how he will behave or who he will befriend."

Miss Bingley's eyes narrowed and she glared at Miss Bennet in a fury. "I know what you are about, *dear sister-in-law*. I have seen your kind before. You have nothing more than a wealthy man and *pin money*, as your improper mother would put it, in your mind. Mr. Darcy will not fall for the likes of you."

"And you think he will fall for the likes of you?" Miss Bennet's tone was positively dripping with scorn, and by this time Darcy could see that she was finally annoyed with Miss Bingley's insinuations. "You say that I care for nothing more than pin money, but what do you care for other than the man's position in society? You are nothing but a social climber who has far too high an opinion of herself, and I cannot imagine that Mr. Darcy is any less able to see through *you* than he is able to see through *me*."

The fury which exploded on Miss Bingley's face told Darcy that she was to the point of attacking Miss Bennet, signaling the time had come for him to intervene.

"Miss Bingley, Miss Bennet," said he, stepping forward to insert himself between the two women.

Miss Bingley turned a false smile upon him—Darcy wondered if she kept it at hand so that she could don it at a moment's notice—but Miss Bennet regarded him evenly and without surprise. Though he had not seen anything in her manner, Darcy wondered if she had known he was close by all along.

"Oh Mr. Darcy," cried Miss Bingley. "Has the time come for you and your darling sister to leave?"

"I think it may be soon, Miss Bingley. However, before I go, I wished to say something to you."

The look of discomfort suggested suspicion that he had heard what she had said, but Miss Bingley allowed no other indication of disquiet.

"Of course, sir. I am happy to help wherever required."

Darcy favored her with a faint smile. "Miss Bingley, I believe I have made my sentiments known to you on more than one occasion. I ask you again, due to the respect I have for and my friendship with *your brother*, that you cease to speak to Miss Bennet in such an unkind manner. It is not only unwarranted, but unladylike. I would not wish to be required to sever my acquaintance with you over so trivial a matter."

A huff escaped Miss Bingley's lips, but she soon mastered herself. Darcy did not know what else he could do; if telling her in a clear and concise manner did not induce her to leave off her quest to become Mrs. Darcy, he did not know what would. But whether she finally understood or not, he would not have her importuning and insulting Miss Bennet when he had the power to prevent it.

"Miss Bennet and I are now sisters, Mr. Darcy," said Miss Bingley. "What is a disagreement between two who share as close a relationship as we?

"Regardless, I believe it is time for us to depart." Miss Bingley turned to Miss Bennet and her lip curled in a sneer. "Miss Eliza. What an illuminating conversation this has been. I assume we will once again speak anon."

Her tone left no doubt as to Miss Bingley's feelings concerning the prospect, but she turned away before anything could be said in response and stomped away. Darcy watched her, and if she would only turn and look at him, the disgust she would see on his face would dissuade her from ever importuning him again.

"I thank you for your defense, Mr. Darcy," said Miss Bennet, drawing his attention. Her demeanor was not only a little amused, but also somewhat stern. "However, I would have you know that it is unnecessary. I have handled Miss Bingley and her supercilious airs and her cutting remarks since they first arrived in Meryton last year at Michaelmas. I assure you that I can continue to handle her."

Darcy reached out and grasped Miss Bennet's hand, holding it as the precious talisman it was. "I am well aware of your fortitude, Miss Bennet. But where I can do something to assist, I will. You must expect me to protect you if you wish to have a happy courtship with me. I take care of those I love."

Miss Bennet watched him, her bearing calm, but clearly softening at his words. His unintended declaration of love for this woman she did not miss, but she also did not respond. Darcy would not press her—he was certain she felt the same for him, but he would wait until she was comfortable enough to tell him herself.

"I am certain you are well accustomed to caring for others, Mr. Darcy. And I have no objection to being cared for. As long as you do not forget my independence."

A chuckle burst forth from his lips and Darcy shook his head. "I doubt I could. After all, your independence is one of the first things that attracted me to you."

Raising the hand he still held to his lips, Darcy kissed it tenderly, his eyes never leaving hers. He therefore did not miss the affection which was the result of his action.

"Thank you, Mr. Darcy. I believe we shall get along famously."

Darcy did not answer. He merely reflected on how it would be a very interesting courtship indeed.

Chapter XIII

The day of the ball swiftly arrived, and Darcy prepared himself carefully, wishing to look his best for the woman he was courting, though still unacknowledged. The thought that she might be similarly preparing her appearance with *him* in mind filled him with impatience. At the same time, he also felt another emotion, which frankly surprised him: desire. He *desired* Miss Bennet, as much as he esteemed and loved her. The happiness he felt at such a realization filled him with hope for the future, such as he had not experienced before.

Cooling his ardor in that moment proved necessary—though he was not yet even in her presence!—so Darcy turned his mind to other things while his valet fussed with the knot in his cravat. Though he wished for just about anything else, he had indeed spoken with his aunt concerning the attendance of Bingley's relations, and though Lady Susan had not desired any closer acquaintance with Miss Bingley than she already possessed, she had decided to dispatch an invitation to Mr. Hurst. After all, she said, if Darcy was to make an attachment with Miss Bennet, Miss Bingley would be closer connected to the Darcys and the Fitzwilliam's, and it would not do for society to think there was some reason why the woman was being held at arm's length, understandable though it might have been. In fact, with their combined support, Miss Bingley might actually find someone willing to marry her.

However, in the invitation addressed specifically to Mr. Hurst—and sent with a servant to make certain it was delivered to his hand alone—the countess had made it clear that there were to be no disruptions by Miss Bingley's instigation. Hurst *and* Bingley had assured her separately that Miss Bingley would not be allowed to make a spectacle of herself. Darcy privately thought they might be underestimating her, but he decided it would be better to simply watch and intervene if necessary.

The thought of Miss Bingley was distasteful, so Darcy turned his attention back to the one who was worthy of contemplation. Darcy had never been one for dancing, though he enjoyed it well enough with the right inducement. And Miss Elizabeth Bennet was certainly the right inducement. He had found the day Miss Bingley interrupted them during their discussion, that she was also fond of dancing.

When the time had arrived for the Darcys to leave—thankfully, Miss Bingley and the Hursts had departed moments earlier—Darcy rose with his sister and thanked his hosts for their hospitality, and Miss Bennet and the Bingleys accompanied them to the door. It was there that Darcy had made the request which had been on his mind during the entirety of the visit.

"Miss Bennet," said he, "should I expect that you, as a sociable young lady, are fond of dancing?"

Miss Bennet smiled and she ducked her head, seemingly understanding Darcy's intent. "I am indeed, Mr. Darcy. I flatter myself that I rarely have to sit without a partner."

Darcy frowned, though his wink told her that his words were not intended to be taken serious. "That could pose something of a problem, Miss Bennet."

"Oh? And why would my dancing habits be of any concern to you, sir?"

"Because I mean to ask you to dance, and I must own that I am loath to share you with any other."

An arched brow was her response. "Share, sir? By my account you have not even secured my hand for a dance yet. Since you are unaware of all of my movements, I might already have accepted another's offer for the first dance. If so, it would be *him* sharing me with *you*."

"That would be a miracle, Miss Bennet, as I have delivered the invitation myself only moments ago. So unless Hurst has preempted my request, I must assume you are toying with my affections."

The sound of tinkling laugher issued forth from Miss Bennet's mouth.

"Do you actually think Mr. Hurst wishes to dance with me? If so, perhaps I should demur in anticipation of the offer of his hand. There is little which could give me more pleasure than a dance with Mr. Bingley's brother."

This time it was Darcy's turn to laugh. "And you would wish for a dance with Hurst more than a dance with me? Though he is married, I am available, and he is dull, while I have it on good authority that I am the furthest thing from dull."

"But he is family, in a roundabout sort of way, Mr. Darcy. It would not do to offend him, though I have no hope of obtaining his regard."

"Miss Bennet," said Darcy, his voice infused with a mock annoyance, "would you please stand up for the first dance with me at my aunt's ball?"

"Of course I will, Mr. Darcy."

Darcy smiled. "Thank you, Miss Bennet. I shall look forward to it."

The woman regarded him, a hint of a smile playing around her mouth. "Tell me, Mr. Darcy, is this what you say to every young woman whose hand you solicit for the first dance at a ball?"

"In fact, you are only the second young lady with whom I will stand up for the first dance, Miss Bennet."

The significance of his statement was not lost on Miss Bennet, but she only continued to look at him, and if his judgment was in any way correct, she anticipated the coming dance as much as he did himself. Darcy considered soliciting her hand for the supper dance as well, but he decided to wait. He could easily do it the night of the ball itself. There was no need to rush. He had all the time in the world

A moment later, Darcy's valet pronounced his attire adequate, and with a smile and a nod of thanks, Darcy exited his room and made his way down the stairs. There, he found his sister waiting for him.

"Brother!" exclaimed she as she bounded up to him. "I see you are ready for tonight's amusement."

Darcy greeted his sister with affectionate welcome, noting that though she was in one of her usual gowns, his little sister was growing far more quickly than he would have wished. She was now tall and fair, honey-colored hair, the rounded cheeks of her childhood giving way to high cheekbones and an oval face which would draw the attention of young men when she came out. From what Darcy remembered of his mother, the resemblance was striking.

"I am quite ready indeed," replied Darcy, all the while thinking that it was a very good thing that he was able to hold onto her for a little longer. He was not ready to part with her yet.

"I am sure Miss Bennet will be pleased with your efforts." Georgiana's teasing manner and the flash of her eyes reminded Darcy of the subject of her words. "I believe you know that I hope your efforts result in a sister for me."

"Shall she not be my wife first?" asked Darcy mildly.

"Oh! Is it truly to come to pass?"

"Perhaps," said Darcy. "But we must follow the established modes, do we not?"

"I care not. As long as she shall be my sister, I can wait."

Darcy smiled fondly at her. "I shall do what I can. For tonight, I expect you to retire at the usual time rather than attempting to wait up to hear tales of the ball."

The pout which stole over his sister's face prompted a laugh, and reassured him at the same time; at heart Georgiana was still a very young woman, after all. She was not ready to leave him yet. In fact, he thought she might like to have Miss Bennet as a sister so well that she would not be in a hurry to leave.

"You will be able to hear the stories tomorrow morning. And I expect that I shall be home very late indeed.

"Besides," said Darcy when she appeared ready to protest, "I believe that Miss Bennet and Mrs. Bingley are much better able to entertain you with stories than your taciturn brother. Shall I ask them if you might visit tomorrow?"

A vigorous nod was Georgiana's response.

"I shall do so, then. But remember, the ladies will be fatigued tomorrow, so you must not go *too* early."

Within a few moments, Darcy had bid his sister goodnight, leaving her to thoughts of romantic tales of the ball, and he departed for his uncle's house. As the location was around the corner from his own house, Darcy allowed himself a brisk walk in the spring evening air, arriving only a few minutes later and before any of the guests had made an appearance.

His arrival at his uncle's house was received with the usual hearty greetings, and the even more typical teasing indulged in by both his uncle and his cousin Fitzwilliam. This time, however, Darcy noted that the viscount was as much the target as was Darcy himself. Within moments, the guests began to arrive and Darcy was able to see the reason why.

The duke of Westfield was among the first to arrive, and he greeted Lord Matlock with pleasure. With him he brought his wife, a handsome woman of about the age of Darcy's aunt, and his youngest daughter, Lady Alice Sutton.

"Mr. Darcy," said Lady Alice as she curtseyed.

The years had indeed been kind to the young woman, as she was now in the full bloom of beauty, possessing a slender, willowy frame and beautiful green eyes. In fact, Darcy thought Georgiana would resemble Lady Alice closely in about four or five years' time—or at least their beauty would be of a similar type. Hopefully Georgiana would also possess Lady Alice's confidence when she came out.

"Lady Alice," said Darcy with some warmth. Her father was a contemporary of his father's, and as such he was quite familiar with the family. "I trust you have been well?"

"Very well, sir," said she.

It was clear he could not hold her attention for long, for as soon as she espied Viscount Chesterfield standing a little further away, her cheeks became crimson, and she looked shyly at him from behind a set of long eyelashes.

"Viscount," said she by way of greeting, though it was clear she could say nothing further. Darcy was amused that the sight of his cousin could render such a poised woman so silent and bashful.

For his part, the look James directed at her allowed for no misinterpretation, and had Darcy not known his cousin to be as proper as Darcy was himself, he might have thought James was ready to scoop her up and carry her off. Instead, he merely approached with quiet calmness and grasped her hands, bestowing a kiss on the back of each.

"Lady Alice," said he, "I can hardly credit my eyes, but it seems to me that you grow lovelier every time I see you."

A soft snicker from Darcy's side caught his attention, and he looked to see his cousin Fitzwilliam watching them with no little amusement.

"Have you something to say, cousin?" asked Darcy quietly.

"I imagine everything which needs to be said has already been said," said Fitzwilliam.

"Oh?" asked Darcy.

"I suggest you keep your insouciance in check tonight, Anthony," said the earl.

He had approached while Darcy had been speaking with his cousin, and the glare he directed at Fitzwilliam was returned with a look of utmost innocence.

"You know I would do nothing to disrupt my brother's engagement ball, father."

"Engagement?" asked Darcy.

The earl favored his younger son with annoyance. "It is *not* an engagement," replied Matlock, still glaring at Fitzwilliam. "However, James's courtship with Lady Alice will be announced tonight."

"Making it tantamount to an engagement," replied Fitzwilliam.

At his father's hard look, Fitzwilliam held out his hands in surrender. "I know, I know," said he, though there was not an ounce of repentance in his manners or his tone. "I shall not make sport with my brother, though I am ever so tempted to indulge. In fact, I am happy that he has found someone to admire. I had begun to wonder if the earldom would eventually pass through me after all.

"Besides," continued he, jerking a thumb at Darcy, "I shall have ample sources of amusement in Darcy here, and I have made no promises about refraining from making sport with *him*."

At that moment, Miss Patterson could be seen to be descending from the stairs, and the three men looked up at her, one with welcome, one amusement, and the other with a slack jaw.

"I seem to remember someone claiming to be able to make sport with *me*," said Darcy to his uncle, glancing at his cousin significantly.

"As do I," said the earl, his voice shaking with barely suppressed laughter.

For his part, Fitzwilliam attempted to resume his previous expression and appear unaffected, little though he was fooling the other two men. Uncle Hugh merely slapped him on the back.

"Son, your admiration is a poorly kept secret. I suggest you go and secure the lovely Miss Patterson's hand for the first set before someone else beats you to it."

Fitzwilliam scowled, but Darcy noted that he lost no time in taking his father's advice, much to the earl's amusement and pleasure. His departure left Darcy alone with his uncle, who soon turned to him and eyed him with speculation.

"And what of you, Darcy? I understand your aunt has invited the lovely Miss Bennet to the ball tonight. Shall you secure her hand as soon as she arrives? She is pretty enough that I do not doubt you will have competition should you delay."

"There shall be no competition," said Darcy. "Aunt Susan asked me to deliver Bingley's invitation myself, and I was fortunate enough to secure her hand at that time."

The earl laughed. "That is the spirit! I am happy you used such forethought. She is a lovely girl indeed."

"That she is," said Darcy, though in a quiet tone which he was not certain the earl could hear.

As the time for the guests to start arriving approached, Lady Susan herded her husband and sons, along with Charity, who was in attendance, to the receiving line, and though she shot a look at Darcy, beseeching him to join them, he shook his head and went off in search of some punch. It was a trial enough to attend events like this in general—he was not about to ruin his present good mood by standing in a receiving line, greeting people he would otherwise not wish to associate with.

He passed the time speaking with the duke, renewing an acquaintance which had lapsed in recent years. All the while he watched for some sign of Miss Bennet as the ballroom filled up. It was not long before the ball was to start that Darcy finally caught sight of her.

She entered the ballroom on Bingley's arm, with her sister holding on to his other arm, and the room seemed to lose its luster with her presence. She was wearing an ivory ball gown which hugged her curves and accentuated her exquisite figure, complete with long gloves extending past her elbows, and a pair of dainty slippers which peaked out from beneath her dress as she walked. Her beautiful mahogany hair was piled on the top of her head, tendrils falling down her back in shimmering waves. And as she drew closer, Darcy could see that in the curls of her hair, she had woven small white sweet Williams, mixed with beautiful blue forget-me-nots, the only part of her attire which held any hint of color.

It is not likely I could ever forget her, thought Darcy.

The exquisite way in which she had taken care in dressing, and in the way her hair was done, with the flowers woven throughout, suggested to Darcy that she had done it for him and him alone. At least it was pleasant to think it, even if it was not completely true.

"Given your reaction to the approach of that young lady, I dare say you have managed to conceal an attachment from society."

Darcy turned back to the duke, eager to excuse himself. The man was watching him, a hint of indulgence in his manner. "You know, I had hoped for an attachment between you and one of my daughters—your father and I often spoke of how wonderful it would be if our children married."

"All your daughters are lovely ladies, your grace," said Darcy.

The duke only laughed and waved him off. "I understand the timing was not quite right. But I will say that your father would have been proud of the man you have become, and he would have adored your first wife. If what I am seeing before me is any indication, I cannot but imagine he would have approved of this young lady too. I shall expect an introduction during the course of the evening."

Then the duke slapped him on the back and retreated, leaving a bemused Darcy behind, grateful for the man's words.

Turning, Darcy walked a few paces to where Bingley was leading the ladies to a location by the side of the dance floor, and there he bowed and exchanged happy greetings with the new arrivals.

"Miss Bennet," said Darcy, turning his attention to the lovely woman on his friend's arm. "Might I say that you look beautiful this evening?"

"Would it be the truth, Mr. Darcy?" asked Miss Elizabeth.

For the first time in his experience with her she was watching him behind a coquettish fluttering of eyelashes, but even that only enhanced her charms in his opinion. It bespoke a shy acceptance of his words and attentions and that she was affected by him, rather than any insincerity of manner in order to gain his attention. She had no need to resort to such stratagems, as he knew she was well aware.

"Anyone who cannot see it can only be blind or bereft of wit."

She smiled at him and appeared ready to say something further when their tête-à-tête was once again interrupted by the arrival of a most unwelcome acquaintance.

"Mr. Darcy, how good to see you tonight."

As one, Darcy and Elizabeth turned to greet Miss Bingley, who was behaving in a demure fashion under the watchful eye of Hurst and her brother.

"Miss Bingley," said Darcy. "It seems you have the knack for appearing in a most particular fashion."

Miss Bingley preened at his perceived compliment, while Miss Bennet, who undoubtedly understood his meaning, smiled behind one hand. It was that action which brought her to Miss Bingley's notice.

"Eliza," said she. For once her words were not accompanied by the sneer she typically used when speaking with Miss Bennet, but even so it was clear she was not happy to see her supposed rival. "I see you have taken my advice and visited my modiste for your dress."

"On the contrary, Miss Bingley," said Miss Bennet, "I had this dress made up at my aunt's modiste. Jane and I have used her services for many years now. She makes excellent dresses."

"It looks wonderful, Miss Bennet," said Darcy.

Miss Bingley only sniffed. "It is adequate."

The musicians, who had been tuning their instruments, began playing the music for the first dance at that point, and Miss Bingley turned back toward Darcy, batting her eyes at him. Compared with Miss Bennet's understated coquettishness only a few moments before, it appeared blatant and overdone.

"I do so love the first set of a ball," said Miss Bingley in an exaggerated fashion. "It speaks of romance and courtship."

"Indeed it does," said Darcy.

Then he extended his hand to Miss Bennet and said, "I believe this is our set, Miss Bennet."

As her small and delicate hand slipped into his, Darcy excused them and they joined the line which was forming, near to the first couple, which happened to be his cousin and Lady Alice. A surreptitious glance back at Miss Bingley revealed her shock, which appeared to be turning to anger. But then a hint of melancholy seemed to settle over her, and Darcy saw that she had finally recognized that she had lost him. Not that she ever *had* him, of course. He could not feel too badly for the woman—she had ignored every hint he had given her, so if she was disappointed, it was her own doing.

As the dancers stepped forward to begin the set, Darcy was arrested by the sight of Miss Bennet's amused smile.

"That was . . . smoothly done, Mr. Darcy," said she.

Though her words were amused, Darcy had the sense that she was, though perhaps not precisely upset, at least a little sorry for Miss Bingley. And he had to own that he had perhaps not behaved with the greatest of empathy toward the woman who was, after all, the sister of his closest friend.

"I apologize for the breach of decorum, Miss Bennet," said Darcy, when the steps of the dance took him close enough to converse with her. "I must own that sometimes I find Miss Bingley's manners to be a trial, but that is no excuse for unkindness."

Miss Bennet shook her head. "I do not blame you, Mr. Darcy. Miss Bingley has been . . . well, she is nothing less than a huntress on the prowl, and she is almost uniformly unkind to me. I fully understand how it might become tiresome."

A sigh escaped Darcy's lips and he appreciated the fact that the dance steps took them away from each other so he could ponder his words. Thus, when they were once again in close proximity, he was able to smile at her and say:

"Miss Bennet, you are too generous. Miss Bingley can indeed be a trial at times, but I should not use our understanding to tweak her nose. I would not have you feel our attachment is lessened through the use of such behavior."

"I could not feel that way, Mr. Darcy," said Miss Bennet. She regarded him soberly, though with a hint of a smile at the corners of her mouth. "I believe I am intelligent enough to know when I have been blessed with a regard which is real and true. Any number of Miss Bingleys could never take that from us, I dare say."

Warmed by her words, Darcy grasped her hand as they passed through the steps again, and he squeezed her fingers, gratified when she returned the gesture. They passed much of the rest of the dance, at times in silence, while in others in lighthearted conversation. Darcy noted that they attracted much attention as they danced; regardless of his recent absence from society and his previous marriage, he was still a public figure and there had no doubt been talk of his future marital status. With any luck, those gossips would understand the lay of the land and leave them to themselves without intruding on their romance.

When the dance had concluded, Darcy took Miss Bennet's hand and escorted her from the floor; her sister and Bingley had danced the first together as well, and they were headed toward a location on the far side of the ballroom, where the Hursts and Miss Bingley were standing. Before they could arrive there, Darcy leaned down to Miss Bennet and said:

"Thank you for the dance, Miss Bennet. It is clear that you were underestimating your abilities. You dance beautifully."

Luminous eyes turned to regard him, and Miss Bennet said: "As do you, sir. I have had the misfortune to stand up with some who have not been nearly so skilled—and one whose dancing was an abomination! It is so much better to stand up with one whom you esteem above all others, is it not?"

"It is indeed," said Darcy. He held her gaze in his own for several moments, and though she was becoming a little flustered, she did not break it off.

"It is for that very reason," continued Darcy after a few moments, "that I would like to solicit your hand for the supper dance as well. Will you do me the honor?"

Miss Bennet regarded him with mock astonishment. "But will that not be taken as a declaration, sir? We shall be the talk of London by morning."

"I find that I care not," said Darcy. "Have I not already declared myself? It is by your wish that our courtship has not already been published far and wide."

"You are correct indeed, sir. If you wish to have the supper set, I shall cede it to you, of course. I anticipate it highly."

They walked up to the waiting Bingley party and for once Miss Bingley was blessedly silent. Darcy, therefore, felt no compunction about continuing their conversation.

"So you have not been asked by anyone else in attendance? I fear I must question the eyesight of the other men of society. Surely they cannot fail to recognize the beauty before them when you walked into the room."

Miss Bennet's cheeks colored, but she looked back at him with exasperation. "Perhaps you are carrying your flattery a little too far? We stopped to talk to no one when we entered the ballroom. As such, I find it unlikely that anyone else could have solicited my hand for a dance."

"A poor excuse," said Darcy, fighting to keep a grin from his face. "I believe had I not known you when you stepped into the ballroom tonight, that I would have hastened to be introduced. I do not doubt your dance card shall be full for most of the evening."

"I hope so. I have a reputation to uphold."

Darcy regarded her warmly, basking in her teasing repartee. "I do not doubt you shall, Miss Bennet. I believe it is inevitable.

It was not long, in fact, before Darcy's assertions were proven correct, much to his mingled smugness and annoyance. Soon there was a flood of young men insisting upon receiving introductions to both Miss Bennet and Mrs. Bingley, and if the dejection at the knowledge of Mrs. Bingley's lack of single status caused an expression of self-satisfaction from Bingley, the sight of Miss Bennet's inability to claim the same prompted Darcy to scowl. In compensation, Darcy was able to overhear several times in which she turned down requests for the supper set, reflecting on his own good fortune to be the possessor of that particular dance.

His relations were no help. Fitzwilliam in particular seemed to relish the ability to introduce her to all and sundry, and if his sly glances in Darcy's direction seemed to indicate an expectation that Darcy would stalk about in a rage, Darcy's responding smiles appeared to cause him to grin all that much more. He had apparently caught on to the fact that Darcy had already made his move, and far from being annoyed at the loss of the opportunity to tease his cousin, he actually saluted Darcy, seemingly content that he would be gaining Miss Bennet as a relation.

Thus, Darcy was able to watch from the side of the dance floor as Miss Bennet, bright light that she was, enjoyed herself dancing with many young men. Her glances at him occurred with great frequency, and he nodded back at her, noting that many times she appeared to wish she was dancing with him, rather than whatever dandy had led her to the floor. That, more than anything else, caused Darcy to grin with smug superiority at whatever man cast annoyed glances in Darcy's direction.

As for Darcy himself, he stood up for a number of sets, though by no means all, as was his wont. His aunt, Charity, Mrs. Hurst, Mrs. Bingley, and Miss Bingley he partnered at various times during the evening, and he also stood up with Miss Patterson later in the evening, just before the supper dance. He enjoyed himself for the most part, even his dance with Miss Bingley, as she was silent for the duration. It was unprecedented, in Darcy's experience.

When at last the time came for the supper dance, Darcy approached Miss Bennet, his anticipation charged for their upcoming set, during which he could once again claim her exclusive company. She watched his approach calmly, and he thought her demeanor indicated as much expectation as Darcy was feeling himself.

"Shall we, Miss Bennet?" asked Darcy as he stepped up to her and extended his hand.

The feel of her dainty hand ensconced within his own was indescribable, so right did it seem. She peered up at him, her heart in her eyes, and Darcy knew that this was where he belonged. Their journey to this point had informed him that they would do well together, but it was only now that he realized how very *right* it felt to be in this woman's company.

Knowing that no words were needed, Darcy led her to the dance floor and they assumed their positions. Soon the music began and they stepped into motion, following the steps of the dance

Forever after, Darcy was able to remember little of that dance at his aunt's ball. The music, the other couples, the very air that he breathed—all faded into insignificance. He could not say how long they danced, or whether either of them ever took their eyes from the other, and for all he knew they might have moved through the steps of the dance, twirling around each other for an eternity.

What he did remember was the feel of her small hand within his, the brilliant hue of her eyes, the sensation of longing and belonging which filled his very being, and the overwhelming love he felt for this exceptional young woman. Perhaps most of all, he remembered the sensation of being at home, which he had had never realized how much he had missed until he once again felt it.

Darcy spent the dinner hour by Miss Bennet's side, refusing to move any further away from her than was necessary. They spoke of many things, their subjects moving from one topic to the next with fluidity, and Darcy felt he had never enjoyed himself so much at a ball.

That Miss Bingley stayed away was a blessing, in Darcy's mind. In fact, she seemed to have garnered the attention of a young man with whom Darcy was not acquainted. But he was tall and seemed to be well favored and genial, and Miss Bingley appeared to be hanging off every word the man said. Hopefully she would see that she had no need to depend on Darcy to raise herself in society.

The meal had ended and the attendees had begun to make their way back to the ballroom when Darcy caught sight of his uncle's butler as he approached Bingley. The man whispered a few words in Bingley's ear, prompting Bingley to frown and stand, following him toward the door.

"Something appears to be amiss," said Darcy to Miss Bennet. "I shall follow Bingley to see if he requires my assistance."

Miss Bennet nodded and rose with him, and he offered his arm to her, noting that she was not about to allow him to leave without her.

They exited the dining room as discreetly as possible, and followed behind Bingley as he was led to a room near the back of the house. And thus, they were in time to hear a man blurt out the news that Bingley had obviously been summoned for.

"Mr. Bingley! It's Miss Lydia—she's run away with a militia officer!"

Chapter XIV

"I beg your pardon?"

The sound of Bingley's question hung in the air, but it was not immediately answered, as the man who had delivered the message was clearly winded, as if he had run all the way from Hertfordshire.

"Thomas?" asked Miss Bennet.

She stepped forward to confront the man, clearly agitated by his appearance. It helped calm the man, as at the sight of her face he attempted a smile, albeit a weak one.

"Miss Lizzy!" exclaimed the man. "Mr. Bennet sent me to beg for Mr. Bingley's help. Miss Lydia has run off with Lieutenant Wickham!"

"What?" demanded Darcy. He stepped forward and looked at the man, saying: "What is this about George Wickham?"

"You know Mr. Wickham?" asked Miss Bennet.

"I do. Who is Miss Lydia?"

"She is my youngest sister, Mr. Darcy," said Miss Bennet, her voice quiet. "It seems she has done something foolish."

Darcy's jaw worked at the knowledge. George Wickham! Darcy had not seen his father's former favorite since he had received three thousand pounds from Darcy in lieu of a valuable family living after

Darcy's father had passed. But his deeds before Darcy had terminated their connection were enough to indict Wickham in Darcy's eyes; drunken parties, gambling, debauchery, seduction—there were no depths to which George Wickham was not willing to descend.

"Andrews," said Darcy, calling the attention of his father's butler.

The man, who had been watching events unfold, snapped to attention at Darcy's tone. "Yes, Mr. Darcy?"

"Please summon my cousin the colonel here immediately. And keep it as quiet as you can."

The butler nodded and turned to leave the room. Darcy turned his attention back to the man, Thomas, who was beginning to catch his breath. Bingley was looking on completely at a loss, while Miss Bennet watched it all, her countenance strangely devoid of all emotion.

"Miss Bennet, please tell me of George Wickham."

Miss Bennet looked at him, a hint of curiosity piercing her stoicism, but she readily responded. "Mr. Wickham joined the militia company wintering in Meryton near the end of October of last year. He immediately made himself agreeable to everyone there, and has generally been well thought of."

"I can well imagine that, Miss Bennet. Mr. Wickham is quite capable of charming all and sundry. His proclivities are only understood when he leaves a place, inevitably leaving unpaid debts and ladies' virtues compromised. He is not a man to be trusted."

"You know him?"

"All too well, Miss Bennet," said Darcy. Then realizing that his manner was rather grim, he softened a little and favored her with a smile. "Had I known of his presence, I would have warned you. Now, what of Miss Lydia?"

Miss Bennet sighed. "My sister is . . . Well, both of my youngest sisters are silly and more than a little vapid, Mr. Darcy. They care for nothing but flirting and officers, though I would not have thought one of them would throw all propriety to the wind. In fact, when I was last in Meryton, I would not have said Lydia favored any officer in particular. She is rather happy to be the recipient of the attentions of several officers at once."

Darcy nodded. He had seen young ladies of Miss Lydia's ilk before, though perhaps not as blatant as she seemed to be. Darcy turned to the messenger.

"And your name is Thomas?"

"Yes, sir," said the man. He appeared terrified, but Darcy was not in the mood to reassure him. Depending on the situation, much might depend upon quick action.

"What further can you tell us of Miss Lydia's relationship with Mr. Wickham?"

"I cannot tell you much, sir," said Thomas. "She is as Miss Lizzy said—eager to flirt and pass her time in the pursuit of pleasure. I cannot say if she favored Mr. Wickham."

"And what happened to prompt your journey to London?"

"Miss Lydia was seen by her sister entering a carriage with Mr. Wickham. Miss Kitty was able to watch the carriage long enough that it seemed to be heading for London. Mr. Bennet sent me on his swiftest horse to beg for Mr. Bingley's assistance to head them off before they arrive."

"How long ago did this happen?" asked Bingley, finding his tongue and speaking for the first time.

"About three hours, Mr. Bingley, or near enough."

Darcy turned to his friend. "Would they be in London yet?"

Bingley thought for a moment before he shook his head. "I doubt it. In a carriage—even a finely crafted one, able to move swiftly—it would take four hours at least."

"And the carriage Miss Lydia entered was a rented coach, sir," said Thomas.

"Then we still have time." Darcy turned to Thomas. "Did you see them on the road?"

"No sir," said Thomas. "But I road like the wind and crossed fields and forded streams hoping to get here more quickly."

"We may still catch them before they get to London," said Bingley.

"We had best catch them," said Darcy. "Otherwise they will disappear into the slums and finding them will be a great deal more difficult."

In fact, Darcy thought it would be nigh impossible to find Wickham if he managed to secrete himself in the maze of streets which characterized the rougher areas of London. Darcy had kept track of the man for a short time after he had severed contact with him, but as Wickham had immersed himself in his debaucheries, Darcy had allowed his vigilance to lapse. There were a few locations he could call on to try to determine the man's whereabouts, but if those were exhausted without any information, he doubted he would be able to find Wickham without engaging the Bow Street Runners.

The door opened and his cousin entered, but he was unfortunately followed by his uncle, with Mrs. Bingley, Mr. and Mrs. Hurst, and Miss Bingley following behind. The butler, who had opened the door for the newcomers, looked at Darcy and shrugged his shoulders in apology.

"What is this, Darcy?" asked Fitzwilliam as soon as he entered the room.

"Wickham," replied Darcy shortly. "It seems our old friend is up to his tricks again."

"Wickham?" asked Fitzwilliam, clearly confused. "But you have not heard from him in years."

As quickly and succinctly as he could, Darcy related what he had been told in a low voice. Hurst and the earl had drawn close to hear what Darcy was saying, and Miss Bennet attempted to keep Miss Bingley and Mrs. Hurst close by, while at the same time telling her sister what had occurred. Within a few moments, Darcy had passed on the pertinent information to the men, and was already making plans as to how he would handle the situation.

"Then I do not see any other option," said Fitzwilliam, once he understood the situation. "If we leave directly we may be able to catch them before they enter the city."

"And if we do not?" asked Bingley. His obvious trepidation suggested that he already knew the answer to that question.

"That is not a consideration," said the earl. He turned to Darcy. "Most of my footmen are engaged in tasks related to the ball, but I have several stable hands in town who can ride out with you. I suggest you make Wickham an offer he can't refuse. Might I suggest Van Diemen's Land?"

Darcy nodded grimly, while at the same time Fitzwilliam said: "Van Diemen's Land is too good for the likes of George Wickham."

"I believe we have our plan, gentlemen," said Darcy, and he turned to Hurst, who seemed to understand what he wished to say.

"I will see the ladies home," said Hurst in a gruff tone.

Darcy nodded in agreement.

"Surely there is no question about marrying her now," interjected Miss Bingley, directing a scathing glare at Miss Bennet. "After this . . . episode involving her silly little flirt of a sister, I would be surprised if any of them were *ever* married."

Darcy glared at her and was about to respond when Hurst spoke first. "Be silent, Caroline!"

"But—"

"Not another word. You should remember, *dearest sister*, should word of this leak out, that *you* are also connected to the Bennets through marriage. Your own reputation would not remain spotless if this became known."

"I suggest you keep it strictly to yourself, Miss Bingley," said Darcy.

"But I have told you before that my intentions are none of your concern, as they do not include you. Do I need to be any clearer than this?"

Miss Bingley colored at the reprimands she had received, and though her jaw was still working with anger, she shook her head and allowed herself to be led from the room.

"Your departure will be noted, Darcy," said his uncle. "But the Bingleys should not raise too many eyebrows. As long as you are able to find them, we should be able to keep this quiet."

"Thank you, uncle," said Darcy.

The earl nodded and left the room, leaving the three gentlemen to the final preparations for their departure. They quickly agreed to change their clothes and meet back at the house as soon as could be arranged.

"I shall also send word to the barracks," said Fitzwilliam. "I can have half a dozen men join us in the search. As Wickham is by all accounts a militia officer now, this concerns the army too."

Nodding, the men turned to leave to return to their homes to change. In truth Darcy would have preferred to simply ride out in his current attire, but with the coolness of the spring evening and the unsuitability of his clothing for riding, it was best for them to have the appropriate equipment. His valet would have him changed in no time.

In a trice Darcy and Bingley were walking down the hall toward the massive front doors to the house, but before they could exit, Darcy was arrested by the sight of the Bennet sisters waiting for them by the door. Frowning, Darcy strode forward, noting that Bingley was approaching his wife. He stopped in front of Miss Bennet, noting her distraught wringing of her hands.

"What is it?"

"I asked Mr. Hurst to allow us a moment," said Miss Bennet. "I wish . . ." She paused and closed her eyes, swallowing heavily, before she opened her eyes. They were filled with tears.

"I have decided that I will release you from our understanding," continued Miss Bennet, her tone speaking to her heartache. "It has not been announced yet, which I can only consider to be a fortunate fact. You have no obligation to me, sir, as I release you with a full heart."

Darcy watched her, his emotions running the gamut between anger and sadness, disbelief and exasperation. But what never wavered was his love for this woman. And he would be damned if he allowed her to escape.

"Miss Bennet, do you wish to end our understanding because *you* wish for it to end?"

"Of course not, Mr. Darcy." Miss Bennet's voice was quiet and she had looked down to the floor refusing to lift her eyes again. "But I will not drag your family name down with my own."

"Please look at me, Miss Bennet."

She visibly steeled herself, but she did look up at him. He could see nothing but concern for him. It melted his heart all over again; this woman was willing to give up that which she desired most in order to avoid hurting him. How could he not love her?

"I shall not end our understanding unless you will not have me, Miss Bennet."

She started a little at his firm statement, but Darcy would not allow her to once again speak her case.

"Miss Bennet, I find that I am completely incapable of living without you. I care not what your silly sister has done. I care not what Miss Bingley has to say on the matter. I care not what the wagging tongues of London shall say. *You* are far more important to me than they. Unless you wish to be rid of me, I shall not go away. Do you wish to be free of me, Miss Bennet?"

"I do not," said Miss Bennet in a soft voice. "I do not wish to ever be separated from you."

Almost without volition, Darcy stepped forward and pulled her into his arms, pressing her cheek against his chest, and fitting her head under his chin like she belonged there. Darcy felt rather than heard her sigh, and he marveled at the exquisite sensations coursing through his body. Every nerve felt afire, her nearness the most addictive opiate.

Then cautiously, worried that she might flee from him, Darcy pulled away a little, and reached down to tilt her head up to him. The sight of her glorious eyes, the unshed remnants of her earlier tears pooling in their corners, unmanned him, it was so beautiful. And with infinite care, slowly so she would have time to object, he lowered his head and pressed a kiss to her lips.

They were soft and moist and were the most delicious thing Darcy had ever tasted. He wanted more, all the while knowing that it was not proper, and he was not yet entitled to it.

At length he broke off the kiss and looked into her eyes. "I shall find your sister and we shall determine what is to be done. I must believe there is some way to manage this situation and ensure that there is minimal damage to her reputation. And unless I miss my guess, my aunt would be willing to help teach your youngest sister to behave. Let us not make any decisions until we know exactly what the situation is."

Miss Bennet nodded and the subject was dropped. Mindful of the time and the need to hurry, Darcy soon guided Miss Bennet from the room, noting that Bingley and his wife had joined them. Darcy handed Miss Bennet into the carriage after Bingley had guided his wife in, and in the dim light he thought he could see Miss Bingley glaring at him from the interior. But he trusted Hurst to handle the matter and keep Miss Bingley in line.

"Do you have something to tell me, Darcy?" asked Bingley.

Darcy shook his head. "I suggest we focus on the task at hand. After this matter has been dealt with, I will speak with you, and with Mr. Bennet."

Nodding, Bingley turned and accepted the horse a groom had brought forward for his use. Darcy idly wondered who had possessed the forethought for such things. Shaking his head of such thoughts, Darcy called out to Bingley as the other trotted away.

"We should meet back within fifteen minutes, Bingley. If we are not here, make for the road to Hertfordshire, for we will have gone on ahead."

"I shall, Darcy," said Bingley, his voice floating back to Darcy through the darkness.

As it was, Bingley returned to the earl's house before Darcy did, and Darcy thought the man must have galloped all the way there and back to have made it in such a time. A group of his uncle's men milled about in the courtyard behind the house waiting for instructions. Into this mass of confusion his cousin strode out from the house, dressed in his regimentals, calling for order and setting the men to their tasks. Soon, they were all mounted and riding out toward the northwest of the city.

"My men will meet us on the road," called Fitzwilliam as they rode. "They will help us search the area for any sign of the libertine."

Darcy nodded and turned his attention to the road. The streets of London were largely quiet, unsurprising considering the lateness of the hour, and the company passed through them as quickly as possible. A fog had arisen during the night, and it became thicker the further north they rode, though it did not impede their progress. It was a shifting, eddying mist, which clung to the horses' hooves and furtively hid in the doorways and alleys upon their passing.

When they reached the north road they were joined, as promised, by several other officers in their regimentals, all seemingly alert, as though it was not the middle of the night and they had not been roused from their beds. The lead man—a sergeant by his insignia—saluted Fitzwilliam as he pulled his horse to a stop. He conferred with the man for a moment before drawing everyone in close.

"Now we will ride north, watching for any sign of our missing lovers. Wickham has ever been a soft man, so I do not expect any kind of resistance from him, but as he has a gentleman's education and a familiarity with a gentleman's weapons, take care if you approach him.

"We all know what a gentleman's carriage looks like, so we will not stop any carriage which looks like it is occupied by a rich man. Hackneys, mail coaches, anything that looks like a hired coach—we will stop all these and question the occupants. As it is late, we should not find many travelers on the roads.

"Be vigilant. If Wickham suspects any pursuit, he may try to pull off the road to allow it to pass. If you see anything unusual, investigate it. The timing is such that it is unlikely Wickham has already arrived in London, so there is no need to hurry. We will take a measured approach and find them before the damage to the lady's reputation is irreparable. Are there any questions?"

A general murmur met the colonel's instructions and within moments, he had the party formed up and on the move into the night. It was immediately evident to Darcy that his cousin was well versed in such tasks, for he was efficient and specific in his instructions, positioning each of the men, ensuring that they understood what their specific tasks were. Within moments, they were moving along, inspecting the road as they proceeded, and moving swiftly, yet without undue haste.

Thus began one of the most frustrating nights in Darcy's memory. The colonel was determined to leave no stone unturned, and no possible escape for his quarry, and he directed the men to ensure this was so. They encountered very few carriages, and what they did were quickly sent on their way when they did not fit the description of what they were searching for. They came across several inns as they rode, and those they found were entered and the innkeepers, eyes heavy with the sleep from which they had been awoken, were summoned and questioned concerning any late arrivals. But for the first hour of their journey, they were unable to find any trace of the fugitives. And as the night grew later Darcy knew that the chances they would find Wickham were slipping away with them.

At one point after they had been searching for more than an hour, they came across a carriage, which in the darkness and mist appeared as a ghost in the night. More importantly it had the look of a hired carriage. Darcy's heart leapt into his throat at the thought they might have actually found who they were searching for.

"Halt," commanded Fitzwilliam as he reined in directly in front of the carriage.

At first the carriage driver did not seem inclined to stop, but as he drew nearer, Fitzwilliam once again cried, "Halt, I say!" and the sight of his scarlet coat, showing dull and drab in the gloom, seemed to convince the driver it would not go well for him if he refused.

"Here, what's this?" demanded the driver.

"We are looking for a hired coach carrying a militia officer with a young woman. Do your passengers fit that description?"

"A man and a woman, yes, but he does not have the look of an officer."

"Stand down and we shall see," said Fitzwilliam, approaching the coach. The driver once again appeared ready to protest, but the sight of Fitzwilliam's hand on a pistol which was stuck into his belt ensured his cooperation.

"You in the carriage!" cried Fitzwilliam as he approached. "Show yourselves."

There was a brief pause and then the coach door opened, and a young man stuck his head out. "Yes officer?"

Disappointment flooded through Darcy's breast. Though the man's form was indistinct in the paucity of light, his hair was clearly blond and his features looked nothing like Wickham's.

"It is not Lydia," said Bingley. He had ridden close to the coach in order to be able to see inside the carriage.

"My apologies, then," said Colonel Fitzwilliam. "Tell me, have you seen any sign of the pair I described."

"No," said the driver shortly. "Now move aside and let us pass."

The men quickly obliged and the carriage moved on, leaving the party to ride on.

"Could Wickham have stopped somewhere along the way?" asked Darcy as they rode.

"That is my hope," replied the colonel, his voice nothing more than a grunt due to the exertion of riding. "For if they have not, then we must have missed them. Even in a slow carriage, they would have been able to come at least this far."

"Then we must continue the search."

Fitzwilliam made no reply and they rode on.

As they continued on and hope began to fade, Darcy considered the situation. The fact of the matter was that he did not know how to act. The thought of giving up Miss Bennet due to nothing more than her sister's foolishness was something he could not countenance, but she had essentially been correct. Society was unforgiving at the best of times;

at least it was for those who did not have the wealth and benefit of societal standing to protect them. An indiscretion by a duke's daughter could be covered up and forgotten with enough money changing hands, but if the secret was betrayed to society, not even that standing would protect the offender.

By contrast, the Bennets had no standing, little in the way of money, and few resources to fall back on. Whatever gossip ensued might be contained to the community in which the family lived, but they would be shunned in that community and there would always be a risk of the story making its way to the wagging tongues of London.

Of course a marriage would salvage the situation to an extent, though not completely. If the perpetrators were not directly in the sight of society, the matter might be forgotten quickly. Perhaps with enough money Wickham could be persuaded to marry Miss Lydia and attempt to make his fortune in the Americas.

The true question, though, was what effect Darcy marrying a woman with a scandal attached to her—albeit one controlled—would have on his standing in society, and even more importantly, on Georgiana's prospects. It would hurt them, without a doubt. But with the Fitzwilliam name backing him, coupled with his own standing and reputation for proper behavior, Darcy thought the damage would be minimal. And if someone decided against offering for Georgiana for so small a matter, then Darcy thought he would rather not see his dear sister married to such a man anyway.

Furthermore, what did Darcy care for London society? Even before his withdrawal upon the death of his wife he had cared little outside the company of a few dear acquaintances and friends. His friends would undoubtedly stand beside him regardless of whatever gossip ensued, and those that did not were not true friends anyway.

The thought of the earl and his reaction gave Darcy pause. He had already approved of Miss Bennet, but that might change if the situation were not resolved in a satisfactory manner. He would not wish to have any hint of scandal attached to the family. Yet, with a little persuasion, Darcy thought that he could gain his uncle's support. Having already being acquainted with Miss Bennet, his uncle had the measure of her character, which could only be a boon.

Still, there was no reason to worry over the matter at present. There still was some hope that they would be able to find the young woman and her paramour and resolve the situation satisfactorily. Miss Bennet trusted him to repair the damage, and he meant to do it.

It was more than half an hour after the incident with the hired carriage that the company came upon a small inn by the side of the road. By that time the chill had settled into Darcy's bones, and he wondered if he would ever again be warm. He judged it only a few hours until daybreak, and as the season was not yet advanced enough for the sun to rise especially early, it was likely time that farmers would be up and preparing for the day; the world would be waking soon.

The inn was insignificant, catering to a clientele which was of a more common sort, and though Darcy thought that he might have travelled past it during his many journeys to and from London, he had never stopped there. The sign which hung over the door was indistinct in the lack of light, and it swung from side to side, swaying and creaking in the light breeze. The paint was peeling from the structure, and it slouched beside the road which gave it its life's blood, looking tired and worn.

Fitzwilliam drew the men to a halt when they had espied the inn and he gathered them around, giving everyone their assignments as he had in the other places they had searched. Three men were sent around to the rear of the building to cut off any escape, while several were dispatched to surround the building and watch the windows.

"This has the look of a place one such as Wickham might frequent," said Fitzwilliam as he sized up the structure.

Darcy grunted, cold, tired, and annoyed that they had been led on this merry chase. "If I know Wickham, a place such as this would likely consume his last available funds."

"Let us hope he has decided to use them here, then."

They pressed forward at a trot. There were no lights through any of the windows at the front of the building, and the common room was dark and empty. Dismounting, Fitzwilliam led the way to the front door and there, he paused and rapped heavily on the oak frame.

"Open this door!"

"Who are you?" demanded a voice.

Turning, Darcy noted the approach of a shadowed man from around the building. He hurried up to them and peered at them from beneath a hood which partially obscured his face, but Darcy could see the piercing blue of his eyes as they watched Colonel Fitzwilliam in an accusing manner.

Then Darcy heard a gasp behind him and Bingley strode up, saying: "Mr. Bennet?"

Chapter XV

The man's eyes widened in recognition and he threw off his hood. "Mr. Bingley?" asked he.

Bingley stepped forward and shook the other man's hand vigorously, all the while exclaiming his pleasure at their meeting. Mr. Bennet seemed to be well aware of Bingley's exuberance, and he smiled, though tightly, in greeting, his visage showing his relief. In the dim light Darcy was able to make out dark hair, greying at the temples, a weathered countenance, and those sharp, blue eyes he had noticed before. This was the father of his beloved.

"I cannot tell you how happy I am to see you," said Mr. Bennet. "I was not certain Thomas would deliver my message so quickly. Thank you, Mr. Bingley."

"It is no trouble, Mr. Bennet," said Bingley. "Of course we are happy to help."

Mr. Bennet looked about, noting Darcy, Fitzwilliam and the other assorted men who were within range of his sight, and he chuckled, though the sound carried a hint of a sardonic edge. "It seems you were able to bring an entire company to apprehend my foolish daughter, sir. I had not thought to hope for more than a man or two."

"The opportunity to see George Wickham gain his just desserts was all the motivation needed, sir," said Fitzwilliam.

Eyes widened, Mr. Bennet said: "You speak of the man with such venom, sir, that I might think that you know him."

"I beg your pardon, Mr. Bennet," said Bingley. "This is Colonel Fitzwilliam and Mr. Darcy. Darcy is my good friend and Fitzwilliam is his cousin. They were present when your message arrived, and were kind enough to offer their assistance."

"We are well acquainted with George Wickham, Mr. Bennet," said Darcy. "Thankfully he left our lives some years ago, but given our presence here, I doubt he has changed in essentials."

"Hmm . . . I doubt he has," said Mr. Bennet. "But that is a story for another time. I have tracked Wickham here—I believe he is inside. So we had best apprehend them before they are able to get up to any further foolishness."

Fitzwilliam exchanged a look with Darcy. "How do you know they are here?"

"I came across the carriage they hired," said Mr. Bennet with disgust. "The man was heading back north when I happened across him no more than fifteen minutes ago. He was able to tell me where he left Wickham and my daughter."

"Very well, let us go to it," said Fitzwilliam, his tone cheerful. "I have a great desire to speak with our old friend Wickham again."

Turning, Fitzwilliam once more pounded on the door, demanding admittance. It was only a few moments later when a short man opened the door and peered at them, anger coloring his expression.

"What is this? Is everyone out and about tonight?"

"We are looking for a young man and a girl who we believe stopped at your inn, good sir," said Fitzwilliam. "The man is a militia officer who has absconded with a young girl. He is wanted for deserting."

Darcy had to hide a smile behind his hand at his cousin's words. It was true Wickham would *soon* be wanted for desertion, but at present Darcy doubted any warrant had been issued for his arrest.

"A pair appeared at my door no more than half an hour ago, sir," said the man. His tone was more respectful, as he had obviously seen the colonel's uniform and undoubtedly understood that there were several gentlemen standing on his doorstep. "But he has not the look of a military man. The girl is a silly one, though, I would wager."

"That is my daughter," said Mr. Bennet. "Could you kindly direct us toward the room they rented?"

The man seemed to hesitate, but he readily asked them to enter and directed them to the stairs. "The room I gave them is the last one on the right. Please refrain from disturbing my other guests."

The four men climbed the stairs with alacrity and had soon gained the upper floor. The hall was not long as the inn was not large, and it was the work of a moment to arrive outside the room. Hand poised to knock, Fitzwilliam paused at the sounds of a struggle within.

"Not until we are married, George!" screeched the sound of a young girl's voice.

"Not if I have anything to say on the matter!" cried Mr. Bennet, and he pushed his way forward and flung the door open to crash against the wall behind it.

The room beyond the door was typical of the quality of the inn in which it was situated; drab furnishings in a room with faded, peeling paint, and the distinctive aroma of the unwashed bodies of those who normally frequented such establishments. In the middle of the small room stood the stark reality of the bed, and there on top of the counterpane lay two struggling figures.

"Lydia!" boomed Mr. Bennet as he charged into the room.

The young lady squeaked and rolled away from her paramour, espying her father in an instant. The paleness of shock fell across her countenance, and she cried: "Papa! What are you doing here?"

"Saving you from a lifetime of misery, girl!"

Mr. Bennet dragged Miss Lydia to her feet and bustled her over to the side of the room where he forced her to begin donning her dress, which lay discarded on the floor. Darcy looked at the girl with a critical eye—she was quite tall and rather pretty, and he thought she looked like his Elizabeth in essentials. She was also still wearing her chemise and other assorted accoutrements which told Darcy that while Wickham had tried to have his way with her, she had been able to fight him off. Her virtue appeared to be still intact.

For his part, Wickham lay languidly on the bed watching Miss Lydia with a leer while she stepped into her dress at her father's command. He was wearing nothing more than his smallclothes, and he appeared to have missed the fact that there were several gentlemen other than her father in the room. That changed with the sound of the colonel's thundering voice.

"Wickham, my old friend!"

Wickham jumped in surprise at the sound, and his face took on a hint of horror when he saw the scarlet uniform of Darcy's cousin. Then he espied Darcy himself and he relaxed slightly. Darcy merely scowled at him; Wickham would find out to his detriment that Darcy was not about to assist his former friend from his predicament. Quite the contrary, in fact.

"Fitzwilliam! Fancy meeting you here."

The colonel only eyed Wickham as a cat might admire a fat, juicy mouse. "I presume you can produce a letter from your commanding officer which would explain why you are so far away from your encampment?"

The words were spoken in a mild tone, but the hard glint in Fitzwilliam's eye spoke to the amount of trouble which had come Wickham's way. For his part, Wickham seemed to sense this, though he attempted to charm his way out of his situation. He scrambled to his feet to meet the colonel, though he presented a slightly ridiculous picture, dressed only in his smallclothes.

"Just on my way back, old man. You have nothing to fear."

"On your way back?" asked the colonel lazily. He stalked into the room, steps slow and measured, and his gaze never left Wickham's. "In a rented room in a small and dirty inn, along with a gentleman's daughter whom you were attempting to seduce? And with your hired carriage already on its way back north, as Mr. Bennet here can attest?"

Wickham's countenance became whiter as Fitzwilliam continued his accusations.

"Unless I miss my guess, I suspect you expected pursuit, though likely not for some hours. You stopped here to have a little fun, after which you planned to abandon the girl, steal a horse, and make your escape, leaving the trail to grow cold, and more importantly, forsaking Miss Lydia here to fend for herself."

"George and I are to be married!"

Miss Lydia Bennet stepped forward, and though she was now wearing her dress and had restored her modesty, it was a little askew, as if the buttons were not done up correctly.

"Tell him, George. George promised to take me to Gretna Green so we could be married. It is what you desire the most, is it not George?"

Wickham was silent, wisely exercising some restraint, though self-control was not one of his virtues. Fitzwilliam, however, was not impressed, as his snort of derision clearly indicated.

"Then why, pray, are you travelling south? Unless its location has changed, Gretna Green is in Scotland, which happens to be north of England."

"George merely has some business to complete in London first," said Miss Lydia with an airy wave of her hand.

"Is that so?" asked Fitzwilliam, turning an amused grin on Wickham, who was looking at Miss Lydia with more than a little revulsion.

"Yes, tell him, George!"

Finally, the provocation became too much for Wickham and he sneered at Miss Lydia, saying: "You are a foolish girl to be tempted by nothing more than empty promises. Why would I marry you? You are good for nothing other than a romp in bed, and you have turned out to be a disappointment in that regard as well. I should not marry you if you were the last woman on the earth!"

A primal shriek issued from Miss Lydia's lips and she darted forward and aimed a kick at his shin. Unfortunately, her aim was no better than her sense of propriety, and her kick went wide, glancing off the inside of Wickham's shin and travelling up to a far more sensitive area. Wickham doubled over with a womanly shriek, but Miss Lydia was not finished; she pummeled at him with her fists and raked him with her claws, and managed to inflict considerable damage on him before her father pulled her away.

Then suddenly the night's adventures became too much for her and she burst into tears, burying her face in her father's shoulder.

"There, there, Lydia," said Mr. Bennet, putting a soothing hand on her back. "Though I dare say you are one of the silliest girls in all England, I do not believe any young lady deserves to be spoken to in such a manner. Let us go downstairs so that you may compose yourself."

"We will take care of Wickham, Mr. Bennet," said Darcy.

Mr. Bennet gave him a tight nod, and though he did not say anything further, the look he gave Darcy suggested he knew something. Or perhaps, that he suspected what piqued Darcy's interest in this matter.

Fitzwilliam and Bingley had each grasped Wickham by an arm and had deposited him back on the bed. He was clearly still in pain, but Wickham was able to glare at the two men with credible ferocity. At least he did until Fitzwilliam scowled at him, which caused him to blanch in response—Wickham was very aware of Fitzwilliam's disgust of his lifestyle, as it had been pointed out to him on a number of occasions when they had been at Cambridge. Fitzwilliam could be an intimidating man when he chose, not only because of his size, but because of his implacable manner.

"Well, well, what have we here, Wickham? In hindsight, does your decision to join the militia not seem a little . . . precipitous?"

Wickham's glower replaced his fear. "My circumstances left me little choice."

Fitzwilliam raised an eyebrow. "And yet you somehow found the money to purchase a commission?"

A glare was Wickham's only response.

"It seems you have learned to hold your tongue on occasion," said Fitzwilliam. "Pity."

"I cannot imagine what this episode is to you, Darcy," said Wickham, turning his attention away from the colonel. "It is not as if I have importuned your precious sister, though I will confess her dowry would be welcome indeed."

In a seemingly casual manner, Fitzwilliam reached out and cuffed Wickham on the side of the head. "I suggest you do not speak of Georgiana, Wickham. If you had attempted anything with her, I would have hunted you down and hung you from the highest tree I could find."

Wickham frowned at Fitzwilliam, but he directed his words at Darcy again. "Why are you here, Darcy? Surely you are not interested in that bit of muslin. If she had not been so eager, I would not have taken her with me."

"It would have been better for you if you had not, Wickham," said Darcy. "I care not what you do with your life, for I have long lost any hope for your reformation. But you absconded with the sister of my friend's wife, which made it my business."

"Whatever," said Wickham with nary a hint of embarrassment. "You have her returned to you—good riddance. We had not been on the road for fifteen minutes when I found myself desiring to throw her from the coach, and it did not signify whether the driver stopped first. I have never met so annoying a girl in my entire life!"

"Wickham, Wickham, Wickham," said Anthony, laughing and shaking his head. "You do not seem to understand that you have truly stepped in it this time. If it had been up to me, you would have been thrown in Marshalsea many years ago, but Darcy here is far more tolerant than I. I believe you have used up even his well of patience."

"You have nothing," said Wickham, attempting a show of bravado. "So I am away from my barracks? I might receive a day or two in the stockade for being away without leave."

"Your testimony against mine?" asked Fitzwilliam. "All I would have to do would be to testify that you were deserting when I apprehended you, and my word would not be tested. Do not suppose you can wriggle your way out of this with your smooth manners. They will not help you in this instance."

"Why can you not simply let me be?" asked Wickham, a hint of a whine entering his voice. "I have given you no trouble since I left Pemberley that last time. Allow me to return to my barracks and I shall not bother you again."

"We shall not because you are a detriment to society, Wickham," said

Darcy. "You do not care who you injure because of your actions, whether it is some shopkeeper which must find some way to feed his family when you depart without paying, or ladies like the one who just left in tears. At least she has been spared the indignity of bearing your loathsome offspring."

"Then we have both been fortunate."

Darcy shook his head. "I shall no longer allow you to prey on the unsuspecting, Wickham. I believe it is time for a change."

At that last Wickham perked up a little, and he looked on Darcy with interest. "If I recall, there is still the matter of that living your father left to me. Perhaps a change in profession *would* be warranted after all."

Fitzwilliam cuffed him again, while Darcy shook his head. "You as a clergyman? Do not make me laugh, Wickham."

"Your father left it to me," said Wickham.

"And I compensated you for it."

"He was far more generous than he ought to have been," added Fitzwilliam.

"I shall not entrust the spiritual wellbeing of the people of Derbyshire to you, Wickham," said Darcy. "You may as well banish such thoughts, for you will never possess a living under my auspices."

"Then what do you suggest, gentlemen?" asked Wickham, his tone as nonchalant as Darcy had ever heard from him.

"I suggest court martial or Marshalsea," said Bingley. Darcy glanced over at his friend and noted the unfriendly glare he was directing at Wickham. It was the hardest look Darcy had ever seen on the face of his friend, and rather incongruous on the normally happy man's countenance.

"I believe Bingley might have a point," said Fitzwilliam.

Wickham began to protest, but Darcy only glared at him, wondering at what his father's favorite had become. Wickham had always been a little too full of himself, expecting everything to be handed to him without any effort on his part. Whether that belief had been borne of jealousy of Darcy's position in life or simply because he was inherently greedy, Darcy did not know, but it had been a facet of Wickham's character from his earliest memories.

"Much though I believe he deserves it," said Darcy, cutting into the conversation, "I believe that I must honor my father's wish one last time."

Wickham perked up. "Then you will gift me the living?"

"No, Wickham," said Darcy. "I shall not. As I said, you are not suited to care for your own spiritual wellbeing, let alone that of any others.

Even if I had any indication at all that you wished to repent of your deeds, I would not countenance such a thing. Instead, I believe you must start a new life."

"What do you mean?"

His tone was suspicious and he appeared to dislike the way in which the discussion was proceeding. And well he should not—Darcy was not about to allow him to go free. Not this time.

"How about a new start in the Americas?" asked Darcy. "You would be free from debt, free from expectations. I want you out of England, Wickham. If you accept a ticket to Baltimore or any other American port, I will arrange for the charges against you to be dropped. You would be a free man."

His nose wrinkled in distaste, Wickham shook his head. "I do not think the former colonies are refined enough for me."

"Would you prefer Van Diemen's Land?"

"*I* would prefer Van Diemen's Land," said Fitzwilliam.

Wickham ignored Fitzwilliam's comment and focused on Darcy. They shared a gaze for a long moment before Wickham looked away with disgust.

"I suppose you are not willing to negotiate about this."

"No, Wickham. This time I cannot ignore your activities. You will accept the Americas, or I will see you shipped off to Australia."

Wickham brought a hand up to stroke the stubble on his chin. "You know, a ticket to America and a new start might be what I need. I can make my fortune there with a few thousand pounds in my pocket."

Laughing, Darcy reached forward and slapped Wickham on the back. "Ever the optimist, Wickham. But I am sorry I must disappoint you. I will not give you any money. You will need to make your fortune on your own."

"But how will I do such a thing?" whined Wickham.

"I care not," said Darcy. "For once you will be required to make something of yourself, or you will not. I will give you a five pound note and a ticket, and whatever happens after will be up to you."

It was a decidedly downcast Wickham who was led from the room a few moments later. Fitzwilliam had put his sergeant in charge of the prisoner's deposition, while one of the men was dispatched to Hertfordshire to carry news of the delinquent officer back to the colonel of the regiment. Wickham himself would be taken to London where he would be incarcerated until a ship was found to carry him over the ocean. Fitzwilliam, with the help of his father's influence, would arrange for him to be released from his commission so he could make the journey. Wickham was lucky, mused Darcy as he watched the man go. If he had joined the regulars, no amount of influence would have affected his release. He would undoubtedly be facing the scaffold.

"Good riddance," muttered Fitzwilliam when the man was gone. "Let the Americans deal with him."

"I cannot agree more," said Darcy.

The three remaining gentlemen left the room and descended the stairs themselves, entering the common room of the inn and finding Mr. Bennet sitting on one of the benches, with Miss Lydia leaning against him, snoring softly. She appeared angelic in repose, and in such an attitude, Darcy thought she looked even more like her sister. It made one forget the fact that she was headstrong and loud, and had attempted to do something very foolish that evening.

"I shall see to our departure," said Fitzwilliam. "There must be a carriage for hire nearby. I think it would be best to get our intrepid Miss Lydia to London as soon as possible."

Darcy and Bingley agreed and the colonel excused himself. The two men approached Mr. Bennet and noted that he had a protective arm around his youngest daughter, watching her sleep as if she had not a care in the world.

"I remember when she was naught but an imp," said Mr. Bennet softly. "She was always an energetic child, happy and carefree, always ready to run about and play, always with a happy smile or laughter at some nonsense."

Pausing, Mr. Bennet looked up at the two men, his countenance troubled and overset with anguish.

"I can only imagine what you two gentlemen must think of me at present. I have not perhaps done my best with my girls, though my two eldest are truly exceptional ladies. But it would have grieved me indeed to have lost my youngest to that man. She is silly, but she does not deserve such a fate."

"It is best to leave such thoughts alone, Mr. Bennet," said Bingley. "We have averted the worst, and I do not doubt that Miss Lydia has learned a valuable lesson here tonight."

Mr. Bennet nodded, but his eyes fell back on his daughter. "Perhaps you are correct, son. Unfortunately, we will need to devise some story to explain her sudden departure. I warned my wife on the pain of losing her allowance not to breathe a word of what has happened, but that stricture will probably not last long. I will need to return to enforce it, I dare say."

"You are both here," said Darcy. "I suggest you tell the truth without divulging any of the specifics. Say that you brought Miss Lydia to visit with her sisters and leave it at that. Without anything further, what talk there is will soon die out in favor of other gossip."

The man cocked his head to the side, seeming to consider the matter. "Perhaps you are right, sir. I believe your name was Mr. Darcy?"

"Darcy is my longstanding friend, Mr. Bennet," said Bingley. "I believe I mentioned him to you on occasion."

This time Mr. Bennet snorted, but it was not with derision. "More or less constantly, I would say. Furthermore, the names 'Mr. Darcy' and 'Georgiana Darcy' have often appeared in my daughters' letters of late, especially that of my second eldest."

It was a challenge; Darcy could see the man looking at him measuring him up as if to determine whether he was a suitable match for a most beloved daughter. Darcy returned his gaze with one of his own.

Then Mr. Bennet nodded, as if to say that he had investigated Darcy and was satisfied.

"Your suggestion appears to be most sensible," said Mr. Bennet. "I believe it would be for the best."

"Miss Lydia is welcome to stay at my house as long as you feel necessary," said Bingley.

Turning his attention to Bingley, Mr. Bennet paused while weighing the offer. He then shook his head, saying: "Thank you for your offer, but I believe it would be best if Lydia was to stay with my brother Gardiner. She would no doubt look on a stay with you as an adventure and an opportunity to attend balls and parties. Not only is she a little in awe of my brother, but Mrs. Gardiner is one of the only people she will listen to at all. Let us not make a holiday out of this situation if we can avoid it."

Darcy nodded; it was a sensible plan. Having met Mr. Gardiner, Darcy had a healthy respect for him and knew that he could curb Miss Lydia's high spirits and even potentially instill a bit of decorum into her manners. And while Darcy had the highest opinion of Bingley, the man was not an authoritarian; no doubt Miss Lydia would have her own way more often than not if she was to stay with him. Then again, Darcy had the measure of Miss Bennet, and he doubted she would be lenient with her sister.

It was then that Fitzwilliam once again entered the room.

"There is a carriage for hire in the nearby village," said he as he crossed the room. "I was able to let its services for the morning to take Miss Lydia to London."

"Thank you for your assistance, colonel," said Mr. Bennet. "In fact, thank you all for your assistance with that scoundrel."

"It was no trouble, Mr. Bennet," said Fitzwilliam, baring his teeth with a sardonic grin. "Though Darcy here had all but forgotten of Wickham's existence, I always suspected that he would appear in our lives again. The opportunity to deal with him for good was one which was too good to simply pass up."

Mr. Bennet, chuckled and shifted slightly, causing Miss Lydia to stretch her legs a little and moan in response. Mr. Bennet patted her shoulder and she quickly settled into sleep again.

"Then I suppose you should thank me—or my daughter—for the opportunity which presented itself."

"I shall thank her as soon as may be."

Shaking his head, Darcy could only laugh at the two men. It seemed they were kindred spirits, and Darcy further suspected that Mr. Bennet would get on well with the earl. The source of Miss Bennet's own sense of humor and intelligence were also revealed—she had mentioned her closeness with her father on several occasions, and Darcy did not doubt that this man had served as the primary influence on her character. Darcy could only thank him for raising such an exceptional woman.

The men settled into quiet conversation as they waited for the carriage to arrive. But it was not long before the talk settled due to their collective fatigue. It was, after all, very late, and none of them had yet retired to their beds that evening. The innkeeper had brought them a pot of tea at some point, but though they had partaken of some soon after its arrival, it now lay cooling and forgotten in the rough cups which had been provided. Bingley it appeared had nodded off, and the colonel was leaning back against the table behind him, his eyes closed—Fitzwilliam was able to sleep in any location, no doubt a skill learned during the many campaigns he had been a part of. For Darcy's part, he was feeling a little sluggish himself.

"My daughter's letters have spoken volumes, Mr. Darcy," said Mr. Bennet, jolting Darcy from his languor. "I have long dreaded the day when I would lose my dearest Lizzy, but the way she speaks of you betrays her esteem."

"As I esteem her," said Darcy. "She is the best woman of my acquaintance."

"Then there is nothing more I can say," said Mr. Bennet. "As long as you care for her like she is your greatest treasure, I will be satisfied. What more could a father want for a beloved daughter?"

"What more indeed?" asked Darcy, thinking of his dear sister and his own dearest daughter Cassandra.

They lapsed into silence once more and Darcy was left with his own thoughts for company. Clearly, he had stumbled upon a singular family, one who did not consider consequence and gain over all other matters. Mr. Bennet had not once questioned him on his holdings, and the fact that he would love Miss Bennet trumped all other concerns. Though they were not of his sphere, Darcy thought he would like the Bennets and their relations very well indeed. Especially Mr. Bennet and the Gardiners.

Everything had been resolved in a satisfactory manner. Darcy was free to continue on with his plans to court, and eventually wed, Miss Bennet. There truly was nothing more that he could ask for.

Chapter XVI

In reality, it was not many more minutes before the sergeant appeared to report the arrival of the hired carriage. To those who had waited in the common room of the inn, it had seemed like it was longer, as it often does to those who are drifting in and out of sleep. Darcy rose with the rest upon being summoned, feeling little refreshed for the few moments in which he had slept, yet grateful for it given the hours in the saddle he was still required to face before he could seek his bed.

Mr. Bennet bustled Miss Lydia—barely awake and protesting—from the room and into the waiting carriage. Darcy passed some coins to the innkeeper for his troubles and went to his horse, and though he glared at his mount for some moments in distaste, he soon mounted and they were off.

"The way you scowled at your mount, I wondered if the poor animal had done anything to offend you," said Fitzwilliam as they rode behind the hired carriage.

Though he fixed Fitzwilliam with a hard look, Darcy thought to ignore his cousin. Unfortunately, Fitzwilliam was not about to allow it.

"Think of it this way, Darcy—it could be worse. You might have grown up a second son, entered the army, and spent many a night half asleep in the saddle, hoping that some Frenchman did not come upon you and empty his pistol into your head while your mind was still encased in fog. Furthermore, the results of the evening were positive indeed. Now you shall not be required to determine whether a scandal in the family will prevent you from offering for the delightful Miss Bennet. It seems to me you have much to be cheery about."

Shaking his head, William only spurred his horse on to get a little ahead of his cousin. Even that did not work, as Fitzwilliam kept pace with him.

"You are not considering holding this against her, are you?"

Darcy turned to his cousin, seeing the frown Fitzwilliam was directing at him.

"I was not," said Darcy. "In fact, I think I might have married Miss Bennet, regardless of the outcome of our search for Miss Lydia. That did not stop her from offering to release me from any obligation."

A low whistle floated up through the air, and Darcy turned and looked at his cousin askance.

"I do not know what to be more astonished by," said Fitzwilliam. "Your insinuation suggests you have a secret agreement with Miss Bennet, which is most unlike you. But that might pale beside the fact that there is a woman in the world who would not hold onto you—and consequently your fortune—regardless of any other concern."

"And yet *she* is such a woman," said Darcy. "She is far more concerned about her happiness and my own to care two figs for my fortune. And as for any 'secret engagement,' it is nothing more than an agreement to enter into a courtship. We have not yet informed anyone because Miss Bennet's mother is . . . excitable. She did not wish to become the center of attention so quickly."

"You had better snap her up, Darcy," said Fitzwilliam. "Any other woman from whom you requested a courtship would spread it far and wide. Miss Bingley would have ordered her wedding clothes had you even glanced at her from across a ballroom."

"I fully intend to," said Darcy, quietly. "There is no other woman her equal in London or anywhere else."

Fitzwilliam slapped him on the back and congratulated him, and then kicked his horse to the front of the column to confer with his sergeant, leaving Darcy with his thoughts. And he had pleasurable thoughts indeed.

The journey back to London was accomplished swiftly, and Darcy retired for a few hours for some much needed sleep. He awoke early that afternoon feeling much refreshed, and dressed for the day, as there was still much to be done. His first task was to speak with his cousin Fitzwilliam concerning the disposition of one George Wickham. It was fortunate, then, that Fitzwilliam had arrived at his house not long after Darcy arose to bring him that news.

Darcy watched as his cousin entered and flopped onto a chair in front of Darcy's desk. Though Darcy thought Fitzwilliam had not slept—or had slept very little—he seemed little affected by that fact as he was grinning and seemingly happy. He soon made the reason for his enthusiasm known.

"It is settled, though one might wonder at the speed at which the decision has been made," said Fitzwilliam. "Of course, father's influence was beneficial, but I had not thought to see generals make decisions so quickly."

"And what has been decided?" asked Darcy.

"Wickham has been discharged in disgrace for deserting his regiment. But your suggestion of transportation to the New World has been met with approval, so long as he is not given the means to return."

"What if he manages to obtain the necessary means?"

Fitzwilliam snorted with derision. "If you put five pounds in his pocket when he boards the ship, I do not doubt it will be gone ere the first night passes. The man's ability with the cards or dice has never been as great as he believes, and I do not doubt that will serve him ill when he arrives in the Americas. Or even before, I would imagine.

"Regardless, there will be a warrant issued for his arrest. Should he ever be found to have returned to England, the warrant shall be enforced and he will be detained."

Darcy nodded. "Then that is well enough. When can he be put aboard a ship?"

A sardonic grin spread over his cousin's face. "That is the best part. There is a ship leaving London tomorrow, bound for New York. Wickham will be on it, and it will not cost you the money for his passage. The war office has decided to pay it, as Wickham is our responsibility as a militia officer."

"Then it is all settled," said Darcy with a sigh.

"Do not blame yourself, Darcy," said Fitzwilliam. He eyed Darcy pointedly and continued: "Wickham has made his own choices, and you—more than anyone—are aware that most of those choices were less than ideal."

"I am not blaming myself, Fitzwilliam. I was merely reflecting on the fact that it is an ignominious fate for my father's favorite. Wickham could have been so much more. It is all so senseless."

Fitzwilliam only shrugged. "You cannot force the horse to drink from the trough. You knew what he was by the time he was fifteen. He has walked the path *he* chose in life. If it has led him to less than desirable ends, it is his own responsibility."

For the next half hour or so, Darcy and Fitzwilliam spoke of that and other matters, and at the end, Fitzwilliam left, citing a need to return to his barracks. It was just as well, as Darcy had other matters to which he needed to attend.

He departed the house after Fitzwilliam left, and within a few moments he had arrived at his uncle's house and been escorted into the earl's study. There, Darcy, after a brief exchange of pleasantries, introduced the subject he had come to discuss—whether his uncle would withdraw his blessing from Darcy's attachment to Miss Bennet.

When he brought up the subject, Uncle Hugh actually watched Darcy with some amusement.

"Tell me, Darcy, would it matter at all if I told you now I disapprove of Miss Bennet and her family?"

"Not in the slightest," replied Darcy. "My heart is engaged, and I have decided that I shall wed Miss Bennet, if she will have me."

"Then I do not know why you wish to canvass my opinion," said the earl. "You are your own man and you will conduct your affairs in a manner which is pleasing to you."

"But I would not wish to cause strife in the family."

The earl regarded him with a shrewd smile. "Or perhaps any more strife than marrying a woman *not* chosen by your aunt will already provoke?"

"I do not care about Lady Catherine's feelings on the subject," said Darcy, albeit a trifle shortly. "I have already broken with the woman and I will not bow down to her wishes, as I have already made plain."

"I did not think you would." The earl fell silent for a moment, and then he sighed and looked Darcy in the eye. "I will not lie and tell you I am not concerned about the actions of this silly sister of your Miss Bennet. But for herself, Miss Bennet is a lovely woman. It will be up to her father to control his daughter, and perhaps this will provide the impetus to ensure she is handled properly."

"She has likely learned a valuable lesson from the experience," said Darcy. "Young ladies in society are often not educated as to the dangers of such men as Wickham. They are coddled far too much. I expect Miss Lydia now knows of the precarious nature of her situation."

"Then it is settled," said the earl. "If your Mr. Bennet would like, I believe Susan would agree to assist. Perhaps the girl can join you and your wife after you are married. She can only benefit from seeing Georgiana's example."

Though Darcy was of two minds of the prospect—Georgiana was a good girl, but the influence had the potential to go *both* ways—he agreed and soon departed. His next stop was to be the Gardiner townhouse, the location of which he had learned from Bingley before parting that morning.

The Caroline Bingleys of the world likely thought that Darcy had never visited a place as common as Gracechurch Street near Cheapside, but Darcy was actually familiar with several parts of the neighborhood, as his solicitor's offices were in the area. The street on which the Gardiner residence was situated was filled with houses that were handsome and well maintained, and if they were not as large and imposing as those in Mayfair, still they were appropriate for their residents' situations. The Gardiner townhouse was a little larger than most, with a stone façade and a warm and welcoming feel that he immediately recognized when he was allowed inside. Darcy presented his card to the housekeeper and soon he was led to the parlor, there to greet the occupants.

Mr. and Mrs. Gardiner were both there, as was Mr. Bennet, his three daughters who were in London, and Bingley. Darcy was greeted with enthusiasm from those in the room, and he entered and sat with them, instantly being made to feel at home among them. It seemed that they were in a cheery mood, other than Miss Lydia who was looking rather chastened. It appeared the fear of God had been placed in the girl's breast, and her manners, so open and forceful the night before, were reflecting that change.

Once the greetings were exchanged and the pleasantries dealt with, they settled down to the business of Darcy's visit. The first subject, unsurprisingly, was the disposition of the author of Miss Lydia's changed circumstances.

"What can you tell us of what is to happen to Lieutenant Wickham?"

Darcy turned to Mr. Bennet, from whence the question had arisen, and said, "I believe that matter has been resolved to everyone's satisfaction."

Then he went on to detail the results of his cousin's efforts that day, explaining that Wickham was to be gone on the morrow, and what measures had been taken to ensure his stay in the Americas would be permanent. That they were all relieved by the news was evident, but Darcy was surprised by Miss Lydia's reaction most of all.

"Thank you, Mr. Darcy," said Miss Lydia. Her manners were still subdued and her countenance downcast—she would not even raise her eyes from the carpet at her feet—but her words were heartfelt and sincere. "I am happy you and my father—and Mr. Bingley and the colonel, of course—were able to find me last night. I have behaved foolishly."

Darcy wondered at her change of heart; he would have thought she would be inclined to fight to have her own way, confessing no wrong, and yet here she was thanking him in a sincere manner for his assistance. Someone had been persuasive indeed.

"You are very welcome, Miss Lydia. I trust you have learned something from these events?"

"Oh, yes, Mr. Darcy," exclaimed Miss Lydia. "I surely have."

A laugh nearly burst forth, but Darcy suppressed it in a cough. It appeared that her high spirits were in no way extinguished. In fact, Darcy was happy that was the case—as he had reflected the previous evening, she was not a bad girl, merely one in need of guidance. He surprised himself when he realized he had become attached to her the previous evening. He would hope her spirits would be tempered by a mature outlook and an expanded knowledge of the world, not be beaten from her by the hands of one such as George Wickham.

"I had never thought to say this," said Mr. Bennet, looking fondly on his youngest daughter, "but I am happy to hear you speaking sense. Now we shall need to work on Kitty to effect such a transformation ion her manners as well."

Miss Lydia flushed, but she also beamed with pleasure, even considering the somewhat backhanded compliment Mr. Bennet had given her. Perhaps all the girl had needed was a little attention from a father who she obviously loved. That Mr. Bennet also loved his daughters was evident, but his method of expressing himself was through teasing. It was not precisely the way Darcy might have behaved, but he could understand that a man might not be comfortable displaying his feelings for all to see.

"And have you decided how to minimize the rumors of last night's events?" asked Darcy.

Mr. Bennet nodded. "For now, Lydia will stay with the Gardiners, though I believe at times she will visit the Bingleys as well. However, it has been made clear that she *is not* out in London, and as such she will not attend society events with her elder sisters."

At that declaration a scowl fell over the girl's face followed by a pout. But she displayed no further reaction, leading Darcy to believe the matter had been made clear to her prior to Darcy's arrival, and that an overt display of rebellion would not be tolerated.

"Perhaps during your stay you might consent to be introduced to my sister, Georgiana," said Darcy, hoping he was not making a mistake.

Miss Lydia's eyes lit up and she squealed with pleasure. "I believe I should like that very well indeed, Mr. Darcy!"

"Then it is settled. Georgiana shall be quite happy to make your acquaintance."

The conversation then turned to other matters and Darcy noticed that Miss Lydia added little to it, as she seemed to be caught in dreamy contemplations of the delights which awaited her introduction to his sister. He made a note to remind himself to make it clear that Georgiana herself was *not* yet out, and that she did not participate in society at present.

After some time in conversation passed, Darcy suggested that they all walk out to the park situated near to the Gardiners' home, a plan which was agreed to by alacrity with the younger members of the party. Mr. Bennet declared his preference to sit in his brother's study with a good book, and Mr. Gardiner indicated his need to return to his office to finish the business of the day. As for Mrs. Gardiner, she declined, saying her children were down for their afternoon naps and she wished to be nearby when they awoke. Everyone else, however, donned their coats, bonnets, hats, and gloves, and departed from the house.

The park was only a short distance from the Gardiner townhouse, and the walk was enjoyable, as the air was warm and the day was fine. While Bingley and his wife walked on ahead, Darcy found himself escorting the two younger ladies, which was no hardship at all—the talk was lively, the ladies bright and pretty, and Darcy found himself enjoying the walk very well indeed.

Miss Lydia swung her free arm as they walked, skipping occasionally, and her chatter was enthusiastic and pleasing. And if her spirits were a little exuberant, overall her demeanor was proper enough that he thought it beneficial to simply tolerate her high spirits—better for her to release pent up energy on a walk than to do it in a crowded London sitting room. Miss Bennet apparently felt the same way, for she watched her sister with a hint of indulgence mixed with exasperation—he expected that it was a common reaction to her sister's behavior, but in this instance there was truly nothing to censure her for. The fact that she had recovered from her experience so quickly was no less than astonishing.

"I will be so happy to make your sister's acquaintance, Mr. Darcy," prattled Lydia as they walked. "Lizzy has told me what a lovely lady she is. I hope I shall not be too embarrassed when we are introduced."

Privately, Darcy could not imagine Miss Lydia being embarrassed about *anything*, but he smiled at her and said: "She will be happy to make your acquaintance too, Miss Lydia. But I should not worry about her approbation; she is a lovely girl, though I will own my opinion is undoubtedly biased, but she is also reticent."

"We shall have so much fun together! I can hardly wait."

Darcy fixed a stern look on the girl, mixed with fondness. "And so you shall. But you must remember that Georgiana is *not* yet out, and thus you will not be attending balls and parties. The theater can perhaps be arranged."

"Oh, the theater is Lizzy's idea of fun," said Miss Lydia. Then she paused, before she continued to speak, saying: "But perhaps it is something I should pay more attention to. I shall need *something* to fill my time now that my father has forbidden me to go into society."

"I dare say it would be in your best interest to broaden your horizons. There is much in this world which is of interest—not everything need center around dancing."

"I would have expected you to say such a thing, Mr. Darcy," said Miss Bennet with a laugh. "Especially given how much you dislike the amusement in general."

A look of utter horror fell over Miss Lydia's face. "You do not like to dance, Mr. Darcy?"

The incredulous note in her voice induced a laugh, but Miss Lydia was not amused. She glared at him with an imperious impatience which reminded him of his aunt.

"I believe Miss Bennet is stating opinions which are not *my* own, Miss Lydia," said Darcy. "I cannot count dancing as my favorite activity, but I am not opposed to it either. I prefer to be well acquainted with my partner when I do dance, as I do not find it easy to make new acquaintances. Besides, dancing is often a tool used by those who wish to move up in society, and I detest those who have nothing more than social standing and money in mind."

Miss Lydia cocked her head to the side and looked at Darcy in obvious puzzlement. "What do you mean?"

Pausing for a moment, Darcy considered his response, knowing he had stumbled upon an opportunity to teach her something of society. A glance at Miss Bennet revealed her curiosity as to how he would handle it, and he smiled at her before directing his attention back at Miss Lydia.

"There are people in society who desire advancement above all other things. Mr. Wickham was one of those, though his method of obtaining that which he desires is much more reprehensible than most."

Shamed cheeks blooming, Miss Lydia looked away. "And I followed in with his schemes. I wish . . . Well, it is evident I must be more discerning in the future."

"Miss Lydia."

The sternness of his voice mixed with kindness, brought her eyes back to his face, and he was surprised to see tears pooling in the corners of her eyes.

"Do not be too hard on yourself. You were deceived by a man who has practiced deceit all his life. What is important is for you to learn from this experience so that you might make a better decision next time."

Miss Lydia nodded while she brought up a hand to dash the tears from her eyes.

"Mr. Wickham is not the only person who uses such things for his own gain, though I suspect you know that he was not trying to make his fortune with you."

"I know *exactly* what Mr. Wickham wanted from me," said Miss Lydia.

"Then you are already wiser. But you also must know that there are many in society who lust after the same things as Wickham. There are many stratagems which are undertaken by such people to gain what they want. You must learn to differentiate between those who genuinely wish to know you from those who merely wish to profit from you."

"But Mr. Darcy," said Miss Lydia, "I have not fortune nor connections to recommend me. Surely I will not be a target for such a person."

"It is true you do not possess fortune, but you have a new brother in Bingley, do you not? Bingley is not of the highest levels of society himself, but he possesses a personal fortune to be envied. A connection to him would be worth much to certain others."

Though she nodded, Miss Lydia soon turned a speculative eye on her companions. "And might there perhaps not also be a connection to *you* Mr. Darcy? Or do my eyes deceive me?"

At his other side, Darcy could see Miss Bennet color out of the corner of his eye, even as she exclaimed: "Lydia!"

"Well, it is not difficult to see!" said Miss Lydia with a huff. "I saw the way you looked at each other when Mr. Darcy entered the room."

Darcy shared a glance with Miss Bennet, noting her embarrassment. He was surprised that Miss Lydia had shown such perception. He had thought he was being circumspect in his admiration for Miss Bennet.

"Miss Lydia, I do admire your sister," said Darcy.

Before he could say anything further, she squealed and darted over to embrace her sister. For her part, Miss Bennet returned the embrace with more decorum, and a hint of indulgence.

"I knew it!" exclaimed Miss Lydia. "In fact, I thought it last night when you found me in that horrid little inn."

Somehow Darcy thought she exaggerated, but her continued babbling allowed him no opportunity to speak further. It was some moments before her chattering slowed.

"Oh, I must speak with Jane!" said Miss Lydia at last. "For I know she must be so happy for you, since you have always been so close."

"Lydia, we have not announced anything concerning the matter yet."

Miss Lydia's eyes widened. "A secret courtship," said she with a gasp. "I would not have thought you would do such a thing."

"It is not a secret," said Darcy quickly, hoping to remove such a thought from her mind. "Your father knows of our attachment and I have his permission."

Miss Bennet regarded him with surprise at such a statement, but she soon turned back to her sister again. "As Mr. Darcy said, we are not engaging in anything of a clandestine nature. But for the moment we do not wish for mama to know."

That brought Miss Lydia up short. "I had not thought of that. Mama would make a big fuss, would she not?"

"Can you doubt it? Think of what happened when Mr. Bingley proposed to Jane."

A grimace settled over Miss Lydia's countenance. "I see what you mean. Very well, I shall keep your secret from mama. But surely we can tell Jane and Mr. Bingley."

This time it was Elizabeth's turn to color, and she looked up at Mr. Darcy shyly. "I am afraid they already know. I apologize, Mr. Darcy, but Jane saw our farewell last night and she would not rest until she knew the particulars."

Darcy regarded her with a smile of his own. "I am not upset, Miss Bennet. I was planning on telling Bingley myself."

"Then I may speak to Jane of the matter without fear!" cried Miss Lydia, and she turned and began to walk away, her pace hurried.

Before she had continued far, however, she halted and turned, looking at Darcy and Elizabeth, a hint of uncharacteristic shyness in her manner. It took her a few moments to find the words she wished to say—or perhaps work up the courage to say them—but when she did, she looked directly at Darcy.

"I am sure I will enjoy having you for a brother very well indeed, Mr.

Darcy. I thank you for helping my father and Mr. Bingley last night, for I doubt my prospects would be nearly so bright if you had not found me."

And with that, Miss Lydia turned away and hurried to catch up with the Bingleys. Darcy was amused to see that the girl was actually skipping as she went, a sight which caused a low giggle to sound beside him.

Darcy turned and looked at Miss Bennet's well-loved face, noting the way she watched her sister, her eyes crinkling at the corners displaying her amusement. It appeared he was to gain several happy and bright people as relations, and though he might once have arrogantly disparaged their situation in life, he now found that he could not wait to lead this woman to the altar. It was a bright future indeed.

"I must own to a little curiosity, Mr. Darcy," said Miss Bennet when they were alone. "How did the subject of our understanding come up with my father?"

"By much the same means as it came up with *your sister*," replied Darcy. "For did she not see something in your manners which alerted her to your feelings?"

"But that is completely different, Mr. Darcy," protested Miss Bennet. "Jane and I are as close as sisters can be, whereas you only met my father last night."

"By his own admission it seems like he also gleaned something from your letters in which you mentioned both my sister and myself."

As Darcy was watching for Miss Bennet's reaction, he was not disappointed to see a blush spread over her cheeks. It was then he decided a little teasing was in order.

"Of course, he might have seen my inspection of Miss Lydia last night and guessed as to its meaning."

The way Miss Bennet's eyes whipped to him was comical, and the astonishment with which she regarded him further increased his amusement.

"Lydia?"

"She *is* a handsome young girl, Miss Bennet. And perhaps more importantly, she truly resembles you, whereas neither of you resemble your eldest sister to any great degree."

In an instant the blush was back in place, and Darcy laughed, noting that Miss Bennet's blushes were very fetching indeed. He looked forward to a lifetime of provoking them.

"You are quite correct," said Miss Bennet once she had mastered her reaction to his words. "Lydia and I do look alike, and my second youngest sister, Kitty, resembles Jane much more closely. Only my middle sister, Mary, does not truly look like any of us, though it is easy to tell that she is her father's daughter."

"I shall look forward to making their acquaintance, Miss Bennet."

Miss Bennet laughed. "You might someday regret that sentiment, sir. We are a disparate group, and I do not doubt that we might be overwhelming for someone of your reticent nature."

"Would you call my uncle or cousins reticent, Miss Bennet? I am quite accustomed to dealing with those of higher spirits, I assure you.

"Furthermore, I will own that I have become quite attached to Miss Lydia in the short time I have known her. Of course her exuberance can be a trial, but I believe that she will be a delightful girl when that liveliness is tempered by restraint. And I believe she will be very good for Georgiana who is, as you know, quite shy."

Mischief twinkled in Miss Bennet's eyes. "Perhaps you have paid your attentions to the wrong Bennet sister, sir."

"No, Miss Bennet," said Darcy, gazing at her steadily and noticing her softening expression in response. "I am quite aware of who is best suited to become my future wife. Though I have high hopes for Miss Lydia's future, I have no desire to redirect my attentions."

"I am quite happy to hear it, Mr. Darcy."

They walked on in silence for some time. Ahead of them, Bingley and his wife walked along the path with Miss Lydia in tow, listening indulgently as she chattered happily. There was nothing further he could want at this time, and Darcy could not be happier about where he had ended up in his life. There had been hardship and sorrow, and he knew he would have been fortunate to live with Cassandra forever as his wife. But life had a way of changing, propelling one toward a path which they would not otherwise of trodden, and though the sorrow had gripped Darcy in its claws for longer than he should have allowed, he was now free of it, able to live his life to the fullest again. And he did not doubt that his life with the woman by his side would be full indeed.

"Miss Bennet," said Darcy, breaking the silence which had sprung up between them, "I find that I must say . . ."

Miss Bennet looked up at him as he paused, and for a brief moment he fought to steady the font of emotion which had sprung up within his breast. She watched him as he did, seeming to sense what he wished to say. He thought she felt all that he did. The knowledge allowed him to smile and find his voice once again.

"I merely wished to declare myself right now, Miss Bennet. I love you so very dearly. I anticipate the day when we might finally be joined in matrimony. But I want you to be in no doubt of my feelings. The timing is completely at your discretion. I only hope you do not make me wait too long."

A laugh met his declaration, and Miss Bennet reached up to touch his face with one gloved hand. Darcy caught her hand in his own and turned it over, pressing a kiss against her palm. She sighed in pleasure, and Darcy anticipated a time when he would do the same thing to her bare hand instead of kissing it through her glove.

"I can hardly wait for it myself. Do not fear a long wait. I find that I am little inclined for such a thing myself."

"That is well indeed."

He gathered her hand again and placed it on his arm, holding it there with his free hand. And they walked along the path, following dear friends and beloved sisters. Overhead birds sang their joyous song of the renewal of spring.

The next day dawned dark and damp, and the weather fit the circumstances quite well indeed, for it would see the end of an association with the Darcy family; this separation would be of a permanent nature.

Though Darcy still harbored ambivalent feelings concerning George Wickham and his place in the history of the Darcy family, there was no such ambiguity about the need for Wickham to make a new start in life in a location far from England. As a young child who had been his constant companion, Darcy had loved the boy, even as he had loathed what the man had become.

Darcy hoped that Wickham would take this opportunity for learning and use the gentleman's education he had received due to the Darcy family's largesse, and make something of himself. Opportunities to build one's fortune were rife in the New World, and Wickham, as an intelligent man—Darcy could allow his former friend that much—could raise himself quite high should he only apply himself.

Unfortunately, effort had always been the issue with Wickham—he was much more interested in having everything handed to him than to work for his daily bread. And life in the New World would require a man to work, as it was much less civilized there than in England.

Breakfast was a somber affair. Georgiana had nothing but fond memories of George Wickham, as he had often taken the time to amuse and play with her. The knowledge of the kind of life he had led saddened her affectionate heart,

Soon Darcy took leave of his sister and entered his carriage, directing the driver to convey him to the docks, and he sat back as the carriage lurched into motion. The streets of London were already teeming with all manner of denizens, workers hurrying along their way, horses, carts, and carriages weaving in and out of the congested streets, mothers and their children walking in the coolness of the morning, and street vendors, crying out their wares to passersby. In all it felt like a normal spring morning.

When he arrived, Darcy took up his hat and his walking stick and exited the carriage, noting the stark reality of the ship sitting alongside a nearby dock. Sailors swarmed over the hull and rigging, checking and double-checking the sails and lines, calling out to one another in rough voices and caustic tones. The captain stood on the deck watching the activity, occasionally calling out to one of his sailors. It looked like it was a well-run ship, a sturdy ship, in which the journey across the ocean might be made quickly and in safety.

"Darcy!"

Turning at the sound of his voice, Darcy noted the approach of his grinning cousin. Fitzwilliam stepped forward and slapped him on the back in greeting.

"I had thought you might stay away."

Darcy shook his head. "I owe it to my father. He saw in Wickham the potential for so much more than he became."

The look Fitzwilliam gave him was severe. "You do not owe him anything, Darcy."

Darcy shrugged. At that moment a wagon pulled up with soldiers in tight escort. It appeared the army was taking no chances that Wickham would be able to escape. When the procession had halted there was some activity around the wagon, and soon the back was opened and the prisoner emerged.

Wickham was much as Darcy had ever remembered him—charming and witty, as he spoke to the soldiers, a hint of the old Wickham who was able to charm all and sundry and on short acquaintance. But Darcy, who knew Wickham better than most—even after having been estranged for more than five years—noted the undertone of uncertainty and even fear which permeated his being. The prospect of the unknown positively petrified Wickham.

When he caught sight of Darcy, Wickham's affected smile slipped a bit, but he quickly recovered and turned in Darcy's direction, with his escort's permission.

"Hello Darcy!" said he when he had approached. "Have you come to see me off? I dare not hope you have come to commute the sentence upon the damned."

"No, Wickham," said Darcy, though he directed a slight smile on his onetime friend. "I believe that new start in America is what you need. And even if I *was* inclined, I have no power over the situation any longer. As you are aware, the army has a say in this matter now. I am afraid that America is now your future."

Wickham nodded sagely, and seemingly without any surprise. "I suppose I have no choice. In that case, I bid you farewell, for I doubt we shall meet again."

"One moment, Wickham," said Darcy as Wickham began to turn away. "I have something for you here."

Darcy held out an envelope to his friend which Wickham eyed for a moment before he looked up at Darcy.

"What is that?"

"It is a note for one hundred pounds which you may obtain when you arrive in New York City. Take the note to the address listed in the interior, and they will provide you with one hundred pounds. That should allow you to make a good start in the New World. What you do after that is your own business.

"But remember," said Darcy sternly, when Wickham looked on him with wonder, "this is the last money you will see from the Darcy family. Make it count, Wickham, and do not gamble it away."

Wickham stared at Darcy for several moments, emotions moving across his face one after another. He seemed to be caught in some well of feeling which he had never before experienced.

"You would give this to me, even after all that has happened."

"You are my father's godson, Wickham," said Darcy. "You are well aware of my opinion of the way you have lived your life, but I have no desire to see you suffer. If this money will help provide you with an advantage when you arrive in the New World, then I am happy to do it."

For the first time since they were children, Wickham smiled in a genuine manner. "Thank you, Darcy. You are a good man. I shall do my best to make you proud."

"See that you do, Wickham. And a word every now and then as to your doings would not be amiss."

Nodding, Wickham replied, "Should there be something to report, I will be happy to do so."

Then turning, Wickham crossed the gangplank to the ship, and with a single jaunty wave, he disappeared below decks. Fitzwilliam and Darcy stood and watched as the final preparations were completed and the ship cast off. Soon it was out in the middle of the harbor where it turned to the south for the journey through the English Channel and to the Atlantic Ocean beyond. Wickham was now gone from his life forever. Darcy hardly knew what to think.

"I knew you would not allow Wickham to leave with nothing more than the clothes on his back."

Darcy turned to his cousin and shrugged. "What I said to him is the truth. My father held him in high esteem. He would have wanted me to do this."

"Your father only held him in esteem because you did not illuminate him as to Wickham's character."

"Do you think my father would have thrown him off if he knew?"

"If you thought your father would have attempted to see to his reformation, why did you not tell him?"

Darcy grimaced. "Perhaps I should have. At the time, however, I did not wish to cause my father heartache by informing him of his favorite's character. Now I am older and wiser, and I might have behaved differently then had I known what I know now."

"It is the way of life, Darcy. If we possessed the wisdom of old age as youngsters, our lives would undoubtedly be much easier."

"Of that I am certain," said Darcy.

The cousins stood watching the ship for some time longer, until it became nothing more than a speck on the horizon and ultimately disappeared from view. When it had, they turned by common consent and began to walk from the docks. Darcy offered his cousin a seat in his carriage, which Fitzwilliam accepted with gratitude.

"Back to your lovely almost-betrothed?" asked Fitzwilliam in a teasing tone.

"Yes," said Darcy. "I could not be happier, I assure you."

Epilogue

The master's study at Pemberley had been Darcy's retreat for many years. It was a large, bright, and handsome room, filled with generations of Pemberley's management records, treatises on farming, and personal favorite volumes which the master would sometimes indulge in when he was not busy with the business of the estate.

Darcy occupied the room one morning, going over some reports of his various investments, but he knew it would not be long before he was interrupted. There was too much happening for his solitude to remain unchallenged, and he knew of one in particular who would undoubtedly decide that talk of lace and finery was too much. In fact, he suspected that the person would insist upon riding out on the estate as an escape.

Chuckling, Darcy sat back in his chair, his reports forgotten in favor of his reminiscences of the recent years of his life. Indeed, life had been kind to him in the last fourteen years, and other than the usual vexations and trials which came with life, he found that he could not complain. He was a healthy, robust, and active sort of man at the age of two and forty, and he had a good and happy woman for a wife, who made his days a pleasure, and filled his nights with passion. There was nothing more he could want in his life.

Children had, of course, followed their marriage, providing Cassandra with siblings and playmates, and the girl had blossomed under Elizabeth's care and attention, growing into a lady who would be much sought after in the coming season. The two were practically inseparable, Elizabeth providing love and guidance, while Cassandra looked up to her as a mother—indeed, Cassandra had never addressed her by any other title.

Thus, Pemberley's halls echoed with the sounds of children, laughter, and the patter of running feet, and Darcy could not be happier. Even now Elizabeth was only four and thirty, so he imagined that they might still be blessed with more children. Darcy was content to take life as it was presented to him, a sharp contrast from those desolate years after he had lost Cassandra.

The sound of running footsteps interrupted Darcy's musings, and soon the door was pushed open and a young boy rushed in. He was tall, much like his father, and on his head was a mop of mahogany hair, unkempt and wild. It seemed he preferred it that way, and he could rarely be induced to brush it. He was perhaps the most serious of the Darcy children, though he also possessed a healthy measure of Elizabeth's playful character as well, though not as much as his sisters did.

"Father!" exclaimed the boy when he had gained the inside of his father's sanctuary. "This talk of lace and other finery will drive me mad!"

"You know your mother is preparing for your sister's coming out next season," said Darcy to the boy mildly. "And do you not recall that you should knock on my study door before you enter?"

His son did not appear to be chastened in the slightest. "But father, when Cassandra begins to speak of dressing *me* up in her finery, that is when it becomes too much to endure. Shall we not ride out?"

Smiling at how he had accurately predicted his son's response, Darcy shook his head. "I am sorry, Robert, but I believe you shall be required to wait. You know that your cousins will be arriving this afternoon. Surely you can amuse yourself until then."

A sullen stare met Darcy's suggestion, causing him to laugh again. It was difficult at times for Robert, he mused. At eleven he was intelligent and talented in many things, but having so many sisters made him long for another boy his age with whom to play. But Darcy and Elizabeth had been blessed primarily with daughters. When Elizabeth's first daughter, Lily Jane, had been born, Cassandra had been ecstatic to have a playmate. Robert had received no such blessings as the next three births had all been daughters. Now that he had actually obtained the long-awaited brother, little two-year-old William was much too young to engage in the activities Robert preferred.

Darcy tried to be as much of a companion to his son as he could manage, but there were times when that was difficult, as the estate and other matters required his attention on a constant basis. There were few other boys in the area with whom Robert could associate, and as a result, the visits of his cousins were always long awaited when they were to come, and long mourned when they left.

"Very well, Robert," said Darcy, taking pity on the boy. After all, there was nothing holding his attention anyway. "Let us ride for an hour or so until luncheon."

Robert whooped and turned to run from the room.

"I shall meet you at the stables, Robert," called Darcy after him.

"I shall be waiting!" the boy's voice floated back to the study.

Shaking his head with fond amusement, Darcy set about tidying up his desk. When that was complete, he left the study to make his way toward the sitting-room where he knew he would be able to find his wife and his eldest daughter, and as he walked he considered those whose lives were so intertwined with his own.

The Fitzwilliams and the Bingleys were both to arrive today, and they both boasted young boys who were of age with Robert. His cousin, Anthony—formerly Colonel Fitzwilliam—had inherited an estate from a great uncle, and had indeed married Miss Patterson, much to the delight of his mother. Their felicity was a wonderful sight to see, and Darcy was content to know his cousin was happy in his marriage, when he had at times worried that Fitzwilliam would not return home at all.

As for the Bingleys, Bingley was as jovial as ever, Mrs. Bingley was serene and beautiful, and now had several of her own children to her name. And Miss Bingley had met a man who had paid her the attention she craved—in fact, Darcy found out later it was the man who he had seen her speaking with the night of his aunt's ball—and she had also married. Though Caroline Powell, as she was now called, was not a close acquaintance, they still saw her and her husband on occasion. Darcy found he could tolerate her presence now. Mr. Hurst was happy, as his wife had given him two sons, and he had furthermore been able to keep Darcy's friendship and, more importantly, access to his wine cellar.

As for others of their families, the earl had married Lady Alice and produced several children, and Uncle Hugh and Aunt Susan, though they were becoming quite aged, were still hale and hearty. The Bennets were also still at their estate of Longbourn, and if Mrs. Bennet was still a silly woman, the marriages of all her children and the promises she had received that she would be cared for should the worst come to pass, had softened her manners to the point where she was at least tolerable, though not with any great frequency.

Mr. Bennet was another matter. Darcy truly esteemed his father-in-law, as he was an intelligent man, invariably good-natured, if a little sarcastic. Perhaps most importantly, Darcy could tell that he loved Elizabeth very much. Their children enjoyed the time they spent with their Bennet grandparents.

As for Elizabeth's other sisters, Mary had married a parson and lived a county over in Nottingham, and Catherine had married the owner of a small estate in Dorset. She was the only one of the family who lived at such a great distance, and as a result, they saw her infrequently.

The youngest Miss Bennet was the longest to hold onto the name of her birth. Miss Lydia had largely lived with the Darcys and the Bingleys after her attempted elopement, and her improvement had been great. As Darcy had expected, Lydia and Georgiana had hit it off immediately and had soon been as close as sisters. Lydia had submitted to his decree that she was not out in town without any protest, and three years later, both young ladies had come out into London society together. The experience had proven beneficial, not only for the young ladies, but for Darcy and Elizabeth, as it had prepared them for the day when Cassandra and their other daughters, would eventually have their own debuts.

Luckily for Darcy's sanity, neither had found a young man who impressed them enough to marry, and they had both stayed that way for their first three seasons after their debuts. Then Georgiana had found a young man she could not live without, marrying and moving into her own home with her new husband. During the period of her honeymoon, Lydia had once again lived with the Darcys, and though she was happy for Georgiana's good fortune, Darcy and Elizabeth had easily seen that she was melancholy, not only for the distance between her and her confidante, but also for her inability to find her own man she could love and respect.

As fate would have it, Georgiana invited Lydia to live with her after her marriage, which Lydia had resisted for some time, due to her desire to allow her sister by marriage time alone with her new husband. But once Lydia had finally been persuaded, Georgiana introduced her to a young man who immediately became infatuated with her and they married, all within a few months of Lydia joining her sister at her new home. Needless to say, Georgiana had delighted in teasing Lydia, claiming she could have found her happiness much sooner if she had only accepted the invitation. Regardless, both lived within fifty miles of

Pemberley, and were often to be found there, or in each other's company.

It was also fortunate that Wickham was never seen again in the country of his birth after the day he had embarked on the ship for the Americas. Though he had promised to keep Darcy abreast of his doings, no letter had ever made its way back across the Atlantic, not that Darcy was surprised. He hoped that his one-time friend had managed to change his ways and make something of himself, but he was not confident Wickham had actually been able to overcome his vices.

When Darcy entered the sitting-room, it was to the sight he had expected—Cassandra, Elizabeth, and Lily were sitting close together, the table in front of them covered with fashion magazines, designs, and all manner of feminine accoutrements. Darcy had to suppress a chuckle; Elizabeth had never shown much interest in fashion of any kind, but the upcoming debut of their eldest seemed to fire her imagination. She could often be found with the two eldest girls poring over designs and patterns, and at times he had even caught her giggling with her daughters as if she were naught but a girl herself.

"Is something amusing you, husband?"

Apparently he had not been as successful as he thought at hiding his reaction to their close conference. Fortunately, Darcy had become adept at deflecting his perceptive wife's wit.

"I had a visit from Robert," said Darcy. "He appears to be distressed at your discussions of lace and other finery."

Lily actually rolled her eyes—she was at the age where she secretly found boys interesting, but professed them to be annoying, her brother most of all—while Cassandra and Elizabeth only looked at one another and laughed.

"He mentioned something about some sort of threat to dress him up in dresses too?"

Cassandra only laughed harder. "He insisted on interrupting us with comments about his horse and other matters, when we are trying to concentrate."

"He was quick to retreat!" said Lily, stifling a giggle of her own. "Uncle Anthony would have been proud at how quickly he led his company to safety."

There was nothing else to do but to join the ladies in laughter. Darcy could well imagine his son's behavior.

As quickly as he had gained their attention he lost it, as the ladies were soon poring over their magazines again, and the discussion of lace was restored. Darcy understood with an intimacy of experience what a gaggle of females in discussion of such subjects could do to a man, and he sympathized with Mr. Bennet, who had not even had the benefit of a son to break up the ever-present chatter in his house.

A pang entered Darcy's heart as he watched the ladies in their animated discussions, knowing that the upcoming introduction to society was only the first step in Cassandra's journey to adulthood. Soon, she would be the belle of every gathering, attracting the attention of young men who would seek to flatter her and woo her, and ultimately she would choose one of those young men, and accept a marriage proposal. Darcy would no longer be the most important man in her life.

The promise the girl had possessed as a young child of three was realized, and Darcy found himself looking at a confident, poised, and beautiful young lady. She looked so much like her mother that sometimes Darcy could imagine that he was talking with her mother. The heartache at the loss of his first wife had long passed, however, and it was easy for Darcy to see that in his daughter, his first wife lived on. And she would have been proud of her daughter indeed.

Then Darcy's focus shifted to his second daughter, a gangly youth of thirteen who was beginning the change to a young woman. Lily resembled *her* mother quite closely, and would undoubtedly be as much sought after as her elder sister when she finally came out. Darcy felt himself fortunate that he had several more years with her before he was forced to face that eventuality.

"You appear to be deep in thought."

Darcy turned and smiled at his wife. He had not noticed when she had risen to approach him, so focused had he been on his daughters. She was the light of his life, and the one he knew would never leave him. He made it a point to tell her how much he loved her on a daily basis.

"Do we truly need to let her go?" asked Darcy, feeling a little wistful, and even a little sorrowful at the prospect.

"She will still be our daughter," said his wife, understanding instantly what he was saying. "Perhaps she might even be induced to settle close by."

"Perhaps," said Darcy. "But the very thought of a man taking our dearest Cassandra away . . ."

He could not finish the sentence, though Elizabeth instantly understood to what he was referring. Her answering laugh was like a balm to his soul.

"That is where women differ from men. You fear releasing her into the arms of another man while I am merely hopeful she will find a loving relationship like I have found myself. What more could we want for her?"

"You are correct, as always," conceded Darcy. He turned and smiled at his wife, putting all other thoughts from his mind. "If she can find a man who loves her as much as I love you, then I shall be very pleased indeed."

"There! Now you have something on which to think other than the thought of losing your daughter, absurd as such a thought might be."

Darcy looked down at his wife, noting the happy contentment, the amusement, and the solid dependability which was so much a part of her character. The years had changed her as they had changed him. Her face was a little more lined than it had been, though she was still as beautiful to him as she had ever been, and the rigors of childbirth had changed her body and added pleasing curves to her frame. She was the one who would never leave him. And Darcy was content.

The End

For Readers Who Liked Cassandra

A Bevy of Suitors
When a chance remark from Mr. Darcy causes Mr. Bingley to rethink which Bennet daughter he wishes to pursue, Elizabeth Bennet finds herself forced to choose from among a bevy of suitors.

A Summer in Brighton
Elizabeth is invited to travel to Brighton instead of Lydia with her dear friend Mrs. Forster. But what is supposed to be a relaxing vacation turns out to be anything but. Amid intrigues and newly discovered love, Elizabeth discovers that there exists in one man an evil so vile that it will drive him to do anything to hurt his hated enemy.

An Unlikely Friendship
Elizabeth Bennet has always possessed pride in her powers of discernment. She discovers, however, that first impressions are not always accurate.

Bound by Love
Lost as a young child, Elizabeth Bennet is found by the Darcys and raised by the family as a beloved daughter. Bound by love with the family of her adoption, she has no hint of what awaits her when she and Mr. Darcy join Mr. Bingley in Hertfordshire at his newly leased estate, Netherfield.

Implacable Resentment
A grudge forces Elizabeth Bennet from Longbourn, necessitating her removal to the Gardiners' home in London. Ten years later, she returns to Hertfordshire at the request of her father and learns that the prejudice has not subsided. Elizabeth must withstand her family's machinations if she is to have any hope of finding her happy ending.

Love and Laughter: A Pride and Prejudice Short Stories Anthology
Those who need a little love and laughter in their lives need look no further than this anthology, which gives a lighthearted look at beloved *Pride and Prejudice* characters in unique situations.

Also by One Good Sonnet Publishing

The Smothered Rose Trilogy

Book 1: Thorny

In this retelling of "Beauty and the Beast," a spoiled boy who is forced to watch over a flock of sheep finds himself more interested in catching the eye of a girl with lovely ground-trailing tresses than he is in protecting his charges. But when he cries "wolf" twice, a determined fairy decides to teach him a lesson once and for all.

Book 2: Unsoiled

When Elle finds herself practically enslaved by her stepmother, she scarcely has time to even clean the soot off her hands before she collapses in exhaustion. So when Thorny tries to convince her to go on a quest and leave her identity as Cinderbella behind her, she consents. Little does she know that she will face challenges such as a determined huntsman, hungry dwarves, and powerful curses . . . .

Book 3: Roseblood

Both Elle and Thorny are unhappy with the way their lives are going, and the revelations they have had about each other have only served to drive them apart. What is a mother to do? Reunite them, of course. Unfortunately, things are not quite so simple when a magical lettuce called "rapunzel" is involved.

About the Author

Jann Rowland is a Canadian, born and bred. Other than a two-year span in which he lived in Japan, he has been a resident of the Great White North his entire life, though he professes to still hate the winters.

Though Jann did not start writing until his mid-twenties, writing has grown from a hobby to an all-consuming passion. His interests as a child were almost exclusively centered on the exotic fantasy worlds of Tolkien and Eddings, among a host of others. As an adult, his interests have grown to include historical fiction and romance, with a particular focus on the works of Jane Austen.

When Jann is not writing, he enjoys rooting for his favorite sports teams. He is also a master musician (in his own mind) who enjoys playing piano and singing as well as moonlighting as the choir director in his church's congregation.

Jann lives in Alberta with his wife of more than twenty years, two grown sons, and one young daughter. He is convinced that whatever hair he has left will be entirely gone by the time his little girl hits her teenage years. Sadly, though he has told his daughter repeatedly that she is not allowed to grow up, she continues to ignore him.

Website: http://onegoodsonnet.com/
Facebook: https://facebook.com/OneGoodSonnetPublishing/
Twitter: @OneGoodSonnet
Mailing List: http://eepurl.com/bol2p9

Printed in Great Britain
by Amazon

54041039R00137